Maybe Crossings

a novel

Gretchen Eick

Blue Cedar Press
Wichita, Kansas

MAYBE CROSSINGS
Copyright © 2015 & 2022 by Gretchen Eick. All rights reserved.
No part of this book may be reproduced or utilized in any
manner whatsoever without written permission, except in the
case of brief quotations embodied in critical articles and reviews.
Inquiries should be addressed to: https://bluecedarpress.com or

Blue Cedar Press
PO Box 48715
Wichita, KS 67201
Second edition 2022 with discussion guide
ISBN: 978-1-958728-02-4
Library of Congress Control Number: 2022945367

This is a work of fiction, with all scenes and characters the
product of the author's imagination. Historical events ground this
story and historical people are referenced—Septima Clark, Fannie
Lou Hamer, James Lawson, the Reverend Kelly Miller Smith,
Bob Moses, and Vedran Smajlovic, the cellist of Sarajevo, but are
the product of the author's imagination and used fictitiously.

Cover photo by Eldred Reaney, 1960, courtesy of *The Tennessean*
Lyrics from "You Have Come Down to the Lakeshore"
by Cesáreo Gabaráin (1936-1991), used by permission
Oregon Catholic Press.
Composition: Caron Andregg/SeaCliff Media Marketing

Printed in the United States of America
IngramSpark

For Edward and the children

PART 1

Don, Cleveland, Ohio, March 2003

Images puncture the oblivion of sleep. They start benignly. His father's face as they pulled into the driveway back home in Buffalo after their whirlwind trip to Nashville when he was twelve. Resolute, determined, strong. Don likes this new version of his dad, feels proud of him. Abruptly the face crumples and becomes frightening. This man peering toward the house from behind the driver's side of the car is out of focus, distorted by the sullen mist of an unceasing rain and the bleary water-streaked glass through which Don, looking out the living room window, sees him. The face is fractured by crevices and canyons deep and unfamiliar, out of place on a man in his mid-thirties, and unrecognizable to this twelve-year-old, who is barely acquainted with grief and not yet able to read its signs.

Almost half a century later, half-awake, he is still that child who cannot read those lines on his father's face.

His mother's face now devours his father's, enormous, cruel and furious, her beauty distorted by alcohol and rage. She is screaming. In his sleep she looms over him eight feet tall, bending toward him like one of those punching balloons that lean so far that you think they must topple, but Mother always rights herself. He is confused. Maybe it's his father leaning in close, body closing from ninety degrees to forty-five before bouncing back, upright, one side of his face swelling blue and purple? He is worried about his father and moves toward him, wanting to place his thin child's body between them, wanting to see his father's face. But when he comes close, the face dissolves, leaving only his mother's fury ringing in his ears as he wakes up. It is a familiar dream, recurring when he is ill and feverish or when he is especially tired. It always disturbs him.

The clock radio's red digits glow 4:00 a.m. He gets up, careful not to disturb his wife, Ann, or Sam the Dog, who is, as usual, sleeping at the end of their bed so as not to play favorites. Stepping over the dog and avoiding the squeaky board on the threshold, he walks softly to the bathroom and then to his study where he settles himself in the brown leather recliner, certain that he will not be able to retrieve the comfort of unconscious sleep. He pushes against the back to raise the footrest and relaxes into the chair's embrace. He covers himself with the plaid woolen throw that makes its home on the back of the recliner for nights like this, thanks to Ann.

Ann, with her fragments of Jung, has suggested that he think about his dreams and identify how each person in them reflects himself. It sounds exhausting. Besides, he cannot imagine himself as that screaming woman who terrorized his father. He prefers to drift in that murky place of deep sleep, unmoored from thought and oblivious to memory.

In his dream he is always twelve. His breath is shallow and his heart racing as he tries to recall what was happening in his life when he was twelve.

February, 1960

For an early birthday present, Poppy-Don has installed a basketball court in the back yard for him and his friends to play on. It is Friday, February 12, 1960, the birthday he shares with Abraham Lincoln, a school holiday. He remembers this because part of him wanted to stay home with his friends shooting hoops on that court. Instead, he is in the car with his father going on their first long road trip together. He has never spent so much time with this serious man who is usually working. He feels okay being here in this protected space together, safe, but he is a little nervous, not knowing what to expect.

He watches the factories and farm fields whisk past the window like a speeded-up movie, watches the road unfurl in front of them, two lanes on either side of the white stripe that leads them to what's ahead. He listens to the radio, idly and without interest. The jingles catch and root in his mind, "In the Valley of the Jolly—Ho, Ho, Ho—Green Giant"; "Pop Pop, Fizz Fizz, oh, what a relief it is"; "I'd love to be an Oscar Mayer wiener, everyone would be in love with me."

After several hours they stop for a burger and a chocolate shake at White Castle. He's been napping but awakes when he feels the car reduce speed and exit the highway. They both are quiet. Introverted, Ann would later call him.

Back in the car after their next toilet stop, he senses his father's tension. He feels apprehensive. He knows his father has a friend in Nashville, the widow of his war buddy, who they are going to visit. But his father never talks about the war, nor does he speak about his semi-annual trips to see the family of his friend. Don can tell that his mother is jealous that Dad is taking him and not her on a trip. He summons up courage and asks quietly, "Can you tell me about these people we are visiting, Dad?"

His dad lets out a long sigh. He checks for approaching cars. There are none. Dad starts talking, only his words don't make sense. Something about his war buddy's wife Cora and son Edward and some eight-year-old girl with a strange name who is Don's sister. He is taking Don to meet them in Nashville.

Don keeps still, tight as the strings on the violin Poppy-Don bought him for Christmas, waiting. He says nothing, staring at his father's profile as though if only he focuses hard enough on that angular, closed face, he can make himself understand. It seems like a long time before his father speaks again. Something about Korea. Don thinks his father is telling him he was married to someone other than his mother, but he says the sister is eight.

Even at twelve Don knows the math doesn't add up, unless his dad was married to someone else *while* he was married to Don's mother, and that is impossible.

"So I have a sister who is eight years old?" he asks, "Just checking." He can feel his heart thumping.

His father nods, eyes glued to the road. "Does Mom know?"

"Not yet. I was afraid she'd prevent you from going with me. I expect she'll be very angry. Your sister lives with Cora because I knew your mom would never accept her into our home and I'd never hear the end of it. We're making this trip because I've decided that it is wrong to have my children grow up not knowing each other. I need to take responsibility for my children, both of them, whether your mother stays or leaves." The color has come back into his father's face and he looks strong.

Don feels confused. He doesn't understand any of what his father has told him. He wishes he was back home with his basketball and his neighborhood friends. He turns his head to the window, watching houses slide past, waiting, not sure for what. Part of him feels sorry for his mother. Part of him wants to take care of his father. His father has always been kind to him, and he loves his father in the default way children love their parents, but until this trip he hasn't known him, although he only realizes that this very moment. Now he thinks that his father has probably been unhappy for a long time.

Not knowing what to do, he climbs into the back seat and says he's going to take a nap. It is dark behind his eyelids, and he pretends to be sleeping. He curls himself toward the seat, away from Dad and the words that disturb the air between them. Dad turns on the radio, dialing it low so the voices are indistinguishable to Don. Eventually he sleeps.

They are entering Nashville. Dad has driven through the night while Don slept curled up on the back seat. Nashville looks quite different from Buffalo, he observes as he wakes up. Signs of spring are already poking their way out of the earth, crocuses in purples and yellows and forsythia bushes budding with small lemon-colored trumpets.

Dad smiles at him. "The sun seems more at ease with itself here than in Buffalo. Maybe Buffalo winters cause it more anxiety. Maybe we'll drop our anxiety here, too," he says. Dad drives carefully through the morning rush hour traffic to get to the south side where his friend Cora lives.

Don is surprised to see crowds of young Negro people gathered on a main street—he counts 124 before their car crawls past them through the blockage of gawking motorists. He wonders what they are doing. Dad drives up to a small white house at the end of the block and gets out, coming to Don's side of the car and opening the door for Don. Don feels pretty uncomfortable, and Dad puts an arm around his shoulders, telling him it will be okay. Then the house door opens and a brown skinned woman with a big smile exclaims, "Arthur, Don! Welcome to our home!" There is a brown skinned boy about his age and a girl who must be the sister, her unusual face pretty and her eyes staring at him curiously.

He doesn't remember much else other than that they all got along, and he liked the boy, Edward, and the girl, Mi-Young, and the kind woman named Cora. He remembers liking Cora's cooking and talking around the table about what they'd seen on the main street driving there. He remembers that by the time they had to go, he didn't want to leave. He doesn't remember much about their trip back home, but he does remember—vividly— their arrival back in Buffalo.

Don hears the soft sigh of the hinges on his study door and opens his eyes half a century later. Sam their dog has pushed open the door to the study and sprawls next to the recliner. Don reaches down and strokes Sam's wiry fur, grateful for his presence. He returns to recalling this memory, one hand still on Sam's head to ground him. What is it Ann always says? That was then and this is now? Sometimes they glom together in an inseparable mess.

He sees his dad nosing the car into the double garage, careful not to scrape Mom's baby blue Buick that Poppy-Don had bought for her. Quietly they unload the car and enter the house through the kitchen. Dad hugs him, thanks him for going on this trip, and tells him everything will be all right. "We are done with secrets, son. I will tell your mother and it will be okay."

Don remembers walking the long hallway back to his bedroom and, when he was safely in his sanctuary, closing and locking his door. He can hear the lock click as it slides safely into its nest in the door. He hears his parents' bedroom door open and his mother's clumsy, shuffling steps as she moves to the kitchen. He pictures her using both hands against the walls of the hall to steady herself. That's what she does when she is really drunk. The smell of cigarettes and gin wafts into his room from under the door. He hates those smells. He hears his father's voice, calm and low, and his mother's, harsh, jagged, and accusing. He climbs into his bed without undressing and pulls the quilt over him, holding the two bed pillows tight against his ears, and repeating silently to himself inside his head the words of the song he had learned from Cora and Edward and Mi-Young, "We Shall Overcome," over and over, until he falls asleep.

Arthur, Nashville, Tennessee, February 13, 1960

Don's father, Arthur, drives his black Ford sedan slowly along Nashville's Fifth Avenue, watching for the turn that will take him to Cora's. His son points to a crowd of young Negroes in four groups who are walking two by two along the sidewalk toward the all-purpose department stores grouped on the next block. He can see the stores' neon signs blinking their names: Woolworth, McClellans, W. T. Grant, Kress. Traffic has slowed to a crawl as gawking riders lean out their windows to call out threats and epithets. The young people appear oblivious. Arthur sees crowds of white people gathered on the sidewalk outside the entrances to these stores. He wonders what is going on. Finally the Ford is through the bottleneck of spectators and he turns right and crosses the railroad tracks. He passes the Piggly Wiggly grocery, the First Progressive National Baptist Church, a barber shop, a veterinary office, and several liquor stores before turning left onto Cora's street.

When he stops the car and steps out, he notices two of her neighbors peering suspiciously from their front windows at this white man and boy. For the first time, he wonders if his presence in Cora's life brings her criticism. Why hasn't he thought about this before, during the seven years he has been making semi-annual visits to this family? He walks Don to the front door which opens before they reach it. There she is, Cora, stately and dignified with a smile in her chestnut eyes that more than compensates for the looks from her suspicious neighbors. He waits until the door closes to hug her, a respectful hug like people give their close friends, both parties leaning toward each other hinged at their waists so upper body contact is minimal. He wonders fleetingly if her neighbors suspect him of another kind of interest in Cora.

His daughter runs to him, arms out, and he lifts her into the air. He is aware that Don is watching closely. Arthur gives the boy Edward a man-to-man sideways hug and introduces Don to each of them. He observes his children eyeing each other warily. Mi-Young's pretty oval face always startles him, she so resembles her mother.

Cora is taking Don's coat and asking if they have had breakfast. He admires how she uses her voice with its lilting modulation and her offers of food to ease the uncomfortableness of this first meeting. He breathes a thank you for this woman, as he has done so many times in the years he has known her.

He remembers the day the letter arrived from Inchon, South Korea from Jindae's older brother, Jinwon. Jinwon wrote that he had been trying to locate Arthur for three years to tell him that he had a daughter born to Jindae in 1952. Jindae had named her Mi-Young, "beautiful daughter." Jindae had suffered from a lung ailment that made breathing increasingly painful. In June 1954 they had lost her to death. The grandparents worked hard to provide for the child, but the war had left their area in economic distress, and mixed-race children faced prejudice in Korea. Arthur's daughter needed a parent. Would he bring her to the U.S. where her life would be easier?

He had left the house and driven for hours, not knowing where he was headed.

At a gas station outside of Youngstown he'd gone to a pay phone and dialed Cora in Nashville, pouring out to her what he had learned.

Cora had started college thanks to his monthly assistance and Booker's military death benefit. Her words had stunned him.

"Arthur, I can raise her. Have them send her here. She can be the sister Edward is always asking me to give him and you can come here to visit her and us. Your wife need not know. Oh, Arthur, God is good! Think of it! You have this precious child who is a part of you and a part of Jindae. And Edward and I can do something for you in return for all that you've done for us."

He could come up with no other solution. He could not tell Milly, and he had no other family to turn to.

He made the arrangements for his daughter to come to the states through the Pearl Buck adoption agency that assisted AmerAsian children of U. S. servicemen who had served in Korea to find homes in the States. Amazingly, Milly never questioned his twice a year visits to his closest friend's widow and child. He didn't tell her that they were Negroes.

He looked forward to those trips to Nashville and "my other family," as he had come to think of them. He found a degree of contentment he had not before known with his daughter, the woman she called "Mama Cora," and Booker's boy.

The house is small and the five of them crowd the living room munching on cinnamon rolls and sipping orange juice. Then he and Cora settle on the couch, to catch up with each other's lives. Edward invites Don to play Monopoly. The boys go off while Mi-Young sits on the arm of the couch, one hand ruffling her father's hair. Cora has given Mi-Young an all- American look by braiding her long dark hair into two pigtails and tying them with red ribbons that match her corduroy jumper. Arthur is pleased by how attached Cora and Mi-Young are and by how much pleasure Cora takes in caring for the child who calls her "Mama."

They talk of this and that: how tall Edward has grown, how

much he looks like his father with his nerdy-smart looks and his new horn-rimmed glasses, how each of the children is doing in school, their out-of-school activities, and each of their jobs. Mi-Young, bored by their grownup conversation, wanders off to find the boys. When Cora excuses herself to see to dinner, which is simmering on the stove, Arthur leans back, resting his head on the back cushion of the couch, grateful to be able to close his eyes. Eventually the smells of ham, red beans and rice, greens, and cornbread mix with the scent of cinnamon and vanilla—she's made her bread pudding!—drift into the living room and down the hall. They bring the children, Edward and Mi-Young calling out, "Mama, how long till we eat?" Don hangs back. Arthur suspects that his son is trying not to show how hungry he is.

Cora pulls her gate-leg table from against the wall and positions the extra legs that support the leaves. There is room for all of them. He watches her apply the thick padding she uses to protect the wood, then a damask tablecloth, the kind his wife uses only for holiday meals. He gets up to retrieve the silverware and plates, and she smiles at him appreciatively. Then she calls them to the table.

Over dinner Arthur asks Cora about the young people they had seen on Fifth Avenue. She tells him that the church she and the children attend, First [Colored] Baptist, has been trying to get the city's officials to end segregation in the downtown stores Arthur drove past. Her pastor, Reverend Kelly Miller Smith, organized a meeting of Negro clergy with the city's officials, but the meeting did no good.

"Most of us shop there," Cora tells them. "They'll take our money but they don't let us sit down to eat or hire us as clerks. Pastor Smith doesn't accept being treated like a fool. He's been holding meetings at the church for the community and other meetings for college students from Fisk University. A preacher from up North's been teaching us about the philosophy of Gandhi, civil disobedience, which means nonviolent resistance to evil. They're conducting their first act of civil disobedience at the downtown stores February 13—which is today! That's probably what you saw."

When Don shared that he'd counted 124 young people, Cora grew visibly excited.

Edward spoke up. "Reverend Lawson says that the segregation laws of Tennessee are against the Constitution of the United States and the teachings of Jesus and that people can defeat evil if they stand up to it and say NO nonviolently."

Cora leaned forward in her chair and reached out to touch Don's arm. What she said surprised Arthur. "You need to love the people who mistreat you, Don, just like Jesus taught. You keep focused on the fact that they're not bad people, they just don't know better. God loves them, too, and is using you to help them understand what is right. You still confront them, yes, because you don't cooperate with evil. But you try to help them see that you, like them, are a child of God."

From the expression on his son's face, Arthur could tell he was confused. He sent a look to Cora that indicated the boy needed more clarification.

"Don, honey, you look puzzled. It's okay to ask if you don't understand." Cora passed him more cornbread.

"Well, I am picturing all these people standing in a store smiling at the people who work there. It sounds weird." Edward and Mi-Young fell out laughing at Don's image of civil disobedience.

Edward clarified, proud to show off. "They don't just smile. They sit on the stools at the lunch counter where they're not allowed to sit because of their color. When they are asked to leave, they say politely that they're going to sit there until they're served." Arthur was impressed by Edward's knowledge. Ah, Booker would be proud of his son.

Arthur's son had more questions. "What if they call the police?"

"Then they'll be carried off to jail. They're trained not to resist being removed or even beaten, just to let their bodies go limp as they are carried to the paddy wagon." Arthur could tell that Don's interest pleased Cora.

"They're jailed for something so little?" Don was incredulous.

"Yes," she replied. "They've agreed to go to jail and remain there, to fill the jails if necessary to get people to think about how wrong it is to treat others differently just because of the appearance God gave them."

Mi-Young was watching her newly discovered brother closely, and Arthur was watching them both. Mi-Young asked if girls were protesting, too. Cora replied that girls and boys, Negroes and Caucasians, "anyone who can stay non-violent can participate, if they can keep cool. You can't react in anger no matter how bad they treat you." His daughter's eyes were big and intent as she listened. He pulled her onto his lap, gratitude flowing through him at being able to participate in this important "family" conversation. Meals around their dining table back home in Buffalo were barren rituals—obligatory compliments on Milly's cooking followed by a litany of complaints from Milly, which Arthur listened to in silence, walking on eggshells. No encouragement to talk, Don wolfing down his food and asking to be excused. He overheard Don say, almost to himself, "You'd have to be very brave to do that."

Usually on his visits to Nashville Arthur slept on Cora's couch but this time Arthur and Don stayed in a motel nearby. It was clean but spare, no television, just twin beds with a table and lamp between them. The man who showed them to their room used a cane, though he seemed to be about Arthur's age. He seemed surprised that they wanted to stay there. "White folks usually stay over on Fourth Avenue," he had said. When Arthur said this would be fine for them, the man had nodded and retreated to his office.

Arthur wondered how his son was doing with the day's new information and experiences. He sought the right words to reinforce his new relationship with his boy. "Don? Maybe we could go over there to those stores and tell the owners we want them to serve everyone without discrimination. What would you think of that?" Even as he proposed this, Arthur wondered if he was being naïve. What did he know about white folks down here? In fact, what did he know about white attitudes back in Buffalo. He was chagrined that he'd never thought about it before this trip. What about his father-in-law's store in Buffalo? Did Poppy-Don serve everyone equally in his stores? Did he have Negroes working for him? He'd never noticed when he'd been in the stores. Could he ask when they returned to Buffalo? He heard Don say quietly, "I think you are really brave, Dad." Arthur wondered just how brave he was, really.

During their one full day together the three children—Don,

Edward, and Mi-Young—seemed to adapt to being part of this new configuration of family. He was proud when Don asked if the kids could walk over to Fifth Avenue and see how the protests were going. Cora's absolute "No" surprised him. He had not seen that anxious side of her before. Cora turned on the small black and white Motorola television so that they could watch the minimal press coverage of what were being called "Nashville's sit-ins." The reporter called the young people "militants" and said much of the city was angry at the students' confrontational methods, "defying the harmony that has always existed between whites and Nigras in Nashville and threatening the prosperity of our businesses."

Cora told them that several truckloads of whites had driven through the neighborhood after Don and Arthur had gone to their motel the previous night, yelling threats, their bravado-bolstered by racks of rifles and Confederate flag decals plastered on bumpers and windows. "Most white folks down here don't approve of whites and Negroes socializing," she had told Arthur when the children retreated outside to the swing. Don was not the only person learning a lot on this trip, Arthur thought.

They left the small shotgun house Sunday after breakfast to drive back to Buffalo. He opened the passenger door for Don, walked around to the driver's side, and, as he was about to get in, turned toward the front stoop to wave good-by. There stood Cora hugging Don, and Don was hugging her back. It was one of those ephemeral, protracted moments that alter a person so that they see with new eyes. It struck him that he couldn't remember ever seeing Milly hugging their son. The force of that realization nearly caused his knees to buckle. Had he been too trapped in his own unhappiness to notice? For a moment time stopped as he clung to the car door, immobilized. My son needs to experience affection. *We have a right to be cared for.* His body jerked once, a surge of electric current passing through him demanding to be acknowledged. Then Don ran down the sidewalk and slid into the front seat, and the moment passed. His knees once again worked. He climbed into his Ford, turned the key in the ignition, gave it some gas, and pulled away from the curb heading for Buffalo, unable to look back at Cora standing there waving until they were out of sight. He knew that he must find the strength to roll away the stone and climb out of his cave of despair. Otherwise, like father, like son, both of them would suffocate from neglect. Resolution quieted the churning in his stomach.

He found himself humming the old hymns he had learned from his mother's days as a Methodist while he drove. He'd made the right decision bringing his children together. His misery evaporated as he imagined his new Self standing up to Milly, insisting that their lives change. As they rode, he and Don spun a scenario of what they would do when Edward, Mi-Young, and Cora came for a week in Buffalo next summer. Both of his children together under his roof! He would not to hide from the truth any longer.

When they were a few hours from Buffalo, his confidence began to leave him, like a fair weather friend, he thought, or a slow leak.

Don, Buffalo, New York, February 15, 1960

It was snowing hard when Don awoke. The branches of the maple outside his window hung low with their weight of wet spring snow. The wind blew the snow in whirlwinds, mini tornados landing and lifting, a confusion of movement, monochromatic and muted. It pushed and pulled the burdened branches back and forth against the side of the house. Don could hear them brushing the brick over and over, like a soft, light brush on a snare drum. Accompaniment for a minor-key lullaby, more dirge than comfort song. He got up and pulled on his pants and a sweater. Then, his stomach growling, he left his room to find some cereal before the school bus arrived.

His mother sat at the kitchen table with a cold cup of coffee and a bottle of whiskey. She was still in her robe, red hair disheveled, eyes puffy and pink. He was afraid of her when she was like this. He looked for a way to escape notice, but she turned, hearing the quiet scuffing of his shoes against the asphalt tile.

"Come here, Don. Mommy wants to talk to you." When she'd been drinking, she talked to him as though he was a small child instead of nearly a teenager.

No escaping. He walked over to the table and sat across from her so that the Formica table separated them. It was his protection.

"Your father told me about his whore and her daughter who probably isn't even his. Those Korean women who hang out with American soldiers are nothing but tramps. He told me he wanted the girl to come here in June with that Negro woman and her brat. Over my dead body! I can't take it anymore. Your father's a loser, a liar, and a cheat. I told him to get out and never come back. Poppy-Don'll take care of us, Donny. We'll be better off without your father. *Don't you ever humiliate your family, Don. Don't you ever, ever do anything to embarrass your family. Do you hear me?"*

She reached across the table, half rising from her chair, leaning toward him, face terrible, hands gripping his shoulders so tightly that he felt her nails biting into his skin. *"Do you hear me?"*

He nodded. "Yes, Mother, I hear you." His stomach cramped and confusion swamped him. He thought he was going to be sick. The chrome legged chair protested with a metallic screech as he pushed away from the table.

He escaped to his room and locked the door, hearing her voice on the phone as she called Poppy-Don and the man down the street who owned a pickup truck. Through his window he saw the neighbor man carrying boxes out to the curb, loading them into his truck, and driving away in the direction of Dad's dealership. The boxes he couldn't fit in his pickup huddled miserably on the disappearing sidewalk.

School had been canceled. All day the unrelenting snow fell darkening and wetting the remaining cardboard boxes until their sides sagged inward and they no longer resembled rectangles at all. He sat or lay on his bed, alert to the sounds of the house. He heard the phone ring repeatedly and Mother's icy Hello when she picked up, followed by the sharp clunk when she slammed it into its cradle. Was that Dad calling? Once he heard her speaking, words slurred but deadly, "...restraining order. You'll never see him again." He remained in his room all day. Mother did not call him to lunch or dinner.

In the weeks that followed, Don sometimes saw his father's car driving slowly past the house. He could make out the lanky man behind the wheel, body curved as he leaned forward, intently scanning the yard and windows, face crumpled and grim.

After some months he stopped coming.

Cora, Nashville, Tennessee, April 1960

It was midnight and the phone was ringing. She ran to get it before it would awaken Edward and Mi-Young. The voice on the other end sounded very, very tired.

She took the phone into the coat closet to muffle the noise so the children would not awaken. One advantage of such a small house, she thought absently, the cord reaches to the closet. She focused on listening.

"I told her. She was very angry, throwing things, yelling. She'd started drinking before we got home. She threw me out of the house, sent all my things to the dealership. Her father's preventing me from seeing my son." Arthur started to weep. "I finally connect with both of my children and find the courage to tell the truth, *my Truth,* and she destroys it all. And there's nothing I can do to stop her." He was sobbing now.

Cora tried to visualize the distraught man far away on the other end of the phone, tried to send him energy and strength. She'd worried when he hadn't phoned after reaching Buffalo, but knew she could not call him. Her weeks were very full with her work, finishing her Master's degree, the kids and the protests that kept growing in Nashville.

"Where are you now?" she asked. "What do you want to do?"

He told her he'd been living at the dealership for six weeks, taking sponge baths in the utility sink, sleeping on the sofa in his office, driving by the house trying to see Don. His staff thought at first that he was arriving early and working late, but it hadn't taken long for the word to get around.

"I can't do this. It's too painful. I'll never see my son again, and I can't stand it. I don't know what to do. I just want to sell the dealership and run away."

"Arthur," her voice was calm. "You are always welcome to come here while you sort things out." She was mentally calculating how she would fit another person into their two-bedroom 900 square foot house. She and Mi-Young shared one room and Edward's room wasn't big enough for a second bed. "The sofa's always ready for you, and you know the kids would be delighted to have you here."

"I'm sorry. I shouldn't have called so late. I've made a mess of everything. Maybe I never should have told Milly the truth." His voice went up at the end of that sentence as though he was asking a question.

Cora's feet were getting cold. She tugged her coat off its hanger and slid down to the floor where she scrunched herself into the fetal position, wrapping the coat around her, one foot in each sleeve. She could feel the hard lumps of boots and shoes underneath her and forced herself to dismiss her discomfort and focus on Arthur. She kept her voice low and calm. It was essential to quiet his panic and affirm that he had options.

She was worried by how despairing he sounded. He had always seemed to her a man burdened by pain—not just the residue from war wounds, but the pain born of too much disappointment, too much loss and neglect, too little love. It showed in his eyes and the way he walked, shoulders slightly rounded as though to protect his center. Her intuition told her he needed a compelling reason to keep living.

She tried to distract him with accounts of Mi-Young's latest accomplishments. When that failed, she told him how she had survived when Booker was killed in Korea.

"I cried myself to sleep every night. I reached for the after-world in my dreams where I could see Booker, whole and warm, smiling on me. I didn't want to live, Arthur. I've never told another soul but it's true. Edward's the only thing that kept me going. I'd look at him with his build so like his Daddy's, his curiosity and intelligence, his love for me and need of me, and I knew I had to keep going for him."

Arthur did not speak so she continued.

"We're bonded by our pain, Arthur, you and me, and by our love for our children. If you sell your business, you can come here and be with your daughter. You'd be doing me a favor if you'd come. You can help me get through my busiest month—my Master's exam's in May. And I need some big chunks of time to study, but I can't afford to hire someone to take care of the kids, and I can't take time off work at the college."

The voice on the other end of the phone hesitated, was silent. Then with great resolve said, "I'll come. I'll let you know when as soon as I figure it out. Thank you, dear friend."

Cora told him she'd be praying for him. She waited to hang up the phone until she heard it click on his end. She knew that such a small thing as not hanging up first was important as it might show him that he still had some power.

Awkwardly she pulled herself up from the floor of the closet and hung the coat back on its hanger. It was a no moon night and she felt her way to the couch, lowering herself wearily. She couldn't yet return to bed. She felt sad for the child, Don, imagining him trapped between his parents. She didn't know Milly but could imagine how wounded and self-protective she must be feeling. Not surprising that she lashed out at her husband with so much anger. Perhaps if Arthur came to Nashville for a time and they had a break from each other, they'd be able to rebuild their former connection, though her intuition told her it wasn't likely.

A voice in her head chided her for opening her home to Arthur when she was barely able to balance the kids, the house, her job, and her studies. *One more person depending on you? Couldn't you at least wait till after your exams?* Other voices reminded her that if she meant what she said, she would just have to trust that God would make a way out of no way. Don't be a phony, Cora. You can see this through if you understand that you're not alone. Pray for strength and trust that it'll come. But Nashville was tense these days, relations between Negroes and Caucasians precarious. A white man moving into a black woman's home might provoke anger from either or both groups. What was she thinking!

She moved to the kitchen, closing the doors to the children's rooms and turning on the dim fluorescent light over the oven. She made some coffee in the percolator, hoping its aroma would not awaken them. She sat at the kitchen table holding her cup with both hands and breathed deeply. Okay, God, you've gotta help me here. She made her mind go quiet and simply rested as she savored the coffee and waited for clarity. She wasn't sure if it came, but she wrote out a list.

1. *Check the Salvation Army for bunk beds for Edward's room.* Edward and Arthur could share that room.

2. *Ask at the high school if they need anyone to help in the shop to teach the boys how to fix cars.* Even if it was unpaid work, she suspected it would help Arthur get his grounding.

3. *Ask Pastor to add Arthur to the prayer circle's list.*

She turned out the light and moved quietly back to the bedroom, sliding in next to Mi-Young so carefully that the child, sprawled in the middle of the mattress, merely turned over exhaling audibly, as she relinquished Cora's side of the bed. Just as Cora was going to sleep, she bolted awake, realizing how disapproving many of her church friends would be, how they'd misread her relationship with Arthur.

It doesn't matter. We're only close friends. Anyway, interracial sex still escapes retribution as long as the man is white. *Where was that thought coming from?* Of course, she enjoyed Arthur's friendship. He listened to her like few people in her world. Once she had felt her appreciation for him cross the line to attraction, but she had quickly reprimanded herself and was quite certain he never knew of her lapse of mental self-control. Everyone knew that love across the color line was dangerous with a capital D, and interracial marriage was illegal. Besides, she had no time for romance and, frankly, no one measured up to the man she had lost in Korea.

The sheets warmed by Mi-Young's small body received Cora's

exhaustion, and she let go of these troubling thoughts. She would have to bank on her reputation in the community. Those who gossiped, let them suck their teeth. Pastor would remind them that Jesus placed no racial boundaries on his instructions to care for one another.

Arthur, Nashville, May 1960

Arthur drove up to Cora's house two weeks later in his black Ford Galaxy towing a small U-Haul trailer behind him. All of his worldly possessions rattled as the trailer moved unsteadily down the street. The neighborhood dogs galloped out front to see what was causing the commotion. Milly had kept the house furnishings, despite moving into a much larger home that Poppy-Don purchased for her and Don. Consequently, Arthur's U-Haul was half empty, which explained the cacophony of ear-damaging noise that accompanied its every move, announcing his arrival. The noise brought Cora to the front door, the kids following close behind.

He felt emotional seeing the three of them wearing broad, welcoming smiles. They were the only people in the world who were happy to see him, he thought. Together they hauled most of his things to the shed out back until whenever he might move into his own place.

For more than a week Arthur remained in the house, sleeping in Edward's room on the lower bunk of the second-hand bunk beds Cora had located at the Salvation Army. He emerged for meals and trips to the toilet but other than that, he slept. On the eighth day he awakened to hear someone knocking persistently on the door to Edward's room where he lay in the twisted sheet that had become his cocoon. He rubbed his eyes, felt the stubble that ranged across his face, and made himself stand. He smelled something foul and wondered for a moment what that odor was. Then he opened the door.

Cora was standing there, shoulders thrown back, chest out, dressed up for work. The look in her eyes alarmed him, and he took a step back toward the bed.

"Arthur Johnson, you are not here to vegetate. You have work to do. Our arrangement was that you would help with the children. For a whole week now all you have done is sleep. That's *not* okay. I need you to help me. The state you're in, Edward has been sleeping on the sofa rather than be closed in a room with you. You stink, Arthur. How long has it been since you've bathed? Now get yourself cleaned up, change your bed, and climb out of that sink hole you're living in."

It was a side of Cora he had never seen. She was formidable. She'd turned into another Milly. He did as he was told. When he emerged, clean smelling and smooth shaven, her expression did not change. She handed him a list of his responsibilities while he shared her house. She also *told* him—she didn't ask him—that he was going with her to church the following evening. Then she left for work. Her parting words were, "I expect you to have dinner on when I return."

As he tackled her list—weeding the vegetable garden, fixing the back screen door, doing laundry, being there when the children arrived from school, preparing dinner—he thought about this new Cora. In the past she was so nurturing and caring. Where did this angry, bossy woman come from? He wanted to resist her imperiousness, to declare himself as a man with a Right to stay mired in the Pit of Despair, feet stuck in the bog. Look at what he had lost! As the day passed, he shifted to looking at what *she'd* lost by taking a deadbeat into her home who made more, not less, work for her and who avoided the other members of the household. By the time Edward and Mi-Young arrived from school, he was adjusting his thinking.

They found him in the kitchen slicing carrots and cubing potatoes for stew. Mi-Young approached him warily.

"Daddy, is this really you?"

He placed the paring knife on the cutting board and squatted facing her so they were eye to eye. "Yes, honey, it's me."

"You were so weird all this week, like you didn't care about us at all. Is it true that you only love Don? That's what my friend Cornelia said. She said parents have favorites and some parents only love that favorite kid."

Arthur reached out to take her in his arms. "No, Mi-Young, I don't have a favorite. Anyway, *you* are my favorite daughter."

"I'm your *only* daughter, right?" she corrected him, frowning. He could see she wasn't going to make it easy for him. "I don't want a weird daddy. I want you the way you used to be."

He was astounded by her directness. He could never have said such a thing to his parents.

Edward entered the kitchen looking for a cookie to hold him till dinner. When he saw Arthur, he left quickly without acknowledging his presence.

Over dinner the four of them sat in silence. The air in the room pulsed as though zapped with a cattle prod. Finally, Arthur spoke. He apologized for being so sunk in self-pity, for stinking up Edward's bedroom, for abandoning Cora when he'd come with a promise to help her out, for being unclean and "weird." He thanked Cora for forcing him out of his bunk and pushing him to be responsible. He could see skepticism veiling their faces. "I'd like to ask you each to keep on me if you think I'm not carrying my share of the load around here. Will you do that? Will you put me on probation?" His questions felt risky. What if they said No? What if they asked him to leave?

As he scanned each of the three faces looking at him, he detected a gradual relaxing of facial muscles. He thought neutrality might be replacing frustration and anger, though he couldn't be sure. Mi-Young was the first to come around, then Cora, and finally Edward, the man of the household. Arthur could feel the sparks Edward's eyes gave off as Edward delivered an ultimatum. "My mom says when you're knocked down, you've gotta get yourself up. That's your only choice. That's how it is at our house. Do you understand?" Arthur couldn't see Cora, his eyes were locked on Edward's. When his eyes darted to hers before returning to Edward, he had the distinct impression that she was suppressing a grin.

"I understand," he said.

The church was red brick and dated from the 1870s. Cora told him that newly freed people built the church, which served as a school, community center, and place of worship. Reverend Kelly Miller Smith was continuing that tradition. Wednesday night worship was full of music. Rich, resonant solo voices soared with verbal encouragement from the congregation, and Arthur felt lifted and carried and set down in a new place. "I am a pilgrim, a pilgrim of sorrow, trying to make this wide world my home.

Don't have no hope, got no hope for tomorrow," they sang. He felt stunned and moved. Whoever wrote that song was telling his story.

A lady on the front row began weeping loudly and waving her arms in the air. Were the words telling her story also? He felt envious as two women dressed in white went to her and held her while she sobbed. A young man, very dark complected and looking like he was in need of a good meal, ascended the steps to the chancel and stood in the pulpit to make an announcement. "Please, y'all, stay after service for Reverend Lawson's training. We've achieved some victories, but there're still many stores that are holdin' out. All of us're needed downstairs in the fellowship hall. Thank you." Then it was time for the benediction and a choral postlude. Voices from the congregation joined the choir, singers rocking back and forth in time to the music as they sang.

Arthur had not wanted to come. The only white person among several hundred brown people? He stood and turned to Cora to thank her for virtually dragging him here, but she'd moved to the front of the sanctuary where the Pastor had his hand on her head while his lips moved. Arthur waited. When she returned, he asked her what that was about.

"I'd consulted Pastor what to do about you and followed his counsel. I wanted to pray with him to thank God for showing me the way to help you move out of your despair." Her eyes were shining. Her honesty and commitment to helping him overwhelmed him and he had to look away.

He followed her downstairs to the fellowship hall. The air in the basement of the old brick building felt swollen with moisture, damp and clammy, and the smell of mildew mixed with the hot grease smell of frying food. Most of the seats were already filled with older people, faces shiny with sweat, many robotically working their funeral home fans. Probably forty people sat in a semi-circle around a tall, medium brown man with enormous serious eyes and high arched eyebrows. His glasses took up a third of his face and his lips looked carved from a lustrous wood. His was a strong mouth.

Cora whispered to Arthur that the man—James Lawson—had gone to prison in West Virginia—solitary confinement—for eleven months to protest against the war in Korea. That caught Arthur's attention. He and Booker had *fought* that war for about the same length of time. When he said this to Cora, she whispered back, "Reverend Lawson's time in prison was a kind of combat, too, nonviolent, anti-war combat."

Lawson recounted the progress the Movement was making in various parts of the South. The assembled adults applauded the successes they'd achieved here in Nashville. Lawson called for volunteers to picket several downtown stores that continued to deny service to Negroes, and Cora raised her hand. Arthur surprised himself by raising his as well. He was impressed with the dedication of the people participating in the Movement and liked the way they supported each other verbally and with physical expressions of care, an arm around the shoulders, a hug, a pat on the back. One thing he was certain of: he wanted to stay near this woman who was doing everything she could to help him recover.

Saturday found him carrying a sign on which was printed in bold royal blue block letters, DON'T BUY WHERE YOU CAN'T WORK. Cora's sign read, WE ARE ALL CITIZENS WITH EQUAL RIGHTS.

"Nigger lover," "Communist," "Go back to Africa and take that white boy with you," the crowd in front of the store shouted at them. A woman wearing high heels and pearls threw a tomato at him. He felt its squishy splat on his neck, then the juice running down his chest inside his collar. Men in the crowd cheered her on and more tomatoes from the grocer's outside display pelted them. He felt angry and scared. He saw Cora up ahead, her crisp white blouse stained red from the tomatoes, her face wearing a kind of half-smile that said she was ready. He was scared for her. And he was scared for himself.

These angry people screaming in their faces made him think of Milly. Over the past two months he'd been trying to blot out Milly's angry face from his memory, to recall the vivacious young Milly he had found so attractive. It was Cora's suggestion. That's what she did protesting, she told him. Picture the people filled with hate as innocent, happy children, before the poison got into them. Focus on one person among them.

Now he tried to do this with a man who looked to be his age, a man wearing slacks and a short sleeved button-down white shirt. The man's head was thrown back, his open mouth spewing epithets. Arthur focused on how that mouth might look on a child sleeping, vulnerable. In his mind he closed the eyes and rumpled the slicked back ducktail hair. It helped, at least until another tomato whacked the side of his head and knocked his sunglasses off. Before he could retrieve them that same man, no longer a sleeping child, deliberately brought his foot down on Arthur's glasses with a decisive crunch.

Cora, Mount Eagle, Tennessee, July 1960

Cora celebrated passing her Master's exams by going to Highlander Folk School for a weekend of training. After Arthur said he wanted to come, she'd arranged for a friend to stay at the house with Edward and Mi-Young. Sometimes it amused her how Arthur trailed after her like a faithful puppy.

Highlander Folk School was twenty miles away in Mount Eagle, Tennessee, and known among folks in the Movement for the dedicated, effective leaders it trained. Their group traveled in the church's retired school bus up the steep mountain roads that wound through undergrowth so dense and green you could feel the chlorophyll spawning. The sun lit up the occasional open fields and sifted through the giant oaks and elms to dapple the roadway with shadow and light. Along the highway they passed a billboard with an enormous photograph of Dr. Martin Luther King, Jr. and the words "MARTIN LUTHER KING AT COMMUNIST TRAINING SCHOOL."

As they turned in to the property with its breathtaking gray-green lake and tall, pointing pine trees, Arthur commented how peaceful it looked. The white man sitting in front of them turned around. "Looks are deceiving. The state of Tennessee has been using everything in its arsenal to close this place down. I won't be surprised if they succeed in the next year."

"Why?" Arthur asked him.

"Well, this is where most of the leaders of the Movement have received their training. It's a place that operates as a true democracy. People here sort out their own answers to the problems of racism and inequality. They're not given answers. And they work together doing the physical labor that is essential to keeping this place open—clearing the grounds, maintaining the roads, washing dishes, cleaning up. It began as a camp where labor unions organized and then shifted to training civil rights workers. To the State of Tennessee, that means it's the center of communist activity."

This will be interesting, Cora thought. Arthur fought communists in Korea. She wondered if the billboard and the man's comments alarmed him.

The first evening they gathered in the large wood paneled room of the main building to meet the leaders of the training. Breezes drifted into the room through the row of open windows. Cora was surprised to see so many whites present and listening attentively. She had expected the participants would be almost all Negroes. When a stately gray-haired, brown-skinned woman walked to the front of the room and everyone hushed, Cora felt excitement course through her. She had read about Septima Clark who was on the staff of Highlander, but to see her heroine in person! Mother Clark had taught school in the Sea Islands off the coast of South Carolina for most of her life. When the state passed a law saying citizens would lose their state employment if they were members of the N.A.A.C.P., she refused to resign from the organization, knowing it would cost her her job, as well as the pension that she'd contributed to for forty years, and her other benefits. She was 58 at the time. After South Carolina fired her, she'd moved to Highlander where she taught her strategies for involving illiterate adults in crafting new, educated futures for themselves—Citizenship School, she called it. Those she trained were starting these schools for adults across the South. Cora wanted to start one in her community.

Seeing this older woman with her intelligent eyes and straight bearing, the powerful daughter of a slave, undiminished by age and seemingly strengthened by mistreatment, Cora felt pride in her race and her gender. Sitting at the feet of Mother Clark absorbing her knowledge and wisdom was the high point of Cora's weekend.

Occasionally Cora would glance over at Arthur and try to read what he was thinking, but mostly she simply delighted in being part of this moment in history.

When they boarded the return bus for Nashville, she asked about his experience of the weekend. He said the best thing for him was seeing so many blacks and whites working side by side and interacting as friends. She liked his answer.

Edward, Nashville, May, 1963

The screen door banged behind him as Edward hurried into the house to answer the phone. Mom and Arthur and Mi-Young were unloading groceries. It was Saturday, and they had spent their morning picketing as a family, then grocery shopping. Since he was fourteen Mom had insisted he and Mi-Young go with her to protests. It was like church, non-negotiable.

"We'll make it an every Saturday thing we do together. But your priority is to finish high school and get into college. After that you can get involved however you choose. Until then this family will protest *together*, on my terms." Change was coming, she liked to remind him, but change takes time. There will always be a lot to protest. He didn't say it but he disagreed. Now is the time.

To his surprise, the man on the end of the phone asking to speak to Edward Hardyway was the Admissions Director from Howard University calling to tell him that, not only did they want him to study there, but also that he was chosen to receive a scholarship that would cover almost all of his tuition. The voice told him to arrive at the end of August for orientation. Edward was jumping up and down when his family trooped in carrying their brown paper sacks of groceries.

After they celebrated, Edward reminded Cora of her promise. "I'll be in college by the end of August, so I can get involved however I choose, right?" His mom sat down abruptly. Her expression was familiar—her mind clicking through her options till she found the best one.

"You don't turn eighteen till December and you have this opportunity for an outstanding education in Washington, D.C. at the premier Negro college where there'll likely be a lot going on. Do your first year at Howard and then we'll see."

Edward felt torn. He wanted to join a group he had heard about that was going south to register voters. But Mama was the boss. Would she ever not be? He'd been involved in the Movement for three years but always beside his mother. As much as he loved her, he knew that one of these days he would have to declare himself and strike out solo.

August 26th, Arthur and Cora drove him to Howard University. Mi-Young shared the back seat with him. Traffic was incredible and they passed car after car driven by Negroes.

"Can there be this many people going to Howard?" Arthur asked. Cora and Edward fell out laughing, and Arthur's face turned red.

"They're going to the March on Washington," Cora reminded Arthur. "We're going there, too, after we get Edward settled in his dorm. We're going to the office of our brand-new senator, Herbert Sanford Walters, to ask him to support President Kennedy's Civil Rights Bill." Cora's face went slack, and she looked sad.

"What's wrong, Mama?" Edward asked. He and Mama had been so tight all of his growing up years; he was skilled at reading her, at knowing when she was feeling blue. He was, after all, her man, responsible for her. Seeing sadness reshape her face, loneliness swamped him, and he realized how much he would miss her in the coming months. Oh, Mama.

"I was thinking about Senator Kefauver who died a couple of weeks ago. He was a good man, one of the very few southerners to refuse to sign the Southern Manifesto. This new man we don't yet know about, but we'll try to persuade him face to face." Clearly Mama was not thinking about missing *him*. For a moment Edward resented how involved she had become in the Movement, wishing her sadness was about leaving him at the campus.

Over their almost eighteen years together they had developed a kind of dance they both participated in. Mama would mention something she wanted him to know about and Edward would jump in to show that he did. Sometimes it was Edward who brought up something he wanted her to know about. Back and forth they danced, one and then the other taking the lead. She was doing it now and he couldn't resist showing off at Arthur's expense.

"Who knows what the Southern Manifesto is?" Edward was starting their special dance now, to distract him from anticipating the pain of living apart from her. Their familiar competition helped pull him out of his funk. He was looking at Arthur in the rearview mirror, fairly certain that Arthur wouldn't know. Arthur's attention was on the road.

Edward liked Arthur, but it was embarrassing to see how much Arthur missed in the news. Mama's commitment to the Movement meant she was a news junkie like Edward. Sometimes Edward wondered if Mama found it frustrating that she was more informed than Arthur, whose job at the auto shop and volunteer work at the high school took up so much of his time.

When no one responded to his question, Edward answered it himself, pleased by Mama's approving smile. "It's the declaration signed by almost all southern politicians that they will resist school desegregation by every means possible within the law." Edward was proud that he knew the answer and grateful that Mama had trained him to pay attention to the news. What's happening directly affects our lives, she'd often reminded him.

They passed the Lincoln Memorial and were crawling along Constitution Avenue watching for Sixth Street NW, according to the map Mama passed him. Howard University was close now.

His mind jumped back to his coming separation from Mama. He was glad that Mama would have Arthur and Mi-Young back home to keep her company. Arthur and she seemed to be good friends, even if his knowledge of the struggle disappointed Edward.

As they turned north on Sixth, he tempered his excitement about attending Howard with a promise to himself. When my freshman year ends, I'll really do *something* with my life.

Arthur, Nashville, September 1963

When Mrs. Mabel James died at 94, her family had called Cora, who lived next door, to suggest "that man" might want to rent Mrs. James' house. The daughter had lowered her voice, Cora told Arthur later, and suggested "It'd look better than sharing your house with that white man. You know how people talk." Cora had laughed recounting the conversa- tion, but Arthur, ashamed that he had not been more sensitive to how his presence might tarnish Cora's reputation as a righteous woman, followed up with the daughter and arranged to rent the place, as is, with the possibility of purchasing it when he'd saved the necessary $10,000. The tiny shotgun house, identical to Cora's, was separated from Cora's by a field where, with the permission of the daughter, they expanded Cora's vegetable garden.

It was Sunday morning, nearly time for church. Arthur had awakened to the birds, washed, and eaten breakfast. It was a normal Sunday. The three of them would walk together to church, and after church they would have dinner at Cora's. Holding his coffee cup carefully, he stood framed by his front door and let the sun tighten the skin of his face. The air was still, hardly a leaf moving, and the butternuts and walnuts out back held tight to their leaves. He would remember September 15th as a beautiful day.

After dinner at Cora's, he returned to his little house, planning to nap before taking Mi-Young for ice cream, their daddy-daughter bonding time.

He pushed open the door, walked the four steps to his television, turned it on, and lowered himself onto the sofa. He turned to CBS. He was trying to pay more attention to the news so he'd be better able to converse with Edward when he came home for Thanksgiving. Harry Reasoner was speaking as the screen showed a large, rectangular brick building with one side blown out and two totally destroyed parked cars. Arthur turned up the volume.

"At 9:30 this morning a dynamite bomb was tossed into the basement of 16th Street Baptist Church in Birmingham, Alabama. Four young girls attending Sunday School died in that blast—Addie Mae Collins, ten; Denise McNair, eleven; Carol Robertson and Cynthia Wesley, both fourteen. One of the children was decapitated by the blast and fourteen others injured. This is the fourth bombing in Birmingham in less than two weeks and the twenty-first in the past eight years. Bombings of Negro churches are becoming common throughout the South. The sanctuary where four hundred people were worshiping was strewn with shredded Bibles, hymn books, and shards of stained glass. In its only remaining stained glass window—Jesus with the children—a hole obliterates the face of Jesus."

The reporter continued narrating, but Arthur had stopped listening. He, too, had worshiped at a Negro Baptist church that morning and delivered his eleven-year-old daughter to her Sunday School room in the basement.

He fled the house, running across the field, paying no heed to the tender growth of fall spinach, kale, and lettuce, crashing into Cora's house. *"Co- ra-a-a-a,"* he screamed. She was standing in the kitchen doorway, eyes fixed on the television, weeping. His arms went around her, holding on for dear life. Mi-Young emerged from Edward's old room that she'd moved into three weeks earlier when they had taken Edward to college. Her face looked confused, and Arthur gathered her into his arms, sheltering her with his and Cora's bodies, terrified that he would be unable to protect his daughter—or this woman who meant so much to him—from the evil that stalked this world. He had not been able to protect his son, Don, or Booker, the man who became his only friend during his year of combat in Korea. He could not voice his terror.

After some minutes he loosened his grip on Mi-Young and

Cora. He moved through the house closing and locking all the windows despite the warm day. He cautioned them to let no one in and asked if he could sleep on the couch in case of trouble. For the first time in his civilian life, he wished he had a gun.

That night on Cora's couch his body shifted continually. His long legs tangled in the afghan and he thrashed about trying to free them. He was like a trapped animal, sometimes shrieking and other times tearing at the afghan as though it was the enemy. His cries brought Cora from her room in her white chenille robe to see what was wrong. She seemed to him a phantom and he shrank from her, burying his head in his arms, facing the back of the couch, shaking with fear. She asked him quietly to please return to his house; he was frightening Mi-Young. Then she walked him back across the field and helped him into bed, leaving a light on in the kitchen for consolation. As soon as she closed the door his nightmare resumed.

It was 1951 and he was in Korea.

Great stabs of pain bounced from one side of his skull to another like a wrecking ball swinging from a fulcrum in the center of his brain. Staccato, unending, the locus of their landing unpredictable, banging now frontally, now on the left, now rear right, a cacophony of continuous, terrible pounding. With great effort he forced his eyes to open. All around him was confusion and noise, explosions and screams. Booker! *Where was Booker?*

Gradually his ability to focus returned. Monochromatic grays shifted to gaudy greens splashed with red. Something was lying a couple of yards in front of him, sprawled and flattened, unrecognizable except for bits of camouflage and the bump he recognized as a helmet. His first thought, an observation removed from any memory of context, was that he was looking at roadkill. Then full consciousness returned.

He heard a sound, a groan become a bellow, become a wail, animal and inarticulate. It was coming from him, wrenched from his core by the thing lying there before him. *NOOOOOOOOOOOOOOOOO.* It would not stop. *NOOOOOOOOOOOOOOOO.* He wiped the back of his hand across his face. His hand came away stuck with pieces of pink flesh and streaks of blood.

A medic crept toward him, mindful of the landmines that were devastating their company. He did something to Arthur's leg and wrapped his forehead, all the while murmuring something that Arthur could not understand, something like "stay....with. me." He felt himself rise out of his body and looked down on a scene from Hell. So much destruction. He noticed strong brown hands attached to the flattened mass in front of him. One hand reached out toward the right, as though trying to retrieve the rifle that had jumped from its grip at the explosion. The other hand reached back, palm up, as though to protect someone behind him.

Arthur began to shake and woke himself up. He stumbled to the kitchen and ran the tap, splashing his face and letting the faucet run till the water ran over the lip of his glass. He wasn't aware of turning off the tap or of walking back to his living room. He sat in the overstuffed chair that, with his couch and TV, crowded his living room. This dream had afflicted him right after the war for more than a year, but, as time passed, he had been able to stifle it, to focus on the Now of his life. Tonight it was back in technicolor and surround sound.

He began to cry, loud, deep groans that crawled from his gut and filled the room. Booker. Once he'd been medivac'd out of Korea and home to Buffalo, he had been unable to grieve for Booker. Milly would not allow it.

Now, alone in his little house, he would grieve his best friend.

He had been twenty-three when they met, a farm boy from Western New York who had done what was expected of him. He had finished high school and trained as an auto mechanic. There had been no money for college. He fixed cars and saved up to purchase a car dealership. He had married the first girl to catch his attention and had a son the requisite nine months later. He had been too young to fight in The Good War, but he was the right age to volunteer to fight in Korea, which he did, despite his wife's opposition. He was sent to Fort Jackson, South Carolina where the U.S. Army was forming the first racially integrated units since the American Revolution.

He had not had much contact with Negroes before Korea, but with one-quarter of the U.S. troops in Korea being Negroes, he began to make up his experience deficit. Booker became his translator, his mediator, his best buddy.

Booker was two years older than Arthur, also from a farm community, also married, and also father of a young son. Their friendship started over a care package Booker's wife sent him, chocolate chip cookies packaged in popcorn so they would make the five- thousand-mile journey from Tennessee to South Korea without being reduced to crumbs. Booker had shared the cookies with Arthur, and Arthur had felt most grateful for Booker's willingness to risk befriending a white boy. Few white boys were showing kindness to Negroes in Korea, integrated army or not.

In time they talked about their dreams. Cora was at the center of Booker's conversation. "I'm so blessed to have Cora," he would enthuse, his face shining with pride. He and Cora were from sharecropping families that had sent them to relatives in Nashville so they could attend high school. Rural areas in Tennessee had no high schools for brown skinned kids. They had met on a Friday evening when their school bands played in a competition at Fisk University.

"There was this pretty dark skinned girl playing clarinet. Ooooo-eeeee! She almost overlooked me. What would a girl like that want with a skinny trumpet player wearing horned rimmed glasses and behaving goofy once he grabbed the courage to approach her. I can see her now weighing whether to turn and walk away. Something held her, maybe that we both were determined to attend Fisk even though no one in our families had made it past eighth grade. Anyway, we started talking. I swear to you, Arthur, from that first conversation I knew we'd get married. Even then she encouraged my dreams and had her own. Best thing that ever happened to me, meeting Cora!"

Arthur was reluctant to talk about his wife, Milly. Listening to Booker talk about Cora and comparing his lack of enthusiasm for Milly to Booker's delight in Cora left him feeling confused and inadequate. Eventually Booker's interest eroded his reluctance. One night on a routine patrol together Arthur told him about the ambitious redheaded beauty he had married when they were both barely twenty. Milly's father owned a Grant's Five and Dime in Buffalo. He belonged to the Chamber of Commerce, was active in the Knights of Columbus, and sent his children to Catholic schools, his four sons to the prestigious Canisius High School. His plans for his daughter's future included a "good marriage" to a man who would keep her in the manner to which she was accustomed.

"I didn't fit his idea of the kind of man she needed, but Milly persuaded him I'd do. She was restless under her Daddy's direction and impetuous. I think she set her sights on me to defy her father. Or maybe it was lust? She'd been saving herself for Mr. Right and said she could tell I was him. I think she'd seen too many movies with tall, dark, and handsome mystery men. Really, I'm no mystery, just shy and quiet." He didn't tell Booker, but he suspected that her attraction to him had more to do with his being in awe of her, grateful that she found him worthy of her attention. He was safe, no threat to her considerable power, born of her social status, good looks, and cultivated charisma.

They had married quickly on a fast timetable that allowed Milly to retain her virginity, although, had her period not arrived, they probably would have given in to their lust before the wedding. He didn't tell Booker that either. On a brief honeymoon to Niagara Falls they had tumbled into bed and, once they discovered where this and that went and how they fit together, they remained there for most of the weekend. The sex was fun and, in what was the most intimate conversation of their marriage, they acknowledged that they didn't understand why people made such a fuss about virginity.

Almost immediately he'd had second thoughts. Milly was a Force. Beautiful and sexy, confident, and brash, she pushed him to get that car dealership, to supply her with the most fashionable (and expensive) clothes, to find them a house. Of course, she was not employed. Her job was to keep the house, cook and shop, do laundry and look pretty for him when he returned from work. She soon tired of the novelty of house-wifing in their apartment. All it took was a visit from one of her friends who asked how she could possibly be happy in such a small, sparsely furnished place. That left her even more dissatisfied and irritable. Arthur wearied of her complaints. Maybe a baby would help, she had suggested? Arthur preferred to wait until their finances improved but, as usual, Milly would not be deterred.

They named their son for her father, a decision totally Milly's. Arthur had no contact with his family, so he had no grounds for objecting. It did help with the in-laws. Grandpa Don, soon shortened to Poppy-Don, would regularly sweep into their place to claim his namesake, carry the child off to the zoo or park and ply him with ice cream and treats. Poppy-Don established an indulgent "normal" that they could not afford for their son, and Little Don enjoyed his adoring grandfather.

Little Don, with Arthur's dark curls and eyes and his unique inquisitive exploration of his world, delighted both Milly and Arthur and seemed for a time to hold them together. But only for a time.

Their relationship was full of drama, introduced by Milly, and withdrawal, introduced by Arthur. He had begun to find her treatment of him humiliating, even infuriating, although he rarely acknowledged those feelings to himself, much less to Milly. Like the good man he was, he held in his frustrations and tried to make it work. When it didn't, he joined the U.S. Army to fight in Korea. In a surprisingly candid moment talking with Booker, Arthur admitted that joining the Army had seemed a way to escape his wife's constant covert criticism and that he wouldn't mind if she found someone else while he was gone.

After he shared his life with Booker, Arthur felt embarrassed and exposed, regretting he had revealed so much of his disappointment. He would never forget how Booker responded: "Sounds like your wife's criticism and neglect were what you were used to, growing up, like me, in a large farm family with a mother stressed out trying to keep food on the table. Sometimes any attention's an improvement over none at all." With those words Booker restored the balance in their friendship. How amazing to be able to talk and listen and not have to choose his words with precision for fear that they would be thrown back in his face to lacerate him.

With Booker there was no judgment. Not even when Arthur met a young Korean woman one summer weekend when they were on leave. He was first attracted to her by the way she threw her head back when she laughed, so very physical. That sudden graceful motion set her long hair undulating and released a four-note, cascading half-scale, barely audible. It crinkled her corners of her eyes and lit her face with a smile. She seemed to be enjoying herself fully and it delighted him to watch her.

Uncharacteristically, he approached her and introduced himself. They sat sipping cold drinks and talking in a patois of English and Korean. He tried to keep up a steady stream of funny comments or playful poses to elicit her laughter. It was a game they played, finding the funny in the midst of war. The young white farm boy who had always done everything right gave not a thought to the facts of his being married and her being Korean, or to the impossibly remote chance that loving her would produce happiness for either of them, given those facts.

When he returned to the barracks, Booker teased him. "This old married man came back early. Gotta save myself for Cora, you know. *You*, now you're a different story. I ain't never seen you so happy, Buddy. I believe God don't want no one to be unhappy, Arthur. Only the Lord knows how much time any of us has to be happy with us here fightin' this war. I'm glad you're happy *now*."

Sunday Jindae brought him to her home to meet her parents, nice, friendly people, very welcoming of him. When her parents went to Sunday evening service at the Presbyterian Church, Arthur and Jindae stayed behind. He took her in his arms and felt himself reborn there on her sleeping mat half a world away from his miserable life. He returned to his unit determined that his future had to include Jindae, no matter how unrealistic and impossible that seemed.

The soldiers in his unit joked about combat being an all or nothing experience. Either you were bored with nothing to do during lulls in the fighting, or you were exhausted by the demands of chasing the enemy and keeping yourself from being killed. There was no middle ground. Unfortunately, this lull was short lived.

Booker. They had it all wrong. It was Booker who should receive the Purple Heart for his bravery trying to save his buddies while wounded. It was Booker who gave his life trying to warn him to stay back in that moment of recognition when he felt the earth give beneath his foot and knew he had stepped on a landmine that would permanently transport him away from the woman he loved more than anything on earth.

They medivac'd Arthur back to Buffalo, to Little Don and Milly. For months he focused on learning to walk again and tried to box up the pain that haunted his days and disturbed his nights. He felt hopeless, barely able to smile at the antics of his son, hardly noticing Milly's efforts to bring him back to life. Apparently, she had not found someone else. His remoteness, emotionally absent now that he was again physically present, seemed to intrigue her. Vaguely he was aware of her pursuing him, as though his retreat into depression stimulated and challenged her. She had little power over him now, but she seemed to like that. Her hands and mouth devoured his body with a vigor he found distasteful, and he remained unresponsive and distant. Why didn't she get it? Why couldn't she see that he needed her to listen in silence, to welcome his tears, and to hold him while he wept for all that he had lost?

At some point the nightmare let go of him. In his semi-somnolent state he found himself remembering how the woman he thought of as his brown angel entered his life. After his physical health returned, he'd felt a sense of responsibility for the loved ones Booker had left behind. He'd left Milly a note the first time he went to find them: "Driving to Nashville to visit the family of my best buddy who died in the war. Back Monday night."

He'd written ahead for permission to come so she was expecting him. He had not expected the six-year-old in short pants and a neatly ironed short sleeved shirt to be the spitting image of his father, down to the small pair of horn-rimmed glasses, too large for his face. The child had thrown open the screen door and run to him, wrapping his arms around Arthur's legs, hopping up and down, then running around him chanting with obvious delight, "You know my Daddy! You know my Daddy!" He'd felt his throat close.

Cora was as Booker had described her, solid, dignified, centered, with a smile in her eyes so warm that Arthur wanted to climb onto her lap like a child and lean into her kindness. She'd ushered him into the living room, motioning him to the couch while she sat in the armchair, drawing the child Edward to her. The boy nestled against her briefly, then slid off to fetch an eight by ten sepia photograph of Booker in uniform, smiling out at them. He looked so real, so natural, his glasses tipped slightly to the right the way he'd remembered. He couldn't speak. This was even harder than he'd expected.

The rest of the day the two adults had talked while the child played in and out of the living room, alternately listening in on their conversation and roaming in his own world. Cora asked a lot of questions saying she wanted to get as clear a picture as possible of Booker's thoughts and experiences in those months when he was so far from her, those months that were his last on earth. She said she was a spiritual person and that his death had not defeated her. She continued to feel his presence now and then. He'd felt jealous when she said this, yearning to draw on his friend's wisdom and caring. Each spoke of Booker reflectively, enlarging the other's understanding of this person they both loved so dearly.

Twilight sneaked up on them as they sat talking, savoring their memories of Booker and grateful to be able to talk about him with another who understood how unique and wonderful Booker was.

Cora named it. "It means so much to talk with you because you really knew him and loved him. Most everyone around me wants me to move on with my life and forget him. I will never forget him, I don't want to do that. And I can tell that you understand." He did and it bonded them. They would remain in contact through letters, and he would set aside some money each month for her college fund, knowing how important it was to her and to Booker that she achieve her dream of a degree from Fisk. Now more than a decade later the pounding inside his head resumes, shells exploding all around him, every footstep fraught with danger, the man ahead of him, his dearest friend, transported to oblivion in bloody, sticky pieces. It goes on and on, the noise assaulting his ears and smoke burning his lungs, his eyes. He cannot escape.

Cora is pounding on his door, calling him to let her in. But he cannot move. There is a heavy weight on his chest and the blood oozing into his eye sockets obliterates his vision. He is trapped in remembrance and grief.

Cora

When Arthur did not come to the door, she used her extra key to open it. He lay there nearly catatonic, his eyes open but sightless. Three years ago, after he emerged from his hibernation in Edward's room, he had told her that Booker's death in that mine field haunted him, but he hadn't spoken of it from then until now. Had the Birmingham church bombing triggered his memories?

She bathed his face, speaking words of reassurance softly, calmly. I should have been a nurse, she said to herself. When he slept, she left his room and returned across the garden to her home, checking in on Mi-Young, who, it appeared, could sleep through anything, including her father's night terrors.

Cora had her own night terrors to contend with when Edward called to tell her that he had responded to the church bombing and the deaths of the four girls by signing up to go to Mississippi with a group from Howard, joining Bob Moses to spend next summer registering voters. Mississippi was known in the movement as "the belly of the Beast" for its violence against people who asserted their civil rights. Numerous people had already died in Mississippi towns for trying to register to vote, dozens of churches had been burned, members of White Citizens' Councils had paid hundreds of threatening visits to black folk across the state. She tried to bargain with her son. Anywhere but Mississippi. Edward insisted that confronting segregation in Mississippi would be a game changer, would bring press coverage and alert the nation to the price one paid for being black in the American South. "Even if I die, Mama, it will be worth it."

He had voiced her worse fear. She lay awake praying fiercely and with anger, *Don't you take Booker's and my child, Lord. Don't you do that!* It was three a.m. before she fell asleep. When her alarm went off at 6:30, she realized she would have to get control of her fear. Edward would not be going to Mississippi until June and would be there all summer. She could not sustain this level of anxiety for nearly a year. She showered and dressed, awoke Mi-Young and got breakfast for the two of them before Arthur knocked on the front door to collect his daughter and escort her to school. His face was gray and he seemed distracted, but other than that there was no indication of the hellish night he had survived. Riding the devil's back, Cora called it. Well, the devil had plenty of riders on this street, she thought.

Just before Thanksgiving the young president, who seemed committed to dialing down the tensions that had brought the United States and the Soviet Union to the edge of nuclear war a year ago, was assassinated in Dallas. He had called for civil rights legislation that would make racial discrimination a federal crime just five months earlier, on the very day that the head of Mississippi's N.A.A.C.P. was assassinated in his driveway. President Kennedy, murdered in Texas, where most cars wore Confederate flag decals as a badge of pride.

When Edward came home for Thanksgiving and then Christmas, Cora tried again to dissuade him from going to Mississippi. It was clear to her that he knew the danger. In fact, he pointed out to her that Alabama was nearly as life threatening as Mississippi, the way protests by groups of black teachers and undertakers, clergy and children were being met with ferocious police dogs and fire hoses whose focused spray was so strong it lifted people into the air before letting them crash on the pavement. Mother and son could agree on the danger but not on what Edward's response to it should be.

Edward held onto his determination to participate in Freedom Summer with a vice-like grip. He argued that the leaders of the Nashville sit-ins had relocated to Mississippi and were working in the Delta where the population was more than ninety percent black, where if people were allowed to register and vote, they could vote into office folks who would take their interests to heart. The Kennedy Administration had even endorsed this voter registration strategy. Her son argued like a lawyer. He even quoted the Fifteenth Amendment to the U.S. Constitution that had been the law of the land since 1870—"The right of citizens of the United States to vote shall not be denied or abridged by the United States or by any state on account of race, color, or previous condition of servitude." He out-argued her. She felt proud of him, proud and terrified. Her son would not change his mind.

Edward left to return to Howard on New Year's Day 1964. Like the preceding four days it was unseasonably warm. That evening Cora collapsed. Mi-Young found her in the bathroom choking back sobs, her cheeks tear streaked, the hair next to her face wet and frizzy, her tears beginning to undo the carefully hot-combed curls she'd acquired at the beauty parlor for their family New Year's Eve celebration.

Mi-Young ran to fetch Arthur, who helped Cora stand up from the closed toilet seat and gently walked her to her room. He removed her socks and shoes and propped her on the bed, half reclining, her head cradled by two plump down pillows. He pulled up the chair next to the dresser and sat down, silently waiting for her to speak. She heard the hum of the neighbor's lawn mower alternating louder, then softer, then louder as the neighbor pushed the mower toward and away from the house, striping the lawn outside her bedroom. The sound was unfamiliar for January 1st and vaguely troubling. Like the world inside her head.

Cora mumbled through her tears that she was so sorry, that she had to be strong for him. His response surprised her. "We're a team," he told her. "You've helped me so many times. Now it's your turn to receive help. And like it or not, I'm the one on the scene to give it to you." He took her hands in his. Mi-Young stood in the doorway. "Is Mama all right?" she asked. "She's going to be," Arthur answered.

There was something about his presence, his calling them a team, that calmed Cora. She wasn't alone in this. Of course, she always had God, but having a flesh and blood person was more substantial. Was that blasphemous? She began to relax as it sunk in that she could share the unbearable burden of her fear with this man who was her closest friend. She began to notice the feel of his strong, workman's hands enfolding hers. *O.K., God, you gave Moses a burning bush and Jonah a withering fig tree. Why should I complain when you give me this white man?* That was her last thought as she relaxed into sleep. Arthur was still there, sitting beside her in the darkened room, when she awoke the next morning.

Six months later Edward left for Mississippi.

June 21st the television news channels reported that three civil rights volunteers had gone missing in Mississippi when they'd driven to investigate yet another church bombing. One of them had been in Mississippi only one day. He was twenty, a few months older than Edward. She tried to handle her fear by keeping busy, too busy to think, but the missing volunteers were all over the papers and the television. Two weeks later President Johnson signed into law the far-reaching Civil Rights Act that she and Arthur had lobbied their senator to support. But their celebrating was restrained. The law did not make it a federal crime to prevent people from registering to vote. It didn't include protection of those like Edward helping them register.

When Edward did not call for weeks at a time, she read everything she could find on Mississippi relentlessly. Finally, she went to talk with her pastor.

Sitting in the tired side chair beside his large walnut desk Cora vented her anxiety, then waited to be reassured. Pastor Kelly Miller Smith heaved a gigantic sigh that seemed to go on forever. He closed his eyes overlong, then spoke the painful truth. "With nearly a thousand young folks, black and white, living and working together in Mississippi this summer, it could get very nasty. We're fighting a nonviolent war here in the South and your son, just like his father, wants to be on the front lines. Prepare yourself, Sister Cora."

That evening after Mi-Young went to bed, Arthur dropped by to check in on them. She asked if they could sit together on her sofa, she needed to draw on his strength to quiet the turmoil inside her. It helped.

On August 4th when the F.B.I. uncovered the bodies of the three murdered volunteers buried in a dam, she thought she would implode from the terror that consumed her all that day, but she got herself together. It was what black women did, she told herself, their only alternative.

Ann, White Plains, New York, Spring 1964

Ann Whitmore's parents were progressive people, Kennedy/Johnson Democrats, supportive of the civil rights movement that was raising consciousness across white America. They were distressed to discover that they had contributed to racism by not noticing it, by merely going on with their lives, unconsciously editing out awareness that privileges were inherent if you were blessed with pale skin. Ann was their only surviving child and she knew they doted on her, supplying her with more than she wanted and cherishing whatever time she gave them. Ann's mother half-joked that she still felt the umbilical cord joining her to her daughter.

At spring break Ann came home from Antioch College and announced that she was going to Mississippi for the summer to teach in a Freedom School. She made her announcement after dinner while they were sitting at the dining room table in their upscale home in White Plains, New York, one of the more elite suburbs of the Big Apple.

Ann's father launched into Do You Realize What You Are Doing, his face unsmiling and grim. He meandered a bit, avoiding stating the obvious: that he feared she would not be safe, that they had not raised her to know how to take care of herself in unsafe situations. "Ann, you are an inexperienced, young and attractive white girl talking of living in rural Mississippi, a state where they kill people for asserting their rights, where most whites will see you as a meddling communist infiltrator." Ann noticed his white-knuckled hands held onto the edge of the table as if he might be about to overturn it. Or were they holding him in his chair to keep him Daddy-like? She took a deep breath and kept her voice low and firm, standing up to her father for the first time in her life.

"We'll be in a group, as many as a thousand of us. We'll always be with another member of the group. They have strict rules to keep us safe. I know I have a lot to learn, but we'll be trained before we leave. One thing I do know. I cannot let this chance to do something really important with my life pass me by. From the way you've raised me, I expected you would understand that." Her zinger hit home. She did not want to be unfair. They had always flooded her with love. They needed to know that she was grateful. She was becoming the competent, independent thinking woman they trained her to be.

She debated whether going to her room or remaining at the table, waiting out her parents, was a better strategy. She decided to stay, banking on her history with them, their reluctance to issue ultimatums, their preference for trusting her judgment.

She was right. They would support her decision. She would go with their blessing, knowing they were terrified for her safety and knowing their Episcopal Church would be holding her in prayer.

During their training in Oxford, Ohio, word arrived that three young volunteers had disappeared in Mississippi. "Disappeared" probably meant they had been murdered by the White Citizens' Council or the agents of the Sovereignty Commission trained to eliminate people who stirred up the blacks to demand their rights. Their disappearance shook them all. This was not like working at Disneyland or on a cruise ship. This was a serious, dangerous commitment. A few of the volunteers decided to withdraw from the program.

Despite her fear Ann and most of the other volunteers

boarded buses and rode into the South, picking up the baton of the Birmingham Children's Crusade of a year earlier and setting off like Don Quixotes to look for heroes and heroines in people commonly treated as worthless.

Maybe Crossing, Mississippi

She arrived in Maybe Crossing, Mississippi, squeezed into the cab of a beat-up black pickup beside Barbara, who was assigned to be her roommate, and the driver. She worried about the engine's wheezing and sighing as it labored through the pouring rain to deliver them to the family that would provide their lodging for the next eight weeks. That was the day the scales began to fall from her eyes as she awakened from what she later called "My Upper Class Fantasy World."

The rain pummeled the earth, denting it with shiny puddles. Rows of tiny, tired shacks faced each other across the pockmarked dirt road. Occasionally a short-haired, long-legged mutt nosed the puddles hopefully, not caring about the rain or anything else, for that matter. Otherwise, the small settlement was apparently empty of human beings. The rain-sound's steady drumming covered all other noise, even the sorry noises of the truck.

The black man driving looked to be the age of Ann's father, his bushy beard graying and his nappy hair salt and pepper. He pulled to a stop in front of the second house on the left of a nondescript crossroad and got out, his overalls fast darkening with the pelting rain. Opening the passenger door, he motioned the young women toward the house. "Move fast or you'll be wetter than catfish," he told them.

The house was tinier inside than it appeared from outside. The room they entered was furnished with a couple of wooden crates, turned upside down to serve as end tables and set next to two rear seats that appeared to have been pulled from some abandoned cars. The "sofas" were draped with worn and faded blue bedspreads that added a bit of color to a room otherwise dreary. The walls were covered in newspaper and one uncovered light bulb swung lazily from a frayed cord that came out of the ceiling.

"Look out you don't hit the light when you walk in here," the man said. The young women stood awkwardly, arms folded across their chests, wet and chilled, even in the sticky heat of a Mississippi June.

"How d'ye do, ma'am," The man in overalls forced a smile at the woman who emerged from the back of the house, a timid, mousy-looking woman, dark skinned and wiry, old before her time, dressed in a ragged house dress of an indeterminate color. Ann wondered what had bleached almost all the color from the dress, the relentless sun or too many washings?

"I be Clarence Jones, ma'am. Ain't you Edna Mae? These here be those civil rights workers you been hearing about. Ernest Washington said you'd be willing to put'em up."

The woman nodded, looking from the black girl to the white, sizing them up while Clarence voiced his gratitude to her. "I know you know what you is doing. We be powerful grateful to you for takin' this chance."

"Set your stuff here," Edna Mae told them. "We got some blankets you can use to make you a pallet tonight." She gestured to the front corner of the room, to the right of the window. "J.B. and Johnny be here soon. They workin' the cotton now. Got the kids in the kitchen if you wanna come meet 'em." She led them to the back room with its table and four mismatched chairs. Ann noticed that the flooring was wood planks covered where the table sat with black and white checkered linoleum that curled up, showing off its frayed edges. On the wall hung a picture of Jesus, the one where he resembles a hippie with a warm, knowing smile as he looks right at you. Three children sat on the floor playing marbles. They stood quickly and ducked their heads, mumbling, "Pleased to meet you, Ma'am," when Edna Mae introduced them, then sat down and resumed their play.

"Set and have some sweet tea," Edna Mae invited. She wiped out two Mason jars sitting on the counter and poured tea from a chipped enameled pitcher dotted with drops of sweat. Ann didn't see a faucet and wondered with alarm where they got water. Edna Mae joined them at the table. "I never caught your names," she said, not meeting Ann's eyes.

"Barbara Betts," "Ann Whitmore," they replied. Barbara, taking the lead, told her that they were volunteers with COFO, the Council of Federated Organizations, here to get the people of Maybe Crossing registered to vote. "With our people more than 90% of this county, if we got everybody to vote, we could put people in office who would do what we want them to do, not just say Yes to what those who own everything want." Ann admired how self-assured and knowledgeable Barbara seemed. Then she noticed Edna Mae was not looking at Barbara either. She was looking at Clarence Jones with a look on her face that said, *What have you gotten me into!*

Later in the summer Edna Mae shared with them her first impressions of them, laughing as she recalled how unaware these young girls were of what life was like for black folks in Mississippi. She had guessed that Barbara was from somewhere in the South by how she talked. Barbara was clearly educated. The little white girl hardly opened her mouth, but from how she dressed, Edna Mae guessed her people had money, probably power, too, from how she carried herself. Edna Mae told them she'd worried that their ignorance would bring the wrath of the crackers down on the people she loved.

Their initial attempt at organizing was a disaster. Edna Mae had invited the neighbors to come by and meet them, but none of the adults responded to Barbara's request that they join her in going to the courthouse to register to vote. Their children, who Ann was supposed to teach, stayed clear of Ann.

That night, lying on a makeshift mattress between the two "sofas" on the living room floor in the moonless dark, Barbara and Ann whispered their impressions of their first day in Mississippi, both admitting that they were shocked by the poverty of Maybe Crossing and feeling very inadequate. Ann edited her observations. She had never had a friend of another race and felt anxious about how it would be to live and work so closely for two months. She was unsure what might offend Barbara so she didn't say what she was feeling—that being here seemed like serving in the Peace Corps in Africa. She did say, "How could people be this poor in the United States of America?" She did not share that she was worried if people here would accept her. Would she, a privileged white girl from New York, have anything to offer them?

Perhaps her dad had been right. If she could have gone home that night, she might have done so, but she could not go home. Phones were in short supply in rural Mississippi, and they'd been told in training that the state government listened in on conversations on their WATS line as well as on the pay phones.

Barbara was whispering something. Ann paid close attention to her. "I'm from the South but I have never seen anything like this," Barbara was saying. "The oppressive heat, houses without screens or electricity or running water, people who can't read or write, who don't know what voting means, even the food—my mama would never feed us molasses on bread for supper."

It seemed to Ann that Barbara wanted her to understand how different Barbara's life in North Carolina was from this. "I go to Shaw University in Raleigh. We're trained to become part of the black middle class, to use proper English, to read the classics, to know and practice good manners. We are taught to be the best and brightest so that we can lift up our down-trodden brothers and sisters. Only these brothers and sisters are so down-trodden I have no idea where to start."

Ann was nodding although Barbara couldn't see her in the dark. Eventually they both fell asleep.

Clarence Jones's pickup, rattling and backfiring, announced his arrival the next morning. When they told him they'd recruited no one, he told them to get in the truck. They were going to COFO headquarters in Jackson where they would plan their next steps.

Thirty volunteers packed the office, sitting on desktops or the floor, or leaning against the walls of the room that in another life had served as a mom-and-pop grocery. Ann worried if she stank of sweat. She and Barbara had not yet figured out how you bathe with no indoor plumbing. She suspected, from the lack of conversation and the glum looks, that the volun- teers in this room were all, like she and Barbara, Day One failures.

A twenty-something brown skinned man in overalls wearing horn-rimmed glasses entered the office and stood in the middle of the assembled volunteers. His face was serious, and he spoke quietly. Not from around here, obviously. Barbara whispered that he was Bob Moses, a teacher from New York who had left a Ph.D. program at Harvard and his teaching career to dedicate his life to the Movement in Mississippi. "He's #1 on the White Citizens Council Most Wanted list."

Bob Moses had them each introduce themselves and say a couple of sentences about what they had done their first day of Freedom Summer. Barbara, looking at her feet and obviously embarrassed, said she and Ann had failed totally. Moses stopped her.

"Okay. So you learned the deprivation folks here live with. They've probably never heard of the Constitution or voting. Many can't read or write. For most of them putting food on the table is a daily challenge. So why would they get involved with you?"

"They have no reason to trust us or to work with us. We are so different from them, so privileged." Ann's voice was a bit shaky but she was speaking up.

"So, how can you find out what matters to them?" Moses's eyes bored into Ann. Barbara came to her rescue. "I suppose we need to ask them," she said. Moses smiled kindly at them. Even his smile was disciplined, barely showing his teeth. Obviously he was an intense, no nonsense person.

"You've got it! *You* must be the students and learn from *them* before they will trust you enough to want to learn from *you*. What you offer them has to be something they see as helping them. Anybody else having a similar problem?" More than a dozen hands shot up. "You will be able to do this, but you must take time to learn about their lives and what they yearn for first. *Then* help them figure out how to get it. The kids will lead their parents. They'll be more ready to take risks, so tend to them, talk with them and listen. God knows they don't want to live lives like their parents'. The Man runs the show, owns the land and the stores, overcharges and keeps the financial records, which they can't read and therefore can't challenge. The Man molests their wives and daughters and has a private army to put down anyone who questions his closed system. The kids know this as well as their parents. What they don't know is that some nice white kids get it and want it to change."

Ann felt she'd been baptized by Bob Moses, pulled up from the water with a new name and calling. She was giddy with excitement. Guided by his wisdom she believed that they could do this work. Her excitement grew when a short, dark woman, plump and charismatic, made her way to the front of the room, her ample backside swaying beneath her house dress as she walked, her face shiny and smiling.

"I think you chil'rens need inspiration for the work ahead of you," she said. "You need to learn in your soul that you, *Ain't gonna let no body turn me round, turn me round, turn me round! Ain't gonna let no body turn me round. Gonna keep on a walkin', keep on a talkin', walkin' to that freedom land.*" Her voice was bold and resonant, rich and powerful, her charisma irresistible.

One by one they stood, clapping on the off-beat and swaying as she lined out for them the rest of the song.

"Okay, you've learned your first Freedom Song. There's lots more where that came from. With Mr. Bob Moses and all of you'uns on our side, we cannot fail. *Didn't Pharaoh's army get drown-ded? Oh, Mary, don't you weep.*" The room was exultant, humming with her energy and confidence. Mrs. Fannie Lou Hamer had let herself loose. Moses told them, "Mrs. Hamer's a good example of what people can do for themselves. She's been a sharecropper and timekeeper most of her life, but they fired her when she tried to register, took away her home, arrested and beat her, leaving permanent damage, but none of that silenced her. Now she leads one of our projects."

As they piled out of the office singing, Bob Moses called after them, "Remember, the people are the experts on their own lives."

Ann was totally star struck. She had never before felt such a surge of strength and conviction. The very air seemed pulsing with possibilities.

A handsome dark-skinned man with a Jamaican accent walked

out beside Ann. They talked about Bob Moses and Fannie Lou Hamer and how impressive they were. His name was Reggie Lewis and something he said intrigued Ann and boosted her excitement even higher. "Personal power's in their blood. They claim it and use it. We can, too. That's why we're here."

To claim her personal power and use it felt thrilling to contemplate. Also scary. She found herself chewing on what Reggie had said during the next few days and was glad when two weeks later her group of volunteers gathered again for a Fourth of July picnic at a local farm, providing time to talk with Reggie. She learned his family had moved to New York City from Jamaica and he attended Howard University.

The summer heat sat damp and heavy on the early evening, and the volunteers sweated away as they danced the Mashed Potato and the Twist. Some of the local young people taught them dances they'd learned from the old folks on the plantations, line dances where you shuffled your feet and swiveled your hips, loose and sexy. Ann danced several of the slow dances with Reggie and then they took their glasses of sweet tea out to the barn where they sat on hay bales and talked.

Reggie told her that he was a descendant of maroons who had fought against the British in successful slave revolts in Jamaica and that his parents were active Garveyites even now, more than two decades after Garvey's death. When she asked what Garveyites were, he told her about the Jamaican who had come to New York during World War I and led the largest movement of black people in history. "My grandfather's proudest possession is a red, black, and green flag of the United Negro Improvement Association, that and his uniform from Garvey's African Army. I grew up hearing that black was beautiful and that we are Africans with a glorious history, that we need to love ourselves and appreciate the beauty of brown skin and nappy hair. I've worn dreadlocks or an Afro since I was eight."

"You weren't born with that hair?" Ann teased.

He laughed, then turned serious. "Down here I am more grateful than ever that my mama taught us to strut our racial pride. This system just beats it out of folks."

Ann heard Barbara calling her to come. Their ride was leaving. All social events for the volunteers ended by eight so that they could return to their homes before dark. Darkness brought out the newly active White Knights of the KKK and the White Citizens' Councils, as well as groups of unaffiliated young rednecks with over-eager trigger fingers. The volunteers knew the rules:

Home before dark,

Call if you know you are delayed,

Tape down the interior light in cars you ride in so that it doesn't go on at night and illuminate you to people in cars that are following you,

Never go out alone,

When followed, drive like a bat out of hell to elude them,

Never get out of your car if they stop you, and

Don't date someone of the opposite race.

Ann thanked Reggie for teaching her an important part of the past missing from her education. "It seems this summer is a series of Before and After moments," she told him. "I feel like I'm walking through doorways into unfamiliar rooms, traveling through one continuous maze. All the furniture of my previous life is being rearranged." She stepped back from Reggie, feeling awkward and wondering if he, like she, was regretting that rule that volunteers should not get involved in interracial romances while here, because such relationships would draw more hostility to the cause. Self-consciously she and Reggie moved toward the vehicles that would carry them to their Mississippi homes, calling over their shoulders, good night.

The following morning before the sun was blistering, Barbara and Ann stood behind Edna Mae's house leaning against the beams that supported her small back porch. From there they could look the length of the street's back yards and see the women hanging washing and the occasional old men rocking on their porches, whittling, or playing harmonica. Kids sat in the dust shooting marbles into small depressions they'd made in the earth. A few women were gathered down at Mary Douglass's place, talking, and Barbara and Ann moved to join them, remembering to slow their pace as they'd been trained so that they looked more like they belonged here. They stood observing the women, who eyed them suspiciously. Clearly everyone knew Ann and Barbara were not from Maybe Crossing. Things got quiet. Then Ann asked what life was like for them here. Most held back, but Hattie was not the least bit reticent.

Fifteen, Hattie looked twenty-five. She was stunning, hair in a soft 'fro, makeup accentuating her slightly hooded gray-green eyes and sensuous lips, clothes put together with a unique abandon—fuchia blouse over a chartreuse skirt with a purple scarf tied around her waist that emphasized her shapely figure. Ann found it hard to take her eyes off Hattie.

"Girl, you want to know about life around here? Well, I'm not scared to tell ya. My daddy left Mama last year just ahead of the night riders. Those scaredy cat white boys hidin' behind their guns and hoods come after him and found me instead. Had their fun with me, they did, all of 'em. Mama thought I wouldn' make it. But I be too mean to let them have the last word. They been comin' back ever since. Long as I play I like their puny little cocks and sloppy pawing, long as there's black pussy for them to fuck, they don't get mean with Mama. I *hates* those puffed up marshmallow mens with their soft bellies and softer brains. They think they be too good to treat us human-like, but they so excited to stick their puny cocks in black pussy they can't hold their seed for a minute." Hattie shook her head back and forth, and sucked her teeth, disgusted. "Nasty is what they are."

Ann concentrated on not showing how shocked she was by Hattie's story. She heard Barbara ask how many others had experiences like Hattie's. Slowly others spoke up. Many of their men had fled, but some had stayed at great personal cost. A man who'd sauntered up to see what was going on explained to the young outsiders, "To speak out when your women are being mistreated, even raped, is likely to result in you ending up at the bottom of the river, your body tied to some old rusty car part heavy enough to sink it. Remember Tom Gray last year?" Heads nodded and Hattie directedan arc of spittle into a pothole with perfect disdainful aim. Someone else added, "Remember those three Freedom Summer volunteers who went missing a couple of weeks ago? Who ain't been found yet?"

That night Ann and Barbara lay in the dark quietly talking of the stories they had heard. Barbara spoke with an intensity that Ann had not before detected in her voice. "It's important to me that you know that not all black people live like this."

Ann turned to face Barbara. A sliver of moonlight glancing through the window lit the space between them. "I know that your family is middle class and that this is probably as shocking for you as it is for me. I just keep thinking that no one should have to live like this. How can our government allow people to suffer such mistreatment?"

Tentatively Barbara leaned toward Ann. "I'm glad you're here," she whispered.

"Me, too," Ann whispered back.

Their nightly conversations erected a curtain between them and their fear—not a wall, for the reasons to be afraid were like giant chunks of concrete blocking a road—but becoming friends charged with looking out for each other lightened the burden of fear. For Ann, an only child, Barbara was becoming the sister she had yearned for.

Several weeks into Freedom Summer Barbara and Ann agreed that they were accomplishing what they came to do. Barbara was organizing people to fill out the voter registration paperwork, prepping them on the state constitution, and preparing them to march together to the courthouse to try to register to vote. Ann was operating a Freedom School, teaching kids and increasing numbers of adults about Black History and their rights under the U.S. Constitution and the newly passed Civil Rights Act of 1964. "The law gives you equal protection under the law, the right to own your property, to stay in any public place on an equal basis with whites, to be hired and promoted according to your skills and not your color, to go to schools closest to where you live, with books and teachers as high quality as those white kids get."

When Ann explained the right to due process, the whole class laughed raucously. Hattie spoke up. "What you talkin' 'bout, girl?

That white man who comes in here and pulls us out of our houses and beats us up or sometimes shoots folks for any little thing—he's breaking *The Law?* Huh! No way! Law may *say* we got due process but they be processing us into the cemetery the minute we claim it."

They'd all laughed, but Ann felt her stomach tighten as the danger she might be putting them in hit her in the gut. She pushed that thought aside and forged on, explaining that sticking together and knowing their rights would give them strength, even power. "There are so many black folks here, so many more than white folks. If you stand together, you outnumber them. There's power in that." The children in her class seemed giddy with excitement when she talked this way, like they could see possibilities for their lives for the first time. It was intoxicating. Unrealistic, but exciting to think about.

Hattie's mother stood in the back of the community center listening. Now she had to say her piece. "You be right that us standin' together scares them crackers. But, y'all notice the truck of peckerwoods driving through Maybe Crossing close on midnight last night? Well…" She was shaking her head, her eyes like knife points cutting into each of them. "We outnumber 'em, but they guns outnumber *us.*"

The nights when members of the White Citizens Council prowled the neighborhood intimidating people and shooting into the homes of folks like Edna Mae who had joined the voter registration campaign, it was not exciting. It was absolutely terrifying. One night Ann felt a bullet disturb the air inches from where she lay sleeping. After that she and Barbara regularly took their pallets out back, where they tried to sleep, challenged the whole night long by Mississippi mosquitoes. They jokingly debated which was their greater enemy—mosquitoes or night riders?—and half expected to catch malaria in Mississippi.

A couple of weeks later four of them were delegated to do the grocery shopping in Jackson one Saturday, Ann and Barbara and Reggie and his roommate "Preacherman." As they climbed down from the white van, Reggie held the door for her. Ann said she was glad to see him. Barbara and "Preacherman" were already in the store. The questions that had been fermenting inside Ann surprised her by flying from her mouth. "If black is beautiful, is white ugly? Do you think all whites are the enemy? Does being a Garveyite mean you only value black people and black culture?" Reggie threw back his head and laughed heartily. Ann felt weak in the knees watching him, he was so handsome and so confident. An older black woman passing by looked disapprovingly at this good looking black man drawing attention to himself by talking so freely with the pretty white girl.

Ann felt embarrassed. Her questions were so transparent. They revealed how anxious she was about how he viewed her, how important it was to her.

When Reggie stopped laughing, he told her she was asking important questions that could not be answered here with all of Jackson looking on. "I'm not avoiding your questions. Let's talk Sunday after the meeting," he suggested.

Sunday afternoon the volunteers convened to report on their work, to sing and be inspired by Moses and Mrs. Hamer, and to relax together. They'd been cautioned that after dark the roads became the property of the Citizens' Council and its private army. Seeing they were running out of time, Reggie motioned to Ann to slip out of the meeting for their conversation. He pulled from his pocket a folded piece of notebook paper on which he had written something. They walked the streets of Jackson's black neighborhood not looking at each other as Reggie addressed her questions. She was impressed how serious he was as he consulted his notes.

"Number 1: I don't think that only black people are beautiful. I think you, for example, are beautiful. But my people have been trained by whites to see themselves as ugly, even repulsive. The dolls available to our children are blond and blue eyed and all the beautiful women we see on TV are white, so we have to re-educate ourselves to value our own women. Number 2: I don't value only black culture. In a country where the majority is white, we're inevitably affected by white culture, even if we try not to be, and we're not likely to get far if we can't recruit supporters from among the whites. Slavery wouldn't have ended without white people joining black people to end it. It's all about the numbers. So, no, not all white people are the enemy. Most of them are just ignorant." He grinned when he said that and Ann felt a rush of attraction pull her toward him. They kept walking but as their arms brushed she could feel the energy flowing between them.

Reggie turned around. They'd reached the perimeter of the neighborhood and dusk was falling. Ann caught sight of a white man a number of yards off on the other side of the railroad tracks watching them. Her stomach knotted. Reggie had seen him, too, and picked up the pace. They didn't talk now, not until the office was in sight a block ahead of them.

"I need to say something else." His voice was low, soft. "I'm very attracted to you. I love your commitment to this struggle and your passion for my people. If things were different, if we weren't in the midst of this revolution that I'm called to serve in..." His voice trailed off and he looked away. "I guess what I'm trying to say is that I can't do this, I can't let myself fall in love with a white girl, not now. And it is very hard not to fall in love with you. It has nothing to do with who you are, Ann. It is who I am and what I must do with my life."

They had reached the office and could hear Barbara and Preacherman yelling for them to get going or it would be dark before they got home.

Ann was quiet in the car, letting Barbara talk about what Ann had missed while she and Reggie were walking. Something about a new task some of the volunteers were being assigned, signing people up for an alternative political party. She couldn't focus on what Barbara was saying. Her insides felt on high alert and unfamiliar.

She hadn't expected Reggie to name his potential feelings for her. She hadn't expected such honesty. She'd never had such an open conversation with a guy her age. When they got to Edna Mae's house, she said she was feeling sick and went to bed immediately, letting her tears come silently, comforted by the muffled, low sound of Edna Mae and Barbara talking in the kitchen.

The next day the deputy sheriff paid a visit to Edna Mae's

house and asked for "the white girl." He was not much older than she was, with sunburned arms and face, which accentuated his blue eyes. He told her she had no business here, "A nice white girl like you shouldn't be hanging around these niggers. It's not safe."

She remained friendly—they'd been trained to treat everyone respectfully. She asked the sheriff's deputy why he treated people so harshly just because of their skin color. Her question seemed to disarm him, especially when she added, "I don't understand this because most of the whites I have met down here had black women caring for them when they were children, cooking their meals, and living very close with them." The deputy shifted position, looked at the ground, and then said he had to go, but that she shouldn't believe those communists directing the Movement.

That night she wrote to her parents about the conversation. She wrote that she could see from that conversation that it was fear, based on a mix of anti-communism and the conviction that the races must remain separated, that drove the violence in Mississippi. She wrote nothing about Reggie.

Edward, Sunflower County, Mississippi, July 1964

When he arrived in Mississippi in June, Edward was already a Movement veteran. After all, he came from Nashville and knew the Nashville leaders who were staffing Freedom Summer. He'd been trained by Reverend James Lawson! His rhetoric was rooted in the church. He was, in fact, thinking seriously of studying for the ministry once he finished at Howard University. Hence his nickname, "Preacherman." On this airless midsummer morning Edward and Reggie Lewis, his roommate, had been assigned to collect signatures on petitions.

Months earlier some from the Freedom Summer leadership team had gone with several local people to a meeting of the Mississippi Regular Democratic Party. As they anticipated, they were turned away, the door slammed in their faces by a burly red faced white man chewing tobacco and spitting the juice at them as he grunted, "We don' 'llow no nigras in the Mississippi Democratic Party!" When he heard this story, Edward had found it hard to keep a straight face. The man juxtaposed "democratic" with keeping out "nigras!"

Mississippi like the rest of the South was basically a one party state. Since the end of Reconstruction eighty years ago Republicans had been scarcer than snow in this part of the world. Participation in the Democratic Party was the only game in town if you wanted to access political power. But black people were denied participation in the openly White Supremacist Democratic Party. That exclusion produced a new strategy: They would organize an integrated Democratic Party by collecting signatures of Mississippians qualified to vote but prevented from registering by Mississippi's Regular Democratic Party. The petitions would call for recognition by the National Democratic Party of a new, everyone-welcome Mississippi *Freedom* Democratic Party (MFDP) as the official Democratic Party of Mississippi. Delegates elected by this new party would carry the petitions to the National Democratic Party Convention in Atlantic City in August. That was where the Texan who inherited the presidency when J.F.K. was assassinated—the man called "The Civil Rights President"— would likely be nominated to run on the Democratic ticket for President of the United States.

Their goal was to collect 35,000 signatures a week, which was why Edward and Reggie had been reassigned from voter registration to signing people up for the MFDP.

Sometimes when they felt especially daring, they entered the cotton fields and approached the laborers to persuade them to sign. That had become increasingly risky and expensive after the legislature raised fines for trespassing to $500. More often they went door to door at dawn, before pickers headed for the fields, and then during the day worked the community centers that Freedom Summer volunteers had set up, ending up at the churches in the evenings. It was tough work.

Mississippi's secret intelligence organization, the Sovereignty Commission, spied on the volunteers, tapped their phones, and sent paid informers to cuddle up to the civil rights workers and report on their activities. Judging by the increase in violence during July, Edward calculated that the whites in power must be worried about the parallel political party strategy. Every time there was a precinct meeting white men turned up sitting in their cars, chewing tobacco and pointing their rifles at any black or white person entering the local Freedom House. In half a dozen towns the Freedom Houses were firebombed, and those not firebombed had been raided.

On this particular day he and Reggie had stayed too long at an A.M.E. church in Itta Bena talking up the MFDP. Day was already headed for China when they began driving home. Reggie placed the petitions in the trunk of the car so they could drive fast with the windows down in the clammy night. And Edward did drive fast, taking those country roads at close to ninety, determined to outrun any night riders. Once they reached the black community where they were living, they would probably be safe, but they still had a ways to go.

The moonless night came on suddenly, like India ink spilling over them, obliterating landmarks. When he glanced at Reggie, Edward could make out only a dark featureless presence in the passenger seat, and it spooked him. Edward was trying to drive without headlights so as not to attract attention, but after skidding off the side of the road a couple of times, he compromised and put on the parking lights. Behind them they saw small glowing dots of light steadily growing larger. Headlights, surely, two cars tailing them. He pressed his foot on the accelerator and the beat up Chevy labored to pick up speed.

Now another light penetrated the darkness, throwing light around the road from its perch atop the police car, causing him to wince as its path momentarily found his staring eyes. Reggie was speaking to him in a quiet voice. "We're only a few blocks from home. Lay on the horn hard and keep going. If we have to pull over, I think we should run for it. Make sure your door is locked and the window up."

Panicked, Edward did as he was told. The shrill, hollow sound of the horn split the darkness, cutting through the black sky like a hatchet. They could sense more than see activity ahead as the men of their community came out onto their porches to investigate what was causing the honking. The car with the flashing light came up beside Edward. Two deputies in uniforms, guns ready, yelled at him to pull over. Seeing no other option, he slowed the car and eased it to the right side of the road where it leaned precariously into the ditch on the passenger side.

"Now! Come out my side!" Reggie flung open his door and leapt from the vehicle, Edward, adrenalin pumping, followed him. They could hear the deputies talking as they approached the car and see the white circles turning to figure eights as their flashlights bobbed with each step. Edward and Reggie crouched beside the fender until they saw a flashlight scanning the car. Then they took off, running toward those porches that they could barely make out up ahead. Shots sang out but they kept running.

"This way. You're almost here. Go 'round back. We got you covered." The voice was familiar, and they did as it directed them. They had reached the last house on Cornflower Road, the beginning of the community of Paul's Bend. Several other houses stood in a flanking formation. Edward imagined the backs of the houses defiantly mooning the cars of the deputies as the search light hit them. The car he and Reggie had abandoned was eerily illuminated by the still circling search light. Otherwise, all was darkness. He was breathless and shaking as they rounded the corner and collapsed against the side wall of the first house they reached. For a moment he thought, stricken with guilt. What Mama would do if he died here in Mississippi?

He could make out voices, the deputies conferring, low and incomprehensible. He heard the sound of splintering glass. One of them must have broken the window to open the driver's door. He heard the familiar sputtering of the Chevy's tentative sparkplugs, long overdue for replacement, then finally ignition followed by the grinding of the gears. He guessed they must be rocking the car forward and back, trying to get it out of the ditch. After a time, the two other cars started up, the searching light disappeared, and he heard the sound of tires kicking up gravel and dirt. Which way were they going? The sound quieted. They must not be coming after us, he whispered to Reggie.

Cautiously, they both stood, peaked around the house, and when they could make out only red taillights in the distance, they walked around to the front stoop. A well-built middle-aged man wearing an army camouflage T-shirt stood on the stoop holding a rifle. "Come on in. You're out of danger for now." He held open the screen door and ushered them into the front room. "Set down awhile and catch your breath."

"Why didn't they come after us?" Reggie asked him.

"There was two of 'em and when they shined their light over here, they could make out a number of us standin' on our porches with our rifles trained on 'em. Didn't want to mess with us, is my guess."

"What'll they do with our car?" Edward asked.

"Impound it. Make you pay $500 to get it back. Then fine whoever picks it up for reckless driving and speeding. That'll be another $250 and $400. My guess is you're looking at $1,150 before you see that car again."

Reggie stood and began to pace. His face looked grim. "We've got to get the car back or at least get to it tonight before they go over it. I put all those petitions in the trunk, remember? If they get those petitions, they'll have the names and addresses of all the folks we've signed up and those people will become targets. Edward, we've got to find where they put that car and retrieve the petitions."

"How can we find the car in this dark?" Edward shifted from relief and elation at being safe to terror at the thought that they could be exposing the hundred people they had enlisted to sign up for the MFDP to reprisals.

The man he thought of as his rescuer was speaking, taking time with his words. He thought it unlikely that the deputies would take the car far tonight. Probably they'd just park it on the nearest side road and return in the morning to go over it. If they were really careful, they might locate it tonight while the deputies were celebrating frightening those "communists."

When Reggie and Edward insisted in going to find the car right away, the closed expression on their host's face changed. "I ain't had much interest in what y'all been doin' here," he said. "This voter registration business and that political party— I been saying it'll only bring trouble to us. But if you boys is willing to risk your lives to go find that car right now and get back all them people's names and addresses, well, I guess I oughta to be willing to risk my own ass. Make you a deal. You get back here in one piece with those papers, and I'll sign up myself."

As they started back to where their car had been, following a map the man had drawn for them showing where the closest turnoffs were, where they might have stashed the Chevy, Edward joked to Reggie that at least they were signing up another member. "No telling how far we volunteers will go for the cause, right?"

It took two hours before they found the car. Their host had been right. It was parked under a eucalyptus away from the road, disguised with brush and pointed toward town.

The car keys were a casualty of their frantic flight across the fields. But the man had loaned them a screwdriver, and Reggie used it to jimmy the lock on the trunk. He shined the tiny flashlight attached to Edward's ballpoint pen into the trunk. There were the petitions. Reggie stuffed the petitions into a brown paper bag they found in the trunk. Edward found the dirty rag they used to check the oil next to the tire iron and passed it to Reggie. "Wrap the bag in this," he whispered. He quietly closed the lid of the trunk and they set off, running as lightly as possible, terrified that a cottonmouth or black snake might be lurking where their feet landed. Edward thought they looked like male dancers making jump after jump, legs stretched wide, leaping across the stubbled fields, as they headed back toward Paul's Bend, accompanied by the chatter of cicadas and the low rumbling of tree frogs. "Look for my light," the man had told them, and sure enough, once they located the small glow of the man's rusty lantern, it guided them home.

He was there on his stoop watching for them. He had contacted their host family and agreed to keep them at his place for the night. "Y'all had enough excitement. Best settle in here, but stay away from the windows." He pointed to the floor beneath the front window where he'd put two pillows and a light blanket. "I don't think they'll come back tonight, but you best lie low just in case they do. If you're flat on the floor you should be safe if they shoot into the house. " Then he signed their petition and walked toward the back of the house, saying over his shoulder, "Guess you know where the outhouse is. Pail of water on the stoop if you want to wash up."

For a moment Edward, imagining the deputies returning for them, thought he would vomit, but he lay down beside Reggie and forced himself not to. Going out on the stoop would be too much to cope with. Within minutes he descended into a dream-haunted sleep.

The following day they got up with the sun and resumed knocking on doors, trying to get folks to sign their petitions. Word had gone out that these two black college boys had gone back to get the petitions in the dead center of the night in order to protect the people. It seemed to Edward that folks treated them differently. Even grumpy old men nodded at them as they passed and seemed glad to see them. Folks in most of the homes they approached invited them in and signed. They told each other they could cope with anything after last night. Anyway, now that their night of terror was over, it made a good story, and it helped their recruiting that they'd become local heroes.

Ann

Ann saw Reggie most weeks at their volunteer gatherings. She watched him interacting with the other volunteers, on the lookout for any signs of a romance developing with one of the black women. Nothing. With everyone he seemed consistently friendly, funny, and focused on what he was here for.

A couple of weeks after their "you're off limits" conversation, they gathered in Jackson to hear what would happen August 19 when the MFDP delegation would leave for Atlantic City, New Jersey and the National Convention of the Democratic Party. Ann leaned against the wall listening and observing people, as she liked to do. She watched Barbara, who was seated beside Hervie Stein, a Jewish volunteer from Chicago.

Ann saw him reach over and squeeze Barbara's hand. Hervie was especially passionate and outspoken, driven to this work by his extended family's experience in Hitler's Germany. He had grown up with his mother's stories of the steady reduction of the rights of European Jews in the 1930s, leading to the establishment of death camps across Europe. He had lost family in those death camps, two aunts and five cousins at Auschwitz and a grandmother and grandfather at Dachau. He believed that what they were witnessing in Mississippi was very like what had gone on in Germany as Hitler was consolidating his power. Never again, Hervie promised, pledging his life to defeat racism everywhere. He was quite serious about it and Barbara had told Ann that she found his commitment very attractive. She had confided that she thought she was falling in love with Hervie.

Ann looked away. She scanned the room for Reggie but could not locate him. It was familiar, this feeling of being alone amidst a group of people. Since the death of her little brother when she was a child, she had often felt she was looking out from behind a transparent, impenetrable shield, like those Colgate Guard-All toothpaste ads on television where people try to reach the person behind the transparent shield but only bounce off it, leaving the protected one safe but alone. That's me, she thought, safe and solitary. Would it always be this way?

She felt a presence behind her and turned to find Reggie smiling at her. The afternoon light danced between them and reflected off his rich brown eyes. She noticed that his eyes were multiple shades of brown—honey gold, mahogany, cherry—and for a moment she stood transfixed, staring, fascinated by all the color glistening there. She decided that the aura of warmth and kindness that drew people to him was rooted in his eyes.

"I was hoping I'd find you," he said. "Time for a walk?"

She nodded numbly, still encased in that transparent, impenetrable Guard-All shield. They moved toward the door and when the screen squeaked, she glanced back into the room where she found Barbara smiling encouragement at her.

They walked in an awkward silence full of things that neither could express. Then a sudden Mississippi rain storm blew in, wind driving the rain almost horizontally. They ducked under the overhanging roof of a storage shed, pressing themselves against the wall and, when that did not save them from a thorough drenching, slid down to sit on the ground abandoning themselves to the cool relief of the rain, laughing like children.

They talked about their work, their small triumphs, their sadness anticipating leaving Mississippi in just a few weeks. Reggie told her about being stopped by the deputy sheriffs and having to locate the petitions before morning. She had already heard the story but had longed to hear it from him. She listened attentively. Then he told her that he had decided not to return to college but to remain in Mississippi to continue the work of registering voters. She asked if his family supported his decision, which led him into a rambling description of his family and their straightforward, sometimes brutally honest exchanges that invariably ended with his father and mother affirming that each of them had to do what they had to do, regardless of danger or disappointing the expectations of others.

"I love that about them, but if I'm totally honest, a part of me would like them to order me to come home. Their inexhaustible support for my making my own decisions ends up setting a higher standard for me than if they said I had to go to law school, which I know is their dream for me. Do you understand what I mean?"

She understood.

The wheezy honk of Clarence's truck interrupted their conversation. Barbara was leaning out the passenger side window calling Ann to come. The meeting was over, and their ride was leaving. Reggie helped her stand up. It was still raining hard, drops pelting the windshield of the truck. As she ran to the truck,

Reggie called to her, "Be sure you notice the raindrops on the windshield, how they leave footprints, just like we do." He was smiling. She didn't understand.

Edward

Edward thought that organizing Mississippi poor folks to take their stories to the national government and President Lyndon Johnson was a brilliant strategy. He got goose bumps imagining the National Democratic Convention hearing the stories of what life was like for poor black people in Mississippi—CBS, NBC and ABC carrying those stories into every living room in America. It would shock the nation and generate momentum for a federal law to protect the right to register and vote. Of that he was certain. President Lyndon Johnson, despite being a southern Democrat, had broken with his party's White Supremacists and strong-armed Congress into passing the Civil Rights Act. Surely, he would support seating the integrated Mississippi Freedom Democrats to represent Mississippi. Volunteers like him and Reggie just had to do the leg work of collecting the signatures of most of Mississippi's black population.

This already hot July morning, while sweat dripped from their faces, tickled their ears, and darkened their shirts, he and Reggie moved from house to house explaining the strategy and collecting signatures. Many people signed with an X and either he or Reggie would print their name next to the X and invite them to come to the nearest Freedom School so they could learn to read and write. Because Mississippi officials refused to register most black people who the volunteers recruited to register to vote, progress on the voter registration front was slow. But forming this alternative Mississippi Freedom Democratic Party, signing petitions, and attending the organizing meetings, gave people hope.

As he and Reggie walked up to yet another tiny cabin, Edward told Reggie that he longed to go to Atlantic City to observe the historic moment when Mississippi's black people showed they could play the game of politics and convinced the Democratic

Party that they should have a seat at the table. "Mrs. Hamer'll testify to the Credentials Committee, it'll be televised, and the world will learn how violently anti-democratic Mississippi is. I want to be there, man!"

"But it's not our part to play. We're not from Mississippi," Reggie reminded him. "It needs to be the people who've paid the price to try to register to vote, the people who lost their jobs and houses and still keep pushing for their rights. We're needed here while they're gone to Atlantic City. Who knows what the Citizens' Councils may try against the folks that don't get on the bus to the Convention?" Why was Reggie always ahead of him in thinking through consequences? Sometimes Reggie's brilliance disgruntled him.

Just ahead they saw ten state troopers surrounding a group of black people. These black people wore suits and ties and carried briefcases. Curious, Edward and Reggie approached, hanging back where they could hear but not bring attention to themselves.

The troopers stood with their legs wide spread and their arms crossed over their chests, holding billy clubs in one hand, keeping the other within inches of their guns. The troopers stood behind the formally dressed black men, where they would not miss hearing a word that was spoken.

Edward felt a mix of fear and pride watching those men in suits standing tall despite the threatening presence of the troopers. He wanted to ask Reggie what they should do if it got ugly but knew they must remain silent and blend into the crowd. He could see pearls of sweat sticking to the forehead of the suited man who was speaking. While he watched, those perfect, shining spheres let go of the man's forehead, elongated and rolled down his nose, dropping soundlessly onto the dirt, one after another, in slow motion like so much in Mississippi, where everything seemed to happen in stretched out time—seconds protracted to minutes, the movement of handkerchief from pocket to face taking forever, the somnolent pace of the people unhurried, every movement slowed to conserve energy in the oppressive heat. Edward held his breath, fascinated by the sluggish parade of sweat beads across the man's face before they descended to the earth.

He wondered what the men in suits were feeling. The air was sodden with a sullen energy that left him anxious. He guessed the men in suits were nervous. They were asking questions of an elderly man and two women. The women wore church dresses and sat on kitchen chairs set out in someone's front yard. The chairs wobbled on the uneven hard-packed dirt. Around the perimeter of the yard someone had planted Black-Eyed Susans, but they slumped, visibly dehydrating, their yellow faces looking down, stems leaning on each other in the unrelenting heat. The eyes of the women darted from the black men in suits to the troopers and back. Occasionally one of them looked over her shoulder to where children peered out from the doorway, standing very still and watching closely. He wondered if the kids had ever seen such well-dressed black men.

Edward heard the men in suits ask about the three missing volunteers and saw a look of terror pass across the face of the man to whom the question was addressed. Then he remembered who these overdressed black people were.

Reggie had told him that the national N.A.A.C.P. had sent a high-level delegation to Mississippi to investigate the disappearance of the volunteers and to learn the experiences of black people who tried to register to vote. This must be them.

The delegation thanked the terrified man and two women they'd been interviewing and moved toward their black Lincoln. The rapid slap-slap of their purposeful steps announced that they were outsiders. The troopers drew in their legs to a normal standing posture and conferred amongst themselves what to do next. Then they, too, strode to their vehicles, only slowly, leaning into the heat.

Edward approached the N.A.A.C.P. delegates to thank them for coming. A younger man of medium height was just about to climb into the car. Hearing Edward, he turned toward him.

"You're very brave to do this," Edward told him.

"On the contrary, we're only here for a few days. You folks who live with this every day are the brave ones. This is a police state, man. Everywhere we go the troopers stick to us like ants on honey. When we went to the statehouse, they had their rifles pointed at us the whole time we climbed those steps, and when we left, they crowded us on all sides, trigger fingers ready, muttering what they'd like to do to us. I thought being a lawyer would protect me, but I learned here that it makes not a damn bit of difference. To them I'll always be a 'nigger.'"

The engine of the Lincoln turned over and began to purr. Some of the other delegates urged "Chet" to get in the car. As he did, Chet called to Edward over his left shoulder, "You be careful." When they pulled away, Edward walked back to Reggie. He was thinking about "Chet" and how scared he seemed. Living here Edward had learned to live past that fear, to walk right into and through it. If you didn't do that you'd be sitting in the fetal position in some cellar rocking back and forth like some crazy person. Come to think of it, maybe acting crazy wasn't a bad strategy.

Ann, August 5, 1964

Ann's eyes were squeezed shut so tightly that the bright morning sunlight could not sneak past her lashes. She knew it was time to get up, but she was reeling from yesterday's news. The three missing volunteers had been found, their bodies dumped in a huge earthen dam along the Pearl River. It was what they had been told to expect back on the day they learned that Mickey Schwerner, James Chaney, and Andrew Goodman were missing. That was June 21st, before Ann and Barbara's group had left Ohio for Mississippi, forty-four days ago. Those forty-four days bracketed all of Ann's time in Mississippi so far.

She'd been told they were certainly dead, so why was she so paralyzed with depression at this gory confirmation? Maybe because confirmation of their murders brought home that Reggie and Edward's terrifying experience—which had become the stuff of myth in the past two weeks—could have had the same outcome? Maybe because rumor had it that the Klan and the Citizens' Councils would be stepping up their violence in two weeks, when some of the volunteers and the 68 delegates that had been chosen to represent the Mississippi Freedom Democratic Party left for the National Democratic Convention? Maybe because Reggie was remaining in Mississippi?

"We gotta be at school in twenty minutes," Barbara called from the kitchen. "Come on, Ann, shake a leg!" Ann felt very close to Barbara. Their late-night conversations in the protective darkness of Edna Mae's front room—the mosquitos had defeated them outside—took them to a place of intimacy that Ann valued greatly. But when she felt alone and depressed, like today, she was jealous of Barbara's relationship with Hervie Stein.

Her legs felt like lead and her head ached from the humidity and the hundred-degree heat. She pushed herself into sitting and willed her crossed legs to support her as they pushed her body up from the floor. She pulled on clean underpants, and a short-sleeved shirt which she tucked into her wrap-around skirt. She folded her pallet, pushed it behind one of the backseat sofas, and walked outside to the makeshift shower, a bucket of water balanced on the Y intersection of the sole tree, a dangling cord tied to its handle so you could tip it to wash off the night sweat. The sun dried her hair and clothes within minutes and lightened her depression. She set the bucket down beside the tree, not taking it to the pump to refill it like she usually did. Last night when they got the news about the bodies, Edna Mae had quietly said that she'd refill the bucket for the rest of the week. Ann figured it was her way of thanking them for the risks they were taking.

Last night Barbara and Ann had stayed up late talking, remembering how they had felt when they arrived in Maybe Crossing. They were already grieving their coming departure from Edna Mae, her children, and the people they worked with. Barbara had confided that she wondered what would happen to her relationship with Hervie once they returned to their separate worlds. They both would be under a lot of family pressure to end it, she was certain. "A Jew boy?" She could hear her mother's voice in her head.

Now Ann shook off the sweat already forming in her hair, put on her sandals, and walked around to the front of the house where

Clarence's truck had just pulled up.

There was nothing remarkable about the rest of the day. Her students were eager learners, as usual. Working with them brought her out of her depression, at least for a time. After school she worked in the library they had constructed in a corner of the community center. She'd stocked it with donated books that Northerners had sent to Mississippi. She tutored a young woman in reading, then gnawed on a couple of ears of corn and savored a peach Edna Mae had sent with her that morning. Because Barbara was collecting signatures with another volunteer, she returned to the community center to prepare for tomorrow's classes while she waited for Barbara.

She was seated at one of the card tables in the library corner, ostensibly sorting stacks of books. She couldn't concentrate. What was she going home to? The question set off an internal earthquake. How could she return to life in her upper-class community, her affluent home, her progressive college? In thirteen days her world would shift seismically, shattering her sense of purpose and replacing it with boredom and depression. She would go from close relationships with Barbara, Reggie, and Edna Mae to isolation in an all-white world where no one could possibly understand how the summer and these friendships had transformed her.

The door to the center stood open. Lost in the forethought of grief she did not notice that someone had joined her. Reggie stood several yards away leaning against the doorway, observing her, his expression tender and concerned. He said nothing, then softly spoke her name. Seeing him she began to weep, her sobs punctuated with "Damn!" and "I don't want to cry!" He slid into the chair across from her and reached for her hands which covered her eyes. He cradled her right hand in both of his. His hand stroking the back of hers felt as light as a feather. When she stopped weeping, he asked if she would like to go for a walk. She nodded, unable to speak, and he led her toward the door, not letting go of her hand until they crossed the threshold.

They walked in silence. She could not muster the probing questions that were her trademark.

"Depressed?" Reggie asked her. She nodded and then added, "And angry that people take lives so easily. That by remaining here, your life's in even more danger. That I have to leave this place, these people, you. That I must re-enter my former world when I'm no longer my former self."

Reggie took her elbow and steered her through a field crowded with cotton plants, their white fluffy bolls so thick that at first glance they appeared to be snow, incongruous in the humid heat of August. A row of pine trees nearly a hundred feet high marked the edge of the field and pointed to the sky like fingers raised in greeting. Reggie led her to them. Selecting the one providing the most shade, he sat down with his back against its broad trunk. She sat beside him, surprised at the cushiony seat the fragrant needles provided.

Ann was bleeding from the undergrowth of cotton that had reached out and snagged her bare legs. Skirts were required for the volunteers, but they made no sense in a cotton field, she thought. Reggie wiped away the blood with his red bandana. From their seats so low to the ground they could see nothing but the frothy cotton. The community center, the school, the church and the mom-and-pop store disappeared from view from this perspective.

She lay back on the pine needles, not caring how Reggie might interpret her abandon. She drank in the scent of pine, the panorama of the field with its overabundance of brown pods splitting as they gave birth to balls of white fleece. Reggie passed her twin pinecones growing from the same twig. "Kind of like us," he said, "twins joined together at their source." He lay down beside her and looked up at the cloudless sky through the loblolly pine's fans of green needles. They heard the counterpoint percussion of two woodpeckers, and Ann pointed out where their red bellies were barely visible high on the tree beside theirs.

"Did you look at the raindrops on the windshield on your way home last night?" he asked her.

She had forgotten. "Why did you want me to notice that?" Ann's gaze was fixed on a large bird soaring and diving and soaring again. "Isn't that a bald eagle?" she asked.

"Woman, you're asking a city boy who knows nothing about

birds. You tell me."

"It is and they're rare. We are lucky to get to see him perform." Reggie reached for her hand and she gave it without reservation.

"Back to the raindrops. I wanted you to notice that they leave footprints when they pelt against the glass—small circles, perfectly round, that remain until the next drop lands in the same space. I never noticed that before this summer. It seemed important somehow, evidence that we each leave our marks, even if only briefly. When you go back to White Plains, you'll leave your mark on the people here and on me, and you'll carry their and my marks with you. That's all."

"I don't want to go back." Her voice was forceful, intense. "I know it's crazy, but I want to stay here with you." She turned her head away from him, torn between re-erecting her Guard-All shield and letting it dissolve completely. When she turned back, he had shifted to his side, one elbow propping up his torso, his face very close to hers. She wasn't sure who moved first to erase the space between them, only that suddenly their mouths joined and her arms went around him. She felt safe. And comfortable. And not afraid.

They remained there under the loblolly pine, banishing the voices inside that called for restraint, for following the rules. They remained until the sun started its fiery descent, lighting the cotton field in pinks and corals. Then, knowing they must hurry to catch their rides, they arose and, holding hands, made their way through the field. Several times as they hurried Reggie stopped to pull her to him for one more kiss. He said they were rehearsing their return to their lives before Freedom Summer. She corrected him. "Everything from now on is 'After.'"

Edward, August 19, 1964

They had signed up 63,000 people for the new Freedom Party. Harry Belafonte, a singer and Hollywood star, had paid for the buses to carry the delegates to Atlantic City. Edward could hardly stand not being on one of those buses. Instead, he and Reggie were assigned to help the volunteers who were returning to their colleges. Reggie was interim project director while the regular project director was at the National Democratic Convention. He took the assignment seriously and Edward, who had decided to return to Howard University by way of Nashville, was at a loss what to do with his time. No reason to collect more signatures now. Their voter registration efforts had been minimally productive, and everything now rode on what happened at the Convention. Instead of recruiting, he hung out at the office, organizing the files and the boxes of papers that remained unsorted due to the summer's frenetic pace.

The first night after the buses left, he and Reggie decided to sleep in the office to guard it. They'd heard rumors that the Klan planned to firebomb Freedom Houses across the Delta while the top leadership of Freedom Summer was out of the state. They informed their host not to expect them.

Edward took pride in making order out of the chaos in the office. This Freedom House was an old store that had been boarded up when they'd arrived in June. The ground floor had become the community center where the Freedom School was conducted. Upstairs was the office.

When darkness crept over the small community, he and Reggie sprawled on the lumpy sofas someone had donated which, along with several folding chairs and a card table, comprised the office furniture.

About two a.m. Edward heard a crash followed by the shattering of glass. He crawled to the side window and made out a dozen men below. Someone was pouring something on the ground all around the building. Others were heading back to their vehicles. He heard the sound of their car engines turning over, then a crackling, hungry noise accompanied by the sharp, acrid smell of gasoline.

"Reggie! We're being firebombed. Come on. We've got to get out of here." He pulled at Reggie until he awoke, groggy and unfocused. He opened the window at the back of the office and climbed out onto the roof of the back storeroom that a previous owner had added onto the building. From there they'd have to jump to the ground, but not until they heard the vehicles departing.

He felt dizzy from the strong smell of gas. He crawled back into the already smoky office, yanked the seat cushions from the sofa and pulled them to the back window and out onto the roof, planning to throw them off the roof and jump on them to break their fall. Only when the first cushion burst into a mass of ragged-edged orange and blue tongues of flame did he realize how absurd his plan was.

"We can't wait," Reggie whispered. He clutched some office files to his chest as he prepared to jump.

Edward jumped first, trying to keep his body relaxed and curled. He hit the ground at least a yard shy of the remaining cushion and rolled away from the house which was already lit up by giant, voracious flames eating its exterior walls. Seconds later Reggie jumped, just as the other cushion burst into flame. The files flew from his hands and blew across the flames, jumping and burning, as Reggie rolled away from the house, barely escaping the rapidly advancing fire.

Edward got up, hobbling on a twisted ankle. He called to Reggie to get away from the trees, that pine needles are very flammable. With great effort Reggie got to his knees, then pulled himself to standing and tested his injured leg. Edward could see by the light of the fire that something was very wrong. The outside of Reggie's left pant leg jutted out at a sharp angle, pushing out his jeans. Edward felt nauseous. He swallowed repeatedly the saliva filling his mouth as he realized that Reggie must have broken his thigh bone. He tossed Reggie a long branch that lay at his feet. Reggie caught it and used it to support his weight as they hurriedly limped away from the perimeter of the fire. Please don't let the branch break. It didn't. Residents of the community emerged from the dark into the flame lit area around Freedom House carrying buckets of water to saturate the ground to stop the fire's expansion. A couple of women helped Edward and Reggie navigate the distance to safety while others formed a bucket brigade, filling buckets at the community pump and passing them down the line of people. The firelight silhouetted them, bodies bending to pick up a bucket, turning to pass it on, turning back to pick up another again and again. Pride in them washed over him. Pride in their capacity for collaboration despite how often life let them down. He remembered participating in a bucket brigade when the church that had hosted this community's Freedom School was torched last month.

It was too late to save the office and the community center. But he and Reggie were safe.

All of our records! All of our books! Nothing but ashes. He remembered his mother collecting books for Mississippi, packing them in sturdy wooden crates and paying the postage to send them to her cousin in western Tennessee, from where they were carried by car. Oh, Mama, I'm sorry, he thought.

A woman helped him stretch out on someone's porch. Another woman was wrapping Reggie's leg with a wooden splint to keep it straight until morning when it would be safe to take him to a black doctor in the next town. Then she wrapped Edward's ankle. They'd given Reggie some home brew to ease his pain and now a man offered Edward some. It burned all the way down and nearly knocked him out.

When the fire died, several men helped carry Reggie into the front room of a shotgun cottage nearby. Then they brought Edward in and laid him next to Reggie. Someone tried to make a joke. "Don't want the skeeters to feast on your tender young flesh."

The last thing Edward remembered, was Reggie's voice subdued and strained by pain, telling him to go to sleep, that he was okay.

Ann

Ann sat on the single step that you climbed to reach Edna Mae's front stoop, taking in the glorious shades of salmon and pink and cream that filled the sky in the moments before it turned to monochromatic gray and white. Clouds converged like groups of women trailing children, gathering to greet each other and then disperse, heading home at the end of the day. Barbara joined her, enjoying the sweet relief of evening breezes ruffling the pines and causing their needles to chatter to each other. The two women did not talk, not now.

Ann couldn't keep from smiling. The combination of her afternoon with Reggie and the excitement of seeing the buses off to Atlantic City left her elated. Hope squatted on her depression. Hope, that thing with wings. She was ready for flight in that magical time when darkness comes on as suddenly as flipping a light switch and swallows the day.

She tried to commit to memory how night comes on in Mississippi, to observe it so closely that after she was back in White Plains, or at school in Yellow Springs, she would be able to summon to her consciousness its bewitching arrival. The birds twittered to each other like people at the theatre and then suddenly went silent, waiting for the light to go out and the astounding star-studded spectacle of the Delta night sky to take over the stage. As closely as she watched she could not name the precise moment when the forgiving, pulsing blackness descended.

She heard the smack of Barbara's hand against her arm. Mississippi mosquitoes. Right on time. Reluctantly, Ann stood. She surveyed the darkness and the few dim spots of light in the homes of Maybe Crossing people, signs of a new defiance replacing their fear. Then she went into the house. Barbara followed her.

Within an hour the quiet of the night was shattered by the shouts of men and the backfiring of their vehicles as they approached the community, tires scattering gravel as they came. Ann knew the routine. She and Barbara lay on the floor so that bullets would have to travel through the wooden walls, not just the glass membranes of the windows, to reach them. Was life always like this, she wondered, the perfect moments followed by chaos and conflict? Then she heard something unfamiliar.

A resonant male voice, deep and rich, loud and firm, defiant, even. *"Get out of Maybe Crossing. This be our town and y'all not welcome here!"* The neighbors were cheering him. *"Not till y'all change your ways,"* the voice continued.

Ann's adrenalin was pumping wildly. She could hear muddled and indistinct sounds of voices conferring. She and Barbara waited on the pine floor. She was imagining a shoot-out. Everyone had guns, the KKK, the Citizens' Council, and most residents of Maybe Crossing.

She heard car engines turn over and the grinding of gears. There must be six or more cars out there. Then she heard the put-put sound of the cars in motion and the deafening honking of car horns. The sound decreased in volume. *Decreased?* This was not part of the script the White Knights of the Klan followed in their previous visits.

She raised up and looked out the window. She could see the red taillights of half a dozen cars heading out of Maybe Crossing. No shots had been fired. Just a defiant verbal ultimatum that in the past would have brought severe reprisals. Was the community's solidarity and the night riders' hesitation a product of this summer's work? Despite the few people registered to vote and the hundreds of beatings and the deaths, was this a sign that change is coming, like Sam Cooke promised in his song?

Edna Mae and her boys emerged from the back room smiling. Together they went out to the road where other residents were gathering in an impromptu celebration in the darkness. Ann could not see their faces but the younger ones were jumping around jubilantly and shouts of "Praise the Lord!" punctured the night. She and Barbara hugged and jumped and shouted, too. It felt good to let out all that relief, all that gratitude.

Edward

With Reggie recovering from a badly broken leg and immobilized by an ankle-to-hip cast, it was Edward who saw to the departure of busloads of volunteers. Reggie remained by the phone in the home of the owner of the mom-and-pop store to receive reports from Atlantic City.

Edward enjoyed being in charge and knew he was good at keeping track of details. He was also good at consoling the weepy young women conflicted about leaving Mississippi. Some volunteers had left before the Convention in Atlantic City, but most were leaving this week, before the results of the Mississippi Freedom Democratic Party's challenge would be known. It was a glum group of volunteers, most of them whites, who he oversaw as they boarded the buses. They hung out the windows waving wistfully as the buses pulled out and headed North.

This particular day the group departing included volunteers he had come to know fairly well. Edward stood beside the Greyhound bus, reluctant to say good-by to Barbara, Hervie, and Ann. Ann seemed very disappointed when he told her that Reggie was unable to come to see them off due to his broken leg. Edward was feeling disappointed also. They had shared the terrors of Mississippi, the heat and bugs, the thrill of doing meaningful work, long-shot work. They had witnessed small changes in the responses of the people they worked alongside. Losing these friends to their separate lives, lived great distances apart, left a chasm inside him he feared would never be filled. How could anyone who had not been here understand what they had experienced in these two months?

The driver shouted, "Last call to board." Edward hugged each of them and stood at the door checking off their names as they climbed the steps and moved down the narrow passage between the rows of seats. He stood with the local people who had come to see them off.

Everyone was quiet as the bus pulled out. He wondered how these people would fare without their white friends' presence attracting national attention to their situation. He wiped the dust and sweat from his face, wished the locals a good day, and walked back to their makeshift office. He could see Reggie in the window watching the bus disappear down the road.

Ann's parents were at the Greyhound station in White Plains to meet her. She wondered if they could see how changed she was. Mom could hardly wait to tell her the news. They'd been watching the National Democratic Convention on television and heard the beginning of Mrs. Hamer's speech. Amazing woman! Then her presentation to the Credentials Committee was interrupted by a press conference at the White House, but there wasn't any breaking news announced by President Johnson, so it hardly merited cutting into Mrs. Hamer's account of life in Mississippi. Luckily, the networks were going to replay Mrs. Hamer's speech that night.

Ann brightened at that. She put her backpack in the trunk and slid into the back seat. Mom wanted to know where her suitcase was, and she explained that she'd left her clothes and suitcase with Edna Mae. "She needs them more than I do."

The ride home was a prelude to what would be for Ann a prolonged experience of frustration. Her parents were interested and full of questions, but trying to explain everything unfamiliar to them was exhausting. When they reached the house, she excused herself to take a shower, not coming downstairs until dinner. Mom had made steak and baked potatoes, green beans with almonds, and a tossed salad with lemon meringue pie for desert. The table was laden with more food than Edna Mae's family ate in four nights. Ann felt nauseous looking at all that abundance and ate little. In the set of Mom's face she read disappointment.

After dinner they moved to the living room to watch coverage of the convention. Mrs. Hamer gave her speech—no notes, just life experience—ending with the statement that if the Mississippi Freedom Democrats are not seated, then she questions America. Ann felt hot tears etching parallel lines on her face.

Cora, Nashville, September 1

Cora stood at the kitchen sink washing the supper dishes. She was humming to herself. It was a trick she had learned to keep her mind off her fears. Her voice was low and barely audible and she hummed one old hymn after another, whatever lodged in her mind. The loud bang of the screen door interrupted her self-imposed state of not thinking, and she shook the soap suds from her hands and wiped them on her apron, moving toward the front door to investigate the cause of its banging. There in the doorway stood her son Edward, smiling big, glasses akimbo, sporting an Afro and wearing a dashiki. She enfolded him in her arms and held on until she felt him moving like he wanted out of her fierce embrace. She loosened her hold on her son and stepped back to study him. He'd grown taller in his months in Mississippi. She scrutinized his face, his front and back, looking for injuries and changes her mother's eye had feared. Finding none, she held him again, reminding herself not to hold on so desperately. He was alive! He looked well! It was over and he had come home.

Then she floated to the phone to call Arthur, who had gone back to his house to change clothes after work, and Mi-Young, who was babysitting. She warmed leftover smothered pork chops, rice and turnip greens from the garden in a skillet, set out bread and butter, and poured Edward a glass of milk. Part of her wanted to resume their old pattern of lively conversation sorting out the latest news, in this case, from Atlantic City, but she told herself not to hover, he must set the pace, discuss the news and tell his stories when he was ready. He seemed uncharacteristically quiet, or could he be depressed? "Mama, thank you for letting me go," was all he said before Arthur arrived, face flushed with excitement. He'd run through the garden and took off his muddy shoes at the front door before entering and pulling Edward into a bear hug.

Her two men sat in the living room while Cora finished washing up. Now Edward began to talk. "You've heard that they gave us only two of the sixty-eight seats reserved for Mississippi? he asked, "And that Mrs. Hamer and Bob Moses turned that down and led the MFDP in walking out of the Convention?" His face sagged with exhaustion and for a moment she could envision how he would look as a much older man. She nodded. Edward almost spat out his next words. "The President was so afraid of losing the election that he kissed up to the white South. It was his fear that he listened to, Mama. For as long as I can remember you've told me not to let fear rule my decisions. President Johnson betrayed the people of the Delta because of fear....and they'd suffered so much finding the strength to set their own fear aside and believe democracy was possible."

Uh oh, Cora thought, my son is coming back to me disillusioned, which is the other side of the coin to fear. Now she abandoned the enormous effort she had been making to keep quiet. "You're thinking that all your work accomplished nothing?"

Edward sank into the sofa. He didn't answer her.

"A lot of the commentators are saying that things are changing in Mississippi and predicting that by this time next year Mississippi will be registering Negroes at the same rate as Tennessee, which would be an amazing accomplishment." She was doing combat with his discouragement.

"If there're any black people left to register!" His voice was angry. Here it comes, she thought.

Edward told them of the firebombing of Freedom Houses and black churches, of the police following the volunteers, beating them, fining them huge amounts of money, harassing sharecroppers who tried to register to vote.

"Did this happen to you, Edward?" Cora had to ask.

"No," he replied, and her intuition told her he was protecting her. That was all right. She needed his protection as he needed hers.

Through the window she saw the full orange harvest moon bathing her garden in a gentle half-light. She noticed how Edward jerked to full attention at the sound of a car pulling up outside. Would she ever know what he had experienced?

Mi-Young was home from babysitting. She pulled open the screen door and jumped into Edward's lap. With "the child" present the conversation shifted and Edward recounted funny stories, like looking for their car on a moonless night and jimmying the trunk to rescue some papers. He left out the deputies and their guns, and they laughed at what sounded like a college boy prank.

That night Cora lay awake in a clammy sweat, imagining what he had edited out of his accounts. She worried where his anger might take him and yearned for the old intimacy she and her son shared in the days when he told her everything. She wondered if she ever would hear the truth about his experiences in Mississippi and wondered if she could bear the truth. Gratitude for his surviving Freedom Summer and pride in his courage filled her. She knew that her son was now a man.

Arthur stopped by the next morning on his way to work to check on her. She said she was fine. She was glad for the concern in his eyes.

Ann, Yellow Springs, Ohio, Fall 1964

Ann returned to Antioch College, feeling troubled and lonely. When he dropped her off at the college her dad had joked that she was returning from war and that there should be brass bands to welcome her. They'd laughed but there was truth in his joke. She felt like she imagined a returning soldier would feel whose wounds were internal, who no one would recognize as a veteran out of uniform.

By mid-October when her period was two months late, she guessed she might be pregnant. She vaguely remembered hearing that the first three months of pregnancies were the most iffy. Maybe she would miscarry?

There was no one to tell so she kept going to classes, but she couldn't concentrate. By midterms her academic performance was uncharacteristically weak. She had a D in Philosophy and was barely squeaking a C in Drama Performance, where the secret she carried inhibited her acting. She felt brittle and anxious and never let her guard down. She took to wearing lose clothing, men's flannel shirts over jeans, baggy coats over the shirts—she wanted to disappear into her extra-large, shapeless apparel.

Most of academia still required women to dress up for classes and meals, but Antioch took pride in being progressive and cultivating in its students a healthy disrespect for authority. Consequently, most of her professors smiled approvingly when she came to class dressed down, assuming that her time in Mississippi had strengthened her resolve to reject authority and think for herself. Most people on campus interpreted her increased preference for being alone to Mississippi. The other Freedom Summer volunteers from the college had also returned noticeably altered. Her roommate had left school before mid-terms so Ann had her room to herself. She monitored when the other women used the shower and showered after they had left for breakfast. Breakfast didn't remain in her stomach anyway. She began hugging towels in front of her when she walked down the hall to the communal bathroom and got naked only behind the shower curtain or alone in her room so that no one would notice the rounding of her belly.

At Thanksgiving she could see that her parents were concerned about her. She noticed that they both seemed older, worry lines creasing their faces. They asked why she was so withdrawn, why she didn't eat breakfast, why she looked pale. She deflected their questions by saying it had been a demanding semester and that she was really tired. Then she retreated to her room.

By Christmas break she was beginning to show, not much, but enough for her parents to notice. At dinner her second night home Dad asked if Mom and he could talk with her. He said the college had sent them a notice that she was flunking Philosophy and getting a D in Drama Performance, and that they were worried about her.

Ann felt her stomach flip-flop. She was mortified to disappoint them. Since the death of her only sibling, she had carried the responsibility for being both son and daughter to her parents. Not that they ever articulated this, no, they would never do that. It was simply something that she knew was her role in the family. She hadn't disappointed them. She knew this. But getting pregnant at nineteen? The only thing worse would be to die like her brother had.

They moved to the living room and she perched on the far end of the dark blue velvet sofa. Her eyes focused on the intricate geometric patterns of the Persian rug. The grandfather clock in the corner sounded its regular, bass notes. She remembered its rhythm comforting and calming her when she was a child. She tried to remember the script she had prepared for this conversation and failed miserably. She turned away from her parents, poised for flight on the edge of the sofa while silent tears sculpted her cheekbones and dropped onto her lap leaving dark splotches on her jeans. Seeing the wet marks reminded her of Mississippi in the rain and set off a tidal wave of grief that she could not contain. She said in a shaky voice, "I'm pregnant." Her tears turned torrential and great gasps for air hacked at the silence, interspersed with groans that she had stored up for the past three months.

Mom slid onto the sofa next to her and held her. Dad moved the side chair so he was across from her, knee to knee. He held her hands and didn't say anything.

After what seemed a very long time, after her weeping had become half-swallowed sobs, she raised her head and wiped her face with the hanky Mom pressed into her hand. It smelled slightly of Chanel No. 5, the fragrance she'd associated with Mom all of her life. That felt comforting. Still, they said nothing, waiting for her sobs to fully subside. Slowly she told them about Reggie, what an interesting and intelligent man he was, how careful they had been to police their attraction to each other. She told them about spending one afternoon together— privacy was difficult—before someone firebombed the office where he was working. It poured out of her how he'd broken his leg jumping off the roof to escape the fire, how he had not been able to see her before she left, how hard it had been to leave Mississippi, and how lonely she was. And then two, now four months of no period.

"Does he know?" Mom asked.

"No. We really like each other. But not like that." Her sentences came in jerky bursts followed by silence, like she was squeezing them out little bit by little bit., "We each have things we want to do. The summer was so incredible." Silence. "I think we helped each other process what was happening. To us and to people in Mississippi." Silence. "I'm not ready to get married. I'm sure he's not…. I don't know what to do."

She left out Reggie's conviction that he could not let himself fall in love with a white girl. They wouldn't understand.

"Maybe we can help you figure out what to do at this crossing point in your life." Dad shifted into his problem-solving default.

Her sudden laughter startled all of them. "I just noticed you said 'Maybe' and 'Crossing' in the same sentence. That's where I lived this summer, Maybe Crossing, Mississippi. It seems funny to think that I am at another Maybe Crossing." She could tell her parents did not understand but that they welcomed her laughter. Perhaps this was a sign that she really could get through this.

She didn't return to Antioch for spring semester. She remained at home with her parents while her body changed shape and her appreciation of family with it. She hadn't known what to expect, but her parents' support was beyond all expectations. One of her friends in high school who got pregnant was expelled from her family and left to cope on her own. Ann wondered what had happened to her.

The only person outside her family who Ann spoke with was Barbara, who was back at school at Shaw University in Raleigh, finishing her senior year and feeling confined by school after their experience in Mississippi.

Barbara was writing and occasionally talking on the phone with Hervie, though neither of them could afford long distance phone calls more than once a month. Hervie would phone on the second Saturday evening of each month, because it was the anniversary of his first real conversation with Barbara. That was sweet, and hearing about it stirred in Ann a moment of longing for that kind of contact with Reggie.

When she told Barbara about the baby, Barbara listened carefully to how Ann was feeling and then tried to tease her out of her funk with, "This baby will be your permanent reminder of Freedom Summer."

Barbara didn't know how to get in touch with the other volunteers. The firebombing of the offices had destroyed so many records. She told Ann that Reggie was regularly mentioned in the SNCC newsletters. He'd been named a major organizer for the planned Selma to Montgomery march for voting rights that was to begin in January.

Ann followed the progress of the march throughout the winter. It made the front pages of the *New York Times* and she imagined his family, living somewhere near her in New York City, must be very proud of him as she was.

It frustrated her to follow events in Selma from her parents' comfortable home in White Plains. She worried about the marchers and about Reggie. When she felt alone and scared, she reminded herself that he was doing important work and that her work was to finish school and provide for their child. She would not distract him with her news.

In mid-March, she was ecstatic when President Johnson asked Congress to pass a federal law protecting the right to register and vote. It would include federal supervision of elections in districts with a history of preventing people from voting. According to the paper such a law would in the future protect the voters they had tried to register. She knew that Reggie's work in Selma, Alabama —and the murders of three more civil rights workers there—was responsible for the President's action.

As her due date grew closer and the baby's kicks made its presence acutely real, she sometimes talked to the child, telling it Mississippi stories, stories of the brave people of Maybe Crossing.

On April 7, 1965, Ann gave birth to a baby girl who she named Keisha, which means Great Joy. Right up to that moment her parents had talked about placing the baby for adoption, but she refused to relinquish this child who represented the most transformative time of her life. The baby was a visible sign of the new world they had been working for. With her caramel-colored skin, narrow nose, and thick, curly, black hair the baby resembled both of her parents and represented that future Dr. King called them to embrace. Live as though the future you desire has already arrived, he preached. Ann was determined to live in that future with her daughter.

She tried to explain to her parents why she could not relinquish her daughter, fearing they would not understand. But they did. At least they understood how important keeping this baby was to their baby. Their opposition evaporated when Ann passed Keisha to them. Her mom had already strategized how they would make it work. "If I quit my job and you transfer to a school here in New York City, I can care for her while you're in classes."

"We can manage financially," Dad chimed in, though he still thought they should notify Reggie. She was insistent. No contact with Reggie.

When she brought Keisha home from the hospital, they settled into their new routine, Ann taking classes at City College, Mom caring for Keisha, and Dad earning the income. It was an arrangement surprisingly pleasurable for all of them.

Don, Buffalo, Summer 1965

Arthur's son Don spent his lunch hours in the diner across the tracks from the steel mill where he had a summer job. Booths lined the front wall of the diner like cubicles, their backs and seats upholstered in dark red vinyl that set off the white melamine table tops. The paneled walls of the diner displayed ads for coke, fat hamburgers, and pie, and a shiny glass display case showed off the mouthwatering selection of pies to those seated at the dappled gray formica counter. The customers were regulars, mostly men in work overalls with soot streaked faces along with a few old guys come for coffee and pie and to flirt with the waitress. Actually, most of the customers flirted with her.

She was small and pretty, vivacious, curvy, and energetic. Don had been observing her. She struck up conversations with her customers and remembered what they told her about themselves. She laughed a lot as she interacted with them. Don liked that. Laughter was in short supply in his life. Even at nineteen he lived carefully, assessing the potential consequences of his behavior, his words, and exercising inordinate self-control so as not to upset his mother and grandfather, who both had the power to destroy him.

The waitress turned her attention to the tall young man who the other customers had teased her about, who they'd noticed watching her. One lunch she startled him by asking, "Aren't you going to ask me out?" He was visibly flustered and wary and didn't respond.

Several days later, he surprised himself by asking her, "Wanna go out tonight?"

He took her for hamburgers, and she teased him, "Did you figure I love hamburgers 'cause I work at a diner?" He felt awkward and embarrassed but persisted, enjoying her confidence and her humor. They went to *Dr. Zhivago* and she cried silently when the lovers were separated. He was smitten. By their fourth date, they could hardly keep their hands off each other. He took her to his house—his family was on vacation for three weeks—and from then on they spent every night together until his mom and grandfather returned.

When he returned to Oberlin College, they wrote letters and saw each other when he came home for breaks, but he never mentioned her to his family. There was something exciting about having this important part of his life to himself and he suspected that had his family known, they would have forced an end to his relationship with Connie. They had big plans for his life. He would become a research scientist finding a cure for cancer or enabling travel to other planets. With her high school education and questionable grammar, Connie wasn't a woman to present to colleagues in those circles. Eventually, he ended the relationship.

Ann, White Plains, Summer 1967

On a warm Saturday afternoon Ann received a call from Barbara. Keisha was napping and Ann stood in the sunny kitchen of her parents' home, anticipating a good catch-up chat. But Barbara's voice was troubled, and she stumbled trying to find the best words as she told her friend what had happened at a recent meeting of the Student Non-violent Coordinating Committee that they both had belonged to for nearly three years.

"Everything's changed," Barbara said. "John Lewis is out of leadership, and James Forman and Stokely Carmichael are taking charge. After a long, heated discussion they voted to make SNCC an all-black organization." Barbara paused and Ann tried to take in what she had said.

"Stokely's been talking about the need for Black Power to counter White Power. He says whites should work in their own communities because all the problems black people face begin in white communities. Hervie and the other whites were told to leave! Hervie's very upset. Preacherman, too. They took the vote when some of us who opposed it had left the room to cool down. This isn't the SNCC that shaped us, Ann. I can't remain in such an organization. I've decided to take a break from the Movement and go to grad school."

Ann's voice was small and brittle, "Was Reggie at the meeting?" "Yes."

"What was his position?"

"He sided with Forman and Stokely." Barbara's voice sagged with regret and Ann could tell how sorry she was to bring her this news. She stretched to reach a kitchen chair, uncurling the cord of the phone, and sank down on it, her legs weak and rubbery. She scooted closer to the wall letting the cord slacken and re-curl.

"So you're leaving the Movement? Going to grad school?" She wasn't taking in everything Barbara was saying.

"Yes, I've done my stint, given it my all, but it has worn me *down*. I need to go back to school where I can read great literature. I don't want to have to watch my back or worry about the politics of the Movement. I've applied to Columbia in Literature and Critical Theory."

"That's really close! I'll get to see you!" Her fingers straightened the cord's spirals and let them snap back, jumping and wobbling, into one long ringlet. Playing with the cord pushed down her feelings.

"Hervie's coming to New York, too. He's enrolled in Hebrew Union. He's decided to become a rabbi." She could hear Barbara exhale, then pause like she wasn't sure where to go with their conversation. "Ann, he's asked me to marry him! Imagine that, a rabbi with a black Baptist wife."

"What are you going to do?" Ann's mouth felt dry and her voice sounded like it belonged to someone who hadn't spoken in a long while.

"I've said Yes, contingent on how this next year goes living so close and seeing each other so often." Barbara's voice changed and Ann could feel her concern moving through the phone cord. "What about you, girl?"

She pulled herself together, refocused and tried to banish the emotions attacking her voice. "I graduate in June. You won't believe this, but my professor made me apply for a national fellowship to do a Ph.D. in Mathematics, all expenses paid if I get it. Me! I figure nothing lost by applying. Never thought of myself pursuing math, but the predictability of math, its stability and lack of drama—all that's appealed to me lately. I think I'd enjoy being a professor teaching math to undergrads on some bucolic campus. Why not?"

She heard Keisha upstairs in her crib singing to herself, a good excuse for ending the conversation. It wasn't that she didn't love talking with Barbara who was her best friend. It was Barbara's news. That Reggie had supported forcing whites out of SNCC dismayed her, but she wouldn't tell anyone. At least it confirmed that she had made the right decision in not telling Reggie about his mixed-race daughter. If he didn't want whites working with blacks in the Movement, how could he embrace his child and her mother?

She must move on with her life for her sake and for Keisha's.

She would graduate from City College and do her grad work at NYU so that she and Keisha could continue to make their home with her parents.

As she climbed the stairs to liberate Keisha from her crib, she closed the door to thinking about Reggie.

Don, Buffalo, Summer 1967

The summer before Don entered grad school, he saw Connie on the street. When she threw him her radiant smile, he felt guilty and aware of how attracted to her he still was. He asked if she'd like to go for a beer. She seemed the same, warm and encouraging, asking about his experience in grad school, his family, his summer job. He'd missed her warmth and lightness. After a second beer he invited her back to his house.

She seemed disappointed when he said that his mom and grandfather were away on vacation, it being August. He could feel her eyes following him as he moved between the refrigerator and the kitchen counter, making them grilled cheese sandwiches and Campbell's tomato soup. It was disconcerting to see so much affection on her face.

They took their meal to the patio where they sat watching the birds swimming the air effortlessly. The patio was fenced and private, for which he was grateful. They sat in two Adirondack chairs side by side and he tried to calm his heart. A sudden rustling in the giant oak that shaded this side of the house pulled their eyes up to where its leaves rattled vigorously. They could see streaks of white and gray among the shaking leaves.

Two male pigeons, tail feathers spread in fans of gray and white, flew at a dowdy gray female again and again, aggressive and persistent. Don felt embarrassed when he realized what they were doing. Connie seemed fascinated. It was definitely a conversation stopper.

When the pigeons departed, Connie reached out and touched his arm. "I'm all right, you know. I love you, but I understand your limits."

He fiddled with his empty glass, turning it round and round. Its solitary ice cube slid from side to side making soft pinging sounds. He didn't know what to say or do. The woman was so honest. He felt the glass moving up and out of his hands. She was removing it, placing it on the end table between them. She sat on the broad arm of his chair, her head turned to face him. Her right hand lifted his hair from his forehead in a gesture so tender he found it overwhelming. Then she kissed him gently.

This woman wore an aura of safety unlike anyone he had known. He yearned to inhabit that unfamiliar safety even as his fear immobilized him. His body jerked involuntarily, mind battling matter. She stood and picked up their glasses, saying she would refill them. When she returned, he pulled her onto his lap and the water sloshed out wetting his pants and causing them both to laugh, their laughter physical and liberating. He kissed the back of her neck, tentatively, then turned her face to him looking at her full on, and the ferocity of his need did not make her look away.

Holding on to each other they navigated their way into the house and up the stairs to his room, where they fell on his bed laughing. Their lovemaking went on for hours, alternately energetic, athletic, intense, and playful, but always unambivalent. He would never forget the freedom he felt that night.

He awoke the next morning apprehensive, bordering on terrified, thinking he heard his mother downstairs. He knew he could never introduce Connie to his mother and imagined the contempt his mother would throw at her. What could he do? He'd made a mistake. He'd taken advantage of Connie's open reception of him, her still-obvious love for him. The facts had not changed: she would never fit in his world. His panic accelerated.

He gathered her clothes, shoes, and purse into a hopeless pile at the end of the bed and then awakened her. He couldn't look her in the eye so he turned away while he pulled on his jeans and T-shirt, mumbling that they would always be the best of friends, that he loved her, only not in a way that would lead to marriage. He let her down, this time for good.

He checked the hallway for signs that his mother had returned early. Nothing. She'd only returned in his head.

He led Connie to the back door, helped her into the car, and drove her home. He couldn't look at her, but his peripheral vision showed a face from which the light and safety had fled.

Two years later he dropped by the diner. It looked the same except for a few new ads on the wall. She wasn't there.

He ordered coffee and apple pie and sat in his usual booth, looking for anyone he recognized. Casually he approached a gray-bearded, pot-bellied man in Carhartt overalls who he thought he remembered as a regular and asked if he could join him. When the man smiled and nodded, he slid into the man's booth. Yes, the man knew Connie, lovely girl. When Don asked what had happened to her, the man told him that she had given birth to a baby boy after her parents kicked her out and had moved away to reassemble her life, maybe to Cleveland? No one knew who the father was.

"She's a good girl, that Connie, a good Catholic! She ain't no whore.

Some guy must of used her and just throwed her away—dirty bastard! Nobody's heard from her. The owner told me she'd tried to raise the boy on her own but couldn't manage. Had to place him for adoption. Close to broke her heart, they say."

Don tried to mask the chill that was traveling through his body. He thanked the man, slid out of the booth, leaving his pie uneaten, and exited the diner, regret and guilt churning his insides.

That child, that son, must be his.

Arthur, Nashville, June 13, 1967

Arthur was coming for dinner as he had every Tuesday and Friday for the past seven years since he had made Nashville his home. "Best nights in the week for me," he liked to say, "Time to relax with my family." Only he wished Cora could relax. She was always doing something. Tonight he and Mi-Young had persuaded her to let them cook for her, since it was her birthday. Of course, what they cooked was less ambitious than what Cora put together effortlessly like an artist playing with paints. Tonight's menu was hamburgers on the grill with greens from the garden, mixed fruit, and potato salad from Piggly Wiggly with a chocolate cake that he and Mi-Young had whipped up. Thank you, Betty Crocker. The cake was waiting, already loaded with candles. He could tell Cora was antsy. She kept getting up and coming into the kitchen, offering to help. Why couldn't the woman relax?

The little house was warm and Mi-Young toted a tablecloth, silverware, plates and napkins to the back yard where he had built a deck shaded by the tallest tree in the neighborhood. Mi-Young was setting the table, when Cora wandered into the kitchen yet again, this time carrying *The Nashville Tennessean*. She was saying something to him that he had missed. Then she started reading to him from a front-page story.

"The U.S. Supreme Court overturned Virginia's anti-miscegenation law yesterday finding for the plaintiffs in Loving v. Virginia." Mi-Young, about to turn fifteen and never willing to be kept out of the adults' conversation, entered the kitchen, characteristically forgetting to keep the screen door from banging. "What is 'anti-miscegin-something?'"

"Laws that ban marriage between people of different races," Cora replied.

Arthur moved to stand behind Cora, reading the article over her shoulder. "Wow, that's big news. Crazy it's taken this long." He was looking at Cora, thinking. Mi-Young liked to tease him that he couldn't do two things at once. She was probably right. He could smell the meat on the grill crisping and headed out the door to turn the burgers. His thoughts tangled in this new information, and he finished his chef's duties robotically.

Seated at the picnic table on the new deck they attacked the meal with enthusiasm. When Mi-Young carried the lighted cake out from the kitchen, her face had that look that Arthur recognized as her I-can-hardly-contain-this-surprise look. Before she started singing Happy Birthday, she grinned at them both and said, "Well, Dad, now you and Mama have no excuse." Arthur knew she was talking about the Court's decision. He'd been thinking the same thing but afraid to say it. Over the years he and Cora had become close and he knew they loved each other, though it had never been said. Sometimes he'd wanted so to take her in his arms but had held back, unsure if she would welcome that, knowing that if she didn't, it could harm, even destroy, their relationship.

He glanced furtively at Cora trying to read her response. She was clearly embarrassed and, when she went on about their wonderful birthday dinner, he knew she was trying to change the subject.

Mi-Young would not be deterred. "Well, at least you should think about it!" she said before launching into her slightly off tune rendition of Happy Birthday to You.

Arthur and Mi-Young finished the washing up, Arthur, agitated and anxious, afraid that if he let this moment pass, he might never again have the nerve to bring it up. Cora was waiting for them in the living room. He called from the doorway that he'd forgotten one thing, then rummaged in her junk drawer searching for something he could use. If he made it funny, she could joke it off and they could resume their regular relationship. Right?

He wrapped his finding in a paper napkin and tied it with a scrap of yellow ribbon he'd discovered in the drawer. Then he entered the living room and placed the small package on Cora's lap. She looked up at him, face confused, then untied the ribbon and unfolded the napkin. There lay a metal twist-em that he had shaped into a ring. He felt scared but it was too late so he plunged on.

"Mi-Young makes a good point. Why don't you think about it. Maybe we can talk tomorrow?"

Mi-Young's melodious laughter burst the silence in the room. "Oh, Dad, you are too much! What a unique proposal!"

Cora didn't say anything. He could tell she was rattled, and Cora was rarely rattled by anything. There being nothing more to say to relieve the awkwardness of his misguided gesture, he said good night and walked through the garden to the neutral quiet of his little house.

Cora, June 13, 1967

She lay in bed talking to Booker in her head. She wanted her first love to know about this new development in her life and communicate his approval. Or not. In the early years after his death she had been able to summon Booker and feel his presence. But for the past few years he seemed far away and inaccessible. Now, nothing was coming through. She guessed she was on her own to decide how to respond to Arthur. Come to think of it, she'd been on her own for a long time, if you didn't count her one-sided conversations with God.

I'll think about it tomorrow, she thought. The words of her least favorite movie heroine, Scarlett O'Hara, coming out of her mouth! Well, I guess I have no one but myself to blame for this predicament, she thought, as she turned off the light and sank into a fitful sleep.

Sometime during the night her face relaxed into a smile.

Ann, White Plains, Summer 1968

Over that year Barbara and Ann spoke regularly by phone and occasionally met in the city over a meal. In early June they met at a hole in the wall Middle Eastern restaurant in the Village, five tables and a tiny kitchen but kibbe, babaganoush, and baklava to die for. Sitting across from each other so close together that their knees touched, Barbara confided that trying to find fault with Hervie and his marriage idea was not working. Ann thought, Lucky Barbara. Lucky Hervie. She imagined how nourishing it would be to build her life with someone who had shared Freedom Summer. Barbara said they loved each other "too much to let little things like race and religion separate us." Ann laughed and squeezed Barbara's hands. She and Keisha and their other friends would provide the support Hervie and Barbara's parents were withholding, she reassured Barbara.

So it was that in mid-June Ann and three-year-old Keisha took the subway to Morningside Heights to Barbara and Hervie's apartment. There a rabbi and a Progressive National Baptist preacher, both rebels within their religious communities for presiding over this mixed marriage, conducted the unorthodox service, which was followed by a feast Barbara and her cousin had been preparing for days. There was fried chicken, potato latkes, stuffed peppers, greens cooked with chicken fat rather than bacon, sweet potato casserole, cornbread and an enormous, braided challah bread that the cousin carried in on a tray to the oooo's and ahhh's of the guests.

Keisha at three was a happy, precocious and outgoing child, who loved to socialize, especially when, like today, she could wear her pink polka-dot dress, matching hair ribbons, patent leather Mary Jane's, and lace-trimmed white socks. She talked to everyone at the reception and stole the show from whatever was going on near her. She moved among the grownups asking them questions, which they delighted to answer. It was a celebrity wedding and the celebrity was Keisha.

Ann loved watching her daughter work the crowd. Keisha was the best thing that ever happened to her, and watching other adults delight in her daughter made Ann very proud. Eventually, worn out from being a social butterfly, Keisha fell asleep in Ann's arms, a sign that it was past time to get back to White Plains.

Several days later Ann was hurrying to class and tripped, her bag flying open, its contents strewn across the sidewalk. Damn it! She checked herself for oozy places. Finding none, she sat on her heels and gathered up all the detritus of grad school, stuffing it quickly into her bag. "Need some help?" The voice belonged to a striking woman wearing an embroidered peasant blouse and blue jeans who squatted beside her and helped retrieve what Ann had missed. "I'm Alyssa. Sorry you're starting your day like this, but your bad luck is my good luck, as I get to meet you. Weren't you at Barbara and Hervie's wedding with that darling little girl? Who are you?

"Ann Whitmore, grad student in Math and late to class. Thanks for the help."

When they passed each other two days later, Alyssa asked if they could go for coffee. To Ann, lonely and consumed with her studies and her mommy work, the chance to get to know another woman who might be friend material sounded like manna from heaven.

Alyssa was easy to talk with and non-judgmental, and Ann poured out her life-changing experience in Mississippi and her surprise by-product of that experience, Princess Keisha, as Dad called her. Alyssa seemed genuinely impressed with the life decisions Ann had made.

"You are one brave woman, Ann. I'm honored to meet you." Alyssa had planned a career in interior decorating but had joined the Peace Corps instead. Before entering grad school she'd spent two years working "up country" in a small village in India teaching women how to plan their pregnancies.

Ann laughed when Alyssa told her that. "Maybe I should have been in India rather than Mississippi," she grinned.

They began meeting for lunch, developing a comfortable friendship over sack lunches consumed on the benches of Washington Square Park, watching people. Sometimes for exercise they walked the neighborhoods of Greenwich Village. It helped to have a friend at NYU.

One Saturday Alyssa invited Ann and Keisha to dinner at the apartment she shared with her partner, Sandra. Ann was curious about Sandra and Alyssa's relationship. She had never known women who were lesbians and could not imagine having the courage to openly love another woman. After that dinner Ann felt slightly awkward around Sandra, both attracted to the relationship she observed between the two women and wary of it, uncomfortable.

Ann dated rarely. She'd met no one who interested her for more than one date. Anyway, men her age were not interested in a woman with a small child. She told herself she was too busy for romance, although on Friday and Saturday nights she missed going out. Sometimes despite her delight in her daughter she allowed herself a pity party. Would her life be forever sexless?

In late July Alyssa proposed a beach trip to Long Island. When Alyssa picked Ann up early Saturday, Sandra was not with her—too much work to do to meet her deadline. Mom had offered to keep Keisha who had a cold, so it was just the two of them heading for the shore.

They lay on the beach soaking up the sun, resting in the shelter of the cloudless blue sky and enjoying the ease of their rambling conversation. Ann paid no attention to the sunburn blooming pink across her back until her shoulders started crinkling like paper when she shifted position on the blanket. Uh-oh, she reached for the blue glass jar of Noxema and slathered it on her shoulders, arms, chest, and legs.

Alyssa reached for the jar when Ann had finished and rubbed the soft white cream on Ann's back, paying gentle attention to the borders where raw skin met the protection of swimsuit. Ann's thirsty skin sucked up the Noxema leaving a cool, menthol feeling in place of the burn.

"That feels so good. Want me to get yours?" When Alyssa nodded and turned onto her stomach, Ann began spreading the cream, moving her hand in circles out from ridge of back bone that divided Alyssa's taut, muscular back into two perfect halves like the wings of a butterfly. The skin rippled under her touch. "You have a lovely back," she said. "Funny how we underestimate backs, don't even notice them, yet they keep us upright and are beautifully purposeful."

"Well, I don't want to be upright right now, or purposeful." Alyssa laughed and some strands of her long hair came loose from the hair pins that held them off her neck. They fell onto her newly greased back. Carefully Ann lifted the hair and re-pinned it. She hadn't before thought how intimate such small acts of caring were.

No conversation now as each turned to the novel she'd brought. Ann found it hard to concentrate, preferring to watch the shore and the children squatting in the sand constructing castles and then darting in and out of the water like sand pipers, their small bodies always in motion. Like Keisha. A wave of missing washed over her. She missed Keisha even in this one day apart. Mom joked that they were "joined at the hip," but Ann thought of it as "joined at the heart."

Vaguely she was aware that Alyssa was standing, gathering her things together and putting on her flip flops. "I can't believe it, but it is already 7:30. We need to get started home," she called to Ann. Reluctantly they shook out the sandy beach blanket and headed for the car.

When Ann called home to tell Mom they would be quite late getting in, Mom suggested they spend the night and come back the next day rather than driving in the dark. She even offered to pay for a motel room. Sandra made the same suggestion when Alyssa called. She could really use the additional alone time to complete her project.

There was one room left at Howard Johnson's so they took it and shared funny stories from their teenager days over dinner and a bottle of wine that they brought back to the room.

Ann told Alyssa how much she had enjoyed the day, a rare treat for a twenty-three-year-old responsible mother. Lying in the welcome cool of the orange and turquoise motel room with the moon checking in on them felt especially luxurious on this, her first night away from her child. She shifted on her side of the bed trying to find the most comfortable position, then settled in like a nesting hen. She pulled the chain to extinguish the lamp light. She lay curled on her side, right arm under her pillow and savored the warm numbness of her sunburnt back under a new layer of Noxema. Lovely to turn off her Keisha-radar for one night of deep, uninterrupted sleep. She was almost out when Alyssa's voice slid into her last fragment of consciousness.

"I need to say something, Ann. I think I'm falling in love with you. In fact, I think I've been in love with you since that first time I saw you crossing the campus."

Ann's mind bolted into emergency alert while her body lay frozen and heavy as stone on her side of the bed. The sheer curtains tossed by the air conditioner's rhythmic bursts of cold danced playful, weightless, carefree—and incongruous—in the window. Moonlight poured through the slits in the nearly closed venetian blinds and lay down diagonal bars across the bed. She couldn't think of anything to say, so she remained silent.

Alyssa resumed speaking, cataloging the things she loved about Ann. She said she had been afraid to tell Ann because she didn't want to jeopardize their friendship, which was very important to her.

Later Ann blamed herself. Hearing how wonderful she was in Alyssa's eyes touched her. Alyssa's words offered caring and solace that part of her craved, especially now when there was no time left over to pay attention to her own needs. No one had ever found her amazing, at least, no one other than her parents. Well, maybe Reggie, but that was so brief and so long ago. Here was her dear friend Alyssa, stretched out on the other side of the bed telling her she loved her.

Ann finally found her voice. "I don't know what to say or think. I love being with you and Sandra, especially with you. I'm flattered that you feel this way. And it scares me."

Alyssa reached over and stroked Ann's hair reassuringly. Then her hand moved over Ann's face, playing with her cheeks, eye sockets, and chin, gently and lovingly. It felt good to be caressed. As her hand moved over Ann's shoulders and tentatively, softly inward across her chest, Ann's nipples stood erect on the hills of her breasts.

She felt like someone else, someone unrestrained and adventuresome, someone whose body could abandon itself to the sheer delight of touch. Could this person be her? Confusion fought with pleasure and confusion won. She closed down. Her body went wooden, paralyzed by too much feeling, like overloaded circuitry that suddenly goes dead.

Alyssa pulled back her arm, yielding most of the bed to Ann's still body. They did not speak or touch for the rest of the night.

Their drive home was silent, the car full of unvocalized noise, a veritable cacophony of questions and confusion. When Alyssa pulled into the driveway of Ann's parents' home, she said softly, "I don't know what this means or how it changes things." Ann mumbled something and escaped the vibrating air inside the car, her thoughts clashing like cymbals.

She felt like one of Mom's orchids, a flower whole and delicate and beautiful, folded in on itself, awaiting the strength to push open its protective covering and bloom. She wondered if she could bloom with the nourishment Alyssa offered her, Alyssa whose friendship she valued more than she could express. What about Sandra, who was also her friend? Sandra would be devastated if she knew what had just happened.

During the next week Ann was in turmoil. Alyssa called a couple of times to check on her, but their conversations were brief and strained. Alyssa did say that she had told Sandra about her attraction to Ann. Ann felt her heart racing.

It wasn't that she disapproved of women loving women. It was more guilt about what it would do to Sandra for Alyssa to leave her for Ann. Would Alyssa even want to leave Sandra? Would Ann want her to? Ann felt more alone than she had since before Keisha's birth. She had learned so much from Alyssa, and she loved her, but was she willing to risk judgment, harassment and discrimination? Was she a lesbian? In the end she chose to walk away. She wrote Alyssa a note.

Dear Alyssa:

Your friendship has meant so much to me and my family and I will always love you and Sandra. I have decided that I am too much of a coward to be able to pursue a deeper relationship with you. That makes me very sad. I hope you can understand.

Love, Ann

It meant the end of her friendships with Sandra and Alyssa. It was a heavy price. Without Alyssa and Sandra, Ann's loneliness rooted deeper, tethering her to the darkness below the skin of the earth. She wondered if she was cursed to be a loner, leaning on her child and her parents and incapable of any other kind of love.

Don was on his way to his dream of becoming a physicist, beginning a Ph.D. program at Columbia. Occasionally he met Hervie Stein for lunch. They'd known each other back in Buffalo where Hervie's father owned a clothing store across the street from Poppa Don's Grants Five and Dime. Hervie invited Don to his wedding and Don, who disliked social occasions like weddings, felt obliged to go. Hervie, he knew, needed his support. He'd heard from his mother the terrible comments Hervie's mother made about the woman Hervie was marrying. And so he went.

The reception in Hervie's apartment was wall to wall people, not that there were so many people, but the place was small. Only one child attended, a little girl who, to his surprise, captivated him. Generally he found children frightening, but this child allayed his fears. Her dark eyes seemed back lit and effervescent, inviting those near her to come in and see the fascinating world that she saw. Before she approached him, Don, the silent observer, took her in—broad, toothy grin, unruly black curls that could not be restrained by barrettes or rubber bands, silky tan skin, and tom boy body that seemed much larger than it was because it was always in motion, filling the space around her. How could this child have so much energy? He watched her moving through the crowd and found her mesmerizing.

Wearing a serious expression, she walked up to within a yard of where he sat on Hervie's overstuffed sofa and stood studying him, as though she didn't want to frighten him by standing too close. After some minutes she began to question him, as he had observed her do with others at the reception. She waited for his answers and seemed to think about them before moving to her next question. Gradually she moved nearer.

"I'm Keisha. What's your name?" she asked.

"Don Johnson. Glad to meet you, Keisha," he replied.

"Where do you come from?" Keisha asked.

"Buffalo, New York," Don replied.

She looked him up and down. "Do you have a mommy?"

"Yes."

"Do you have a daddy?" Her brown eyes seemed to be looking into his soul. The easiest thing was for him to say Yes, but her steady, sober gaze required honesty.

"I have a daddy, but I haven't seen him for a very long time," he told her.

Keisha thought about his answer. "Is he dead?" she asked. "I don't know," Don replied.

"It makes me sad that you don't know. I don't know my daddy, either." She was standing next to him now, close enough to touch him if she reached out her hand.

"Is your mommy good to you?"

Another zinger compelling him to be more honest with this child than he had been with his peers and maybe even with himself. "My mommy has a sickness that makes her mean sometimes," he told her.

The child was standing very still, her surfeit of energy controlled and focused as she studied his face intently. "Maybe you could share my mommy. She is really good to me and she isn't sick so she isn't ever mean."

The child held out her right hand to him, palm up. "Mommy says when I'm sad. I should hold her hand 'til the sadness goes away. You can hold my hand."

She amazed him. How could she know about his sadness? It was as though this child, who couldn't be more than three or four, intuited that he needed special handling. He extended his hand. They moved closer for their hands to meet. Hers was so tiny and soft in his. His long, muscular fingers enclosed it with reverence. She led him around the room introducing him to the other guests as "my special friend." After a while she told him she had to go, it was past her bedtime, and she was sleepy. She gave him a hug.

"Thank you," he said to her back as his personal pink cherub receded, navigating her way between the legs of the other guests to find her mother. He saw a tall, dark haired, attractive woman scoop the child up into her arms wearing a smile that nearly broke his heart.

He looked away. When he looked back, they were gone, elevated pink polka dots slipping out the apartment door.

Feeling isolated and lonely was familiar to Don. He lived his life according to a rule he had followed for so long that he had no idea where it came from: *Avoid what you don't know; what is unfamiliar can hurt you.*

An idea bubbled up inside him, new and enticing as fresh-from-the-oven yeast bread—he could take action to see the child and her mother again. Had the child called forth this willingness to let his old rules for staying safe lapse? He knew it was absurd to attribute such power to a three-year-old. For some time he puzzled over the changes he felt stirring inside.

After several months, he found the courage to call the attractive, serious woman with the stunning smile who the child said was never mean. Hervie's wife supplied her phone number. His heart was pounding and his hands sweaty when he called and asked her to dinner. She declined. Too much to do preparing for her oral exams.

Didn't she know how hard this was for him? Maybe he never should have called. What was he doing building dreams on the momentary friendliness of a little child? He should know better.

Before she hung up, he needed to know that his memory of the small person in pink polka dots with the curious, quizzical expression and probing questions was real. He asked, "How is Keisha?"

He could tell by the way the woman fumbled an answer that his question threw her. He guessed that she had not expected him to remember her child's name.

"Keisha's fine," she told him, then she added that the child had talked about a man with no daddy and a sick, mean mommy, a man she had talked with at the wedding. "Might you be that man?"

"That's me," he admitted. "Your daughter is remarkable."

"I know," said Ann. Then she added, "Maybe call back in a couple of months?"

The country was in chaos with frequent protests against the war in Vietnam and rioting in the nation's center city neighborhoods. Ever since Dr. King's assassination in April and Robert Kennedy's in June, the country had been out of control, so polarized that people were hospitalized from the response of police to their protests. The worst situation was in Chicago at the National Democratic Convention, but, actually, the chaos was happening around the world—student riots in Japan, Paris, Czechoslovakia, Mexico City. And now Richard Nixon would become President, elected after disclosing on the weekend before the election that he had a secret plan to get the U.S. out of Vietnam. The intense conflict between conflicting ideals stirred in Ann a desire to get involved as she had in Freedom Summer. After her oral exam at the end of the month, perhaps she would make time to join the anti-war Movement.

The day after her exams, the phone rang and Mom called that it was for her. She'd slept in, exhausted. The deep voice on the phone sounded vaguely familiar as it congratulated her on her being All But Dissertation.

"Who is this?" she asked.

"Keisha's friend, Don Johnson," the voice said and she could hear the smile. "You said I could call after your exam, right? I'd like to help you celebrate, maybe bring dinner tonight for you and Keisha?"

Clever way to hit on me, she thought to herself. How could she turn that down? "I suppose you know that my family includes my mom and dad?" Maybe that would daunt him.

"Actually, I was thinking of dinner for all four of you, plus Hervie and Barbara and me. How would that sound?" He had covered all the bases and, though she'd rather have spent the evening watching mindless movies, she agreed that he could come, with dinner, Chinese would be nice.

She wasn't sure she remembered what he looked like. Oh, well. It was only one evening.

He arrived with Barbara and Hervie loaded down with entrees

for the seven of them. He was very tall with dark, curly hair and Marlboro Man rugged good looks. Keisha welcomed him as though their conversation at the wedding had taken place yesterday.

Mom and Dad seemed impressed when he got down on the floor and played Chutes and Ladders with Keisha. Ann, however, was suspicious. Could he be a child molester or one of those men clever enough to know the way into a woman's pants is through courting her children? She retained a reserve around him that verged on coldness. But she had to admit it was generally an enjoyable evening. They even watched *The Sound of Music,* so she really shouldn't complain.

As he was leaving, he turned to her, face serious, and asked, "Have I offended you in some way? I was really trying to make this an evening of celebrating your achievement, but you seem really wary of me. Keisha said you are not a mean mommy, but you seem angry to me. Please forgive me if I've not done this right."

She stepped out on the front porch where they could speak without the rest of the family overhearing them. This was embarrassing. She dealt with it the way she dealt with most things, blunt honesty. "I have been hard on you and ungrateful for your thoughtful gesture tonight. It isn't your fault. It's mine. I've worked so hard to do it all—the Ph.D. and raising Keisha and being a good daughter to Mom and Dad. When I passed my orals, I just wanted to collapse, sleep all day, and watch silly movies. I think I'm suffering from Doctorate Traumatic Stress. I know I will get over it and I do sincerely apologize for taking it out on you. I wouldn't blame you if you walked away and never came back. Maybe Keisha and I can take *you* out to eat next week to make up for my bad behavior?"

To her surprise, he simply said. "You name the time and I'll be here to pick you up. Call me." He passed her a slip of paper on which his name and phone number were printed in block letters. How did he happen to have it already written out, she wondered? Then he walked down the steps and to his car, calling over his shoulder, "Get a good sleep tonight."

She did not know what to make of this man.

In the weeks to come they saw each other frequently, usually with Keisha and often her parents included. She was surprised to discover that he was a private person, that his over-the-top dinner the night after her orals was an aberration for him. The gentle chemistry between them was what Ann needed. No pressure, no drama, just friendship. By their third month, Dad commented that Don seemed to smile a lot, and, when she passed his comment on to Don, Don agreed, saying that being around Ann and Keisha made him happy. Then he flushed and changed the subject. When they hung out at Ann's parents' house, Keisha took charge of Don, taking him to her room to play with her toys, to the park down the block to push her on the swing, soliciting his help to teach her how to ride her scooter, and serving him pretend cookies and tea on her dolly tea set—muddy water and a messy paste of play dough with chopped leaves that he said was the most delicious fare he'd ever been served. The tall, private physics grad student threw caution to the wind with the child, carrying her on his back as he crawled across the living room playing Rajah Riding Elephant and twirling her around the back yard so that her body flew up and out, sailing on the air as she spun. They both clearly loved it.

When he told Ann that his only family was his unhappy alcoholic mother and his grandfather back in Buffalo, Ann, whose experience of family was of support and acceptance, felt her antennae go up. She was not interested in a relationship of care taking for a neurotic, unhappy person. Yet those words did not fit Don, at least not when he was around her and Keisha. He was obviously a good person, and she loved the bond he and Keisha had built. Most importantly, he was taking it slow with her. Too slow, she was beginning to feel. Would the man ever make love to her? The few men she had gone out with seemed to assume that as a mother—a post-virgin woman—she would put out on demand. With Don it was the opposite problem, despite Keisha referring to him as "My Love Daddy" the other night at dinner.

One winter evening after reading four books to Keisha and

tucking her into bed, Ann closed the door to Keisha's room and found Don standing in the doorway, very close to her. Before she could think she reached up and kissed him on the mouth right there in the upstairs hall with its generations of Whitmore and Sullivan family photos looking on. He responded to her mouth eagerly and steered her down the hall to her room. She had the sense to call out, "We'll be down shortly, Mom" before turning the handle and backing into room all the way to her bed, where they collapsed, lying very close and caressing each other. When his long fingers slid between her legs and found her moist and pulsing, she whispered in his ear, "I've been waiting." By the time they were ready to leave each other's bodies, the clock on her nightstand read 1:08. Mom and Dad had gone to bed hours ago.

The next morning Ann sat in the kitchen nursing her coffee and puzzling over how Don had known which room was hers. Later, when he came by for supper, she asked him. He blushed and said, "I asked Keisha."

Ann, White Plains, New York, March 1970

Ann had completed her dissertation and successfully defended it. She would be hooded at commencement in Washington Square Park in May with Mom and Dad, Barbara and Hervie, Don and Keisha there to applaud her. In March, she received an offer from Baldwin Wallace College on the west side of Cleveland: a tenure track appointment as Instructor of Mathematics, the only woman in the department. She was elated but also concerned what this would mean for her relationship with Don. Being two years younger than her, Don was still working on his degree. He took her out to dinner to celebrate receiving the offer.

The restaurant was crowded, and it was not easy to hear what he was saying. Twice she asked him to repeat what he had said, and twice he did, the second time his voice audible above the clinking of silverware and china, audible, indeed, to the people seated at tables near theirs. "Tomorrow will you go with me to the courthouse to apply for a marriage license?" It was a unique way to propose, but Don was a unique person. She reached across the table and took his hands, holding them firmly. Then she told him how happy his proposal made her, how she had been distancing herself a bit from him, trying to prepare for life without him, how numb and self-protective, and, yes, miserable she had felt, her heart breaking at the thought of leaving him.

She was vaguely aware that the other diners had grown quiet during their conversation, forks midway to mouths, eyes on Don and her. She was uneasy, embarrassed, wishing they would all just disappear and leave them alone together.

Suddenly Don stood and walked around the table, pulled her to her feet and kissed her passionately on the mouth in front of the entire restaurant. She was stunned. He was an introvert who valued privacy, who was never demonstrative in public. The restaurant crowd erupted in applause and their waiter brought out a bottle of champagne "on the house." At that moment she knew that she would never truly understand this man who she loved, this man capable of such surprising shifts and changes who was willing to risk trying the unfamiliar for her.

After his display of passion in the middle of the restaurant Don seemed to shift shape, retreating like a turtle into his impervious shell, eyes seeking a place of sanctuary from which he could study his environment. Tonight he had been willing to be studied by all these strangers in order to give her a remarkable, romantic moment that she would never forget. She squeezed his hand and whispered, "Thank you."

While Don felt his pants pockets looking for his wallet, she thanked the waiter, apologizing for creating a scene. She sensed Don's anxiety and wondered if he might be missing his wallet. She reached surreptitiously into her purse, felt for her credit card, and brought it out hidden in her closed hand, never taking her attentive eyes from the young waiter's face. She reached for Don's hand and slipped him the card as gracefully as that Olympian relay racer he admired passed batons. For an instant he looked confused, then grateful as a dog for leftovers.

"Don't apologize," the waiter was smiling at her, clearly

oblivious to her covert pass. "My boss says people are always hungrier for the possibility of romance than they are for delicious food, even the tasty options on our menu. He's going to ask the food reviewer who was here tonight to include your engagement in his review. It's good for business. If the reviewer is a romantic, it might even earn us an extra star."

PART 2

Don, Cleveland, Ohio, March 2003

Sam, the dog, ambled after him down the half-flight of back steps and out the door to the yard. The yard glowed, whimsical, full moon reflecting off the March snow and starlight falling through the bare branches of the old oak. They walked to the back lot, their nightly ritual before bed. The man checked for observers in the brightness of the night, then unzipped and, together, dog and man released a stream of what was held inside. Satisfying. Don treasured this ritual. Time to let his thoughts sidle where they pleased before returning to the house.

They were an odd pair, Sam, the dog designed by a committee, Ann liked to say, built low to the ground, short black and brown fur with an incongruous white face that no one could call beautiful. Most people responded to Sam with laughter. Don, on the other hand, wore his 6'4" body with elegant remoteness, angular, purposeful, a thinker. No one would imagine him peeing in his back yard alongside his dog.

He looked up at the star speckled sky and sighed, marveling and moved. Then his seasonal sadness returned. He let it out rarely, almost always when he was alone, and always this week in March, the approximate anniversary of the child's birth. Now he brushed off the snow from a worn wooden lawn chair and sat down. A voice in his head dismissed his feelings with facts:

You have a successful career; you have a wife who you love and who loves you and is your best friend; you have an accomplished, delightful daughter, no debt, and students and colleagues who admire you. What more could you want? *My son.* And not to feel guilty about what I did.

The quiet, preoccupied manner he had cultivated ever since he was twelve had worked for him, allowing him to share an emotionally undemanding life with Ann while preserving his secrets. Recently certain memories pushed to the surface, demanding his attention like an abscess needing to be lanced. Why now? he wondered. He was a scientist and accustomed to concrete answers, but here in the back yard of the Shaker Heights house he had shared with Ann for more than thirty years, he could think of none.

He leaned back in the chair, gathering his jacket around him, regretting he had left his warm wool scarf on the hook inside the back door. He let Sam's leash fall to the ground, but the old dog remained beside him like he knew he was needed.

Don calculated how long it had been since he'd seen her, nearly thirty-five years. He thought of her as the person who taught him to trust, at least sometimes, the woman who prepared him for Ann. He looked up at the stars, fastening his eyes on the Seven Sisters, really only six as one of the sisters had separated and been lost. He imagined Connie as that sister, separated from family and people who cared about her, left to fend for herself alone with a baby, *his* baby. He wondered where she was, whether she had married, had more children, whether, indeed, she was still living. He wondered too if she still loosed the laughter he could hear now inside his head as hot tears furrowed his cheeks.

Somewhere in this world he had a son. His only biological child. He and Ann had tried, but the only time she'd been able to carry a baby to term, their baby boy had died at birth. For more than a year their silent grief took up all the space when they were together. He hadn't told her about his other son, it hadn't seemed necessary, and he'd feared how she might respond.

What had become of his nameless son who would be thirty-four by now?

It had been for the best, hadn't it, deciding to break it off with Connie before their passionate attraction to each other could take root and limit what he could achieve? At least it had been best for him. He was never able to answer that question decisively, which was probably the real reason he had never told Ann.

He stood and looked up at the full moon. The bare branches of the oak fractured the night sky into angular, irregular shapes, like pieces of a hard-edged puzzle. His stomach contracted as a question, unbidden, pushed its way up and pierced his heart. Does my father ever stand, solitary and grieving, howling at the empty-faced moon?

He wiped the back of his sleeve across his eyes to wipe out the memories freezing damply on his cheeks. He whistled to Sam, who trotted up amiably. Together they went in, and he closed and locked the door.

Richard, Evanston, Illinois, March 21, 2003

He was tall, very tall, and had to bend down to talk with most people.

Only then could they see the hairless strip of skin that ran like a pathway from his forehead to the back of his head, fortified on either side by springy brown curls. The contrast of those defiant curls with the vulnerable balding space made his appearance rather striking, even remarkable, and marked him as someone who might surprise.

He carried himself with the confidence that comes, if they claim it, to large people, confidence born of others feeling slightly overwhelmed by their physical presence, so imposingly *there* taking up such an extravagant amount of space. Not that he was fat, no. He was big. Long arms sprouted a heavy crop of curling hair that covered his torso and legs, legs encased in made to order pants, pricey but his only alternative. Feet, huge, size 15. Hands?

Ah, his hands! Long fingers in perfect proportion to the palms curved down from the knuckles to make music, rarely to do manual labor, but hands like those should be protected from such routine activity, preserved for what they did best—coaxing sound from pianos and vocal chords, orchestras and choruses.

It was Friday and his classes were over for the week. He walked across the still snow-covered campus, irritated that the weather was so damn cold. Heading south on Campus Drive he nearly collided with three of his students, wide-eyed freshmen with crushes who gushed, "Hi, Dr. Allen. How are you today?" He smiled without showing his teeth, trying to communicate boundaries. He behaved impeccably with female students and would never entertain the thought of taking up the invitations that experience told him languished accessible beneath their gushing. He hurried on, glancing over his shoulder to be sure they were not following him to the coffee shop. But they had rounded the corner heading for the library. Safe!

A colleague approached from behind him, calling out, "Hey, Rich! Got plans for the weekend?" Now they were walking side by side and Richard was fast processing how he could exit the conversation. When the colleague asked him to go for a beer and Richard declined, the man tossed a barbed remark as he peeled off toward the faculty parking lot. "So Dr. Allen doesn't like coeds *or* men. Okay, see you Monday."

Could no one understand that as a composer he had to capture the music when it chose to appear? It irritated him that no one ever got it. He was *not* a boring man. He simply required solitude to play with the tunes and dramas unfolding inside his head and to structure them, give them sound and voice. That's what composers do. That's why Northwestern had hired him.

He stepped up his pace, plowing his way through the snow, deciding to stop at his apartment to leave some books before going to the coffee shop. The apartment was a third-floor walkup, its rear balcony looking out on

Lake Michigan. That balcony was why he'd chosen the place. That and the Arabica Robusta coffee shop three blocks away.

The balcony would be his composition sanctuary where he would sit and dream up melodies, inspired by the view. It was big enough for his electric piano, which meant he could orchestrate whatever inspirations lodged in his head right there, converting melody to multi-phonic music on his back porch. A great idea, except that warm spring days seemed to elude Evanston. For now, the piano sat on his kitchen table, and he had to do his head work at Arabica Robusta.

He tucked a tablet of composition paper into his briefcase along with some No. 2 pencils, freshly sharpened, and hurried down the stairs, out the door, and into the surprisingly light late afternoon. Snow in these longer days of spring annoyed him. He leaned forward, hugging his arms to his sides to conserve warmth, nearly dropping his briefcase that contained little other than composition paper—tissues for his chronically drippy nose and a bundle of student papers held together with a large metal spring clip whose foldable wings would probably by now have snagged and torn his composition paper. He was in a foul mood.

The aroma of assorted java brews inside Arabica Robusta diverted him for a moment. He let the fragrance of strong, dark coffee stir his sensual self. He scanned the crowded room and located an empty table against the back wall on which he placed his briefcase to claim the space. Only one chair. Good, he could work without interruption. He got in line to order his mocha grande with an extra shot of expresso. But when he carried it carefully back to his table, the one chair was gone. More precisely, going. Lugged by a young woman in bold glasses, hair pulled into a loose, bushy ponytail, wearing tired blue jeans topped with an oversize green wool hand knit sweater. His mother was a knitter and had raised him to notice things like the cables that ran down her sleeves as identifiers of Quality.

Quality or not, he approached the table, picked up his briefcase rather dramatically, threw his muffler around his neck, pulled on his leather gloves, and stomped out of Arabica Rustica heading back to his apartment, steaming, his irritation growing as some of the foam from his mocha grande slid onto his right leather glove and dripped down his wool jacket. This was not supposed to be how his first Friday after Spring Break would end!

It was tricky holding the mocha and his briefcase and striding forcefully while avoiding icy patches on the sidewalk.

He heard a voice behind him, a pleasant enough voice, not too high and using multiple pitches. He had an ear for voices.

"Wait! I'm so sorry. I just didn't notice your briefcase. We were having a meeting and needed one more chair. I'm truly sorry. I've put it back, so do return, please."

He stopped abruptly and turned to look at her, the mocha sloshing out the hole in the plastic cover again. Damn! It was the green cables woman, and she hadn't thought to put on a jacket before running after him. A horrible thought crossed his mind: She must be the spontaneous sort who acts and speaks without thinking. He licked the over abundant mocha, weighing his options. He really preferred working at the coffee shop on a Friday. Most thirty-somethings would be celebrating the end of the week and working solitary amidst a crowd of happy people was preferable to working solitary in his apartment. It created the illusion that he had friends.

And she had such an earnest look.

"I accept your apology." Did he sound pompous? "I prefer drinking my coffee in the shop so I can get some work done. I will return!"

"I don't think the Philippines is still waiting," she was grinning. He felt confused and embarrassed, and his mocha was getting cold. "Sorry, that was gratuitous. You said what General MacArthur said as he escaped from the Philippines. I found it funny. Chalk it up to my weird sense of humor." Shivering she hurried back to Arabica Rustica and held the door for him. He mechanically followed her.

His table was already taken and her meeting was breaking up. "Oh, dear, I really messed things up," she said.

He noticed another table with two chairs on the opposite side of the room. "We could sit there," he suggested. Where did that "we" come from?

They maneuvered the distance to the back of the room, bodies turning this way and that in the minimal spaces between the tables. She picked up her briefcase and jacket along the way. They sank into the chairs and she was up again to fetch coffee. When she returned they played Getting to Know You.

"So what do you do?" They spoke simultaneously. "You first," he said.

"Assistant professor of history. Been here one semester." Interesting, she clipped her sentences.

"I'm new here, too. Assistant professor of choral music and I compose as well when inspired." They moved through the usual questions—Where did you get your passion for music/history? Do you prefer teaching or research? Her question, "Are you a people person?" intrigued him and he found himself answering with an honesty that surprised him.

"Not really. I like all the people who live in my head. They're the people I'm closest to. I like to work in places like this but with my earbuds in place."

She didn't seem surprised. "I understand that," she said. "Some days I can spend ten hours on my computer writing about this or that figure from the past who fascinates me. I imagine conversations with them and how they must've looked."

Dark had begun to crawl over the city without his noticing. "I must go," he said, looking at his watch.

"Me, too," she replied, reaching behind her to lift her jacket off the back of her chair.

"Where do you live?" he asked her, then felt flustered realizing that she might think he was coming on to her.

"About four blocks from here, near the lake."

"Which building?" He was stalling for time, wanting to prolong the conversation.

"The Alhambra."

"My gosh, I'm in the Trianon across the street." His face brightened.

"Then I guess we can walk home together." She moved to the door with rapid, strong steps, like a woman on a mission, all businesslike and professional, the green cables hidden under her black wool coat.

"Yes," he said to her back. He hoped she didn't notice the excitement in his voice.

They were quiet as they walked, both hunched against the wind off the lake. Richard was rehashing their conversation in his head.

"Sometime I would love to hear one of your compositions." She spoke all in a rush, paused, and then appeared to apologize. "There I go again intruding. I'm sorry. This was a lovely way to end the day. I guess I just didn't want it to end."

That honesty, again. He watched her fish in her shoulder bag for her keys as she walked up the sidewalk to the entrance to the Alhambra. The wind blew her hair out of the ponytail and swirled it across her face.

His legs on autopilot kept walking toward his building across the street.

Abruptly he stopped, not yet to the curb, as his mind caught up with the new information he had received. He could enjoy a conversation with someone who, like him, was an interior person. He could meet someone intelligent and accomplished and she could enjoy listening and talking with him. His mind was processing all this with uncharacteristic rapidity, which left him anxious. He was trying to come up with a response to her, to this afternoon, before it all slipped away into his fat file of lost opportunities. Suddenly he made an about face and walked quickly, almost cantering, to her door, which she had just opened. She looked back at him, and he was surprised to see disappointment filling her face. Her expression confused him but he pushed on.

"I want to see you again," he blurted out. "I don't know if you have anyone in your life. I don't know much about you at all. I don't even know your name, but I would really *like* to know you." He was looking straight into her eyes while he talked.

They both heard a soft sound and he felt something wet, warm, and slimy on the bald place, above his forehead. Reaching up, his leather glove encountered something slippery that shone white on the brown leather.

"I think a bird shat on my head," he ventured, and they both started to laugh.

"Why don't you come upstairs and I can clean you up," she said. And he did.

Keisha Johnson, March 22

Finding herself walking up to her apartment with a man behind her whose name she didn't even know for the purpose of disposing of bird droppings on his head seemed weird and incongruous to Keisha. After the last time she had sworn off romances with academics. Why had she invited him to come up? Oh, well, she had the baseball bat next to the front door, a can of mace in her kitchen cabinet over the sink and her black belt in Karate. She was prepared if this proved to have been a dangerous mistake. Anyway, he piqued her curiosity, and she had enjoyed talking with him.

On the last flight she forgot to tell him to watch his head. The ceilings were lower in the stairwell from there to the roof. She heard a crack as he banged his head on the lowered ceiling that he had not seen. "Damn!" he said. Then, "Shit!" as a trail of blood slid over his forehead and down his cheek, barely missing his right eye.

"I think I've cut my head."

She unlocked the door to her apartment, ushered him into the kitchen, and wrapped ice in a dishtowel, which he held against the cut while she gingerly wiped off the bird droppings with a moist paper towel. Maybe this wasn't a good idea after all. Then, feeling sorry for him, she resumed asking him questions and, while he was answering, put a pot of water on to boil some pasta and offered him a glass of wine. Might as well make the best of it. He stayed for an hour and then left wearing her Rite Aid butterfly bandage on his head, the last one left in the box.

Awaking the next morning she stretched out in the middle of her queen-sized bed. She loved to take up the entire space, to stretch like a slow-motion cat and hold that stretch before relaxing into the sensation of Egyptian cotton sheets against her skin. Her thoughts turned to Dr. Richard Allen and their hours together.

Then the phone rang.

It was her mother, calling to say she would be in Chicago next month for a conference and would love to take Keisha to dinner. How was the new job? Was Keisha happy? Had she met any interesting people?

Keisha knew that "interesting" was code for "marriage prospects." She felt irritable. She wanted to get back to reviewing the evening. Making up an excuse, she ended the conversation and lay back against the pillows, hoping she hadn't hurt Mom's feelings and annoyed at herself that how her mom felt about each of their interactions still mattered so much that it could derail a whole day. She would call back later and suggest a restaurant where they could meet.

Back to Richard. Was he "interesting" in the way Mom meant it?

Certainly he was pleasant enough, quirky and safe, no need for the mace or bat. It was refreshing to meet someone interested in her experiences and not just wanting a one-night-stand. He'd seemed especially interested in her travel outside the U.S. and her upcoming trip to the Philippines, asking a lot of questions and seeming wistful that he'd not traveled abroad.

When they parted, he had shaken her hand, that's all, and she had noticed how lovely his hands were, nails trimmed short, fingers long and strong. You could tell a lot about a person by their hands.

The smell of coffee reset her reverie. Mentally she thanked Mom for the timer-coffee pot that she'd set before going to sleep. She was out of bed, showered and dressed in ten minutes. Coffee in an insulated carrying cup, briefcase in hand, she was off to the library. She relegated sorting out Richard Allen to the bottom of her things-to-do list.

Later, sitting in her carrel her mind wandered to her relationship with Mom. Mom was so close to Dad, so bonded in an unemotional, I-know-without-you-telling-me intuitive sort of way. Keisha sometimes felt like an outsider around them, a Left Brainer in a household of very organized Right Brainers. She was proud of Mom, one of the few women of her generation chairing a university department of mathematics and seemingly able to do it all—marriage and family, teaching, publishing—a master at multi-tasking.

Keisha had made a painting when she was four that Mom had framed and hung in her bedroom. Keisha had painted a tree so big it took up the whole page with many branches laden with leaves. The teacher had printed KEISHA'S MOM in the lower left and Keisha had printed her name on the right. Mom had loved it, taking it to mean that Keisha felt sheltered and protected, which she did, only she hadn't drawn herself in the picture. She and Mom were closest when it came to protecting Dad.

Keisha remembered going with Dad to visit Grandma Milly and Poppy-Don in Buffalo, staying by his side and holding his hand as he talked with his "mean mother," determined to protect him from her. A ridiculous idea as she was only what? Maybe four? Mom didn't like Grandma Milly, either. Even now when Grandma Milly was confined to an upscale nursing home where they dressed for dinner wearing their finest jewelry and pretended they could hear the conversation around their tables, where they drove their power-scooters back to their lonely, elegant apartments, Grandma Milly seemed menacing, she and Mom agreed.

The library was quiet, and few students or professors hung out there on Saturdays. Deep in its bowels on floor 5B, five floors down, she worked for several hours. Then her eyes began a power struggle with her will, lids sliding down, jerking open, sliding down again. After four or five rounds, she gave in and allowed her folded arms to rest on the desk, her head turned to the right atop them. She'd allow herself a catnap. Her unconscious then took over, delivering one of those dream sequences where you are trapped and can't escape.

She was back at American University in Washington, working late in her office. Someone was knocking persistently. She was afraid and wanted to run, but there was only one way out. She walked to the door and opened it. There stood Andrew and his wife, and they were both smiling. She pushed the door closed but they kept on knocking. How could she get away? She tried the large window. Too heavy, she couldn't lift it. She looked in the closet for a door in the wall but there was none. The knocking grew louder and louder and the lights were flickering on and off. "Dr. Johnson? Sorry to disturb you. We're closing in ten minutes."

A student worker checking the stacks was trying to awaken her. She twitched and sat up, stuffed her laptop and papers into her briefcase, and shrugged into her jacket. The dream had disturbed her and the darkness of the stacks at dusk was not where she wanted to be to think it through.

Walking back to her apartment she was unaware of her surroundings, letting her feet intuitively take her home while her mind fastened its teeth on the dream. Damn! Why was he still infiltrating her dreams? She'd left AU and come to Northwestern to escape this man she'd been infatuated with for four years, this man who would never leave his wife and had told her so from the beginning. Four years of seeing him after their co-workers had left for the day, four years of departmental social events where the wife chatted amiably to her while Keisha barely managed monosyllabic responses, a thick, foul, interior fog having overtaken her brain. Why wasn't she free of him yet?

She climbed the four flights to her apartment, let herself in, and collapsed on the couch still wearing her coat. When she closed her eyes, a memory came back. It was both the most magical day of her adulthood and the most devastating.

They were on their way out of Washington to a cabin in the West Virginia woods for a rare day together. Their words were halting, dribbling back and forth, made trite by anticipation. The iced coffee in the thermos she'd prepared for them remained undrunk on the back seat of his car. The hour in the car was calming, tires humming against the road like a familiar song you hold in your head endlessly, comfortingly. The summer heat was rising, and they rolled down the windows to let the breezes lift their hair. As the car climbed the last stretch of dirt road to the cabin, she could hardly breathe.

The small, dark wood cabin lay nearly hidden by the woods, crouched beside a stream. Sharply angled birch and oak branches obscured its shuttered front and smashed the sunlight into irregular pieces that shifted with the breeze like shards of broken glass. He guided her through the living room and off to the left to the bedroom. She could hear the silence of the woods and feel the chilled mountain air penetrating the warm day. They found the waterbed with its gentle motion that met and cushioned their own.

In between making love they walked in the woods to catch up with their trembling bodies, leaning into each other, talking little, staying in the moment. She was not yet aware that this day would change their relationship forever.

Their lovemaking was memorable. They moved together fluidly and with delight, but when the afternoon shadows elongated across the bed, Andrew looked at his watch and got up hurriedly, pulling on his clothes, calling her to get up and dressed; he had to get back home for dinner with the family. She felt the thud of her heart and head colliding as she came to full consciousness that his play script had a very different story line than hers.

That afternoon marked the end of her delusion but not of her obsession. Their lovemaking in the years that followed continued to be sandwiched into the time left after accounting for his children's soccer games and other family responsibilities. Accommodating to the time he had available eroded her confidence. She was no longer the quirky, charismatic, distinctive, and funny woman she had been. Now she was furtive, chronically disappointed by his unavailability, and more and more depressed. She had been a success in everything she had tried before Andrew. Could that be why she allowed herself to be sucked in and spat out again and again in this relationship, an underlying belief that her self-inflicted emotional battering was a temporary setback, that in the end surely she would win him?

Sitting there on the couch in her Evanston apartment, she felt a resurgence of the self-loathing that during those years left her wanting to shower and scrub her body until it bled. She stood, walked into her bedroom, and sat at the foot of her bed staring at the wall opposite her. She had walked away from Andrew finally, cleared out, found this job at Northwestern. She'd left so quickly that there was no departmental farewell party, no good-by. She had been very proud of herself. It had taken two years of therapy to reach that point. Okay. Now she had to banish the memories which held onto her brain like a tick to its blood source. She would not let those memories sabotage her life here.

Deliberately she removed her shoes. Deliberately she threw first one and then the other at the same spot on her wall. The force with which they hit dented the wallboard, leaving a puckered circle five inches in diameter.

Another memory surfaced. She was back home in the bathroom of her apartment in Washington after spending what time Andrew had available making love on the floor of her office. She was holding her hand mirror behind her so she could see the ugly red brush burn from the carpet imprinted on her back and bottom. Did he intentionally inflict these marks on her the way ranchers brand cattle, as an outward and visible sign of his power over her?

Now she went to her closet and pulled out all of her shoes. She piled them on the floor at the end of her bed. Then she went into action, throwing each as hard as she could at the wall, grunting, "Damn you" with each pitch. The puckered circle grew wider, and the wallboard cracked, then gave way at the point of impact, leaving a dark hole.

She started to move the dresser, to drag it in front of the hole. Then she stopped, considering, and moved it back where it had been so that the hole drew attention from any vantage point in the room. "It's my mantra," she said out loud, a tangible reminder that never again would she allow herself to be diverted by any man from what she wanted in her life. Never again would she be a pathetic, needy woman who sold her soul for a relationship.

She put her shoes back in the closet humming to herself and then singing that Helen Reddy song Mom had taught her in her *Free to Be You and Me* period. She danced around the bedroom belting it out.

If I have to, I can face anything. I am strong (STRONG)…

A noise grabbed her attention. It sounded like someone in the apartment below was poking a broomstick against the ceiling. She lowered her volume back to a hum. But she wouldn't stop smiling.

Richard

It was Saturday morning, no classes to meet. Richard got up early and put on a pot of coffee, strong. He turned up the volume on his Bose so that Mahler filled the apartment. He walked back to the kitchen for a sweet roll to go with the coffee and stood looking out at the Lake. March 23 and another spring snow. Would this winter ever end? He moved to the living room and sat on his overstuffed sofa with a book to read for a break, but he couldn't concentrate. He was thinking about Keisha Johnson, wondering how her Saturday was going. Though he'd learned her name, they hadn't exchanged emails or phone numbers.

He turned on his laptop and went to the university website, Faculty, keying in Keisha Johnson under History Department. There she was. Nice picture. Hair down and a tangle of curls, skin a luscious café au lait, smiling broadly. He added her to his contacts and on impulse sent her a text. "Have plans for this afternoon?"

His phone binged a few minutes later. "Library all day. Tomorrow? Excursion to the Museum of Science and Industry?"

Twelve words but they made his day. He texted back, trying to seem cool, "Ur on. Leave 12:30 for the El?"

They met outside her apartment building and walked to the El, both complaining about the prolonged winter. The train into Chicago came right away and they found seats together and plopped down.

"I've never been to this museum, have you?" he asked.

"No, but my mom is taking me to lunch in a month, and from what I have read of it, it's the kind of place she and Dad will have been to. Brownie points for saying I've been there and seen the exhibits they find spectacular."

He laughed. "Tell me about your parents."

"Both academics. Mom at Case Western Reserve, math. Dad, physics, at Cleveland State. Also does consulting, not sure what about. They're introverts who've been together a long time, at least thirty-four years," she gave him a knowing smirk he wasn't sure he understood. "They love each other and probably never loved anyone else, steady, private people who follow the rules."

"Like me?" He was referencing their conversation at the coffee shop. "Is that like you? I thought you were ready to start seeing the world, head off for parts unknown."

"Part of me is ready, at least to think about it. Another part likes my routines, maybe is stuck in them. But going to a science museum with a woman I have just met is not part of my routine, so I guess I am taking baby steps away from being your father. Are you close to them?"

"Very when I was little. Less as I developed more independence and became more of a puzzle to them. What about you?"

"Dad's a pastor, recently retired after forty-some years of preaching every Sunday and taking care of everybody's problems. He never complained about it, but I know he is enjoying laying that burden down. I used to go with him to visit shut-ins when I was a kid. Sometimes he'd help them to the toilet, clean them up, feed them—I found all that rather scary."

"What about your mom?" Keisha was braiding and unbraiding the fringe on her wool scarf. Was she nervous? he wondered. The train was above ground now whizzing past the backsides of sad brick tenements where the occasional sheet waved at them, frozen flat in the March cold. The train had filled with people. Students with backpacks stood holding onto the backs of the seats and chatting. Occasionally one of them turned suddenly and Richard had to duck to avoid being whacked by a backpack.

"Mom's a social worker with hospice," he continued.

Keisha had turned toward him, and he noticed how intently her brown eyes read his. "Sounds like they have similar vocations. Do they have any time for each other?"

He hadn't really thought about this before. "I grew up thinking marriage was like having play dates with your best friend several times a week. That seemed to be how my parents had time together, a couple of hours and then back into the world of work."

"Is that why you prefer the people and music inside your head?" She had stopped playing with the fringe, and it crossed his mind that her eyes were beautiful.

"You're one perceptive woman! And you have a good memory. Actually, I think I just am that way, not because of my parents or in reaction to them, just part of who I am."

The train pulled into their stop. They reapplied outer wear and gloves and set off on the windy walk toward the Lake and the Museum, deciding to start with the prenatal exhibit.

After an hour of remarking on the array of fetuses enclosed in glass and walking through a huge model of the birth canal, Keisha suggested they rest their feet in the cafeteria where their conversation resumed.

"I don't think I've ever thought much about 'The Miracle of Birth,'" Richard commented.

"More of a 'Miracle of Death' person?" she asked, smiling rakishly. "No, just preoccupied by how people have lived their most productive years." He was looking at her intently. Was she making fun of him? She was funny, but he would not be ridiculed. "Are you making fun of me?" He asked her outright.

"Oh, no, not at all. I'm sorry. It's my sense of humor." Her face went serious. He could see that she felt regret. He smiled, relieved, and she smiled back.

They drank their coffee slowly and agreed they had seen enough for one day. Back to the El station, the subway ride to Evanston, the walk to their street.

This time he invited her to see his apartment. She said she liked not having the extra flight of stairs to climb and enthused over his back balcony. He put on music and suggested they call out for Mediterranean food since a light snow had begun. She agreed. He was feeling good, enjoying prolonging their time together. It had been a long time since he'd spent an evening with a woman. They chatted about their work and books they were reading.

When she rose to leave, he walked her down the stairs and across the street, which she seemed to appreciate. She was playful, making a game out of stepping only in his large footprints. When she slipped on an icy patch, he took her arm to keep her from falling and held on till they reached her door. Then he asked if he could kiss her. He could tell she was nervous by her attempted joke—that she was glad they both had eaten garlic. As soon as she said it, she tried to take it back.

"My inappropriate sense of humor again." He was glad she was nervous, and he wasn't deterred. The face she lifted to him was smiling.

During the next few weeks they saw each other regularly, trading off cooking dinner for each other. He was traversing unfamiliar ground with Keisha. She said what she thought and expected honesty in return. She was passionate and expected passion in return. She disturbed his familiar pattern of retreating when people pushed for a response from him. Sometimes he felt off balance, uncertain what he felt or how to respond.

He'd grown up in a family of caregivers and at sixteen had

declared himself to anyone close enough to hear him, "I will not be a caregiver. It takes too much of a toll." When this assertion provoked no opposition from his parents, he chose to pursue a more insular career—music, especially composing. There he could claim that time to himself was an inviolable necessity, a demand of his profession. Still, he felt conflicted. The norm in his family was putting others first. Was he wrong to reject his family's default of helping others? They talked about this one evening sitting together on his sofa eating pizza.

"You do understand that I don't want you to be a caregiver to me?" she asked. "Of course you need to retreat into your private place to make mental music." He liked that. "Just don't retreat when we're together to avoid honest interaction with me." He detected an unfamiliar intensity in her voice as she said this.

That was fair. But was it asking too much of him? He had been comfortable, if sometimes lonely, in his insularity. Yet, when he stayed *with* her, not retreating, their conversations went to a depth he had not before experienced. He loved the way she thought and how she listened to him sort out and articulate his thoughts.

One Sunday he lay in bed after she'd gone out to the local bakery for croissants. He propped extra pillows behind him, pulled the duvet up to his neck, and let his mind amble to the only serious relationship he'd tried, which had come in his late twenties. It hadn't lasted long. She was older and had a seven-year-old son. It was obvious that the woman hoped he would be a father to her boy. They'd been a couple for six months, though Richard never moved in. He'd enjoyed the boy and rather liked the idea of being part of his life. But the mother's neediness pushed him away, trumping what they had in common, which was mostly the sex. He'd found her boring and, vaguely restless, had ended it, barely noticing her absence from his life, though he had missed the boy.

After that he'd gone out with a number of women, robo-dating one of his married friends called it. Too many perfunctory dinners at friends' homes with women they were certain were "just right" for him. But never had he been drawn to the intimacy of waking up beside another person, seeing their hair scattered haphazardly on the pillow, smelling the damp warmth of a loving night on their skin, and feeling tenderly responsible for them.

Never before now. Before Keisha.

He got up and pulled on his jeans and a sweater and moved to the living room. With *Ella Fitzgerald Sings Cole Porter* playing, he sprawled on the floor, eyes closed, listening to the music washing over him. He visualized the dreamy smile that illuminated Keisha's face in sleep, recalled the soft noises she made as she shifted position, felt her legs scissoring beneath the covers for the pure sensual pleasure of sheet sliding over skin. Sometimes she turned, half-asleep, and buried her face in the chasms of his body, where his arm and side met or where his thighs came together. She would caress his stomach, rhythmically moving her thick, springy hair back and forth, back and forth to pleasure him. Sometimes he thought his chest would split open for the tactile joy of hands, tongue, and crotch sliding, rubbing, nuzzling, pleasuring, neither in a hurry, no anxious pressure to produce or withhold, just becoming, in transit together. He wondered if his parents ever experienced this. Lately he'd found himself noticing elderly couples walking together holding each other's arms or gay couples turning to look at each other as they walked, talking. Was this the Greatest Show on Earth? The best kept secret? That it was so easy and uncomplicated if you simply let yourself feel, let yourself attach, stopped being so afraid?

Keisha, April 18

They were in her apartment, in the bedroom. She could use another hour of sleep, but Richard was sitting up, scanning the room, noticing things. She saw him staring and answered before he asked about the hole in the wall. The truth. Abbreviated but honest. He thanked her for telling him.

He got out of bed and moved to her dresser, picking up two

photographs in a hinged gold frame.

"Who are these people who have had a front row seat to our lovemaking?" he asked.

"Mom and Dad. Over on the desk are Grandma and Grandpa Whitmore, Mom's parents who we lived with when I was small. I think I've told you about them."

He came back to the bed and sat beside her. "Were you adopted?" he asked.

She laughed. She could imagine where this conversation was going. She'd been through it more times than she cared to remember. People revealed a lot about themselves by how they worded their questions from here on. She decided not to make it easy for him. Let him find his own words and squirm a little. It would tell her something important about him.

"No, I'm not adopted." She felt like she was doing research, waiting to learn which box to tick on her survey form, which category to place him in.

"I saw a film once about a South African woman born to white South African parents, only she was brown skinned. Is that what happened to you?"

Keisha didn't know whether to laugh out loud, hit, or kiss him. His response was one she had *never* heard before.

"No, Richard, my mom is my biological mother. She married Dad when I was five, though he was already a part of my life when I was three."

"Do you know your biological father?" He was looking at her, obviously interested.

"No. Mom showed me a picture of him in a magazine when he was in Chicago marching for fair housing with Dr. Martin Luther King, Jr., not far from here. In the article he was quoted as saying that these white neighborhoods of Chicago were more racist than Mississippi."

"So he was a civil rights activist?"

"Yes. So was Mom."

"But you never met him?"

"Correct. Mom says he was a major leader in the Movement doing very important work and she didn't want to distract him."

Even as she said this Keisha could hear how hollow an explanation it was. Surely Mom was smart enough to come up with something better!

Richard was smiling at her, about to make one of his jokes. It was a new skill he was cultivating. "Well, you are certainly a distraction!" He paused for her approving grin. "What does your dad look like?"

"Tall, dark, and handsome, West Indian, hair in dreadlocks, if I remember correctly."

"I never thought about your racial identity before. How do you identify yourself?" His face looked surprised and puzzled. She wondered what he was thinking. And if he would tell her.

"It depends on what age I am. As a little kid, I identified as white. In grade school the other kids were all white and I assumed I was, too. Then one day in fourth grade when we brought Valentines to give away, a boy gave me one that was mushy and another boy teased him about liking a black girl. It was new information. Years later reading DuBois' *Souls of Black Folks* I read about his similar experience, only in his case the girls excluded him from their Valentine giving. It was chilling for him and made him feel 'other.' But, for me? I wanted to hit the boy who was teasing. Probably said something to put him down."

"Do you know what became of your biological father?" He was listening closely, and she thought his eyes looked caring.

"Mom says he joined the Black Panthers and managed their feeding program for kids and a program for teens that taught them their constitutional rights. Mom's friend Barbara kept her updated on what he was doing. He was drafted and served in Vietnam. I guess he hated that war. Did you know we dropped more bombs on Vietnam than were used by the Allies in Europe in World War II?"

Keisha recognized that she was doing what she often did when a question brought her up against unresolved feelings: abstracting what was personally painful by making an historical observation.

She continued. "Anyway, I find him very interesting and wish I knew more, but I think his story is lost to history."

Richard looked puzzled. "But aren't you a historian? Can't

you research it?"

"I probably could. I guess I moved on. There was a period in my life—teens and college—when I identified with him almost completely. I gave my parents a rough time, dismissed them as irrelevant to the struggle. I was active in the anti-apartheid movement just before Nelson Mandela was released from prison and was the youngest member of a collective in New York City that addressed racism around the world. But when I went to grad school, I had no time for anything other than studying. About the only things left from that time in my life are the posters in my office of Malcolm X, Angela Davis, and Mandela. And my convictions."

"I want to be sure I understand. You thought of yourself as black during your teens and twenties." He looked at her and when she nodded, he continued. "Did you feel conflicted about your racial identity?"

She sighed, irritated at how naïve he was, how naïve most whites were. Of course she felt conflicted! She supposed she would have to draw him a picture. Then if he still didn't get it, well, that would be the end of what had been a nice interlude. She tried to keep her voice low and switched to her teacher self as she launched into the education of yet another white boy.

"Like a chameleon I took on the coloration of my surroundings. I could be the violinist Keisha Johnson, straight A student—white—or the rebel quick to notice racially barbed remarks, writing my own raps with hip hop music blasting—black. Fortunately, my mom and dad understood and let me work it through for myself. In some ways it's been harder in academia where white colleagues assume that my race privileges me and black colleagues presume my degree of white ancestry gives me advantages. Add to that the normal competitiveness of the academic world and I have found it hard to have close, personal friendships with colleagues."

She wondered if he could understand. It is so hard to be understood when you live in a skin that bridges two traditionally hostile identities. When you live in a country where color shouts preconceptions that are far from the much more murky and conflictual truth. Oh, God, she was weary of having to explain herself. Why couldn't she just *be herself?* She felt self-protective and her eyes moved to the hole in her wall. She was who she was and there would be no changing that.

She got out of bed and walked to her closet, pulling on her Saturday clothes, then went to the kitchen for coffee to let herself cool down. She returned with two steaming cups, passing him one before seating herself on the floor leaning against the dresser. It was his turn to feel the discomfort.

"What do you think about all this, Richard?" Her eyes scrutinized his face.

"It's very interesting to me," he began. "I am a musician. I love the music of *Show Boat* with Julie, the biracial singer married to a white man even though it was against the law, a woman who paid a heavy price for 'passing as white.' One of my favorite operas is *Madame Butterfly* with a Japanese woman who bears a son from her love affair with a white soldier, and the soldier abandons her and his child. Then there is *Othello*."

Her anger was building, and she interrupted him. "Is this a musician's version of 'Some of my best friends are mixed race?'" She stood and left the room, face averted from him.

After several minutes she returned and sat back down. She would hear him out.

"What I was trying to say is that race and ethnicity coming between people has been a theme in some of the music that most stirs me. I don't know why this is true. It just is."

She could see he was embarrassed and uncomfortable, but he wasn't leaving or changing the subject.

He continued. "One of my colleagues was talking with me Friday about working on an adaptation of DuBose Heyward's 1921 play about mixed race Native American, African American, and EuroAmerican people in South Carolina. It's titled *Brass Ankle* referring to the ankle shackles people were forced to wear. Do you know Heyward? He and his wife Dorothy wrote the play *Porgy* that became *Porgy and Bess*."

Keisha smiled listening to him. One of the things she liked about their relationship was the way they learned from each other, building on each other's knowledge in a way that she found quite stimulating. The intellectual Keisha wanted to pursue this. She stood and went to her laptop. "I was reading an essay yesterday by Alice Dunbar Nelson about being mixed race titled 'Brass Ankles Speaks.' She never published it and it is raw with her own rejection by both whites and blacks. Painful to read.

I'll email you the link so you can read it." She opened her email and sent him the essay.

Then she forced herself to return to probing his feelings. "How do you feel about my being mixed race?"

He was silent. "I don't want people to hurt you. I think that is the core of what I feel. And before today I had not thought about that happening to you."

His answer touched her but she remained wary. "People still do hurt folks like me. Cops pull us over for 'driving while black' and sometimes strangers come up to me and ask me where I'm from. When I say 'Cleveland, Ohio, U.S.A.' they look surprised, like the only people they consider Americans have pink skins. It makes me angry. I know things are much better than they were a generation ago, but it's still annoying and unfair." She stopped, suddenly overwhelmed by the feelings behind her words. She needed a break.

She got up and walked to the bed, extending her hand to him. "I think it is time to change the subject. Let's get some brunch."

Richard

He stood beside her in her tiny kitchen making a salad while she cooked a cheese omelet. They both were quiet. Their conversation troubled him. He wondered if his responses had disappointed her. He didn't want to disappoint her. He'd learned so much about her in that hour talking. She was such a complex person and strong, forceful like his mother. The way she ended the conversation and directed them to get brunch,

Mom had done the same thing so many times when something made her uncomfortable, and the family would follow her lead, like he was following Keisha's.

What happens next? Whose move is it? Maybe, given her history with men, witness the hole in the wall, she would be ready to run. He didn't want that. He wanted them to keep going, working things out, making a path by remaining connected while they learned about each other's painful places.

"Can you pass me the mushrooms, please?" she asked, turning toward him.

Instead, he took her in his arms, just holding her gently, not letting go until the smell of burning toast pulled her away.

Keisha

That night she slept fitfully, assaulted by memories she had consigned to a remote Not to Be Revisited place in her brain. The conversation with Richard had cracked open the door to that place and sharp-edged fragments pushed past the barricades she had erected against them.

She was twenty and home from college for the summer. She'd gone to bed in her girly room, her stuffed animals from a decade ago still piled on the rocking chair and ruffled rose-colored curtains waving in the window. She remembered Mom was wearing a pink polyester pantsuit and she was crying. Mom had been on the phone with her friend Barbara before she'd come into Keisha's room. She'd sat on the edge of Keisha's bed and told her that her birth father had died in an accident. "So young and so sad," she kept repeating. She would provide no details. It was unlike Mom to refuse to talk openly. It troubled Keisha and confused her.

Another shard of repressed memory resurfaced, from the following fall. She was in the campus library, looking at newspaper articles from the previous May, part of a research project she was doing on the lives of Freedom Summer volunteers after 1964. She was looking for her father. She found an obituary in the

Philadelphia Inquirer for Reggie Lewis, 32, who died May 13, 1985. No details. An article in the *Inquirer* dated May 14, 1985 told of the Philadelphia police firing tear gas into a row house that was the headquarters of MOVE, a Black Nationalist group that worked to energize the black community through celebrating African culture, teaching Black History, and growing black-owned businesses. The article said that police fired, "thousands of rounds of small arms fire into the building for ninety minutes. They then tried to remove two roof structures by dropping a four-pound bomb of C-4 and Tovex onto the roof. This started a fire that eventually consumed the entire neighborhood" and killed eleven members of MOVE, whose bodies were unidentifiable. There were only two survivors.

According to the obituary, her father died the day of the police attack. She had already discovered that he was living in Philadelphia and part of MOVE. It had to be him.

She awoke in a cold sweat, unable to tolerate the pain that threatened to consume her even now, all these years later. She turned on the light and lay in bed, forcing herself to remember what happened next in the half-light of her bedroom.

She had cried for days over her lost chances—never to know the whys of her father's life choices, his accomplishments and regrets, his experiences and thoughts. She kept imagining his horrible incineration in that row house in a working-class Philadelphia neighborhood, assaulted with military weapons, as though he and his friends were the enemy in a war. *Why hadn't Mom told her about him? Why had she lied?*

She'd gotten up in the middle of the night and driven home to Cleveland, marched into the kitchen where Mom was making breakfast, and screamed accusations at her, face frozen and unfamiliar from rage. *"How could you not tell my father I existed? How could you keep me from knowing him? How could you lie to me about what happened to him? Parents are supposed to tell their children the TRUTH, but you lied. I'll never trust you again."*

When Ann had told her she was only trying to protect her from pain, Keisha had interrupted her. *"You* are not in charge of my life. That ended when I grew up. *You* don't decide what I will know about myself. I wanted to know him. You had no right to deny me that. All I have is a photograph of a burning city block with a row house that became my father's tomb." The words keened out of her gut with an intensity and sound neither of them had ever heard before. Then she'd stomped out of the house, slid into her car, and screeched out of the driveway, driving well over the speed limit and not stopping until she reached the campus.

In her dark bedroom that night nearly half her lifetime later, the lamp on the end table provided a circle of light, sparse comfort, as she sobbed.

Ann

The full schedule of Ann's meeting in Chicago kept her downtown in the conference center until noon on Sunday. She and Keisha were to meet for lunch at one. At noon she took the elevator to the eleventh floor to gather her things so she could be checked out when Keisha arrived. She checked under the bed, pulled out the drawers, and looked behind the bathroom door to be sure she had not left anything. Her clothes were folded neatly in her roller bag. She reached into the inside zipper compartment to pull out a bottle of ibuprofen. Her head was pounding. Her fingers located a stiff piece of paper and she pulled it out, not expecting to find a photo of Keisha at age twenty.

She'd been looking for that photo, the one she had carried with her during the four years they had not spoken. She sat down in the velvet armchair and studied the photo. Her beautiful daughter looked out at her, dreadlocks reinforcing her saucy independence. From the date stamped on the lower left by the photographer, it was taken a month before Reggie died. Before she lost Keisha.

Don had kept his relationship with Keisha going by sending simple notes of support and love and calling every week, regardless of whether she would accept his calls. But Ann had been too devastated to do that. Instead, she sank into her work, her students, her writing, and her depression.

The phone in the motel room rang. It was Keisha downstairs, ready for lunch. She tucked the photo into the zipper compartment of her purse and slipped the purse over her shoulder. She picked up her coat and briefcase and pulled the roller bag behind her to the elevator. Thank God her prodigal daughter had eventually returned.

Keisha

Mom beamed when she saw her standing in the lobby of the hotel. Keisha loved seeing the look of pride on Mom's face as she studied her daughter before enfolding her in a big hug. Mom looked well, still fit and attractive at nearly sixty. They were eating at the restaurant in the Omni so Mom checked her coat and bag at the front desk.

They settled into a booth and, before they looked at the menu, Mom pulled the picture out of her purse and passed it to Keisha. What was she trying to do? They'd never talked about that time, never.

"Where did you find this?" Keisha tried to keep her voice normal. Had Mom been remembering their huge fight also?

"In the pocket of my roller bag. I carried it with me everywhere in those years, but I haven't seen it in, maybe a decade? Weird to find it this morning. Maybe it's my reminder to tell you how grateful I am that you came back."

Keisha felt uncomfortable. But like Mom she was a believer that coincidences were more than that. Tentatively she told Mom that she'd been thinking about that time just last night, after an intense conversation with the new man in her life. She chose her words carefully. She didn't want to revisit all that pain. After all, the point was that she had come back to Mom and Dad. They had patched things up. She chose words that would serve as a segue to slide their conversation away from the alienation of those years to the present and Richard. She anticipated that Mom would be all ears to hear about him. She was. Keisha commended herself for an effective strategy.

Mom took Keisha's hand. "I want to hear all about him, but I also need to share that I've always felt that Grandma and Grandpa brought you back to us as their last act on this earth."

Keisha didn't know what to say. In a way it was possible. Her grandparents had been killed in a car accident when they were in their early sixties. She remembered Mom had phoned, breaking their silence, her voice so tiny and fragile that Keisha hadn't known who was speaking. She'd squeezed out the awful news and then begged Keisha please to come home. It was the only time—other than when Mom gave birth to Keisha's dying baby brother—that Mom had fallen apart. Keisha and Don together had brought Mom through that grief and Mom knew it.

"If you hadn't come home, I don't think I could've made it." Mom's voice was soft. Then her face changed expression and she asked in a peppy sounding voice, "Now, tell me about Richard." Mom and I are so alike in how we deal with pain, she thought, remembering how she had shifted the conversation with Richard last night when her feelings threatened to overwhelm her.

The waiter had been hovering the background tapping his pencil against his notepad. Now he moved in to take their order.

Don, Cleveland, Ohio

The Cleveland Plain Dealer barely made a noise as it landed on the front steps, so shrunken it was compared with a decade ago. Don went out to get it, Sam padding along beside him companionably. He divided the paper, keeping the front page for himself and passing Ann the society pages and obituaries, watching for her expression of irritation, as predictable as death and taxes. Wait for it. Here it comes.

"When are you going to enter the twenty-first century and realize that women are as interested in the real news as men!" Seeing his grin, she realized that once again she'd been ensnared by her husband. Ah, how he loved to play with her short-fused feminism.

She sighed and scanned the obituaries before turning to the word scramble and Sudoku. No one she recognized today, although there was someone from Buffalo about Don's age.

"Did you know a Connie Riegler in Buffalo?" she asked him.

"I don't remember any Rieglers," he replied returning to an editorial criticizing U.S. aid to Israel.

"You might know her." She read aloud the obituary just in case. She knew that being interrupted when he was reading annoyed him and figured she would get back at him.

Riegler, Connie, 53. Lakeview, Buyer for Macys, BA and MBA from Baldwin Wallace College. Born Buffalo, NY, November 28, 1951. Loving mother to daughters Andrea Musleh and Allison Solo. Memorial service Saturday, April 26, 10 a.m. at Mandley-Vetrovsky Funeral Home, Fairview Park. In lieu of flowers, contributions to Catholic Charities.

He reached for the paper. The photo showed a genial, smiling white haired woman looking straight into the camera, eyes twinkling like they knew a happy secret. Could this be his Connie? He felt his chest constrict at the thought.

After his classes he sat in his office at the computer doing a Google search for Connie Riegler. Not much more than what was in the obituary, but he did find an address on Lake Shore Boulevard, one of those old high-rise apartment buildings looking out on Lake Erie, he surmised. He wrote down the address and the time and place for the memorial service. Driving home from the university he tried to locate her building, which wasn't easy in early rush hour traffic. He decided to attend the memorial service. He owed her at least that much.

Andrea Riegler Musleh, Cleveland, Ohio

Mom's apartment faced the lake, spacious and quiet. Andrea

sat with her sister on the cinnamon-colored leather sofa Mom had purchased fifteen years ago, when she'd finally saved enough to leave the little house in Fairview Park, the house where they had grown up, after leaving Dad.

They were remembering things about Mom.

Allison, her younger sister, said she didn't remember Dad at all. Andrea remembered him. Especially his smell: Beer. She'd developed a life-long aversion to that smell, one whiff making her nauseous. She remembered coming home to find him in his recliner in the darkened room surrounded by an ever-widening circle of empty beer cans, tossed on the floor around him like a wall. To this day dark rooms brought back the anxious churning in her stomach that she'd felt returning from school to find her father, Frank Riegler, in a stupor, breath giving off that stale, sour smell that hung hopeless in the darkened room where this bear of a man hid out in silence, the shades and drapes drawn.

Mom had told them he wasn't always like this, that he'd been a nice man when they'd met, but began drinking more and more after she became pregnant with Andrea. Mom had persuaded him to go with her to Father Joe, the Jesuit priest who had helped her when she first moved to Cleveland, nineteen and pregnant. Mom hadn't told them about being pregnant until a year ago. She told them Dad had cried with the priest, words torn from his throat in a wild storm of emotion, so much sobbing he was hard to understand, something about not being worthy of being around babies after what he'd done. Then just *"No, No, No."*

Mom had stayed with him for nine years. Somehow he made it to work most days and his paychecks provided plenty for them to live on. But beer cans littered the floor most evenings and he barely ate the dinners she prepared for him. By the time Andrea was eight and Allison five, he was following the six packs with shots of whiskey and rarely spoke.

One night he yelled at them and threatened them with his belt. Mom had set her face, gone to their rooms, and gathered up their things, whatever she could carry. She packed the car trunk and the front seat methodically, silently ticking off which files to take, tucking the checkbook into her purse along with the key to the safety deposit box. She put the girls in the back seat, locked the doors, and backed down the driveway while Andrea and Allison peered out the back window at their nice suburban home and the angry man shouting at them from the front step.

Mom told them he wouldn't hurt them. He just felt really bad about himself. "Your dad is sick and we can't help him get better. Each time he comes out from his alcoholic dead zone he feels worse about himself. He's trapped in his pain. I've tried to be enough for him, but I'm not." Years later she told them that on that night she'd pictured him stumbling into their bedroom and getting his pistol. Not that he would hurt any of them on purpose, but, "A man in that much pain with that much alcohol distorting his thinking for nearly a decade might do anything for relief, deliberately or by accident."

She found them a small house at 4220 West 223rd, only two bedrooms and the elms and catalpas in the front yard were diseased and dying. But the house didn't smell of beer or sound of a desperately unhappy man who couldn't erase his war memories, no matter how much he drank.

Andrea remembered how Mom made that little house a welcoming refuge for them, establishing family traditions like Saturday morning pancakes with whipped cream and real maple syrup, even strawberries when they were in season. They biked together along the flat back roads developers hadn't yet discovered. They made up songs and stories. Gradually, Mom said, they lost that haunted look.

It was already dark outside and only a couple of lamps were on in Mom's apartment. Twilight, Mom's favorite time. Allison was tired. She stretched out on the couch with her head in Andrea's lap, and Andrea stroked her hair as she fell asleep, like Mom used to do.

Oh, Mom, how much I miss you. She sent loving thoughts into the universe, troubled that she didn't know where to direct them. Why must death be so secretive? She longed to know where her mother was, certain that such a dynamic and purposeful woman could not simply disappear like vapor into the air.

She returned to remembering. It seemed to help.

Mom found a scholarship for older women wanting to go to college and enrolled in classes to earn her Bachelor's and then Master's degrees at Baldwin Wallace. Andrea remembered her coming home at the end of long days of work and classes, turning the knob quietly so as not to awaken them—only Andrea would try to wait up for her—greeting Mrs.
Spaak, the neighbor who babysat, paying her, and standing on the stoop to watch Mrs. Spaak walk down the street to her own house. Some mornings Andrea found Mom asleep on the couch still wearing her coat and shoes, no energy left to navigate the short distance to her bedroom. Remembering, she felt a rush of gratitude for her mother.

Mom started working at Macy's selling shoes, but once she'd earned her B.A. she became floor manager and, with her M.B.A., chief buyer of ladies' wear. By then they were in high school and she was able to sell the house and purchase this apartment by the Lake, where they all lived through college to enable her to afford to send her girls to university.

The past fifteen years had gone so quickly and brought so much change. Andrea's marriage to Karim Musleh, a Palestinian student she'd met at Case, and Allison's marriage to Tony Sollo, a tenor sax player like Allison who she'd met when her college jazz band went to Italy for a jazz festival. Then two years ago the arrival of daughters to both Allison and Andrea. Andrea was grateful that Mom got to enjoy her granddaughters, even for so short a time. Mom had arranged to spend time with her grandkids so that their parents could have romantic weekends by themselves, though Andrea suspected Mom would use any excuse to be with "my grand girls," as she called them.

The Christmas before last they'd gathered here in Mom's apartment for the usual combination of Italian and Palestinian dishes Mom liked to cook in honor of her sons-in-law for Christmas eve. The living room was festive. Colored lights framed the glass double doors to the balcony, and white lights twinkled like tiny candle flames on the Christmas tree and danced in the room, reflected in the glass doors.

Mom said she had something she wanted to talk to them about.

That was when she told them about coming to Cleveland pregnant and alone at nineteen. She'd tried to raise her son on her own, but ultimately had to place him for adoption with Catholic Charities. She'd started crying, and they'd sat on either side of her, arms around her. She wanted to locate her son, to know that he was well and happy, and she was asking for their help.

Andrea had been shocked. She thought she knew her Mom as well as anyone, yet here was Mom telling them that she been pregnant at nineteen and that she had given her child for adoption. It didn't help that Allison was acting all lovey-dovey with Mom, saying this made them even closer. Why did Mom need to locate this other child, anyway? Wasn't it enough that she had two daughters and sons-in-law and grandchildren?

Later that evening Andrea had asked if Karim would go for a walk with her and poured out to her husband her feelings.

"Do you think your feelings have anything to do with your jealousy of Allison when you were children?" he'd asked her. "Or with how you always felt so responsible for your mom, being the oldest child? Tonight this unknown, your brother, became the oldest. I would think that would be hard on you." She had burst into tears and he had held her while she cried.

"It will be okay, you know. Your mom loves you very much. You're the children she raised and bonded with. Whoever he is, he won't replace you." How was Karim so wise? She could always count on him to help her see things more clearly. Just recalling that Christmas eve walk and conversation helped salve the void of loss she was feeling. She missed Mom so very much, but at least she had this lovely man beside her. For a moment she regretted accepting Karim's mom's offer to host Tony, Karim, and the children at their house "so you and your sister can do the important work of remembering together, uninterrupted in the next few days." She would like for him to hold her tonight, but his mother was right. She guessed she knew where Karim got his wisdom.

In the morning over coffee and oatmeal from Mom's kitchen cabinets, Andrea and Allison resumed their conversation where Allison had fallen asleep on her lap.

"I can't believe she's gone. It's been like one of those nightmares that seem to go on forever," she told her sister. "How could she go so quickly?" Allison had flown in from Detroit as soon as she could after

Mom's test results had come back, but it was Andrea, living thirty minutes away, who had gone with Mom to the doctor and been with her when they learned the prognosis.

"She had that hacking cough we noticed at Christmas. Remember?

Well, I'd stopped at Macy's to get a birthday gift for Karim's dad and ran into one of Mom's friends. The woman asked about Mom's health. Apparently she'd missed several days of work. That's so unlike her, so I insisted on going with her to see Dr. Goyle." Andrea's eyes strayed to the balcony and the Lake, and she held her coffee cup half way to her mouth, stopped by the memories from taking a sip. She'd probably told Allison this several times but repeating it helped it sink in.

"Then everything changed. When we went back to talk with Dr. Goyle several days later, the expression on her face scared me. She sat next to Mom and held her hand. She looked so kind and caring. Then she said, 'Connie, the news is not good. I don't think you have much time ahead of you in this life. Your lungs are...' I don't remember the rest. I think we both stopped listening. I brought Mom here and called you. Then I called Macy's to tell them she needed to take her accumulated sick leave. I called hospice to get the bed delivered. And you came, with Antonia."

"Thank God we had the girls here with Mom." Allison surveyed the room where the hospital bed still stood facing the balcony, set where Mom had wanted it so she could see the Lake and watch her granddaughters play.

"She was amazingly accepting that she was dying." Andrea hoped that she would be that accepting when her time came.

Mom had asked them to call Father Joe. The rectory phone number was in Mom's address book and Andrea had called. Father Joe was recently returned from a decade of pastoring several small congregations in Baja, California, northern Mexico. Of course, he would come.

The oxygen tube comfort care running to Mom's nostrils seemed to keep her comfortable. They talked as much as she could, wanting to hear more of her life, trying as best they could to pour out their love on her as she had poured out hers on them. They read and sang to her.

When Father Joe arrived, the two of them talked, Mom's voice reduced to a whisper. He administered the Last Rites with the family, augmented by Karim and Tony, gathered around her. "This is a good death," Mom had whispered as they stroked her hair and her mottled hands and feet. "Please try to find your brother," she added. "I am so glad for each of you."

That was all. Three weeks after the news from Dr. Goyle that wrenched them from their lives and rearranged their world, Mom was dead.

They had each made the sign of the cross on her forehead.

The husbands took the girls back to Karim's parents while Andrea and Allison waited for the mortuary with its awful gurney and black plastic container into which they slipped her, Loving Mother, 53, carefully, gently. Andrea could not help thinking that this last of life's actions was disturbingly ordinary, like taking out the trash.

Father Joe returned the next morning to help them make arrangements.

Mom had told them she wanted a simple pine box, a cremation casket, the least expensive way to be buried. Andrea had stayed up late working at Mom's desk on an obituary. On the desk she'd found a bright yellow sticky note with a name, address, and phone number in Mom's distinctive script: Don and Ann Johnson. The address was local with an exclamation point writ large after "Cleveland, Ohio." The names were not familiar to either of them. "Should we let them know?" Allison had asked. "Later," Andrea replied.

Don, April 26

He took the morning off, inventing an excuse to miss his

departmental meeting so he could make the memorial service. He was not Catholic, though he had attended mass with a friend decades ago. He sat in the back, alone, and watched while the priest said mass and then invited the congregation to share their experiences of Connie Riegler.

One person after another stood to recount some interaction with her. Many told of her small kindnesses to them. Others shared how her humor helped them. People from Macy's, from her apartment building, from Fairview Park. He didn't see any of her siblings, though of course he wouldn't recognize them anyway. The place was packed. An older Palestinian man, a black and white checkered scarf draped over his shoulders, told of his first meeting with Connie, how she had honored his family by reading about their culture and the history of their country of origin. He said he was proud to share a grandchild with her.

Lastly her girls came forward together, arm in arm, to thank people for coming. The one resembled his Connie, and for a moment he felt a rush of emotion. They closed the service singing a song they said their Mom had taught them in the tiny house they had grown up in, where they—he couldn't make out the words, something like, "rebuilt our family." They sang the first verse together, one keeping the melody going when the other could not continue. The congregation joined in, reading the words printed in the program.

You have come down to the lakeshore,
Seeking neither the wise nor the wealthy,
But only asking for me to follow.
You need my hands, my exhaustion,
Working love for the rest of the weary—
A love that's willing to go on loving.
Oh, Jesus, you have looked into my eyes.
Gently smiling, you called out my name.
On the sand I have abandoned my small boat.
Now with you, I will seek other seas.

The priest walked to the back, swinging incense as he moved

in his spotless white vestments. He stood behind Don when he gave the benediction. Sitting there in the last row Don was overcome with regret and unable to stop his tears.

Ann, Cleveland, Ohio

The red light blinked on the answering machine and the beep-beep-beep of the alarm system greeted Ann as she opened the front door. Automatically she walked straight ahead to disarm the alarm system, then took off her coat and hung it in the hall closet. She placed her wet shoes on the mat awaiting them in the entryway, set down her briefcase, and relaxed into the sofa. She hadn't enjoyed the conference in Chicago as much as she ordinarily enjoyed professional conferences, but her afternoon with Keisha had been lovely. Their several hours of real conversation over lunch and during a brief walk in Old Town left her buzzing with the joy of connecting well with her only child.

Keisha had told her about her trip to the Museum of Science and Industry, describing the prenatal exhibit with intricate details. Ann had thoroughly enjoyed her daughter's extended description, convinced that adult children sharing the details of their lives with their mothers was evidence of intimacy. And Ann wanted so much to be close to Keisha, especially after the years they'd been estranged. Now she leaned back into the large back cushions of the sofa and was grateful.

Keisha had even told her about Richard, the musician who taught at Northwestern and lived across the street. Typically, Keisha left off the subjects of many of her sentences, speaking in that shorthand way she talked when her mind was overflowing with so much to say. "Went on the El to the Museum, then back to his place, dining in since it was snowing. Really nice man. Reminds me of Dad in some ways—tall, lanky, and private."

They had laughed at that word "private," which they agreed applied to Don Johnson more than to just about any one they knew. "Next time you come to Chicago, you'll have to meet him."

"Next time" sounded promising. She'd never push her daughter to marry, but Keisha's biological clock was running, and they so hoped to be grandparents someday.

Keisha rode with her to O'Hare and stayed till she was through security, which was a caring gesture that Ann appreciated. Ann flew in and out of airports including O'Hare many times a year, but having Keisha accompany her was deeply gratifying. She still missed daily contact with her daughter, missed seeing her smile and that unruly hair that kinked into a mass of ringlets in wet weather, missed her long stride and the intently focused look on her face as she scrutinized people or things.

Sitting on the sofa in the house she'd made her home for three decades, Ann closed her eyes and savored the day, glad to be back. Then she forced herself up and into the kitchen to start dinner, knowing Don would be home soon. She cut up veggies to stir fry and a chicken breast putting the pieces to sizzle in the wok. She poured boiling water over a pot of rice and let it simmer, covered, on the back burner. She pulled several pieces of fruit from the produce drawer on the left side of the frig and set about making a fruit salad. She was almost finished when she heard the security system beep to announce Don's arrival. The answering machine began its message. So like him to check the answering machine even before removing his coat and so like her to do everything else first.

She walked into the living room smiling, glad to see him, as she heard, "Dr. and Mrs. Johnson,"—in her mind she corrected the speaker, "Dr. and *Dr.* Johnson"—"You don't know me but my name is Andrea Musleh. I am Connie Riegler's daughter. Mom died last week after a very brief illness, and in going through her things I found a sticky note with your name and address on the top of her 'to do' list. I don't recall her talking about you, but I thought you should know about her death." There was a long pause. "This probably sounds very strange. Anyway, if you don't, don't know her, I'm sorry to bother you. If you do, my sister and I are staying at Mom's cleaning out the apartment this week—

(312) 668-4321—if you want to call. I apologize for not calling before…"

"You have five seconds remaining," the mechanical voice announced. Then CLICK.

Don raised his head, and she could see that something awful had rearranged his face. He looked suddenly older, haggard, and distraught.

"What happened?" she asked him. Then she bolted back to the kitchen where she could smell the vegetables beginning to char. She turned off the burner and returned to the living room to find him sunk into the sofa, doubled over and stricken.

She sat beside him and reached for one of his hands. It lay unresponsive in hers. She waited for several long minutes, then softly said, "I'm here." She waited some more. She could tell that he was searching for words, trying to order them into sentences. She knew that this was the worst of all social requirements for him, having to speak without time to process his thoughts. Finally he began, pausing an uncomfortably long time between each sentence that he squeezed out. "I have never told you this…I wanted to, but I couldn't…You know I love you and am very happy with you…" He was cracking his knuckles one by one and then starting over, though they were done cracking.

"Before I knew you I met a girl one summer back in Buffalo…She got pregnant and her family threw her out…" He was turning his head side to side, eyes closed, as though trying to deny the memories.

"I didn't know about it until years after I'd broken up with her…" More head shaking. Like a metronome, back and forth. "She had a son and tried to raise him, but she couldn't make enough money to support him, so she had to place him for adoption…She died last week. I went to her service while you were gone. No son, only her two daughters." His breathing was audible, as though he was carrying a too heavy burden.

She hadn't seen him so distraught since their baby was born and lived only an hour. He covered his face with his hands and sobbed, while she patted his shoulder, murmuring, "It will be all right," like one does in times like this.

Like this? What had she ever experienced like this? She tried to take it in. Her husband of thirty–three years had loved another woman before her, a love that left him devastated all these decades later, a love he'd never told her about. He had a son somewhere, unknown to him, his only biological child. He was loaded with guilt and pain for not helping this woman raise their child, for forcing her to give him up for adoption.

She observed her own reaction and thought how different it would be if she was younger. She might have railed against him, threatened by his love for this woman, self-protective and wounded. But at fifty-nine she had no doubt that her husband loved her and she him. She could see that this man she loved was suffering more than she had ever known him to suffer. She kept up her litany, "It will be all right," modifying it slightly, "We will be all right."

After what seemed a long time he spoke again. "I was so wrong about her. All those people at her service talking about her, how funny she was, how she helped them, what a success she'd made of her life despite very little money and no support. I dismissed her as not good enough for what I wanted to achieve. But she went to college and grad school and lived a good life. I was so wrong."

Ann was reconstructing the situation. College man with big plans gets girl with no future pregnant and abandons her. Such a common story. She could feel anger rising in her against him, as though she and Connie were one woman, Universal Woman, faced with the universal problem of male privilege.

"So are you crying for her or for yourself?" She said it very softly without thinking, but he heard.

He was accustomed to his wife's truthfulness, one might say tactlessness. But she knew that this was a low blow. He stood abruptly, wiping his eyes, grabbed his coat, and opened the door.

"I'm going out for a while." His words hit her like a slap.

After the door slammed, she returned to the kitchen and served herself some charred stir fry, forgetting about the rice and fruit salad as she ate alone, deep in thought and feelings.

Don

He walked fast without thinking where his feet were taking him. What had he done? It irritated him that Ann was so perceptive **and** so tactless. Maybe he *was* sobbing for himself. Didn't he have that right? He'd lost the first woman he had loved, forever. He would never know his only son. To contact her children, he would have to own up to his role in their mother's misery. Yet not to contact them was to leave himself dangling forever, pulled under by this secret grief.

Who would ever respect him again once they knew? Ann would probably leave him. Keisha, too. He had shamed his family. It would get out to his colleagues. He had built a reputation for being an ethical person, not taking grants from companies whose business preyed upon the poor and defenseless. But with Connie he had behaved shamefully, unethically. He had avoided facing it for all these years, but in his core he knew that walk- ing away from his responsibility for Connie was a personal failure that would taint the rest of his life.

His ability to think rationally unraveled as he walked, terrifying to a scientist.

He rounded the corner walking fast and nearly knocked down a young woman who couldn't have been more than twenty. "I am so sorry," he muttered, meaning it so intensely that she, like Ann, reassured him in that mother-soothing voice, "It's all right. Really, it's all right."

He slowed down. He had to do something to make this pain go away.

He played out his options in his head.

1. He could walk into traffic and hope that a bus or car hit him so hard that he never awakened.
2. He could go back to the house, sneak in and hide in his study until he was able to think more clearly.
3. He could hail a cab and go to Connie's apartment and confess everything to her daughters, asking them, acting

in her stead, to forgive him.

4. He could call Andrea and ask if he could come by
   tomorrow evening. He could bring a gift or open a
   bank account for Connie's grandchildren, as penance.
5. He could find a…

He found himself in front of St. Peters. The officiant at the Sunday evening mass, according to the signboard, was Father Joseph Malick, the priest who officiated at Connie's memorial service.

Option 5 remained stillborn as, out of options, he turned right and entered the massive gothic building. There were not many people present for mass. He looked at his watch. It was 7:30, thirty minutes into the service. Perhaps he could approach the priest after the service? He wasn't a Catholic, but surely confession was confession and sinners, sinners regardless of denominational affiliation. He sat in one of the empty pews at the back breathing heavily and trying without success to slow the pounding of his heart.

Father Joe swung the incense and blessed the small band of stalwart worshippers, held up his hand in the benediction, and dismissed them, walking slowly up the chancel toward the back of the church, his skirts moving languidly. He passed the pew where Don was sitting, hunched and disoriented.

"F-f-father?"

Father Joe looked to his right and seemed to recognize the older gentleman from yesterday's memorial service. Same coat, same watery eyes and tear-furrowed cheeks, the look of a person in great pain.

"Can I help you, Son?"

It was disconcerting to be called "Son," such an intimate name, yet also comforting and Don needed comfort.

"I hope so, Father. Can we talk?"

"In the Confessional or in my office?" "Either would be fine."

"Wait here till I hang up my robes. I'll be back." It felt like a long wait.

The air was chilly in the cavernous sanctuary. When Father Joe returned, he was wearing black slacks and a black turtleneck with a sports coat on top, the cross around his neck the only evidence of his calling, other than his eyes. He ushered Don into his office, a nice enough wood paneled room with several overstuffed chairs that you sank into when you sat on them, so that you felt embraced....or smothered.

Don took a seat, paused, then haltingly told the same story he had told Ann just an hour or two ago. He could see from Father's expression that he was interested and welcomed Don's account. When Don finished, Father Joe spoke.

"I knew your son when he was a toddler. Lovely boy. Dark hair and eyes, very curious, and tall, as I recall. Connie attended services here and sought help from us to be able to keep him, but it was more than she could handle. She came to me desperate, and I got her to the social worker at Catholic Charities. She came back to see me the day she handed the child over to the adoption worker. You're correct; it nearly broke her heart." The priest looked away, his eyes focused on something distant that Don could not decipher. Don shifted in the embracing chair, his eyes never leaving the priest.

Father Joe continued. "But God often makes a way out of no way. I think that's what happened for Connie. Next time I saw her she was married to Frank Riegler, but Frank had seen and done too much in Vietnam and was not the survivor she was. When alcohol consumed him, she moved out with their girls and rebuilt their lives all on her own, going back to school, and receiving promotions at Macy's. But you heard much of that yesterday. What is it you want from me?"

"Forgiveness!" The word lunged from Don's throat tearing through his mouth and bursting into the room, its urgency surprising to both Don and the priest.

Father Joe was silent again. "It seems to me you have some important choices to make. Do you know them?"

"To put this behind me or to seek to know Connie's children, including my son?"

"That's part of it." The priest was nodding encouragement.

"To return to my wife and ask her to travel with me in this?"

"That's part of it, too."

"To tell our daughter the truth and risk her rejection?"

"I think you don't need me to do anything but help you listen to yourself. If you're willing to, can you tell me what it was in Connie that so attracted you?"

"Her laughter and her lightness. She could transform simple things into reasons to feel delight. She saw their possibilities."

"That's lovely. In our tradition we believe those who precede us into death can still provide us guidance. Do you think you could ask her to help you learn to see in this way? She yearned for you to see the possibilities within her and loved you very much, I know. She never criticized you to me. I think she would like helping you in this way now."

Don was silent. This was a different way of looking at death. Could he embark on a course so radically unfamiliar?

"Father, I think I need to go home now. I'll think about what you've said. Can I come again if I need to? I think I'll need to."

"Of course." The priest shook his hand looking into Don's eyes with empathy. "You will find your way," he said.

Don returned home after dark. Ann was already in bed. She'd left the bedside lamp on for him. He gathered his pajamas and slippers and the quilt from the cedar chest, tiptoeing so as not to awaken her, and moved into his study. There he sat for a long time before pulling out the sleep sofa and wrapping himself in the quilt. Finally he fell into a fitful sleep.

He awakened at 3 a.m. to the vivid dream that had haunted him since his childhood— his mother, weeping and furious, telling him, "Whatever you do, don't bring shame on your family." He remembered her verbally pounding this into him in those confusing, terrible days after his father's disappearance from his life when he was twelve. *Don't bring shame on your family.*

He sipped some water, made a trip to the toilet, and returned to the safety of his still-warm quilt, yearning for the refuge of sleep. About seven he stirred, hearing the familiar sounds of his wife getting ready for school. He had closed his study door, and she did not disturb him. After a while he heard her leave the house and the purr of her car backing down the drive.

He got up and called his office. He canceled his classes for the day, asking the department secretary to post a note on the doors of his office and classroom saying Dr. Johnson had the flu and would not be in. He warmed a cup of cold coffee in the microwave and made himself a bowl of raisin bran. He was ravenously hungry and realized that he had had nothing to eat since Sunday brunch. Then he went back to his study, to figure out what to do. He was there all day, the silence a sanctuary.

Ann

Ann got home around 5:30, calling to Don as she came in the door. She'd noticed that his car was still parked in the same place, and when she'd phoned his office, she'd heard that he was out sick. She was worried. Coming upstairs, she knocked at his study.

"I'm here. I just need more time to figure things out," he said through the solid oak door.

"Can I be of help?" She balanced between concern for him and confidence borne of her long knowledge of this man that he would come through this storm.

"Not yet," he said.

"How about if I bring you some supper? I made some beef stew in the crockpot. Would that sound good?" She was clinging hopefully to his words, "Not yet." That implied sometime. Hearing his "Okay," she moved to the kitchen and returned with a bowl of stew and a warm muffin that she set down outside his door. "It's here when you're ready. Is Sam with you? I don't want him to devour your dinner."

"Thank you. He's here."

She walked back to the kitchen, listening for the creak of the door opening. She heard it. OK. One step at a time.

Don

Don slept in his study Tuesday night also, emerging only to make a call to Connie's daughters, who were out, which forced him to construct a message. He thought he had figured out what to do but decided to sleep on it. He slept less fitfully that night but with the same disturbing dream of his mother yelling at him. His mother was in her mid-eighties now and hard of hearing. Even in her present frail state he felt afraid of her. Other than his obligatory weekly call, they had little contact.

Wednesday morning neither he nor Ann had classes, so their pattern was to have breakfast together and head to their respective campuses late morning. He surprised her when he emerged from his study at 8:30, their usual time, and sat down at the kitchen table after pouring some coffee.

"Could I talk to you about what I want to do? Do you have time now?" His voice sounded tired.

"Of course." She slid into the chair across from him holding her coffee in both hands, looking directly at him. He wasn't looking at her, focusing instead on his coffee.

Then words sprang from his mouth, running through the space between them. "I want to go to meet her daughters. I want you to come with me, if you will. I want to tell them that I knew their mother and that she asked me to set up trust accounts for her grandchildren. There are two of them, both of them toddlers."

He paused, took a breath, and continued, now raising his head, his eyes meeting hers. He looked fierce, resolute. "I want to establish trust funds for each grandchild, to pay back for what I should have done for Connie. I was thinking of $10,000 apiece. What do you think?"

He would expect her to object, to say they couldn't afford this, and he'd be prepared to meet such objection head on. It was their pattern.

Ann stood to refill their coffee cups. "I don't know what I think," she said. "It would be a thoughtful gesture, and we paid off the mortgage last year and are in good shape for retirement. But it isn't The Truth." She nodded her head a couple of times while she sought the right words. "Help me understand why you don't want to tell them The Truth?"

"They've just lost their mother. That's a lot to be dealing with. I don't know if they know about her, our, my son." His amended wording felt strange and made him uncomfortable but in his relationship with Ann being truthful was bedrock.

"This way I don't have to bring Keisha into it. I have done a lot of thinking about it, and I think this is best."

Ann reached across the table and touched his hand. "Then that is what we'll do," she said. She could see that he had underestimated her. For the first time in several days, he smiled.

Andrea

The phone rang at 9 a.m. in Connie's apartment. Andrea, sleeping in Mom's bed, reached it first. A soft voice asked, "Are you Mrs. Riegler's daughter? I'm the Hospice social worker. I was calling to see if I could come by and see you and the family today. Would that work for you?"

Andrea had hoped for another hour of sleep without Nawal climbing on her clambering for breakfast. Karim's mother was still keeping the girls overnight so she and Allison could go through Mom's apartment. The lease was up on the 31st, a week from yesterday, and they wanted to get things taken care of before then. Allison had to get back to Kansas City and her music students, and Andrea preferred going through things together rather than having to confer by phone about distributing Mom's possessions. She was reluctant to take time for the hospice social worker, but more reluctant to tell the soft voiced lady that they didn't want her.

"We're trying to go through Mom's things before my sister has to return to Kansas City, but I guess we could take a break at, say one? Would that work for you?"

She was hoping it wouldn't, but the woman responded cheerily, "That'll be fine. I look forward to meeting you both."

Andrea entered the guest room to rouse her sister, taking a

moment to admire how lovely Allison looked sleeping, curled up, knees almost to her shoulders, hands grasping the quilt and snuggling with it under her chin, childlike. Add a teddy bear and pacifier, and she could be either of their daughters supersized. She smiled.

She was so glad they'd been able to be here with Mom in her final three weeks, so glad to have their children playing in the room as Mom let go of life. Mom always said that death happens as part of life. She'd admired cultures that recognized that and gathered everyone at the bedside of the dying so they did not go alone into their final night. Mom got her wish.

Tears welled up in Andrea's eyes and she blinked them back, then reached out to touch her sister's hair.

"Time to rise and shine, Sweet Pea."

Those were Mom's words slipping so easily off her tongue.

They ate a meager breakfast of toast with peanut butter, using up the last of the milk in their coffee, which they carried to the living room where they started on Mom's highboy, the first piece of furniture she bought with her own money after she left Dad. Allison began sorting the cabinets while Andrea worked on the drawers. While they worked, they talked. The items Mom had kept evoked specific memories and laughter. One o'clock arrived in no time.

The hospice social worker was short with very white hair cut in a bob the way Mom used to wear hers. The resemblance brought Andrea a fresh stab of grief. She noticed that the woman was maybe a decade or more older than Mom. Apparently, the woman was good at reading faces.

"I can tell you're wondering how someone my age still does this work when I should be rocking on the porch and knitting, right?" Her smile was disarming. "Let me explain. Hospice is required by law to do bereavement work with the families we work with, but our bereavement counselors are over extended, assigned to work with as many as 475 families at any one time. So, they bring people like me back into service part time.

I'm a veteran; 35 years a hospice social worker! But I'm not here to talk about me. How are each of you doing?"

Her expression shifted to caring concern.

Andrea spoke first. "I think we're running on adrenalin. It happened so fast. Even though I live in Cleveland and saw her every week, I didn't see this coming. I keep expecting her to come out of the bathroom or around the corner, that everything will be back to normal, and the past three weeks nothing but a nightmare."

"Everything we're going through brings up memories," Allison added. "I feel like I'll never be able to stop my tears. Frankly, even seeing you come into the apartment made my heart accelerate. You kind of resemble Mom, with your beautiful white hair."

Andrea was glad that her sister had the same response to seeing this woman. The hospice lady smiled knowingly.

"You'll have these feelings for a long time, I suspect. It's really good that you're both here for this important week, going through this together. Tell me about your mom."

For the next hour the stories poured out of them. Sometimes they laughed, sometimes they cried. The hospice lady just listened. When the stories slowed, she told them what to expect in the months ahead—crying jags, times of depression, thinking you see her on the street, feeling orphaned, maybe sensing her presence, even feeling physically ill with symptoms mimicking Mom's. Then she stood up to leave. She knew they had work to do, she said, and would check in at the end of the week. Before she left she told them where they could get packing boxes and gave them a printed list of Goodwills, veterans groups and church thrift shops in the area that accept donations they might want to make. Then she was gone.

She was helpful, they agreed as they got back to work. By 5:30 they had cleaned out most of the living room, packing things in boxes labeled ANDREA, ALLISON, and DONATE. Large black trash bags filled with discards leaned against one wall, eerily recalling the bag that had carried Mom's body to the mortuary.

"She didn't tell us how guilty we'd feel getting rid of Mom's special possessions," Allison observed.

Their husbands arrived together with carry-out and pitched in to sort Mom's books. Karim reported that he and Tony planned to take the kids to the park in the morning. He also reported that they'd been doing some research at Catholic Charities, trying to track down their name-unknown brother. He'd located a social worker who promised to check the files from 1971 and see if she could locate Mom's records.

That news startled Andrea. Might they actually know something this week? Could they cope with yet another huge change in their world telescoped into such a short time?

"I'm starting to feel I'm living a soap opera," Allison said. "Couldn't we take it a little more slowly?"

"Karim was only trying to help, since you and Tony will only be here this week." Andrea's irritation showed. She knew that once her sister went home, the bulk of the work of handling Mom's affairs would fall on her and she resented it, though she didn't want to get into it with Allison. They needed to support each other now more than ever.

Their stress and exhaustion was visible, and she could see in Karim's face that he was worried about her. The husbands left for Karim's folks' house. "Take good care of each other," Karim said as he kissed her goodnight. "Call us if you need anything."

Tuesday they made more progress. They went to the bank and opened Mom's safety deposit box, finding her important documents and a small, yellowed envelope containing a dark brown curl of toddler hair. She and Allison had both had white-blond hair till age five. It was clear who this curl must belong to. They shared the same thought—a source of DNA!

When they returned to the apartment, Mom's answering machine was blinking. People from Macy's just hearing the news had called to offer condolences. Father Joe was checking in. The last message was from an unfamiliar male voice.

"This is Don Johnson. I got your message and was wondering if my wife and I could come to see you while you're both in Cleveland. Please call me back. It's important."

He left his number.

They tended to details all afternoon, stopping the paper and phone, redirecting Mom's mail, ordering multiple copies of death certificates to send to her financial institutions and the IRS. By evening they were both worn out, weary of this emotional process of sorting, and missing their own lives. It was too late to return Mr.—or was it Dr.?—Johnson's call. Instead, they asked their husbands to bring the children and have dinner with them. For a short time they felt normal.

On Wednesday Andrea called Dr. Johnson. A woman answered, "Yes, I'm Dr. Johnson." When Andrea said who was calling, the woman said, "You want the other Dr. Johnson, my husband Don. Just a minute."

Andrea told him that they could meet the Johnsons either that night or the next, but the movers were coming Friday for the furniture.

"Tonight, then? At 7?"

She hung up feeling slightly irritated with this person who they didn't know who wanted them to make time for him when they were running out of time. But they had too much to do to spend time wondering what the Johnsons wanted.

Mom's apartment was dramatically changed and disassembled. It disturbed her to see this space that had been Home looking antiseptic and barren, unrecognizable without Mom's things, most of which were now boxed or bagged. She was glad Nawal and Antonia would not see the apartment like this. Let them remember Grandma's place as it had been.

At seven the buzzer sounded, and they buzzed back to admit an attractive, conservatively dressed older couple.

Don

When Don and Ann arrived at the apartment on Lake Shore Boulevard, he expected to find a space that would give clues to Connie's life. Instead, they entered a virtually empty apartment— furniture stacked against one wall, no photos or paintings, white walls already spackled to cover the nail holes. There was no place to sit other than the floor, so they stood awkwardly.

He could see that the daughters were distracted by all they had left to do. So he didn't waste their time. He explained that their mother had set up a trust for her grandchildren with Don as the trustee. He would send them the paperwork in the next week.

Ann stood off to one side, watching. He imagined she was trying to learn what she could about Connie through observing her children. Even Ann would not learn much in this sterile room, he thought, especially in so brief a meeting.

Andrea and Allison appeared stunned and moved by his revelation. They said they were shocked that their mom could have saved so much money, but that "generosity and advance planning are characteristic of her." There was an awkward moment, then one of them—the oldest?—corrected her tense, "*were* characteristic of her."

He wrote down their contact information and told them he'd be in touch soon. Ann said how sorry they were for what the women were going through, and that was it.

As they left Connie's apartment Ann reached for his hand and held on.

Ann

He came back to bed that night. Lying awake listening to his soft snoring, she thought about this man she loved, this man she would never fully understand. Luckily, she'd been perceptive enough to realize that he needed space and separateness, needed to thrive on his own. Maybe they both did. Once he called her his rock—she'd said a watering can was a better analogy. She provided shade and regular watering, and comfort when his sadness returned. In reciprocation, he grounded her, listened to her, and loved her and Keisha. Theirs was a comfortable relationship that allowed each to pursue their work, raise their child, and expand their minds, rewarded by this balance of parallel play *and* moments of strong connection.

She smiled and flushed as those moments came back to her. It astonished her how a man so private and self-controlled metamorphosed into a skilled lover who, without restraint, explored every part of her eagerly and with an abandon that never ceased to take her by surprise. Their physical relationship was surprisingly different from the steady, reliable partnership that characterized them as a couple. Body to body they labored like something giving birth, rocking and sighing, slippery with sweat and sweet from the juices they squeezed from each other. When he erupted inside her, she could feel the empty places inside filling up with him, like a beach blessed and nourished with the wet froth of incoming waves.

There had been only one time they had nearly come apart, when she had finally carried a fetus to full term after so many miscarriages. They had been so excited. Keisha helped pick a name for the baby: Julia if she was a girl; Jonathan if a boy. Ann had been to the doctor for her last prenatal visit that afternoon. The doctor said everything looked good. In the night her water broke, and Don drove her to the hospital, leaving Keisha with Ann's parents who had driven to Cleveland from New York for the birth. After nine hours of labor, she delivered the baby, a boy. But something was terribly wrong.

Baby Jonathan's skin was a disturbing shade of blue. Exhausted, she had reached out to hold him. The expression on the doctor's face and all the activity in the delivery room—the sounds of slapping and suction and lowered, concerned voices in consultation—told her with an awful certainty what her mind's eye brought vividly into focus: that other boy, her little brother, lying blue and lifeless by the side of the pool. She saw Don's face, lined and vacant, as though covered by a gray veil, and grief overpowered her.

When she went home from the hospital a day later, she entered a house that sheltered four adults, each caught in their own losses. She and Don retreated from each other, keeping up a modicum of conversation that neither listened to. They continued to provide for Keisha's needs. But they no longer leaned on each other or found in each other a refuge. The distance between them had been most obvious at night when each clung to their side of the bed, their backs shields protecting them from each other, and the mattress between them a widening no man's land.

She remembered her mother and father talking with them about their own experience of the death of a child. They suggested counseling and meditation on specific passages of scripture. She and Don had tried, but each of them was submerged in their individual loss.

She couldn't recall when or how they came back to each other. Keisha had helped. Lying in bed now it made her chuckle to remember Keisha's creative efforts to reconnect them. Eventually she—and Don, too—had swallowed their loss and picked up the pieces of their lives. Perhaps living in the Pit, their feet caught in the clay with only a dirge to wail in insular despair, simply grew old and boring. By a grace she could not explain, she had felt herself lifted up and, like in her dad's favorite Psalm, set on a rock with a new song to sing.

She did not know how it happened for either of them, but one day standing in the kitchen fixing breakfast she had observed to Don,

"It seems we have come through this. Right?"

He had nodded and opened his arms. They had held on to each other, grateful beyond words to be Home.

Like many oldest or only children, Ann had learned early to swallow her losses. They were like empty air pockets taking up space inside her. From childhood whenever she was feverish a troubling nightmare would puncture her restless, overheated sleep and demand attention. In her dream she was filled with small holes of nothingness that threatened to crowd out her vital organs. It was as though she was made of Swiss cheese. She would awaken disturbed and fearful.

The death of her five-year-old brother created the first of those empty pockets. As the surviving older child, she had tried to compensate for her brother's absence. She focused on doing everything right. From age eight she accepted that it was her responsibility to hold her family together and to achieve what her brother and she together might have achieved had he lived. Her parents worried about their super responsible daughter. They tried to reassure her that they loved her no matter what. They praised her unstintingly, even when she slipped momentarily from the path of productivity, even when she became pregnant at nineteen.

She filled up with other pockets of loss. As an adult she would give names to what she had lost: Her playfulness, her irrepressibility, her longing to be taken care of, her desire for a wild and reckless love affair, her baby boy and all those other potential babies who never made it past a few months in utero. Then, on one awful night, her parents.

They had been her anchor, readily talking with her about anything, sharing what they had learned about coping. They taught her to rely on a system of beliefs—that the Universe is benevolent, that leaning on the Lord will carry you through anything, that you must suspend your disbelief because believing helps you cope. It was utilitarian and sensible.

When her parents died and she felt the lights go out, Don had been constant in his quiet support, and Keisha had come back. She had found her way out of grief, though she still missed her parents terribly. It was her mother who had taught her to dismiss her losses from her memory by acts of will that reframed her past; a loss was an opportunity to learn and grow. Using these strategies she had learned to push ahead with her life and stay indomitably in the present.

Now, leaving Connie's apartment hand in hand, Don and she had once again made it, together.

Edward

The distinguished gray haired brown skinned man stood outside Connie's apartment, preparing himself for the face that he would not see when the door opened. Then Connie's friend Edward knocked at the door and waited. He had not come to see her daughters all week, knowing they would be enclosed in the sacred space their mother had so recently vacated, going through her things and reliving their life as a family. He had not wanted to intrude. Now, however, the moving men had requisitioned the main elevator and were using it to move out furniture and boxes. He knew it was now, or miss the opportunity to see her daughters, and, through them, pay his respects to his deceased friend.

The door opened. Andrea, the taller of the two stood facing him with a quizzical look on her face, eyes squinting slightly. Her mouth opened into a smile as she recognized the man from Apartment 1601, her mother's dear friend. Years ago Mom had invited Edward and her daughters for dinner so that these people who were so important to her would get to know each other. It had been such a lovely evening that she made it an annual tradition.

"Please, come in. It's so good to see you," Andrea said, hugging him. "We're nearly finished going through things."

He stepped in, his eyes scanning the room seeking the familiar, but the familiar was gone, wrapped in newspaper and packed in boxes or on its way out of the building in the capable hands of the movers. He sighed. Then he turned to Andrea and took her hands in his.

"I know this has been a very difficult week for you and that you're ready to get back to your own life and probably also feeling very sad to let it go, this place and the material goods that were so important to your mom."

"Yes," she managed, tears shining on her cheeks. "I'm so glad you've come. You were so important to Mom."

Andrea turned to the bedroom and called her sister, who was sitting cross legged on the carpet catching up with work email, so engrossed she hadn't noticed that the conversation in the next room was not with a mover, but with Mom's special friend. Allison set her laptop to one side, got up, and went to hug Edward.

Allison walked to the sliding doors that opened on the balcony. Leaning against the inside wall was a two-foot-tall carving made of dark mahogany wood, lithe, with curves that your hands wanted to caress. It was actually two separate carvings but connected, indeed, carved out of one piece of wood. She picked it up and brought it to Edward.

"Mom found this when she was shopping a month or so ago, before she got sick, and was really excited about it. She said it reminded her of her friendship with you. Here it is, a gift to you from Mom, wherever she may be. There's a note she wrote to you taped to the bottom."

Edward received the carving. Silently he read the note while his hands caressed the firm, silky wood. "Carved from the same wood, polished and glowing with age, inseparably connected forever," Connie had written in her uniquely vertical handwriting. He recognized the origin of the carving: Africa, probably Zimbabwe, where Connie had hoped to visit before she died. They were silent for some moments.

"I wanted to see you both before you leave this place. I wanted to share with you something your mother wanted to be sure you knew."

"About our brother?" Allison asked.

"Yes. She was close to finding him, just hadn't take the final steps. She was afraid to disrupt his life or yours. We talked several times about her dilemma, wanting to know him and especially to know that he had a good life, that she'd made the right choice for his life. She worried that he'd be angry with her for abandoning him. In the end, I think she wished she'd not been so fearful, that she'd been able to find him while she still had time."

The girls exchanged glances. Andrea took charge of the conversation. "Mom told us a year ago. Our husbands have been working on locating him."

Allison jumped in: "Would you join us if and when we meet him? You and Mom were such good friends, and I know that you've done a lot of counseling. You could help us bridge the awkwardness and kind of stand in for her."

They both looked at him intently, hopefully. Edward smiled, enjoying the different ways each of them resembled Connie. "You *are* your mother's daughters," he said. "Of course, I will."

"There's something else we want to share with you, something about Mom we just learned yesterday or the day before— sometime this week! The days are all merging. This is such a confusing time, and we've been working so hard that I can't keep straight what day it is." Andrea spoke with great weariness, and Edward felt concerned about her.

Allison recounted the story Andrea had begun about the trust funds for the grandchildren. "It's so like her, but we've no idea how she could've saved that much money. Did you know about these trusts?"

Edward smiled, glad that Connie's daughters were receiving this welcome news now, when the pain of her loss was most acute. "No, she never told me about setting up trust funds. But I'm very glad to hear it. Who's the administrator?"

Andrea rooted in her purse for the man's business card. "Here it is. Dr. Donald Johnson. Funny, he's a physics professor!"

The name startled him, but there must be thousands of Donald Johnsons. He needed to let them get back to work. "I hope you'll call me, if you find your brother or anytime you need to talk. You know I was a pastor before I retired and once a pastor, always a pastor. In this case, once Connie's friend, always your friend. I must be going," Edward said, "Time to check the mail." He smiled wistfully. "You know going to the mailbox is a ritual of retirees in this building. Your Mom would join us on Saturdays when she wasn't working. We go at 11:20, precisely the same time each day, and make sure we're properly dressed, shoes shined, hair combed. Your Mom used to tease us about it. She thought we should put out cheese and crackers and red wine since it was such an institution. She joked that many a relationship had probably gotten its start in the elevator heading for the mail…. I will miss her."

He hugged them both and passed them each his card. Standing in the hall holding his very special gift, he looked back, surveying the nearly empty apartment, site of so many evenings of good meals and even better conversations. "Please stay in touch," he said.

As the elevator closed behind him, Edward was caught in his own thoughts. The name of the trustee was a common one, but it was also the name of a person he had known briefly when they both were children, known and lost contact with, someone important to his family. Probably it was just a coincidence.

Richard, Evanston

On a Saturday in June Richard awakened early, a melody playing in his head. He was out of bed in a moment and sitting at his keyboard, earphones on, to capture it. Keisha was still asleep. Returning to his closet to throw on some clothes, he tripped over a pair of Keisha's casually discarded shoes and surveyed the disheveled chaos of his bedroom. Her clothes littered the floor and half a bottle of Merlot stood uncorked and precarious on the bedside table. He grimaced. This was a definite downside to his relationship with Keisha. Now that they had begun spending weekends together, her casual way of operating was beginning to annoy him. He was an orderly person who made the bed within five minutes of getting up, except, of course, like today when a tune had to be captured. By contrast, she held several thoughts on different subjects in her head at the same time and shared them helter-skelter so that often he strained to follow her conversation. She called it multi-tasking. But sometimes he didn't want to make the effort and instead simply let her ramble like one of those toys for young children where each button you push produces a recording on a totally different topic: A is for Apple, 1+1=2, Listen to the melody.

He made a mental note to raise with her the way she distributed her clothes around the room, sometimes tossing them on a chair but more often simply dropping them, as though discarding an idea, only clothing was visible, disturbingly so for a tidy person like Richard. Sometimes, like now, her behavior triggered in him the feeling of being out of control, and that made him uncomfortable. His need for order kicked in when the press of work sat heavily on him. Like now, the end of his first year at Northwestern. Student evaluations had been tallied and provided to him in one of those scary manila envelopes with CONFIDENTIAL stamped on front and pack. They had not been bad, but a few students had complained that he had seemed distracted for the second half of the term, *i.e.* since Keisha. He received a contract for next year—he'd jumped that hurdle!—but he knew his Chair wanted him to have more compositions copyrighted and scheduled for premier performances. That meant a lot of work over the summer. It was imperative he protect his time for composing.

He felt the slow burn of irritation and tried to head it off by bringing her coffee, which he hoped would get her out of bed and off on her usual Saturday at the library. When he returned with the coffee she was in the shower, singing slightly off-key. She emerged wrapped in an oversize pale blue towel with another towel around her head. Tendrils of her dark hair escaped the towel edges, as irrepressible as she was. He felt conflicted. He did love her, indeed, he had begun to use the "L" word fairly frequently to describe how he felt about her, at least in his head.

He took control. "I'm composing," he said, foreclosing any proposals for a more frivolous use of the day.

"Fine. I have to write up the research I did last week. Want to meet for supper? Or would you rather be alone tonight?" She'd run a brush through her tangled curls, pulled on a red tank top and jeans and her large silver hoop earrings before he replied, in a somewhat snarky tone, "I may need the whole night and then some." He felt relieved that she did not seem the least bit possessive of his time.

"It was a good night," he said remembering their lovemaking and the experiments he'd not tried with anyone else. He wasn't sure she heard him as she was off to her apartment, coffee in hand after a quick kiss. "Have a great day," she called as the door clicked shut.

It irritated him that this woman could so easily distract him, as though he was a teenager with a crush. He'd never been this vulnerable in a relationship and the timing was off. This year was crucial to his career, a year to make a name for himself here at Northwestern, yet here he was drawn to her even when he was annoyed, wanting to set boundaries while wanting to spend the entire day in bed together.

Later that afternoon he went for a walk along the lake front, planning what he would say to her—that he needed more space for his professional work, that while he thought she was wonderful, he wanted to try seeing each other less frequently so they could both get done what they had to do. He returned to his apartment feeling better and went to work on a composition.

Sunday morning she didn't call or text. He texted her at three to see if she was free for a conversation. No reply. Then at seven she texted back. "Old friend in town. Went for lunch and walked Old Town. Come over if you like."

He felt put out. He'd made no plans, waiting to hear from her. That was the problem. He had no control over his life anymore. Frowning, he started out the door, down the stairs, and across the street to the Alhambra, buzzed her, grumpy when he heard her cheery voice call him to come on up. He climbed the four flights, further irritated that he was somewhat winded by the time he reached her door.

She opened the door wearing jeans and a frothy white blouse, looking stunning. Gold hoops swung jauntily, winking through her thick hair. He visibly startled at the sight of her.

"Like it? I found it in Old Town. How was your day?" She kissed him and walked in front of him into her living room.

"Keisha," he said, recovering his grumpy, serious mood, "We need to talk."

She seemed surprised. "What's wrong? Want a glass of wine and humus and pita?" Typically, she operated on several levels at once and it confused him.

"Nothing, thanks. I just need to talk with you." He sat heavily on her side chair and she disappeared into the kitchen, returning with her wine glass, sitting on the sofa and looking at him with those dark and probing eyes.

"I think we're seeing too much of each other. This is moving too fast for me. I need my routines in order to get my work done and feel good about my life." He was pleased how articulately it came out.

"That's fine with me, Richard." She had shifted to cool, professional. "I guess I had some of the same feelings. That's why I didn't get back to you yesterday or today. Why I went out with

Melanie."

Her response surprised him. "You mean you don't want more time with me?"

"Well, sometimes I want more time with you, but for now I also have work to do to get ready for my time in the Philippines and to prepare for my courses. I'm also going to see my folks, and it feels like the summer is half over."

He had forgotten she was going to the Philippines. "Why are you going to the Philippines?"

"I told you I applied for a fellowship to study relations between the Moros, Muslims in the South, and their Christian neighbors. I'm looking for parallels between Native Americans' and Muslim Filipinos' experience of being colonized by Christians. The parallels may be weaker than I'm anticipating, but I'll learn a lot and see a part of the world I've never visited."

"Isn't there a war going on there?" It terrified him to think she was going into a war zone so cavalierly oblivious to the danger she was putting herself in.

"Yes, but we're traveling in a group so we should be safe. I'm fascinated by conflicts between groups of people. Maybe it's not so different from your interest in music that grows from such situations."

"I don't think it's the same at all. I like to study from the comfort of the library or my apartment, not in the midst of a war zone!" He sounded quite indignant and had begun to pace the floor.

"Anyway, it'll give us a block of weeks apart, which will probably be good for us." She added, "Then when I come back we can see what
amount of contact feels good and what feels too much. Richard, you seem upset. Is there something else?"

"I'm not sure. This morning I was feeling overwhelmed by your things strewn around my bedroom—like you'd invaded my personal space. And I was annoyed that you expected to spend the day with me when I had other things I needed to do. Now you say you wanted time off, too. I feel out of my depth, Keisha. It's been a long time since I have been in a relationship, and I don't do relationships well."

She laughed. "I'm not exactly a professional in that area. You're different from anyone I have known in the past, and I'm different with you. I'm not obsessive with you. That feels good. I like the absence of drama—though right this minute there's a fair amount of drama! I don't feel that I have to be constantly working to please you. Am I misreading you?"

Before he had time to respond, she went on. "I'm quick to read 'No Vacancy' signs even if they're not there. I told you about my long-term relationship with Andrew. Well, I swore I'd never do that again, never stay with someone who isn't available. If you're saying that you're not available, Richard, I'd rather hear it now than be surprised some time in the future."

She was standing and her face wore a closed expression, withdrawn and cool, like she'd pulled a curtain across the space between them.

Her statement brought him up short. "I don't know if I'm available. I'm not Andrew or like him in any way. In fact, I think he's a jerk. I really love our time together, but this morning I felt kind of panicky, like you were in control of where this relationship is going. I wanted to run. I think I'm feeling scared. I don't want to lose you, Keisha, but I don't know what to do with you." His face was pained and intense.

She sat on the edge of the sofa, stiff-legged as though ready for flight. "I really appreciate your truthfulness," she said. "Perhaps we've overdone it, talking or texting every night until late, spending the weekends together."

It struck him for the first time that she seemed breakable. Her voice sounded strained when next she spoke. "I leave July 6th for three weeks in the Philippines, coming home by way of my folks in Cleveland. Do you think that will give you…us…enough time apart?"

Her words stung. He felt confused. This was what he wanted, right? But to think that she would be leaving in three weeks and gone for more than a month…?

"Keisha, is this what you want?"

"I'm not sure I want it, but it's here, want it or not. I accepted this grant and have bought my tickets, so maybe it works to give you more time." Suddenly her face lit up and she flashed him a broad smile. "It'll give you time to discover how much you miss me!"

He melted. "I really care about you," he said.

"I really care about you, too. We're set then? Do you think we should have any contact during these weeks?"

"Talk about things moving fast and feeling out of control! Keisha, sometimes being around you is like being caught in a tornado! *Don't move so fast!* I came over here to talk about giving each other *some space,* not a nearly two-month separation. You're my best friend as well as my lover. Can't we still be both, recognizing that we each have a lot to do in the next couple of months? I understand you will be half a world away—in a war zone! *Of course,* we should have contact! I need to know you're all right! I also don't want to be sidelined while you're off flirting or hooking up with someone on your Philippines trip. Isn't it possible for us to take a baby step away from the rapid escalation of our relationship, *just a baby step,* and evaluate as we go along?" His face was flushed. He was not about to lose this woman, and he was working damn hard to keep her from bailing. He couldn't understand how she could be so insecure. It must be Andrew. His dislike for the man escalated rapidly.

He pulled her to him, relieved that they had declared themselves, managed their first relationship crisis, and discovered they could stay connected even as they gave each other some space. It felt scary how close they had come to walking away from the best relationship he had known—their conversation scared Keisha, too, according to what she'd told him.

Their love making that night was awkward and tentative.

The next evening his phone rang. It was Keisha. "Are you going to be around for a little while? I'd like to come over."

He could feel the tightness of anticipation as he replied, "Oh, Baby, I'd like that." *Where did that come from?* He had never called anyone "Baby." Just part of his metamorphosis, he guessed.

In a few minutes she knocked at his door, one of the perks of living across the street from each other. He poured them each a cup of coffee, his strong and dark, hers with milk, and they sat close together on the floor leaning back against the sofa listening to Big Mama Thornton wail, *Everything Gonna Be All Right.*

During the two weeks before she left for the Philippines, he helped her run errands, purchase her malaria medication and sunscreen, and she listened with interest to his latest composition, giving feedback when he asked for it. She seemed generally delighted by what he had written. He started missing her even before he took her to the airport, and, as he watched her walk away, he yearned to go after her.

They would not see each other until she returned from her travels in mid-August.

Keisha, The Philippines

She didn't tell Richard. She knew she could handle it, and she went calmly, eyes wide open, no delusions, no expectations. For all his preoccupation with the music roaming his head, for all his anxiety that their relationship was moving too rapidly, she knew that Richard loved her.

Knew it and believed it. That strengthened her resolve to continue with her planned trip to the Philippines after she discovered Andrew's name among the other participants. Even boarding the plane she wasn't apprehensive.

It was so like Andrew to arrive late and enter the plane after the other passengers were seated with their seat belts fastened. Bestowing his bad boy smile like a royal bestows waves, he moved down the aisle with confidence and grace. He greeted a couple of people as he came toward her and then stopped at 21B, Keisha's row, tucking his backpack in the overhead bin and sliding into the empty seat across the aisle from her. He said something about being so glad she was on this trip and that she was half his motivation for going. Ah, Andrew, always full of blarney, casting compliments like he was sowing grass seed…or fertilizer.

She gave a minimally polite reply, then opened her book, which she appeared to find fascinating. He took the hint and turned to the woman seated to his right, striking up an animated conversation. He was plying his trade. She recognized the script. A wave of self-doubt hit her so hard that her paperback tumbled to the floor. She retrieved the book, and, with it, her plan for how to handle moments like this. She inserted her ear buds so that she would not hear the conversation across the aisle, and settled into her seat, eyes closed. She was pleased to find that the strategies she had thought out in advance of the trip came to her aid promptly now. Eyes closed she could think about Richard and the four months they had known each other.

That first hour on the plane sitting near the man who had disassembled her life, she established a pattern she would use for the rest of the trip: be polite but cool when she had to interact with him, bring to mind special moments she and Richard had shared as a kind of mantra when the power of Andrew's physical presence disquieted her, and use the music on her playlist that Richard had put together for her to transport her to a zone of peace.

Once they arrived in Davao and headed South by bus, she chose to sit with the Filipino woman who was their tour guide. Enjoying her company, Keisha gravitated to her during each bus ride, absorbing all she could from her in conversations both historical and personal. Keisha's curiosity saved her once it kicked in. She delighted in learning about people and their histories, in this case the Muslim majority and the Christian minority of Mindanao, the Philippines' largest island. Her curiosity was as reliable as clockwork, unleashing a chain of questions that led her, and those who kept up with her, on a stimulating journey of discovery. Most of the time her curiosity kept her thoughts focused so that she was aware only peripherally of Andrew's flirtation with another trip participant.

Naturally, there were times, usually at the end of the day, when, exhausted by all she had learned, she sought to relinquish some of the control she exercised so consciously and consistently during the daylight hours and relax. One night near the end of the trip she was sipping orange juice on the porch of the mission school where they were lodging. She was alone, although Elvie, their guide, had cautioned them not to be alone, ever. Another bomb had gone off in the marketplace in town and kidnappings of foreigners occasionally occurred. Just a year ago Gracia Burnham had been released after being kidnapped by Abu Sayyaf with nineteen others and held for more than a year. Two of the hostages were beheaded and Gracia's husband and a Filipino nurse died in the crossfire of a rescue attempt.

"You shouldn't be out here alone." Andrew spoke so quietly she hardly heard him. He was standing behind her. In the moonless dark she could not see his face, only the outline of his body. "I'm glad for this time with you. I need to know why you left without saying good-by, without any explanation. I've missed you." His voice seemed heavy with regret, even self-pity. "Will you tell me?"

Keisha heard a soft scraping sound and realized he was pulling up a chair near her. She sighed audibly. Perhaps she did owe him an answer. She remained silent, forming what she wanted to say in her mind, kneading the words to shape them, intent and focused.

"There was no future with you, Andrew. Unfortunately, it took me four years to realize what I should've known from the start. You were never interested in building a life with me. I was just a diversionary romance that siphoned off your yearning for adventure and consequently made your marriage more tolerable—maybe made it more satisfying? Loving you brought me so much misery. I was a wreck. I lost my joy, my capacity for delight, even my curiosity. I had to get away. Rapidly. So I did."

"I never lied to you about my commitment to Darla, did I, Keisha? I tried to be very clear about that and that I loved both of you. When I weighed my options and considered my boys, I was clear that I would choose my marriage. I didn't deceive you. Maybe *you* deceived you?"

The darkness gave them permission to speak unaffected by the other's facial expressions. She listened closely and thought about his words.

"You're correct. You did not deceive me. But you did *use* me, use my blind love for you, my obsession with you. I've felt very angry at you for that, Andrew."

"Was it my responsibility to prevent you from deceiving yourself?

Does loving someone include that? Was it your responsibility to tell me this before you disappeared from my life? Does loving someone include *that?*" His voice was small and jagged.

She remained silent for a time, thinking back on her months with Richard and her years with Andrew. Then she spoke. "I don't know. In my life, Love has come like rain to dry ground, sometimes stormy and passionate, sometimes gentle and nourishing. I feel its wetness wash over me. I drink it in. I marvel at its presence. But I've never considered whether its footprints leave responsibilities."

"I'm sorry I couldn't be what you wanted, Keisha. I wasn't merely using you. I gave you all that I could in my circumstances. I'm sorry it wasn't enough."

"And I'm sorry I ran away without explanation. You're right. I was deceiving myself, and I was right that it's better that we're not together."

They were quiet. She could hear the breeze ruffling the leaves of the hibiscus bushes and soft scuffling sounds of small animals scurrying to and fro beyond the edge of the porch. A solitary star poked its head out of the cloud filled sky, winking at them.

They stood simultaneously and moved toward each other. Cautiously and without passion they hugged, the way one hugs a former spouse, reservedly, carefully. Then they turned and went inside to their separate rooms, each mulling Andrew's question about what responsibilities come with loving.

Richard

It was late July. Richard, his parents, sister, brother-in-law, two kids, and Black Lab were at the lake house they had rented in Wisconsin. The long lake sprawled placid and listless in front of the house, its surface reflecting the sky like a sheet of glass. He found himself observing Sue and her husband closely. He watched Hank fitting the kids with life jackets and Sue running back to the house for drinks before climbing into the rowboat and helping Hank paddle. So much responsibility. How could they have any time for each other with the demands of their children?

That evening the rest of the family went to pick blackberries, while he and Sue stayed at the house washing dishes. He had been telling his sister about Keisha. Now he changed the subject and asked her how being married with children worked for her. She stopped washing the silverware, holding the dishcloth in her right hand, and he could hear the drip-drip of the water from the dishcloth hitting the floor. Sue didn't notice, and he wasn't about to mention it. She was concentrating. When she spoke, her words poured out.

"It's crazy most of the time, so much to do—the kids are in so many activities that I need to remember to transport them to and from, and Hank's work places a lot of demands on him, what with the airlines calling him in unpredictably. I end up neglecting my job, which leaves me feeling guilty. All the things I think of as perfect parenting—idyllic dinners around the dining room table, reading together before putting the kids to bed, vacations and birthday parties that are unique and fun, homemade bread, home-sewn Halloween costumes—well, it's just *hard to do it all*, almost impossible with both of us working, and we want to work, need to, really. Something has to give."

The troubled frown on his sister's face worried him. He hadn't been prepared for this answer.

She wasn't finished. "Some weeks what gives is my temper, some weeks one of us gets sick. Last April we were called to the school because Rob had been bullied and finally hit the kid. Allie is mercurial and regularly into a twit over one or another of her girlfriends who hurt her feelings. It never ends. It's *hard*. Period."

She wrung out the dishcloth and wiped down the stove. Richard wondered if she regretted getting married and having the kids. It sounded like she did.

Sue washed out the dishcloth and draped it over the faucet. She went to the refrigerator and pulled out two beers, opening one for each of them, and they sat at the kitchen table nursing them. Then she continued as though she'd read his mind.

"Still, I'm not sorry, and I wouldn't want life without my little family. If I take time to pay attention, almost every day there's something that reminds me why it's worth it. One of the kids says something like, 'Mommy, I won't ever forget this day,' or plants a big sticky kiss on my cheek saying, 'Mommy, I love you sooooo much.'"

She studied him. "But families are not for everyone. I know how much your work means to you, and you've been single for a long time. Maybe it's not in the cards for you, little brother." She grinned, teasing Richard. "Just don't call me up and tell me how great your life without kids is, at least, don't call me on the days when mine is a shambles thanks to all of our family chaos!"

Her comments stayed with him. He felt ambivalent about the whole idea of marriage and children. Yet there was also something that drew him as he watched his sister and her family fishing and swimming together, making S'mores over the open fire, singing in the car, and cuddling on the sofa. But then these activities would be fun to do *with one's friends*, wouldn't they? Did they really require children to make them special? Without children he and Keisha could go into Chicago for a night of clubbing, spend the night in a hotel if they had partied overmuch, take exotic vacations. With kids they wouldn't be able to afford to do those things.

Interesting. He kept including Keisha in his head when he projected Fun Things to Do in the Future. But, children?

When he returned to Evanston, he wrote a love song for Keisha, a politically correct love song—no references to future or children, just sexually explicit descriptions of their lovemaking, borderline pornographic. Setting this to music was really *fun*. He also went online to look for a possible cruise in the Caribbean they might take over Christmas break. He smiled to himself, full of self-satisfaction, imagining his sister's contrasting Christmas chaos.

He met Keisha's plane carrying roses and his love song with its references to her perky breasts and the hot place between her legs. He was smiling broadly. When she insisted, he performed the song for her back in his apartment with his keyboard and "my other instruments."

She said she was amazed by how risqué he was becoming. "Where did the cautious, restrained, unadventurous man I met at Arabica Rustica go?" she asked.

It was a very nice homecoming.

He thought about her question a few days later. He *was* changing, but his changes were not core changes—he still was who he was. He recalled his Dad preaching that the name of God was Yahweh, meaning, "I am who I am," and how that gives the rest of us permission to be who we are, unique individuals, each made in God's image. This was his dad's theology in a nutshell, and Richard could recite it verbatim, he had heard it so often.

OK, he said to himself. I am changing in ways I want to change. I want to try new things more often. I like Keisha's willingness to examine other ways of seeing. But I am who I am, "old Richard" and "new Richard," the same person, a person who keeps on growing.

Keisha, late August

Keisha sat on a bar stool in her kitchen gazing at the pregnancy kit she'd purchased yesterday from the drug store and used a few minutes ago. She'd waited until she got back to Evanston to give much thought to the fact that her period was late. Now it was the only thing she thought about. She must be three months pregnant! That explained why her breasts were sore, why she felt tired and occasionally nauseous. But they'd been so careful to use protection.

This was not a convenient time for a baby. Their relationship was just budding. It needed time and space to bloom. On the other hand, at thirty-seven, time was running out if she wanted children, and she knew that she *did* want children, even if she raised them alone. Once before, with Andrew, she'd thought she was pregnant. She'd concluded that an abortion was her only option, but it turned out to be a false alarm. Could her body be tricking her again? She walked back to the bathroom to take another look at the stick. No ambiguity there.

She spent the next hour reviewing her options while she drank coffee and forced down some granola. Abortion was out. Adoption also. She *wanted* children, and a baby with Richard's genetic inheritance would have a lot going for it. But would this baby be welcomed by Richard or scare him away? She didn't want him to leave, no, please, not that.

By noon she decided she must tell him, regardless of his response. She texted that she needed to see him. It was important. When he texted back to come on over, she crossed the street and climbed the stairs, anxiety wrapped around her so tightly that she felt she was suffocating.

She entered his apartment, sat down across from him, and went straight to the point.

"I need to tell you something—I think I'm pregnant. I've thought about it a lot, and at my age, I really want to have the baby and keep it, even if it means raising it alone. You don't have to be involved if you don't want to be." Her voice sounded like she was reading an abstract. Damn, why couldn't she ease into things rather than spitting them out so tactlessly?

Richard stared at her like he didn't recognize her. *"How can you be pregnant?"*

She shrugged her shoulders. "A hole in the condom? It certainly wasn't something I planned!"

"Keisha, I don't know what to say. We've known each other five months. I feel very close to you, but I'm not sure I'm ready for *this* level of commitment. A *baby?"*

Neither spoke for some minutes. The silence was loud and complicated. Thoughts and feelings bounced off each other like bumper cars, unspoken and confusing. Keisha prepared herself for not being chosen.

"I need to get some air," he told her, avoiding eye contact. She noticed that his hands were trembling.

He arose suddenly, slightly off balance, and lurched toward the door.

Richard

The ease of their reunion after six weeks had calmed his anxiety about where the relationship was going and where he wanted it to go. Now confusion buried him. He felt trapped, disoriented, blinded, as though caught in his recurrent nightmare: expected to conduct a difficult symphony whose score he'd never seen. The only thing he was sure about was that he had to get out of there.

How could she be pregnant? They'd been meticulous about using birth control. They had been separated nearly a month. Wouldn't she have known before she left for the Philippines? Had she deliberately kept it from him?

He walked briskly south along the lake for more than an hour sorting and resorting his feelings about this new information. Mostly he felt terrified. Betrayed. And cornered. He would be expected to do the right thing, marry Keisha and raise this baby with her. But did he want to be married? Did he want a baby? Did he want both at once and so soon? Hadn't she heard how much he did *not* want to be a caregiver?

He sat down on a wrought iron bench facing the lake and got out his phone, punching in her number. "Keisha, I need to know when you knew you were pregnant."

"I was suspicious before I left for the Philippines but not sure. I knew you wanted space and I didn't want to alarm you so I decided to wait until I knew for sure. The baby is due mid-February."

"Thank you," he said, and hung up.

Keisha

Wisps of a breeze fluttered the curtains in his apartment and carried the sounds of late summer, kids calling to and laughing with each other as they walked home from the community pool, dogs barking, the irritating singsong calliope recording that announced the ice cream man, the roar of the crowd on the neighbor's television as the baseball game went into extra innings tied up.

She sat as though turned to salt, like the wife of Lot who looked back longingly. She made a mental note not to look back, only forward. She would survive this and keep going. She was good at compartmentalizing her life, feelings visited only when the moment was right. Problem solving was her default.

As the afternoon shadows lengthened, her emotions grew more insistent. Disappointment, fear, and, yes, anger. She'd been increasingly clear that this relationship was The One. Their time apart had been good for both of them, good in affirming how much they enjoyed each other and how well they had managed that crisis of needing more space. Her optimistic self had imagined Richard smiling warmly at her news and sweeping her into his long arms, proposing marriage, or at least moving in together, and pledging that he would do his part raising their child so that they both could continue their careers. Instead his behavior was rejecting. He was withdrawn, and unavailable. Had she invented her Richard based on what she wanted rather than on who he really was?

Had she fallen for another unavailable man?

She sat without shifting position, listening for the sound of his foot falls on the stairs. She waited for some time. Then she collected her keys and her shoulder bag and left his apartment.

Except for that one terse call, she did not hear from Richard, not that evening or on Sunday. She resisted the urge to text or phone him. Her emotions ricocheted from fury to self-doubt back to fury. She could be observing a match at Wimbleton, Fury 10, Self-doubt 15.

Monday, she altered her regular route walking to the University so she would not bump into him. Tuesday, no word. Wednesday, she awakened from a dream in which she was hitting him over and over again while he stood looking at her blankly. Her anger was growing. How could he dismiss her like this? She dragged herself through Thursday, knowing that her lectures were disorganized and her set face a dead giveaway that something was very wrong. Everyone she passed averted their eyes. She wondered, Why doesn't anyone ask me what's wrong? Why am I fated to mess up intimate relationships?

Still, she did not try to contact him. Her pride stirred her anger into volatile combination.

When she checked her email Thursday evening, she saw that he had written. Angrily she hit Delete before reading it. Then, in a panic of regret, she searched her deleted mail to recover it. It said simply, "When can we talk?" No explanation of his four-day silence. She did not reply.

Friday afternoon most faculty left early. Not Keisha. She reverted to her former habit of working late, even on Friday, returning to her apartment after eight p.m., tired, frustrated, and irritable. She had deliberately not checked her texts. When she did, she found seven new texts from Richard. They had come in out of order.

> *"It was touch and go for two days."*
> *"Couldn't get her heart to beat properly. Kept using shocks on her."*
> *"I left immediately for home."*
> *"Finally on Wednesday she was out of the woods."*
> *"Dad called while I was walking. Mom had a massive heart attack. Going into the hospital for a quadruple bypass."*
> *"Semester starting next week and I haven't written my syllabi."*
> *"Barely made our dress rehearsal for tonight's community concert. I hope you'll come."*

She tried to make sense of the out of order texts. Tonight. That must be *tonight!!!* His debut end of summer concert conducting the community orchestra was tonight, and she had missed it while she gorged herself on self-pity. He had good reasons for not being in touch. How terrible these days must have been for him. And she had not even treated him like a good friend, hadn't checked on him to be sure he was all right.

She dashed from her apartment jogging most of the way to the auditorium despite the heat, arriving winded but in time for the final number. She slipped into an aisle seat on the last row. Seeing him in his tux, his oversized body moving in an intricate dance as he conducted, moved her. Hot tears coursed down her cheeks, and she did not try to stop them. She loved him. Period. If it must be as a friend, she would find a way to cope with that.

As the auditorium emptied, she remained in her seat, hoping he would look for her and see that she had come. But he didn't. Not trusting her emotions, she left the auditorium and walked slowly home.

She phoned her parents needing reassurance. She hadn't told her parents that she might be pregnant when she was there a week ago, wanting Richard to be the first to know. She and Richard had talked of spending Labor Day weekend in Cleveland where they could meet each other's parents. She'd been so excited for him to meet Mom and Dad. But Richard's distress changed all that, she supposed.

At the sound of Mom's voice, Keisha fell apart. She heard the click of someone picking up the extension phone and imagined Mom motioning for Dad to get on so he would be included in this crisis. Now it all spilled out.

Mom did not interrupt her as her tears and anger and despair poured out. It crossed Keisha's mind that Mom knew this story first-hand, and probably hoped her daughter's life would follow a different trajectory. I've disappointed my folks, too, she thought.

"How am I going to cope with this, Mom?"

"You will."

"Will the Department ask me to leave?"

"Not in this day and age! Many female professors are single moms." Mom's voice remained level and calm, for which Keisha was grateful.

"Apparently he didn't want to see me tonight after all."

"You don't know that, honey. People were probably clustered around to congratulate him. He probably expected you to find him after the concert."

"I've made such a botch of this. His mother was having heart surgery and I never contacted him, I was so wrapped up in my own needs."

"All will be well, Keisha, I know that. Give it time. Focus on what you need to do to get ready for the start of the semester. Maybe send him a note apologizing for not realizing what he was going through with his mom."

"Mom, that's so your generation, not mine."

"Sorry! Listen to your heart, Keisha, not your fear, and get some rest, Princess."

Mom's use of that expression made her smile.

Before they signed off, Dad spoke, typically attempting to add some humor, "If you want me to come beat him up, I'll be there in a heartbeat."

She was very lucky in her parents.

An hour later Richard buzzed her apartment and climbed the stairs, ducking his head on the final flight. He sat beside her on the sofa and shifted position so that he was facing her. He took her hands in his and looked at her intently. "This has been a hell of a week."

She explained about his texts coming in all jumbled and five days late, and how she had not realized what he was going through. Then she listened as he told about his time with his parents in the hospital. He told her how close he had felt to his family, all gathered around Mom's bed remembering things from their collective past. Then he told her about the responses he received to the concert. He was glowing with excitement. He did not mention her being pregnant.

"I am really tired from racing back to get prepared for the concert and staying up most of last night trying to write my syllabi." He laid his head back against the sofa and in a moment was asleep. She gently turned him, propping pillows under his head and stretching his legs out. She kissed the top of his head, a noncommittal, friendship sort of kiss. Then she went to her bedroom, climbed into bed and slept. At least he'd come to see her.

In the morning her anxiety awakened her. She was up, dressed, and had coffee and oatmeal made before Richard stirred.

She wondered if he'd told his family about her. She knew she was a strong person, but it felt like Richard had all the power now—like Andrew—and she felt like a pawn to be moved or removed. She didn't like that.

When he finally woke up, they sat at her kitchen table eating in silence. Finally, Richard spoke.

"I need you to know that I'm still thinking about you being pregnant. Mom's emergency took priority, then my concert, and now starting the semester. I need more time before I'm ready to talk about it. Your friendship's very important to me. That won't change, no matter what."

Her anxiety rose. Good friend. Great! "Shall I cancel the trip to Cleveland over Labor Day?" she asked, eyes not meeting his.

"No, but with Mom recovering, I'd like to spend the bulk of the time there with my parents, if that's OK with you."

So, they would go and spend most of the time with their respective parents. She resisted saying something sarcastic. Give him time, Keisha, she told herself.

Keisha, Labor Day, Cleveland

Two weeks later they were sitting in Don and Ann's dining room, talking with her parents over breakfast. She sensed approval of Richard, at least from Mom. Dad was cooler, reserving judgment. She picked up their empty dishes and carried them to the kitchen where Mom had begun the washing up.

Mom put her arms around her, hugging her tightly. "You're so right for each other! And he's so like your Dad, a basically kind, intelligent person who clearly loves you." Mom joked about Keisha, like her, falling for tall, lanky men.

"Only mine still has all his hair!"

"That's a low blow, Mom," she replied.

Richard

Upstairs in the guest room Richard carefully unpacked his keyboard, unfolded it, braced the wobbly X support with wedges of cardboard and sat for a moment before it as though in a trance. Gradually the notes he sought came into focus, in his fingers first, then his mind, and he began to play. His body curled toward the keyboard, swaying like a tree in the wind, long legs bending and flexing, keeping their own time. His beautiful hands fluidly reached and stretched, moving across the octaves respectfully, reverently. Sounds leapt and eased from his touch, cascading and colliding in harmonics new to him, then lingering to prolong the beauty of the moment.

He never knew what he was doing when he composed. It was as though he was overtaken and transformed, used by something, someone. The room filled with the music of Richard and the Unknown Other. He opened himself, let his fingers be led, and when the final notes hung on the air, his body folded, exhausted, head nearly on his knees.

After some moments he reached for his composition pad. Now his brain kicked in as he wrote what he had heard and played, scribbling rapidly and nearly illegibly before the Other moved on.

Don

Downstairs in the family room Keisha's conversation with them ended mid-sentence as the glorious sounds from the guest room swirled down the stairs. Don found himself holding his breath, afraid to move lest his energy might thwart the magic dancing in the air. When the music stopped, he exhaled audibly.

"My God, what was that?" Ann asked looking at Keisha.

"Richard," Keisha answered, smiling.

Later that evening, after Keisha and Richard had gone to bed, he and Ann lay in their queen-sized bed talking over their time with Keisha and the father of their soon-to-be-grandchild. It had been a good day. Now that he thought about it, the past several months had been phenomenal. Still, he felt a nagging doubt that he wanted to express to Ann, but she spoke first.

"He's a gifted young man." Ann was smiling happily. "I'm so glad they found each other. He seems so right for Keisha."

Her optimism irritated him. "You always give things a positive spin and ignore the negative warning signs. He may be a gifted musician, but don't make him into a paragon of virtue, Ann. Keisha's in love with—and pregnant by—a man who's not committed to taking responsibility for her pregnancy. He's stringing her along. Why can't you see the danger that I see in this for Keisha?"

"Maybe because growing up with my parents was so different from growing up with your mom?" she replied quietly, which further irritated him. "Do you think that is why you get stuck to the dark side?"

"I'm not stuck to the dark side. I'm being realistic. Denying Richard's lack of commitment to Keisha and the baby is being a Pollyanna. Our daughter needs a man who will take responsibility for his actions."

It was not a new argument between them, and it was an argument he found hard to win, not having the experience in the Movement that Ann invariably cited to excuse her lack of realism. He anticipated correctly what she would say next.

"I try to live expecting Good to triumph. I learned that in the Movement, and it's carried me through a lot of difficult times. I'm choosing to believe that Richard will sort out what's best for the three of them. We don't have to agree on this, Don, but let me keep my positive thinking. If I'm wrong, I'll deal with it then."

He was not so sure about that. He knew Ann would be devastated if Richard abandoned Keisha. As for himself, it violated his code of conduct to not take responsibility for messes you made, no matter how talented you were. But he wouldn't voice this to Ann, knowing she would remind him that *he* had not stepped up to take responsibility with Connie, so who was he to judge Richard?

In bed they talked about Keisha, remembering her childhood

and her teen years. Ann had tried to steer Keisha. Don always figured Keisha would make her own mistakes, regardless of their advice. He'd been right on that one. Their daughter would listen and then do what she wanted to do. Now, she was pregnant and committed to a man who was unclear about his commitment to her.

Strange, he and Ann had separately dealt with similar crises when they were much younger than Keisha. They'd each walked away, Ann from letting Reggie know about her pregnancy, and he by simply going on with his life, as in the dark about Connie's pregnancy as Reggie had been about Ann's. Keisha was choosing to handle it differently.

They would just have to trust that she knew what she was doing.

"I just hope he realizes how lucky he is," he said, but Ann was already asleep. I never get the last word, he thought as he turned off the light.

Richard, Evanston

He awoke before dawn. His eyes were drawn to the eerie yellow-green blinking of his digital alarm clock and the alien half-light it gave off. Keisha teased him about using an alarm clock. "Just set your phone and enter the 21st Century!" But Richard liked the old fashioned-ness of a clock, visibly counting off the hours, letting him know where he was in the greater scheme of things. It was an anchor. Now, as it blinked 4:00, it seemed to take on personality, defying him to return to sleep. Sometimes he liked this time when most of his world was asleep. He lay reflective, letting his mind amble, savoring the images that bubbled to the surface.

He fleetingly took note of Keisha's soft sleep sounds, sent some thoughts of gratitude into the Universe, and returned to his reverie. He thought about his parents. Dad seemed restless in retirement after a life in ministry. Mom worried about him and confided to Richard that she feared Dad was suffering from depression now that he was not called on to take care of others

24/7. Funny, he'd been so relieved to retire and have time for himself, yet he seemed to find the freedom disorienting.

Then there was Mom, planning to return to working at Hospice as soon as she recovered from her bypass surgery and even in recovery acting like she was twenty years younger. He wondered if she was projecting her fears about herself onto Dad. He made a mental note to call them this weekend.

The green light said 5:03 and then 5:47. He began feeling uneasy, longing to quiet his mind, but sleep remained elusive. At least he didn't have to make an 8:00 class, it being Saturday. The soprano notes of sparrows answered by the bass of the morning dove caught his ear as the window across from his bed languidly filled with a muted, creamy light. He listened. He remembered the first time he had awakened to the music of dawn, age seven, sick with chicken pox and pulled from sleep by the bird sounds which had thrilled him ever since.

When next he awoke it was midmorning. Keisha was up and gone from the bedroom, presumably tackling the morning with her usual optimistic energy. He could smell coffee and cinnamon. She must have already been to the store and picked up their Saturday treat from the bakery. The phone was ringing. He heard her answer it, voice muffled so as not to awaken him. When he emerged, moving with the deliberate slowness that was his morning default, she looked up from her book and beamed. Her smile changed the room and stopped him in his tracks. How was it possible for a smile to have such power? It split the air, releasing particles of light that danced in the sunlight and delighted his eyes.

"You had a call from someone in Cleveland, a woman, who asked if you would call back today. Andrea Musleh is her name. I told her you were taking advantage of it being Saturday and sleeping in. She said No problem, but asked me to be sure you got the message to call her. Want scrambled eggs and cinnamon rolls?"

Their day slid away easily as their Saturdays usually did, now that they had established their own little rituals. Simple things, really, patterns that said they belonged to each other: a leisurely breakfast, time in parallel play, Keisha reading history while Richard worked on a composition, then gathering up the laundry for one to do while the other mopped and vacuumed. Saturdays ended watching a movie cuddled together on the couch. Sometimes they'd miss the end of the movie, their own moves on couch or carpet much more compelling.

On Sunday they called their parents, worked on school stuff, each in their own apartment, and worked out. The issue of her pregnancy lay dormant.

Not having any idea who Andrea Musleh was, Richard forgot to return her call. Wednesday morning in between his classes he was looking for quarters for the vending machine when he found a dog-eared scrap of paper with her name and number in his pants pocket. He made the call later that afternoon while sitting at the desk in his office, a pick-me-up coffee in hand.

"Ms. Musleh? This is Richard Allen. I understand you were wanting to talk with me?"

The voice on the other end of the phone was soft and a bit shaky. He wondered if Andrea Musleh was an elderly woman.

"Please, call me Andrea." He could hear her sucking oxygen and he pictured her sitting with her oxygen tank, its white tube clamped to her nostrils by small ridges. "I don't know where to start this conversation. You and I are related. In fact, we're brother and sister. My sister and I have been doing research trying to locate the child our mother had when she was nineteen and had to place for adoption. We believe you are that child."

He stood up from his desk, then sat down again heavily. His breathing was shallow. His first thought was that she must not be an elderly woman with emphysema after all. He could almost hear his brain rapidly rearranging the data and hoped it would finish quickly so he could make a sensible response.

"Are you still there, Richard?" Her voice sounded concerned. "I'm not wanting to upset your life. Mom died of cancer last spring before she had located you. She asked us to find you to be sure you're all right and to let you know how much she loved you, how hard it was for her to place you for adoption. That's why I called you last week."

The space between them sizzled with tension. He pictured his life and this woman's, each in a cocoon separated from each other by a thin membrane. He felt confused and stupid. Why couldn't he say anything? Finally, he pushed out a sentence.

"I've always known I was adopted, but never was interested in pursuing my birth parents."

"I understand. It's just that, now that we've found you, we'd so much like to meet you, really for Mom's sake. She was a wonderful woman." Her voice changed, tightened, like someone fighting tears. He tried to channel his Dad to help her feel better, but being nurturing wasn't in his repertoire.

"I'm glad to know that your mother was a good woman, and I'm sorry that she died." He chided himself for not being better at this pastoral stuff. "I think I'll have to think about this before I respond." Should he ask any questions? He spoke again before she responded. "Where do you live, Andrea?"

"My husband and daughter and I live in Cleveland, where Mom also lived. My sister Allison is in Detroit with her husband and daughter. Perhaps you could come to visit us? No pressure. I understand you need to think things over. It's strange for us, too. Until a year ago last Christmas we didn't know anything about you, or that you even existed."

His response was guarded. "Let me think about this for a few days and then I'll call you back. OK?"

"Of course," she replied. She passed on her email in case he wanted to contact her that way. "We miss Mom a lot and somehow this seems to be necessary for us to let her go. I understand that it's a shock. I hope you will call back."

Cleveland! Where his parents lived. He felt a wave of guilt as he tried to imagine how his parents might feel about these biological relatives entering his life. He couldn't think clearly. No, not now. He made a lame excuse that enabled him to end the call and carried his coffee into the men's room where he dumped the whole cup into the sink. He watched the coffee give off steam as it circled the drain. How could it still be hot? Everything before talking with Andrea Musleh felt like it occurred ages ago. His day was suddenly out of focus.

She had promised "our mother" she would find him and see him. *Our mother.* The words jumped out like a kettle drum entrance. That he shared another mother with this unknown woman was hard to incorporate into his view of himself.

He was in bed when Keisha got home from her night class at nine thirty. "Are you all right?" she asked him. He lay curled up like a child, his eyes tightly closed.

"I don't know." he answered.

"What's happened?" She sat on the bed beside him, her hand on his leg.

Haltingly he told her about his conversation with Andrea Musleh. Keisha stoked his forehead, listening attentively. "How do you feel about this news?"

"I don't know," he repeated. "I'm trying to figure that out. I always knew I was adopted. Mom and Dad never tried to hide that from me. We're a pretty happy family, not a lot of drama. I didn't think much about whose genes I carry. I don't want to hurt my folks. I want them to be secure in knowing that I'm their son. I'm certainly glad my birth mother gave me life, but I don't know if I want to get involved with this other family. It's too much. I don't want these complications. I've felt happy lately, and I don't want anything to intrude on this little bubble of quiet bliss we've been inhabiting. But it seems that the bubble has burst. First there's the baby and now this contact with my birth family....*I don't like all these demands that I alter my life!* They want us to get together, to meet up, at least one time."

"You know, with a baby coming, it might be good to learn what we can about your genetic background." Keisha was problem solving.

She had a point. But he wasn't ready. He didn't call Andrea, not for a week, then another week, while he mulled over what he wanted to do.

Andrea

Andrea called Allison. Her voice was shaky. "I spoke with him." She could hear Allison exhale. Sometimes she didn't like being the older child, always expected to be responsible. Like now. Well, she'd done it, she'd located him, called, made the effort to reconnect.

"What's he like?"

"Pretty distant. Polite but not exactly warm and fuzzy. Actually, he didn't say much. At least he knew he was adopted. He said he'd have to think about whether he wanted to meet us."

"What do we do now?" Allison's "we" irritated Andrea. It wasn't "we" who called Richard.

"Wait for him to call back. Maybe he won't."

PART 3

Cora, Nashville, September 2003

Cora hurried to the phone to answer it before it stopped ringing. Cell phones rang so few times before cutting off and frequently she had to hunt for hers. In her early-80s she was still spry, still positive, friendly, and supportive, still teaching part-time at the college. Even her hair was still dark, thanks to her little secret—but finding her phone in time to take a call, that's where she knew her age was showing. Her students teased her about being a typical technologically challenged "mature" person.

"Hello?" Good, the caller was still there.

"Hi, Mama, how are you?" Ah, it was Edward! How glad she was to hear his voice.

She started down their usual conversational trajectory, sharing their mutual frustration with President George W. and his two wars that were pulling young men and women of color into costly fights they couldn't win in Afghanistan and Iraq. "The British and the Russians tried unsuccessfully for a decade, and anyone who knows that history knows trying to change these people into clones of us won't work. All these young folks maimed and…"

"Mama," Edward interrupted her. "I have some news."

He told her about the death of his friend, Connie, about his final visit to her apartment and his conversation with her daughters. "Mama, Connie had set up a trust fund for her granddaughters. Now, I knew Connie very well, and I've never known her not to be generous, but I also have never known her to have much money. So I asked them how they had learned about the trust funds. They said a man and his wife had come by to let them know, a Dr. Don Johnson."

The name was vaguely familiar. She waited for him to say more.

"I thought about that name, a pretty common one, and then I went online and researched all the Don Johnsons in Cleveland. It kept me occupied for the better part of a day, but like you always tell me, Mama, we retired people need something to occupy us!"

"Now, Edward, I don't know anything about retirement, son. Remember, your Mama is not retired! But tell me what you found."

"I found a Dr. Don Johnson on the faculty of Cleveland State. The paragraph bio gave his publications and presentations at conferences but nothing about where he grew up, so I did some more research. Mama, *he grew up in Buffalo.* I found an obituary for his grandfather, a local businessman, who died in 1990 preceded in death by his wife and survived by his only daughter, Mildred, and grandson Don."

Cora took the phone into the kitchen and sat down at the table while her mind clicked through these pieces of data.

She cried rarely and always in silence, not wanting to disturb anyone with her emotions. But now her voice cracked and her face felt tight from the effort to hold back tears.

"It *must* be him! Oh, praise the Lord! Arthur and Mi-Young will be so happy! ... *if* we can get him to respond to us. He lived with his mother many years, and she probably filled him with poisonous thoughts about his father. We don't know if a successful university professor will want to find his lost family. Come to think of it, he wouldn't know we're all family now. No telling how he'd feel about that... I guess we have to trust that God is good, and that Don is still the Don we knew so long ago. Oh, Edward, I'm so glad you tracked him down."

Now she was thinking about Arthur, how devastated he would be if his son didn't want to see him. Over the decades she had reminded Arthur that his son didn't know where he was so *couldn't* be in touch. What if now, with Edward's sleuthing, Don *could* contact his father and chose not to?

Almost like he'd read her mind, Edward responded, his voice cautious. "There's a slight problem, Mama. I emailed Dr. Don Johnson and told him who I was and how we are connected. I told him his father was still living but frail and that you and he still live in Nashville and would very much like to see him. That was two weeks ago. He hasn't written back. Perhaps he was away or behind in his email, or perhaps he didn't recognize the name on the email and never opened it."

"Perhaps he didn't want to revisit his past," Cora added. "Maybe we should wait to tell Arthur until we know more? What do you think we should do?"

"I located an email address for his wife and have just emailed her, not with any of the details but just that I'm a friend of his father's. I hope to hear back from her. I'll let you know when I have news, Mama. Now, what about you? How're you doing?"

Their conversation meandered with news of church friends, the College, life in Edward's apartment building, his work with ex-offenders, each one's health, the state of the nation, and Arthur. When they clicked off, she was still at the kitchen table, nursing her third cup of coffee as she savored the conversation, its promise, and their relationship, mother and son and close friends.

Keisha, Evanston, Early October

Keisha's body was changing visibly. It was hard to disguise the swelling she wore out in front as though she'd swallowed a melon. She tried to disguise it, but long sweaters and oversized sweatshirts just didn't work in the continuous heat of Indian Summer. Classes were underway, and she knew her students were spawning speculation like oversexed salmon. She had to do something.

She ducked into Target, furtively approaching the jewelry counter.

Like her mom, she prided herself on Truth Telling. Now she felt like she was about to commit a felony. She told herself that a white lie to a clerk she'd never see again was preferable to a raft of queries from students and colleagues.

"May I help you?" asked the clerk. The woman behind the jewelry counter smiled at her.

"I'd like to look at your plain gold bands," she told the woman. Damn, it had to be a middle-aged woman and not some frivolous teen-ager preoccupied by pimples and boyfriends. She could feel her face flushing and was certain the woman could see the fetus swimming aimlessly in her belly. The *fatherless* fetus. She felt a rush of anger at Richard. What was it with men? They could readily *make* babies, but when it came to taking responsibility for them, that they left to the women. They are nothing but irresponsible babies themselves! Don't they realize that women don't have this choice, especially not recently with a bevy of pro-lifers encircling clinics carrying giant posters with four-foot-high photos of freakishly enlarged fetuses. As though pregnant women aren't aware of the fetus inside them and need to be reminded!

She'd had dreams recently of the fetuses in those photographs. Giant, furless, sloth-like creatures encased in skin and floating in a gravity-less room that expanded uncontrollably. In the dreams she was that room and they were taking over her body. She would awaken screaming and shaken, the moment before her body exploded into thousands of bloody bits, as though one of those plastic explosives that were killing so many in Iraq and Afghanistan was implanted in her uterus and set to go off momentarily.

Maybe her pregnancy did resemble carrying an IED in her body.

Maybe being pregnant this way transformed her into a kind of suicide bomber. Surely it would change her life forever, change her physically, emotionally and behaviorally. One of her friends who she'd confided in said, "You'll never get a full night's sleep once the baby comes!" Awful thought. The baby would change her relationship with Richard, too. Likely he would disappear from her life. Or he'd shift to "Godfather Richard," and she would become the sexless Madonna-mother of this child he did not want or claim. His guilt would drive him away from her, probably to another woman, who she would have to welcome to her apartment when "Godfather Richard" came to visit his "godchild."

Suddenly she was aware of someone talking to her. The woman clerk had brought out a box with gold wedding bands, each nestled in its own tiny blue velvet cubicle. She was watching Keisha, her expression curious.

Keisha looked at the rings, scanning them cursorily. This was not how she wanted to receive a wedding ring. She picked up one, narrow and plain, then another with a gem embedded in its wider band. The woman was talking to her.

"Some women like those. You can choose the stone to match the birth month of your baby." She was smiling gently at Keisha. No deception was necessary. Was it that obvious?

Keisha set both rings back in their cushioned environments, thinking that even the ring she chose would feel the impact of the fetus that would soon explode from her womb. Life in a velvet box versus life scratched and dulled from changing diapers, washing tiny clothes, cleaning snot off faces and dirt from hands and caked food from highchairs, dressing and undressing a little person. Was she really ready for this? But unlike Richard, she had no other option.

It was the embarrassment that bothered her, people, including her students, looking at her ripening body and thinking that she had had unprotected sex, maybe that she had schemed to deliberately get pregnant, and that the father of her baby didn't want her. Everyone knew people had sex, but being black, single, and pregnant carried a whole other set of stereotypes that she hated. Men seemed to think it was okay to speculate about single moms, to see them as "easy hos" and come on to them. She'd read that these women were raped more often than childless or married women. Well, she was now one of those women, all because of a hole in a condom.

Her mom had suggested on the phone that morning that she get a ring and wear it to forestall unwanted questions. "Sweet Pea, you're a strong, competent woman with a great career, a brilliant mind, and a caring heart. People can see that and that won't change. You will be all right."

She'd added almost as an afterthought, "Has Richard made any decisions?"

That was another thing. Keisha hated that Richard had all the power. She was carrying the baby and she would give birth, experience that tearing explosion of blood and pain. She didn't have the power to decide anything other than how to conceal that she was going to be a single mom.

The woman at the jewelry counter was speaking to her quietly. "... honey, a lot of us. Mine turned twenty last week and I am so glad she's in my life. Not that it isn't hard. Some lonely times. But it's still a blessing, in the long run. When are you due?"

"February." There it was. The truth. Couldn't even hide it from a stranger. She glanced at the woman's hands, avoiding her eyes, afraid that her warmth and solidarity would make them the same, Dr. Keisha Johnson reduced to a single mom clerking at Target. She felt panic rising and it tasted metallic. She turned from the counter and walked as fast as she could out of the store to her car. There she sat for some time sorting out what she was feeling. The woman had been kind to her, helpful, letting her know she was not alone in her situation. Why was she so undone?

She had the air conditioning running in the car so it took her several minutes to realize someone was tapping on the window of her car door. It was the clerk, her face transparent with concern. The window groaned as Keisha lowered it.

"I just wanted to be sure you're all right." The woman was smiling at her.

Keisha nodded. "Thank you. I was rude in there, just feeling panicky, I guess. I'm not going to get a ring after all. I don't want to make it easy for him. I won't lie or dissemble. This is *our* baby, and if he doesn't want her, or me, that's his loss." It all came out in a rush.

"You go, girl! Absolutely right. I didn't get a ring till my daughter was in school. I thought the teachers might treat her different if they knew I was a single mom." She patted Keisha's arm encouragingly. "I gotta get back to work now. Just needed to check on you. You be all right. You want to talk some time, you know where to find me. Funny, me selling wedding rings, huh?" She gave a slight wave and ran back into the store.

Keisha heard her cell phone buzzing. It was Richard calling to see if they could have lunch.

"Sorry," she said. "I already have plans. Another time." She clicked off, turned the key in the ignition, and drove out of the parking lot, stopping at her favorite Vietnamese restaurant. There she ordered her favorite Bun noodle dish and savored every bite.

She was thinking about the woman at Target and her mom and the women she'd met on the reservation, about how strong they were and clear about what they valued. She was thinking how glad she was that she wasn't a man.

Richard

Richard walked briskly along the beach and out onto a pile of black rocks thrown against the shoreline of Lake Michigan. The rocks looked casually strewn, as though the gods were rolling dice, but the wire mesh supporting them hinted that they were there to prevent erosion. It was much earlier than Richard usually arose, not even 6 a.m. He heard the hum of a dump truck moving slowly along the shore, and the clatter of rocks tripping over each other when the driver raised the truck's back bed and unloaded reinforcements. Funny how he'd never thought of the work that goes into preserving the shoreline. Somebody's job is to keep the lake from nibbling away at the beach, he thought with surprise. Meanwhile the rest of us enjoy the sunrise over the lake and walk or run the area daily without ever thinking that what we enjoy rests on someone's labor. He wondered idly how the drivers of those trucks viewed their work—deadly dull and demanding or a service to others? Probably it depends on the day, he thought.

He selected a rock with a flat top broad enough to make a seat and lowered himself to it, facing the lake. Streaks of pink and peach clung to the sky and filled the horizon. A soft blue subtly and irreversibly was taking charge, dissolving the pink and peach while he watched.

Everything changes, he thought, and there is nothing we can do to stop the changes.

He played in his mind Frederick Schiller's brief poem about the fragility of everything, the poem Brahms had set to music in *Nanie*. He remembered only fragments, which he spoke out loud:

> *The gods weep, the goddesses all weep that beauty passes, that perfection dies.*
> *that even beauty must fade, even the perfect must die*
> *….Only the mother raises a lament.*

That last couplet, so beautiful, so profound, always moved him. Why had it come to him this morning?

Everything around him was changing and he could do nothing to stop it. His birth mother had wanted his biological half-sisters to meet him. Had she raised a lament for her son, for him? Could she do nothing but weep as she gave him up?

Keisha's body was changing. He could not ignore it, this baby growing inside her, their baby. He could not ignore how it was changing her. She was more reserved, more quiet and introspective. He suspected that she was preoccupied by how this baby would change her life.

The love that flowed so easily between them was no longer so simple. It seemed to be solidifying, like blood exposed to air. Were they losing it? Had the gift they both had treasured been called back with the gigantic change of conceiving a child? Was it doomed to leave them, like the glowing pink and peach sunrise leaves as day settles in? He did not want to lose that love, so unlike anything he had ever experienced. He didn't want Keisha to withdraw. He wanted her quirky humor to flow, her springy curls to tickle his chest, her thoughtful caring for him to be there forever. Yes, he even wanted her irrepressible honesty to bring him up short and make him reconsider.

Now he recalled another poem that he had always loved: Shelley's Ozymandias, the monument to a majestic leader of another time, now forgotten, lying in the dessert, little left of it but the inscription.

Was their love a colossal wreck, eroded until nothing remained? The thought terrified him.

He heard someone calling out to him. It was the driver of the dump truck. He had left the engine idling and jumped down from his cab some yards from where Richard perched on the rocks. "Have you got a light?" the man called to Richard. "I left my lighter at home and it'll be a long day without my smokes."

Richard didn't smoke but he felt his pants pockets trying to be accommodating. "Sorry. Say, how often do you deliver rocks to this shoreline? I never noticed before that they're not just here naturally."

The man smiled. He was probably Richard's age but looked older, his face dark and wrinkled by regular exposure to the sun. Probably does construction work, Richard surmised.

"You and everyone else. Everybody thinks these rocks just come up out of the water like plants from the ground. Funny. That's not the way it works. You have to cultivate the coastline, take care of it, for it to reward you with nice beaches to walk and for kids to play on. Well, thanks anyway. Have a good day." He turned back to his truck walking bowlegged like he'd seen too many Marlborough Man commercials. He opened his cab and hopped up, waving as he turned the truck to head north.

You have to cultivate it, take care of it, to get your reward. Could that be the case with his relationship with Keisha? He allowed himself to do something he'd resisted doing, to look at the pregnancy from Keisha's perspective, or what he assumed was her perspective. It must be scary, anticipating the pain of childbirth and the constraints the baby would put on her life, her teaching, her scholarly work, just when she was hoping for a promotion. It'll be hard for her, especially now, obviously pregnant and self-conscious about it. But she said she wanted the baby regardless of whether I did. Both Keisha and I were wanted babies—inconvenient babies, but babies our mothers wanted to bring into this world. Keisha's mother had her parents to help raise her, and my birth mother had Mom and Dad, who took me on and made me their own. Who will Keisha have? Feeling uncomfortable, he dismissed the question.

This baby could be placed for adoption. Something about that thought disturbed him. Adoption had worked out well for him, but you never could know. What if it was placed with parents who didn't love it, parents who wouldn't sacrifice so that it could have opportunities? What if the adoptive parents split up? What if they were alcoholics or druggies or political extremists?

He knew no one who was genetically related to him, no one who had the same expressions or walked the same zigzagging way, no one who instinctively resonated to musical sounds like he did. What if this baby carried any of these traits of his? Why was it so hard for him to commit to raising this baby with Keisha? Something stopped him short. He could come up with no answer to that question.

The truck driver had said you have to cultivate and take care of the coastline, even though no one notices, if you want the reward. What's the reward?

Maybe it's feeling good about yourself, about what you've accomplished? He certainly didn't feel good about himself right now. I'm a coward. Keisha's friends and family must find me contemptible. Keisha probably feels that way, too.

For months he'd been stuck in indecision while her body expanded. By now everyone was noticing. And wondering. And making judgments.

A colleague had asked him just last week if they were expecting a baby. He'd muttered something unintelligible and fled to the restroom, remaining there over long, trying to assemble a response for the next person who asked. He failed. Later when he met that colleague heading out of the office, the man had smiled at him knowingly, sympathetically, and said something about, "It'll change your life. But it's worth it. Best thing that ever happened to Angie and me. Congratulations!"

He'd left the office fuming, feeling trapped in other people's expectations and wanting to hit the man. Or to immediately move out of his life and into another. He'd thought about literally moving, but he was lucky to be hired for this job and to get a contract for next year. Moving would almost guarantee he would be consigned to a career directing church choirs, adjuncting for very little pay, and taking a second job to pay his bills.

No, he didn't feel good about himself these days. Afraid of a baby, afraid of marriage, afraid of meeting his biological half-sisters, afraid of committing to any of it. Afraid of losing his autonomy, the power to decide things for himself. That's funny! I have been unable to decide anything important for months but I'm afraid of losing the power to decide? It was all crazy-making. All he knew was that he didn't know, not yet, what he wanted to do.

Maybe I could do more cultivating of my love for her, take better care of her. At the very least, it would keep hope alive while I'm stuck and unable to make a decision. It could buy some more time.

That felt like a modicum of resolution, a baby step. OK. How do I do this cultivating? He got up off his rock seat, dusting the remains of dead seaweed from the back of his pants, and climbed down to the beach. Instead of striding back the way he'd come, he headed for the shops clustered along Michigan Avenue. He stopped at the florist for an oversize bouquet, careful to select trumpet lilies in oranges and burgundies, her favorites.

He stepped into the dress shop whose funky blouses she especially liked and picked out a pale blue poet's shirt with eyelet trim around the collar and yoke and big sleeves with a long, full body that would come to her thighs. "She'll look beautiful in that," he told the clerk, smiling. The clerk smiled back indulgently.

His last stop was at the bakery where he bought her favorite cinnamon rolls hot out of the oven and, resisting the temptation to have one right there, walked up the street to her place, phoning ahead to tell her he was on his way.

She greeted him at the door to her apartment, still in her nightshirt, hair like an untamed mane. "You're up early! I don't know when you've been up, out, and back on a Saturday morning before I'm out of bed!" She was smiling. "I smell cinnamon rolls! And *flowers!* And, what's in the box?" He pushed it into her arms and watched while she opened it, her face reflecting that special delight that accompanies receiving gifts for no reason other than that someone loves you. When she saw the shirt, she squealed with excitement and threw her arms around him, causing him to lose his grip on the flowers for a moment, but he retrieved them before they hit the ground. "Why?" she asked him.

"I'm trying to take care of you, in my own way," he replied.

Don, Sarajevo, Bosnia, Mid-October

He sat in the back of the science auditorium of the University of Sarajevo, trying to pay attention to the lecture but finding his mind wandering. He was stiff from over much sitting and still recovering from jet lag. The seats were ancient and uncomfortable. Most of the money coming into Sarajevo for education was going to the two new universities that were about to open. Maybe he wouldn't attend any more of these international conferences.

He had come to this one because of a newscast almost ten years ago during the Bosnian War. It was early in what would become the longest siege in European history, the siege of Sarajevo, forty-four months of shelling that nearly destroyed this city that had been so cosmopolitan, so cultured, such a model of tolerance, of Muslims, Christians, Jews, and atheists dwelling in harmony. One of his graduate students was from the former Yugoslavia. The young student had come to his office one afternoon to tell him of a remarkable man standing up to the power of darkness with only his cello on the streets of devastated Sarajevo.

"I don't know why, but I knew I had to tell you this, Dr.

Johnson. My hope was almost gone from me but then I hear about this man, Vedran Smajlovic." The student had told Don the story, and Don had never forgotten it.

"While snipers murder people who look for water or firewood, while bombs explode in the city markets and playgrounds, killing so many innocent people, this man plays beautiful, haunting classical music out there in the streets in sight of the snipers. Dr. Johnson, it's no accident that he plays Tomaso Albinoni's *Adagio in G Minor*. It is a message not to give up. A composer named Remo Giozotto found a fragment of this composition in the rubble of the city library in Dresden, Germany during the horrible bombing of that city by the Americans in World War II. On the fragment were four notes only, but from that Giozotto made a new Adagio. And the cellist plays it, day after day in the streets of my suffering Sarajevo. Do you understand?"

His student had looked so intently at him, and Don, feeling deeply moved, had only been able to nod. Now he was in that same city, still marked by the siege, seven years after the war's end. He wanted to walk its streets, to visit the markets and playgrounds where so many died, where the cellist found the courage to send forth his song.

The sound of applause brought him back to the conference proceedings. He had to get out of this auditorium. He stood and excused himself, climbing over the people seated beside him and leaving the auditorium as the next speaker was being introduced. He caught and held the door as he exited so it would close quietly. He sat down in one of the armchairs clustered in a nearby sitting area. Then, deciding to check his email before heading out to walk the city and realizing that the only internet connection was in the computer lab on the second floor, he climbed the stairs and located the lab.

He found emails from Ann and Keisha and a couple dozen from Cleveland State. Most of his email simply consumed kilobytes. He deleted it. Then he deleted all his SPAM and DELETED mail. It felt satisfying to clean out his mailbox.

He opened Ann's email and read about her life back home. After she asked about the conference and how he was feeling, she wrote, "Do you know an Edward Hardyway? I got an email from someone with that name who said he's a friend of your father." Then he read further.

"Mr. Hardyway says he's been trying to reach you. He had emailed you but received no response."

He stared unfocused out the window at the apartment buildings sprawling around this urban campus. Beyond them an army of white rectangles, markers of lost lives, climbed the hills and surrounded the city. He tried to recall any such email. That name, Edward Hardyway, sounded familiar. When he was in college, he'd tried to find his father's friend Cora, who they'd visited in Nashville when he was twelve, but he'd been unable to recall her last name. They were introduced to him as Cora and Edward, nothing more. Something in the recesses of his mind felt a flicker of recognition at the name Hardyway that accelerated his heart.

"Shall I respond?" Ann wrote. "I was afraid it might be one of those scams."

He needed time before answering her.

He walked out of the university building across from the Holiday Inn where they were staying. The hotel and the university buildings were still pockmarked from more than three years of shelling. The young Bosnian grad student who picked them up from the airport had told Don that the University of Sarajevo kept conducting classes all through the siege while, from the hills that surrounded the city, heavy artillery and snipers shot anything that moved. The devastation still scarred the buildings and drew him outside.

The conference organizer had told them not to walk anywhere other than on the streets. Thousands of land mines, planted amidst the gravestones on the hills surrounding the city during the war, lay buried there, awaiting the pressure of a careless step to set them off. That might deter most people from wandering the city, but not Don, not today. When some- thing upset him, he walked it through, as though perspective would seep up from his soles. As he set off to climb the hills he vaguely remembered his father saying that his best friend, Cora's husband, was killed by a land mine in Korea.

He stayed on the streets.

After an hour he turned back and walked downhill to a bookstore near the university. It sold the *International Herald Tribune* and Bosnian coffee, thick and strong. There he could pretend to read the news and give himself time to process the confusing images running through his head.

The bookstore had only four small, round tables. He selected the one farthest from the door next to a window that faced the street and settled there with his coffee. It was a sunny afternoon. With the sun slanting through the window, lavishing his table with moving light, he allowed himself to remember the last three days he spent with his father when he was twelve. On the rare occasions when he allowed these memories to come, they always stopped at the point when he and his father had walked into their house in Buffalo, returning home to his mother's fury and the end of his world as he had known it.

So much in his life he had lost—Connie, his son by her, the potential for a relationship with his half-sister, with Edward and Cora, his father, Baby Jonathan who had died at birth, Poppy-Don... His losses washed over him as he sat in that bookstore near the University of Sarajevo, watching the afternoon retreat until the sun came at him, horizontal and piercing through the window.

He knew he was feeling sorry for himself and should know better. He had Ann and Keisha, who loved him, a career in which he had excelled, and his mother. Mother. Mother descending into the special hell of alcoholism and dragging him with her. Not that he drank. No, not since college. But he knew intimately the behavior of addicts and sometimes wondered if the trauma and behaviors of addiction passed to the next generation by some mysterious invisible umbilical cord. Sometimes it felt that way.

Mother had been so beautiful as a young woman and so vivacious. He recalled the pride he had felt when his friends at school would comment on how lucky he was to have a gorgeous mom. But after she threw Dad out, she became harsh, sometimes even violent, her moods shifting suddenly with no warning. They might be having dinner together and something would set her off. Once she threw the coffee pot, breaking a window. Another time she hit him hard across the face when he said that he would like to see his father. The house for all its material comforts felt like his own secret chamber of horrors, the only safe place, his room with its door locked from the inside.

Poppy-Don had intervened and tried to get her counseling, went with her to AA, and persuaded her to sell the house and move back into her parents' home, so Don could have his grandfather nearby. Poppy-Don had truly been a good grandfather, seeking vigilantly to protect Don from his mother's rages and to supply him with stability and care.

Now he remembered Poppy-Don picking him up from high school one afternoon at the start of his senior year. He'd slid onto the ivory leather seat of Poppy's golden Cadillac, glancing left, trying to read Poppy's profile as they pulled away from the school.

"Your mother's having an especially bad day," Poppy'd said. "I've taken her to the hospital to see if they can help her. I know how hard this is on you. It's hard on all of us. She just seems lost, unable to control herself." Poppy drove him home, made him a snack—Mom never tended to such things for him—and then sat down with him while he ate to ask what he wanted to do with his life. When Don said he wanted to be a scientist and that he dreamed of finding a cure for cancer, Poppy had offered to pay his way to college and grad school to make it happen. Then, in the most personal conversation they'd ever had, he told his grandson that he didn't know what more he could do to stop his daughter's appalling descent into alcoholism. It was the only time either of them had named her affliction. After that conversation, Don felt lighter. Someone understood. He was not crazy.

Poppy-Don got him out of the house and into college and grad school, paid for him to travel in Europe, bought him his first car, and welcomed Ann and Keisha into the family, although not at first—not until he realized that if he didn't welcome Ann and Keisha, he would lose Don. At first Poppy had said Ann was not a suitable match for him and made a remark that questioned her morals, having a child without being married, especially a black child. Don remembered with pride declaring himself to Poppy-Don in Poppy's dark green study in the back of the old Victorian house they shared. *"You will not talk like that about Ann and Keisha. You will not."* He was standing very close to Poppy and towered over him.

Poppy's eyes had given away his fear that his grandson, who he loved so much, was about to walk out of his life. Don was prepared for this confrontation. Without stepping back he said exactly what he had planned to say: "I love you, Poppy, and I'm very grateful for all you've done for me. But I let my mother remove from me my father, and I will not let you, or her, or anyone remove me from Ann and Keisha, who are the center of my life."

Poppy-Don's face had shown surprise and then resignation. He stopped making critical comments about Ann and Keisha and made an about face remarkably quickly. Indeed, his change of behavior taught Don an important lesson. Sometimes people can change, and not permitting others to bully you can be a catalyst for their changing.

He had stood up to his grandfather and his mother, drawn his line in the sand, and established boundaries, which was good, essential, something to take pride in. So why couldn't he shake this perennial sadness?

He carried his empty coffee cup to the older man behind the counter whose face carried a nasty war scar. He tucked the *International Herald Tribune* under his arm and walked back to the University's computer lab. There he emailed Ann. "Yes," he keyed, "Invite him to the house. The chance that he knows my father makes it worth the risk that it's a scam."

His plane landed in Cleveland promptly at nine p.m. four nights later. He felt exhausted from the flight and from his nights of dream-troubled sleep. Seeing Ann there to meet him carrying flowers brought a smile. It was a custom he had started when meeting her flights, but she had begun to do it for him a few years ago. He felt grateful for her thoughtfulness. No other men were greeted with bouquets! They kissed and she slipped her arm into his. Walking to the car, he told her he loved her. He probably should tell her more often he thought, as her face lit up.

Lying in bed together he told her about his trip and, just

before she turned out the light, she told him that Edward Hardyway was coming the following night to join them for dinner. Despite his exhaustion, he felt his energy surge before he crashed into dreamless sleep.

Ann, Cleveland

When she opened the door to Edward's ring, they stood looking at each other quizzically. "Do I know you?" she asked him.

"It certainly feels that way to me," he replied. "I doubt you went to Howard, but are you part of the United Church of Christ?" he asked, following her into the living room.

That wasn't it. She felt mildly disoriented, unable to identify where she'd seen him before. They were still offering each other options when Don entered the room—The YMCA? The library on Hayden? The Woodmere Trader Joe's?

She glanced at her husband, imagining how this stranger would see him—a serious man, dressed casually, his thick, wavy white hair curling over his collar and accentuating his resemblance to an aging hippie or Michael Caine. She liked to watch people interact. The two men shook hands, eyes locked on each other. She could almost see their minds sorting remnants of memory for identifiers.

She offered Edward a glass of wine—of course, Don would have cranberry juice—and left the room to fetch the drinks, calling back that Edward shouldn't say anything important till she returned. When she returned, she and Don sat on the sofa and Edward on the love seat sipping their drinks. Edward was explaining that he had come across Don's name and done some web research, which had led to this particular Don Johnson. He didn't mention that he got the name from Andrea, guessing that Connie's granddaughters' trusts were none of his business and not wanting Don to think he had a pecuniary interest.

It took only a few minutes for them both to realize that they were, indeed, childhood friends, connected through Don's father, Arthur, who, Edward told Don, had become Edward's stepfather. They shook hands a second time, more warmly, below-the-surface emotion rendering them a bit awkward.

Ann, watching them, thought to herself that men approaching their sixties seemed to have their emotions wired more sensitively than at earlier times in their lives. Fortunately, she kept this thought unvoiced, though the feminist side of her smugly noted that it was a shame that it takes so long for men to discover the importance of feelings.

Over dinner Edward caught Don up on the Nashville family.

"Your father's slowed down, but he's well for his age. And my Mama continues to amaze all who know her...82 and still going strong, still teaching and her hair dye keeps people guessing her age. I don't think they would have thought about marrying if Mi-Young hadn't teased them about finding excuses not to. Have you had any contact with your father since you were 12?"

Don shook his head. "I heard nothing about my father after we came back from Nashville. For a while I would see him driving past the house very slowly, looking out the car window, probably trying to see me. I know he tried to call, and my mother would not let us talk. I'm glad he and your mom married."

Ann asked, "Do you have other family, Edward?"

"I was married briefly in my late twenties, when I finished Harvard Divinity School, but we mutually decided it wasn't working and divorced. My work for the church consumed most of my time and energy after that, with some good friends and a couple of short-lived relationships thrown in. I've done a lot of international travel and get to Nashville to be with Mama and Arthur two or three times a year."

Ann thought she saw Don wince and made note to ask him about that later, after Edward left. She wondered what would it be like to have a stepbrother living in the same city, unknown to you, but regularly seeing your father, the father you've not seen since you were a child?

"My surrogate son is a young man I mentored for many years. His family adopted me, and I'm "Godfather" to them and to the children of two of my Harvard friends. I retired a year ago from active ministry and began volunteering with a prison ministry as a counselor, part time. I'm thoroughly enjoying being free of people's expectations." Edward smiled. "Forty-three years of meeting people and watching their behavior and expressions alter when they find out what I do was more than enough. You can imagine—their language changes, they censor what they're about to say, and treat me like I am a cross between St. Francis and the Thought Police. But my life is good. And it just got a lot better! The lost has been found, my brother."

Edward said this so fervently that Ann could feel the emotion in his voice. She felt deep gratitude for how comfortable Don and Edward seemed together, despite their knowing each other so briefly so long ago.

Their conversation turned to next steps. Don said he wanted to see his father as soon as possible.

Edward suggested calling right then to let Arthur and Cora know that they had found each other. Don agreed, then asked, "And my, *our* sister? What's happened with her?"

"She's fine. Living in Atlanta now."

Ann brought the landline with its speaker phone to the table, along with a luscious chocolate mousse. But neither man was interested in the mousse. As Edward dialed, she slipped into the chair next to Don's and held his hand.

Cora, Nashville

Cora picked up the phone on the second ring, her face lighting up when she heard Edward's words, *"I found him!"* She turned up the volume on the phone and set it to speaker. Then she passed the phone to Arthur who had dozed off in his recliner. She gentled him awake and put the phone to his good ear, barely able to wait for his facial expression when he heard who he was speaking to.

She could hear an older man, voice wobbly with emotion, saying, "Dad? This is Don, your son."

Keisha, Evanston

Keisha checked her phone the next morning to discover a text from Mom. "Good news. Call me." When she phoned, Mom told her about the emotional reunion the night before. "Your father is happier than I've had ever known him to be, almost giddy, and frequently moist-eyed. We're flying to Nashville for the weekend. Would you and Richard like to come, too?"

She had so much to do for her classes, and she was up for promotion and had to get her paperwork in by the end of next week. She couldn't go. "I'll come in two weeks, Mom, OK?"

She found it hard to believe that her father and his stepbrother had been living in the same city for decades. She'd known since childhood that her dad had been separated from his father by Grandma Milly, and that Dad didn't even know where his father was. She found it hard to imagine her reserved father overcome with emotion. She had never seen him cry, not even when he came home from the hospital after Baby Jonathan's birth to tell her that her baby brother had died. Not even at Poppy-Don's funeral. She remembered the funeral especially well. She'd sat beside him holding his hand all through the service. She'd felt so responsible for him. But he had remained dry-eyed and remote. She could see him with his distinctive way of carrying himself, tall, straight-backed, leaning slightly forward, as though meeting whatever was coming with his brain first and only later his gut and heart. Oh, Dad.

She'd been making breakfast, but now she sat down at the table and wept for him. And maybe for herself. Why is there so much pain in people's lives, even people who are loved so much? It surprised her that she was crying. She thought of herself as a person who feels things deeply, but, like her dad, she rarely cried, even in this crisis of her pregnancy with Richard's ambivalence. Back to Dad. How would this private, unemotional man cope with what promised to be a very emotional reunion?

"I need to be with my family in the uncertainty of their lives and mine." She said it aloud.

An hour later she called Mom back. "I'm coming, Mom. I found a seat on a flight that gets in at five on Friday."

Cora told him that Don and Ann would land in Nashville Thursday evening. They'd canceled their Friday classes so they could have a day with him and Cora before Keisha and Edward arrived.

Arthur sat in the kitchen peeling potatoes for Cora, who was cooking a company dinner. "Wish you could just run next door and pick some greens," she joked. They'd sold the house Cora and Booker had bought and moved to a spacious apartment with elevator access several years ago to make living easier as they aged. The apartment was spacious and homey and better for both of them, but there was no garden. He had taken to using a cane, though he told people that, "my beautiful wife," as he regularly referred to her, could run the stadium steps at the University if she had to.

"Will he be angry with me for leaving? I keep telling myself to be prepared for him to be angry." Arthur held the peeler mid-air, concentrating hard on how his long-lost son might respond to him.

"Honey, I figure this is our chance to out-do the prodigal son's homecoming. That's why I'm cooking up a storm." Cora leaned down and kissed the top of Arthur's head. "He may feel some anger, but we can work that through. The miracle is your finding each other, and both of you know that. Maybe you should make a list of what you want to ask him, what you want to talk about."

He squeezed her hand. "You know, somewhere along these past forty years I realized how lucky I am. I used to think I was so unlucky—Milly, Jindae dying, losing Don, leaving all my worldly possessions—but that's changed. I don't know how or when, it just changed. I have you, and Edward, and Mi-Young and her girls, and a new life here. It doesn't get much better than this, and then on top of all that happiness, here comes Edward finding Don!" He blinked rapidly.

Cora was smiling at him. "I sure am glad you got that figured out before you get any older, Old Man. Some things you got to get right *in time*. Now, have you got those potatoes right?" They laughed and went back to work on supper.

Don had said they'd take a cab from the airport. Arthur sat beside Cora, watching the news and waiting to hear his son's footfalls climbing the stairs to the apartment. Everything was ready for supper. After a while Cora stood and offered her hand to help him up. He must have missed it. Darn his deteriorating hearing! Together they walked to the
door and opened it. There stood his son with a nice looking woman. For a moment he thought he would fall over. His knees went weak and he held tight to Cora's arm to get his balance. Don reached out for him and held onto him. Then he looped Arthur's arm through the crook of his and steered him to the couch. Arthur noticed that the women were chatting amiably.

Arthur looked at his "boy," taking inventory: taller than me, must be 6'4" or 6'5", and built lanky like me. Has all his hair, like me, and it's white like mine. Distinguished looking. He looks like a professor. Not much reminded him of Milly. Whew! That was lucky. He could see that Don was giving him the same examination. He didn't look angry. That was a good sign. So much to catch up on. I need to take it slow, not overwhelm him. *Oh, God, thank you.*

Dinner was delicious, of course, and the women bustled about in the kitchen getting acquainted. Occasionally he could hear Cora laugh.

Afterward, he and Don sat on the sofa side by side, Don on his right at Cora's suggestion, "so you'll be close to his good ear." Arthur unfolded his list and began going through his questions, making notes after each one so he wouldn't forget Don's replies.

His son had done so well in life, not only a professor but developing those machines they're using now to knock out some kinds of cancer. He felt very proud.

Sometime in the conversation Don draped his arm over his father's shoulders, and Arthur patted his hand. It felt so good. He'd made a note that he wanted to tell Don why he had not come back for him. He guessed it could wait until tomorrow.

Cora and Ann did their own talking sitting at the kitchen table. Ann learned that Cora had been involved in the civil rights movement. When she told Cora that she had been part of Freedom Summer, Cora asked her excitedly.

"Did you know Edward in Mississippi?"

Ann was silent, reconstructing her months in Mississippi. She recalled the young man they called Preacherman who was from Nashville, *Reggie's roommate!* Could Edward be Preacherman?

"I don't know. We each thought the other looked familiar when he came to the house, but neither of us could place where we'd met. Freedom Summer ended so abruptly in all that chaos of the Convention and everybody leaving Mississippi to return to college. So many of the records we kept were burned when they firebombed our Freedom Houses. How different it would be now with Facebook and email to locate each other."

For a moment she let herself imagine how their lives might have turned out if she had remained in contact with Reggie. Don't go there, said her mother's voice in her head. She made a mental note to ask Edward about his Freedom Summer experience. She was distracted. What had Cora just said? "...growing up without his father and without any information about him or why he wasn't around. When my first husband died, Edward needed to ask me over and over again why his daddy wasn't with us. I don't imagine Don had anyone to ask about his father."

She pushed away the excitement she'd felt at the thought that Edward had known Reggie and forced herself to stay in the present. "For as long as I've known him Don has carried a sadness that I thought came from his alcoholic mother continually cutting down his father. That woman isn't functional without a fifth of whiskey within reach. Frankly, I've tried to stay away from her. She's toxic. I don't know how anyone can be around her without feeling crushed and deflated. You can imagine what she said about me, a single mom with a biracial child." The depth of her anger at Milly surprised her.

Cora stood wiping her hands on a towel looking at Ann. "Poor woman. I wonder why she lived such a miserable life. I've prayed for her over the years, that she would be able to replace liquor with the Everflowing Streams."

Ann was stunned. *"You prayed for Milly?* What do you mean by Everflowing Streams?" She wanted to have that centered strength that radiated from within Cora, but Cora's God-talk made her uncomfortable, especially when she wasn't sure what it meant.

Cora sat back down, pulling out a second chair on which to rest her swollen legs. She tossed the red-checkered dish towel onto the counter. Then she spoke. "Well, honey, I believe opportunities for healing are all around us, like Everflowing Streams that bring nourishment to people and creatures on every continent. It may sound naïve, but I know from my own life that if you let yourself drink from them, let yourself bathe in them, you can let go of what keeps you down and find peace. I believe there are streams for all of us, and we are charged with finding them and letting others find theirs without getting in their way. People like Milly seem to prefer staying parched, and that makes me very sad."

"Arthur was as low as a body can be when he moved here, but he accepted the love our little family and our church gave him, and gradually let himself trust that there was a way out of no way. He kept walking, one step after another, and eventually located his Stream. By then he'd found the courage to drink from it, walk into it, and let it cleanse him. Of course, he had Edward, Mi-Young, and me encouraging him, caring about him. Losing Don nearly crushed him—a habitually lonely man losing the relationship with his son that he'd just begun constructing." She was shaking her head. "But it *didn't* crush him. And today he is rewarded, praise the Lord."

They sat at Cora's table across from each other. Cora was looking at her with such softness. She gazed into Cora's eyes as though discovering there the Everflowing Stream. She reached for Cora's hands and they sat in silence.

Ann felt certain that this conversation was one of the most important she would ever have.

Later, after she and Don had stretched out on the guest room bed, she listened in the moonless dark while he told her about his time with his father, his voice low and reverent. Then she told him about her conversation with Cora. "You know how lovers say they are lost in each other's eyes? Well, after sitting in the kitchen tonight looking at Cora, I think we're found in each other's eyes." She turned to look directly at Don, seeking his eyes, but his eyes were closed and he slept.

Arthur

Don said his mother lived her life in a very small box. Milly, the beautiful redhead who had everything, reduced to living in a box, no one wanting to be with her. Why is one life prolonged in such misery and another, like Jindae's, snuffed out so prematurely? He wished he was more like Cora, more certain that God weeps with us in our sorrow. But he could not believe that. Something capricious and wonderful that he could not ascribe to Chance or Destiny or The Divine had brought Jindae to him, had brought Booker to him, had brought Cora and Edward and Mi-Young, and now Don. Something terrible had taken Jindae and Booker and removed his son from his life. It just *was*. He could not make sense of it. He could only feel gratitude for this second chance with his white-haired child.

He felt on the middle shelf of the bookcase next to his chair for the small, faded, black and white photo of the farm he grew up on, the picture of his parents and their brood of children posed on the front steps. He found himself in the picture, off to one side, leaning against the column that supported the porch roof. His parents struggled so to provide for this family, and even when this picture was taken, he was moving away from them. He'd lost them over the years largely by choices he'd made. Maybe his choices caused him to lose Don?—choosing to take him to Nashville, choosing to tell Milly that he had a daughter, choosing to flee Buffalo and remake his life here. And if he had brought it on himself? No point dwelling on it now. Gotta keep moving as long as you're above ground, as Cora liked to say.

He smiled thinking about his wife and best friend. Then,

missing the comfort of her presence, he rose stiffly from the recliner and shuffled along the dark corridor to their room. He slid carefully into bed beside her, glad that her snoring was not disturbed by the low groan of the bedsprings. Then he, too, slept.

In the morning he watched his son interacting with his wife Ann. He liked the way she put her hand on his knee, the way he put his hand on her shoulder, and especially the way they listened to each other. He liked the way Don spoke of his students, some of whom had become his friends. He was observing closely. He needed to know that his son had lived a good life, without him.

Cora served breakfast on TV trays in the living room.

"Tell me about your children, Son," he'd asked after a lull in the conversation. He could see pain on Don's face before he answered. Then Don told him about the death of their newborn, Baby Jonathan. He noticed Ann looking at her husband intensely. Then Don continued and what he said seemed to surprise Ann.

"I had another son, too, Dad, born to a girlfriend when I was in college. But I didn't know about him, and when she couldn't manage raising him, she placed him for adoption."

Arthur was smiling, but thinking that smiling might seem inappropriate, he tried to explain. "I was thinking that both of us had a son who was lost to us. You and I have found each other. Maybe someday you'll find your son, too."

Arthur was observing himself as well as his son. Now he was swamped with a wave of feeling. He was learning to just let the feelings come. Invariably they stayed a while and then moved on, recycling, sadness to joy, curiosity to regret to gratitude, and back again to sadness. When the feelings sat too heavily, he excused himself— "my old man's bladder"—to find sanctuary in their small bathroom where he sat on the closed toilet seat and, when he recovered, flushed, to protect his pride. He suspected Cora was onto his bathroom game.

Edward and Keisha shared a taxi from the airport and arrived in time for supper. Arthur was surprised to see the two of them chatting like old friends. His granddaughter could be the child he and Cora never had together, he thought, and loved her at first sight. It was obvious that she was pregnant, and no one mentioned it, so he didn't ask, just wondered. He liked to use his old man's prerogative to flirt with pretty young women and remarked with a wink that Don's women, like his, were extraordinarily smart *and* beautiful.

After supper Keisha sat next to him on the sofa at his request so that he could learn about her life. She told him about her trip to the Philippines, her work on an Indian reservation, her teaching. Then she said she wanted him to know that she was going to have a baby in the New Year and that the father was a good man, a musician, who didn't yet know what he wanted to do about their baby. Arthur reached his arm out to nudge her closer to him. Nestled in his brown-spot freckled, old man's arms, she cried and he held her. When she recovered, he whispered, "Tomorrow you will meet *my* love child, Mi-Young."

It was exhausting watching these beloved people interacting in his home. He noted Keisha's obvious concern for her dad and Edward's way of observing closely, analytically. He guessed that Edward had figured out a lot about each of these folks, maybe more than they had figured out about themselves. Returning from the toilet on one of his trips, he stopped at the chair Edward occupied, patted him on the back and whispered with a wobbly voice, "This wouldn't be happening if it wasn't for you."

By the end of their second evening together his heart was so full that he forgot to tell Don why he had left Buffalo and his twelve-year-old son.

Richard

Richard felt a bit uncomfortable with his decision to remain in Evanston rather than going with Keisha to Nashville. He liked her family, it wasn't that. He had wanted to come with her, because it was clearly very important to her, but he was ambivalent about being included in this intimate family time, uncertain just what relationship to Keisha and her family he wanted, now and in the future, after the baby was born. He didn't want to mislead her or her family.

He got up early Saturday morning and went out on his back balcony to compose. Lake Michigan lay before him, serene in the October sunshine. He waited, but his muse would not come. Eventually he moved back indoors to his kitchen.

Instead of melodies, meals came to him, and he wrote them down: Swedish meat balls, chicken korma, eggplant parmesan, beef in wine sauce. He left the apartment to shop for the ingredients, purposeful and focused, and spent the rest of the day cooking meals that he packed into plastic containers, the right size for two portions, each labeled and stored in his freezer. It would make life easier for Keisha when she returned.

Keisha, Nashville

Keisha had not pieced together the intricacies of how the members of this extended family were connected. When her grandfather whispered about his love child, she'd been taken aback, trying to sort out what he meant but not wanting to cause embarrassment by asking. Later, helping Cora with the dishes, she asked Cora about Mi-Young, and learned from her about Arthur's brief love affair in Korea that had produced Mi-Young and brought Arthur and Cora together after Cora offered to raise the child.

"It's funny how love comes back to us, Keisha," Cora said. "In my experience it's the best gift life gives us, whatever way it comes."

Keisha found herself conflating Cora and Edward with her birth father's family, pretending that she was learning about her Lewis roots through knowing the Hardyways. She knew that was ridiculous, the Lewises being Jamaicans by way of New York City and the Hardyways southerners, Tennesseeans. But it made sense in a way and filled a longing in her to connect in some way with her father's people.

She asked Cora if she could hug her, and when Dad walked into the kitchen to get a drink of water, there they were, holding each other. She said to them both, "My Gran Cora. I like that."

Mi-Young

After the dishes, they all gathered in the living room. Don asked Ed-ward about his sister, Mi-Young, and the room grew suddenly quiet, the ebullience of the day deflated like a punctured balloon.

Cora began the story, obviously very proud of her daughter's accomplishments. "Mi-Young was an amazing child and grew even more amazing as an adult. She was twenty when President Nixon went to China and reopened a relationship between the U.S. and the People's Republic after decades of no contact. She wanted to learn about her mother's people, so in college she took a Korean history course and ended up majoring in East Asian languages at Georgetown University in Washington. She speaks Chinese and Korean fluently! With her somewhat Asian looks, language skill, and strong academic background in East Asia, she was a hot commodity as the U.S. government developed its new relationship with China. Even before she finished her Ph.D., the State Department recruited her.

She joined the Foreign Service and in the Carter Administration was Press Secretary at the new U.S. Embassy in China. In President Reagan's second term she was made Deputy Ambassador to South Korea."

"Wow!" Don interrupted. "Was she able to find her mother's family in Korea?"

Arthur picked up the story. "She found Jinwon, her uncle, who was working in Seoul, and through him located several other uncles, aunts, and cousins. They told her about conditions in the North. Their family was from a town near the border with North Korea. The area was still rural, quite a contrast to what Mi-Young experienced in the rest of the South, where the country was prosperous and the people educated. In 1990 she met a North Korean refugee, fell in love, and married him."

"We really like Son Chi," Cora added. She moved to the buffet to retrieve two framed photos which she passed around. Son Chi was a tall, handsome man with a broad face, narrow nose, and smiling eyes. Their wedding picture showed Mi-Young, oval faced with long, wavy black hair and hazel eyes standing beside him, beautiful in a traditional Korean dress.

"They were married at the U.S. Embassy," Cora explained. "Mi-Young hoped to raise awareness in the U.S. and elsewhere to the conditions North Koreans lived under. She asked her Korean family to help her get across the border with a camera. Because she spoke Korean fluently, she thought she could get information and photographs and that, as a high ranking official at the U.S. Embassy, she'd be believed. But they refused to help her because of the danger she would be in. They feared for her safety. I think they knew that her looks marked her as not fully Korean and therefore suspicious." Cora looked at Edward and Arthur, checking if they wanted to pick up the story. When both shook their heads, she continued.

"She was hugely disappointed and decided to leave diplomatic work and move back to the U.S. to monitor human rights in North Korea without the limits that working for the government placed on her. She was determined to raise awareness to conditions in that country. She took a job with Human Rights Watch and Son Chi worked with the American Academy of Science."

Arthur interjected, "They had three children, all girls, Dae who turns thirty next spring and the twins, Li and Kim, who are—26?" He looked at Cora who nodded. "We saw them regularly while they lived in Washington. We were so glad she was back in the U.S., but she was frustrated. She wanted to do more for the people of North Korea."

They were tag-teaming the story. Edward stepped in. "She lobbied Congress and the State Department, telling them what she knew about the North and trying to persuade them to support groups working to free people from the prison camps in the North, camps like the one where Son

Chi had been held. She made fact finding trips to Korea and even met with Chinese dignitaries at the UN, but the Chinese would not acknowledge the situation in the North because of their alliance with North Korea and our government's official policy was to support South Korea but otherwise not get involved."

Cora resumed the story. "When the CIA recruited Son Chi to work undercover in both Koreas, Mi-Young wanted very much to do the same thing, but her appearance was against her. She's visibly Arthur's daughter, clearly not full Korean, and Korea is a very homogeneous country. Like her Korean family the CIA told her that she wouldn't be able to work in the North. So Son Chi took the job with what Mi-Young calls 'The Agency.' Of course, she couldn't tell us anything, what he'd be doing or where he'd be posted. I'm not sure she knew." A pained expression took over Cora' face.

"Son Chi went missing five years ago. The CIA gives out no information, other than to caution us that in such cases it's best to keep it secret that our son-in-law is missing."

Arthur's face, so like Don's in the high forehead, long nose and strong chin, looked very old, its myriad of intersecting lines a roadmap of grief. "Today God has answered my prayers in bringing you back to me, Don. But your sister is separated from the person she loves most."

The mood in the room was somber. It seemed such a hopeless situation.

After some minutes, Cora spoke.

"We'll see Mi-Young and Li and Kim tomorrow sometime around noon! Dae followed her mother into the Foreign Service and is posted to the U.S. Embassy in Thailand, so she can't come, but the twins are taking off work at the hospital to drive here with Mi-Young. Mi-Young followed the twins to Atlanta two years ago. She hasn't sold their house in Washington in the hope that Son Chi will return one day."

"She continues doing human rights work out of her home in Atlanta," Edward added. He suggested they have a moment of silence, after which he asked for blessings on Mi-Young, Son Chi, and their daughters and thanked God for Don and Arthur and, indeed, all of them finding each other.

"It comes in handy having a minister in the family," Cora teased her son.

Ann

While Keisha played Scrabble with Grandma Cora and Don and Arthur, exhausted by hours of talking, sat together on the sofa, mostly silent, Ann and Edward retreated to the kitchen to talk.

She discovered that Edward was indeed the Preacherman she'd worked beside in Mississippi, which led to extensive story telling about life there in the summer of 1964. At a lull in their Mississippi memories conversation, Edward asked her to tell him about Keisha.

"I noticed you watching her over dinner," she replied. "Let me guess.

You're wondering how Don can be Keisha's father, right?" Edward was embarrassed.

"Oh, I'm quite used to that, as is Keisha. Keisha is my continuous blessing from Freedom Summer. I discovered myself pregnant some months after returning to college. Remember how Dr. King used to tell us to live our present as though the future we desire is already here? That's what we have done, Keisha and I... and Don. Don came along and fell in love with both of us—I sometimes think he was more in love with my precocious three-year-old than with me! Well, we became a family. He and Keisha are very close."

"I can see that," Edward responded. "She's a remarkable young woman."

Ann wondered if Edward was connecting her with Reggie. She wanted to tell him more, to tell him that Reggie was Keisha's birth father, to learn what Edward knew of Reggie's life after Mississippi. But she couldn't. This weekend reunion was about Don and his father. She would not distract anyone in this family from that. Maybe later she and Edward would remember Reggie. Or maybe sometime she would tell Keisha that Edward had known Reggie and let the two of them have that conversation. Or maybe not.

Don

Don awoke before dawn. He had slept poorly. He felt his mind would explode with the colliding images and voices contesting there. He decided he must get up and walk to quiet the chaos inside and sort through all he had learned in this incredible day and a half.

He got up and pulled on running shorts and a T-shirt, grabbed his walking shoes and tiptoed out of the apartment. He sat on the steps to put on his shoes. Then he started walking, he knew not where; anywhere would do.

The neighborhood was mostly residential, small apartment buildings like the one Cora and Dad lived in alternating with shotgun homes, mom-and-pop groceries, liquor stores, churches, and gas stations. Along the street lay empty liquor bottles still in brown paper sleeves, crumpled and glistening foil potato chip bags, and used condoms, artifacts of urban America.

He picked up his pace, jogging along the uneven sidewalk. His head was pounding. As each foot landed hard on the sidewalk, the noise inside his skull grew louder and more insistent.

He heard his Mother, brutally furious, shaking with rage as she told him never to embarrass his family! He was a child again, ashamed of his father but unclear why, torn between his mother's fury, his father's quiet calm, and Poppy-Don's take-charge confidence that dismissed his father and papered over his mother's deepening madness. Following his grandfather's instruction he had erased his father and replaced him with Poppy-Don. Or did his father erase himself from his life?

Here was his father, an old man who had found solace with a new family who cherished him. Had his father ever missed him? Tried to locate him? Now he felt angry and abandoned. The pain he had locked away came crashing through his body. He felt his knees buckle and had to sit down, right there on the sidewalk. It was all so confusing, and he felt like a twelve-year-old again, powerless among powerful adults who manipulated his life and laid out his future without consulting him.

His sadness held him as he sat there, lost in grief. He

abandoned any effort to push it away. Layers of loss weighed him down, pushing him into the Nashville sidewalk which cracked and opened to receive him. He felt buried alive. Images of what might have been formed vividly in his brain. His gorgeous mother before the bottle, his father on their intimate road trip to Nashville, Connie laughing and lovely at eighteen, his and Ann's babies who never made it and the unknown son who did—each image dissolved when he reached for it.

The final image was terrifying: An old man grubbily dressed lying in a hole covered with dirt and rocks and debris, forgotten, uncared for, desolate, and fated to lose everything he loved. His body shook as he wept.

He had no idea how long he lay there in the hole made by the giant crack in the sidewalk. Gradually other images came to him: Cora lovingly caring for his father, for all of them; Edward persistently looking for Don and finding him; his father, accepting him with heart overflowing; Ann sagely supporting him throughout his journey of self-discovery; Keisha watching him closely and coming to him before she went off to bed to hug him and whisper, "Daddy. I'm so proud to be your daughter."

When his trembling stopped, he stood up, taking his time, dusting off leaves and dirt and noticing the stiffness in his legs. Calm came over him and his despair lifted. He had no idea where he was. Somehow his feet found their way back to the apartment of his father. Somehow, he found his way home, only recognizing it as he stood out front gazing at the building in the early morning sunshine.

A siren slashed through the stillness and an ambulance raced up to just beyond where Don was standing. Confused, he could do nothing but stare as the emergency crew assembled the gurney and dashed up the steps with it, emerging some minutes later bearing on the stretcher an old man who looked vaguely familiar.

Cora

When she leaned over to kiss him awake, Arthur's his lips were
cool and blue. His eyes were open but unfocused, and he didn't
even startle when she screamed, "Call 911!" Within moments
Edward was on the phone. Ann had rushed into their bedroom
and sat on one side of Arthur massaging his arms while Cora spoke
forcefully into his good ear. *"Don't leave us, my love. We still need you!
Stay here, Arthur. Don't leave me."*

When the emergency workers loaded Arthur onto the gurney,
Cora grabbed her robe and followed, barefoot, climbing into the
ambulance, all the while keeping up her litany, calling Arthur back
from wherever he had gone. She took some consolation from way
his lips curled upward in a half-smile. Gazing out the ambulance
window she noticed a tall, disheveled man with white hair standing
on the sidewalk, gaunt and dazed. For a moment she felt confused.
He looked like Arthur twenty years ago. Which was Arthur? As the
ambulance began to move, she returned to her work. *"Stay with me,
my love. Stay!"*

The air in apartment crackled with unaccustomed acceleration
as each resident emerged from sleep to throw on the clothes
they'd worn the night before and lurch into action. Edward
brought Cora's car to the front of the building, and they filed out,
Keisha taking time to tape a note for Aunt Mi-Young saying that
they were at the hospital. Keisha slid into the back seat as did
Ann, after she gently helped Don, dirty and chilled, into the front
seat.

At the hospital they filled the small waiting room and sat in a
silence fraught with the intensity of their individual prayers and
worried thoughts. In a room down the hall Cora sat beside Arthur,
calm and determined. She would give Arthur what she had been
unable to give her first husband, Booker: *Presence.*

Mi-Young

Mi-Young and her daughters arrived at the apartment around
eleven o'clock, having left before dawn and making good time.
She swiveled her svelte body from under the steering wheel and

unfolded her long legs, standing and stretching. She was a stunning woman at 50, looking barely older than Li and Kim, who also emerged from the car stretching. Kim ran up the steps to Grandma Cora's apartment, saw the note, and ran back down, a concerned frown distorting her pretty face.

"They're at the hospital, Mom. It doesn't say which one of them is sick."

Twenty minutes later the three women walked into the waiting room, where Edward was the only person she recognized. There were two women, probably mother and daughter, and a scruffy looking white-haired man in torn running shorts and a dirty T-shirt whose arms and legs were covered with scratches. They all looked exhausted and worried. To her surprise Edward introduced the man as her brother Don. She was alarmed by Don's appearance and worried about Daddy and Mama, still not sure which of them was in danger. Edward was introducing her to Don's wife and daughter when the doctor stepped in to give them a report.

"Arthur has suffered a stroke," she told them. "But a few minutes ago, he opened his eyes and spoke. So far, he seems to be unimpaired, although we're running more tests. We're going to get him up within the next couple of hours to check mobility." The doctor had a kind face and she smiled encouragement at them. "He's probably going to make it, thanks to the determination of that woman. She just won't let him go. We'll hold him over night and, hopefully, release him tomorrow. He's a very lucky man."

"We're all very lucky," Edward said.

Relief made them silly. Don's daughter joked that her aunt and cousins were meeting the slovenly side of the family, and they all laughed. The group from the apartment certainly looked rumpled and unkempt, Mi-Young, thought and when her twins caught her eye, she could tell they were making the same observation. Then Edward explained that they'd followed the ambulance with no time to shower and barely time to throw on yesterday's clothes. They had a good excuse for looking bedraggled. Probably hungry, too?

Don's daughter—she hadn't caught the young woman's

name—offered to get some food from the cafeteria for them all. Edward passed her his credit card and suggested Mi-Young's "girls" go with her, calling after them, "Bring back something healthy for the elders, please."

In the absence of the younger generation, Mi-Young began to get acquainted with Don and Ann. She felt awkward meeting him like this after so many years. Thank God Edward was there to help bridge their lives.

When Mama Cora entered the waiting room wearing blue paper slippers and a hospital gown that the nurses had provided her with, her bathrobe on top and her hair disheveled, Mi-Young thought she must have heard it wrong. Was Mama a patient, too? More laughter and explanations.

Mama could not stop smiling as she told them about Arthur's comeback. "I'm holding on to this man as long as I can," she told them.

Ah, Mama! It was so good to see her.

Mama turned to Don. "He wants to see you. He knows you leave tomorrow and wants to have as much time as possible with you."

For a moment Mi-Young was eight again and jealous, but only for a moment. She'd had her daddy's daily attention from age eight until she went off to college. Of course, Daddy needed time to catch up with Don.

The "girls" came back with bagels and coffee, and they all settled into the waiting room for breakfast and "getting to know you." In twos the family was allowed to visit Arthur, and she and Edward went in first. The nurse instructed them to confine their conversations to ten minutes. By evening, with the doctor reporting that Arthur was doing surprisingly well, the family returned to the apartment, leaving Don to be their sentry at the hospital.

At the apartment the evening was surprisingly low key. They read, played games, and munched pizza alone or in pairs, enjoying the newness of being family and the relief that Arthur's life was not in danger. Keisha phoned Richard, and Edward spent time online changing his return flight so that he and Mi-Young could stay for the following week to help Mama care for Arthur. Ann offered to come back to help. They made plans for all of them to spend Thanksgiving together in Cleveland. Between Edward's apartment and Ann and Don's house there was enough room for them all.

She sat with Edward in the kitchen sipping wine and catching up. "Have you had any word from Son Chi?" he asked.

"No, but thank you for asking." She could hear the sadness and resignation in her voice. Okay, time to face the facts. Who better to name them with than Edward?

"I've begun to accept that he won't be returning. Mama went through this and Dad also, and both of them had less than half as long with the person they loved as I've had with Son Chi. I think it's time for me to let him go. When things settle down, I'll probably sell the house in D.C. I miss him terribly, but, you know, there are things that we cannot change."

Edward held her close. There was nothing to say. Then they got into the freezer like they had as children and found the ice cream. It had been a family tradition, although not one Mama encouraged—ice cream eaten out of the carton to help you heal hurts, physical or emotional. On this momentous night they would enjoy this ritual, just the two of them.

For once, Mama had gone to bed early, leaving the kitchen clean up to the younger women. It was a sure sign of how shaken Mama was by how close she had come to losing Daddy. After the ice cream binge, like when she was a small child, Mi-Young climbed into Mama's bed and wrapped her arms around her.

This new configuration of family that filled the apartment was beginning to feel comfortable. They certainly did fill the apartment. Keisha—she liked her name—slept with her mom in the guest room, Edward on the sofa, and the twins on sleeping bags on the living room floor.

Don

He'd asked to spend the night with his father, ostensibly so that Cora could get some rest. In fact, he needed that time. Indeed, *both* of them needed that time to begin their recovery.

That night in the quasi-darkness of Arthur's hospital room, he and his father talked, dozed, and talked some more. There was something magical about the half-dark of that room holding and sheltering the two of them as they talked. Don, sitting in the recliner beside the bed, holding Arthur's hand, told his father about his recurring sadness, how long it had been part of who he was, how he had not understood it until the last few days when he realized how much he had missed his father. Then he asked in an embarrassed, childlike voice, "Dad, did you miss me?"

Arthur didn't hear him, not even when he repeated the question, so Don walked around the bed to put his mouth next to Arthur's good ear and tried again, despite the voice in his head telling him how funny he must look asking such an intimate question in such a loud voice. He wondered if the nurses were having a good laugh at him. Finally, Dad got it. He could tell because Dad turned his head to look directly at Don. "It's on my list, only I keep not getting to it," he said.

He motioned for Don to sit down. This would take some time. Then he told Don what had happened to him in Korea—about Booker and Jindae—and why he had come to Nashville after Milly denied him any contact with his son. Dad told him about his regret that he'd been absent from his son's life, his anger at Milly and at himself for walking away, and his depression. "I thought about going back to Buffalo and forcing her to let me see you. I even imagined how I could kill her and kidnap you, but I knew that was crazy. In the end, after some years, I let it go, all that anger and despair. I had to. It was eating me alive. I had to trust you'd be all right."

Their conversation was transformative for Don. He learned that his father loved him, that anger and years of separation could not alter that. In the hours before dawn pushed away the darkness, the hospital room and Don felt lighter.

He was vaguely aware that a nurse came in to check Arthur's vitals at dawn, while Don lay sprawled and sleeping in the too-short chair that he had pushed as close as possible to his father's bed. Arthur was asleep, too. They were holding hands.

He thought he heard someone saying from far away, "This is why I love my job."

Richard, Evanston

Richard's anxiety over whether he should agree to meet his half-sisters had been growing ever since he had called Andrea Musleh. He couldn't decide what to do.

He knew another plane trip was not in his budget, but he needed to talk with his parents. Needed to talk about this upcoming reunion with people he was genetically related to. Needed to talk about the baby.

He called home while Keisha was in Nashville. No one answered. Typically. His parents were always out. He left a message saying he needed to talk with them and wondered if he could come next weekend. Anticipating their Yes, he booked the last seat on an inconveniently early American flight with a layover in Memphis, the last seat available. Then he called back and updated his message with his arrival and departure times.

He completely forgot that Dad had told him they were taking off that weekend to visit his sister's family. He opened his calendar to enter his itinerary and there it was, Dad and Mom at Sue and Hank's. Great! He had just bought a non-refundable ticket to Cleveland! Damn it! Now what?

Keisha texted Sunday evening, eager to tell him about her time in Nashville. Five months pregnant, she was showing despite baggy sweaters and loose jackets. He had resisted her invitations to feel the baby kicking and had barely looked at the sonograms that showed a tiny girl-child swimming inside her. Yet he needed her in his life, needed her friendship and her strength.

How she could be so calm and centered when this baby would bring chaos to her life? When he asked her, she simply said she wanted a child and this was as good a time as any. Her mother had done it and she had turned out just fine. Furthermore, she was excited to be bearing a child that he fathered, regardless of the role he wanted to play in the child's life.

His folks called back. Dad spoke first, "Richard, it sounds like this is really important."

"Honey," his mom said, "you come ahead. We'll postpone our trip to see Sue and Hank and the kids."

"Are you all right, Son?" Dad's concern was evident in his voice. "I'm not all right, if I'm honest, Dad, but I want to talk with you in person, rather than on the phone. Are you sure it'll work for me to come next weekend?"

"Of course."

"Then I'll be there for dinner on Friday. We can talk then."

"We're holding you in prayer, Son," his father said as they hung up. Richard felt vaguely embarrassed. He wasn't sure what he thought about this prayer stuff.

His plane was an hour late. Dinner was waiting. He could read his parents' worry in their artificial cheeriness. Over dinner they chitchatted about his work, Mom's health, Dad's new retirement routines, the latest in Sue and Hank's lives. When they asked about Keisha, Richard breathed deeply and started in. Might as well talk about what was really on his mind. That's why he'd come. He laid his desert fork on his pie plate, leaving the pie untouched.

"OK. Well, Keisha is pregnant, five months pregnant." Their faces broke into smiles.

"Wonderful news!" Mom said.

"Or is it?" Dad asked.

"Keisha wants the baby. I love her and she's really good for me. But I'm not sure I'm ready to be a married couple, much less a couple with children. We only met last March!" He walked to the kitchen to refill his water glass, returned to the dining room, and began pacing the length of the room, towering over his seated parents. "I'm not sure I would be *good* at parenting. My biological father certainly wasn't! I don't want to walk out on her, but I'm a loner who needs privacy, and I've seen how it is with Sue and Hank—no privacy, no space that others don't intrude upon, and absolutely no time alone. Sue has to lock herself in the bathroom to get away from the kids! I don't know if I will ever be ready for that. I feel like I'm being a self-centered jerk to say this, but it's what I've been feeling. I don't like myself this way but don't know what to do about it."

Richard knew that in forty years of counseling couples his father had helped many conflicted people sort out their choices. But was he expecting too much to think Dad could counsel his son? He heard his father's voice and tried to catch up with his words.

"…when I felt the same way. I was afraid my relationship with your mom would be ruined by having children, who would siphon off energy and attention that I wanted her to give me. When your mom was ready for a baby, I wasn't, and when she told me she was pregnant, I was upset. Then she miscarried, and, to my surprise, I felt sad at the loss of this potential baby, very sad. I even wondered if my not wanting this baby had caused it to be lost. I know better than that, of course, but that was my feeling."

Richard's Mom broke in. "The doctor told me he doubted I'd be able to carry a baby to full term due to problems with my uterus. When I told your father that, I thought he would be glad. He hadn't wanted a baby. But he'd changed. He was devastated! Imagine how surprised I was by his response."

Dad resumed their story. "That's where Sue and then you came into our lives. We started investigating adoption and soon we had Baby Sue, three weeks old, and two years later, Baby Richard, only you were nearly a year and a half, already walking! Being parents brought us closer, the opposite of what I'd expected. We were a team as parents, and we worked hard to remain a team, not to make it your mom's job. You were such blessings in our lives. And you continue to be. I tell you this only to say that things change, feelings change. One day you may discover that what you thought you didn't want, you do want. Life is full of surprises."

"But the point is that *at this point I DON'T want to be a father!*"

"Talk some more about why."

"Like I said, I may be a bad one. It's in my genes."

"Wait a minute. Just because you were not raised by your birth father doesn't mean that he was or is a bad person or a bad father. As far as we know, he may never have known you existed." Dad's face was fierce.

"What *do* you know about him?"

Mom jumped in. "That he was 22, Caucasian, highly educated and intelligent, dark hair and eyes, and tall. That's it. You could try to get the records opened and locate him. We could help you do that."

"He hasn't needed me for 35 years. Why should I need him now?" Now he was pacing the room.

"Maybe you don't, maybe you do. Only you can decide that. It sounds like you blame him for letting you be adopted. Is that right?" Dad looked very serious.

Richard felt distressed. This wasn't the way he'd imagined their conversation. It was coming out all wrong. He tried again, sitting down at the table and drinking the full glass of water before he spoke.

"This decision about the baby is tangled up with another decision I haven't told you about. I recently heard from two sisters whose mother died suddenly of cancer. They said she'd been looking for me because she was my birth mother. They want us to meet. I feel so damn conflicted." He sat down heavily. "*You* are my parents. *You* are the ones who cared for me, loved me, and provided what I needed. I have never felt interested in locating my birth parents, either of them, and certainly I've never been ready to claim them as my family. The last thing I want is for you to worry that you will be replaced by people who never did a damn thing for me!"

"Whoa, Richard!" His father's voice had an edge Richard remembered from when he'd been caught smoking in the downstairs bathroom at fourteen. "Your birth mother gave you life and loved you deeply. We know that she tried to raise you alone but couldn't do it, couldn't make enough money to pay for childcare and housing and food. She went to Catholic Charities out of desperation, out of love for you and concern that you be raised by people who would love and provide for you. I remember the social worker telling us that her decision to place you for adoption was very hard on her."

Mom spoke up. "We know that we are your parents, Richard, though I love to hear you state it. I guess like most adoptive parents we have sometimes worried that our kids might prefer their birth parents. But generally we've felt quite secure with you and with Sue. We want most of all for you to be happy. If locating your birth parents or siblings can give you more information, even if it can expand your circle of family, we've always said we would support that. And we mean it."

"Mom, never in my life did I question whether you or Dad loved me and would continue to love me no matter what."

"Not even when you ran away from home and I gave you a major spanking?"

"No. The knowledge that you loved me was bedrock for me."

"Now that you know we are OK with you meeting them, does that

make your decision easier? We could even go with you, or meet them on another occasion. We are related to them, too, you know. Our son is their brother." Mom seemed much more okay with this than he'd anticipated. He sat staring off into space. His internal compass was not working.

"Keisha suggested that I meet with them, if only to discover family health history, since the baby's health might be affected by that history. Perhaps I could do that, meet with the sisters. Whether there would be future meetings I can decide after I see how I feel in that initial meeting."

"Sounds like a wise decision. And the baby?"

"I don't know. I could be its 'Godfather' and contribute to its upbringing financially and through that relationship, rather than marrying Keisha."

Richard's father spoke, his voice intense and his words direct.

"What are you running away from? Fear that you won't be a perfect father? A perfect husband? Well, I can assure you that *you won't be either a perfect father or a perfect husband.* Look at me! My work constantly came first, caring for parishioners took priority, whether we had a vacation planned or an Easter family dinner or whether you or Sue had school performances or parent-teacher conferences. I let you and your Mother down more times than either of us can count. That's the way it is. *We do the best we can with the information we have at the time and end up disappointing each other again and again no matter our good intentions.”*

"Remember the Christmas eve you had chickenpox and I was irritated because you were to play Joseph in the church pageant that night?"

"Remember the vacation trip we'd planned to take to Disney World off season? The church roof caught fire, and we had to turn around and drive back home, totally missing Disney World."

"Remember the party for your graduation your Mom planned? I was called away because a parishioner was rushed to the hospital, having attempted suicide. I didn't get to any of the party. *I missed your graduation celebration!*" Dad was on a roll.

"Shall I keep going?"

Hearing his father list these disappointments like a litany of regret, Richard was tempted to respond after each item with, *For this you are forgiven.* He wanted to throw humor into the conversation, but seeing the seriousness on his father's face, he decided that joking would be inappropriate.

"Dad, I only remember these things when you remind me of them. Mostly, I remember you reading to me, us talking over supper, and the games you played with us to get us to learn new vocabulary. I remember vacations we did take and seeing your tired face when you returned from yet another emergency you had helped with. You were and are *a good father.* I could not ask for a better one."

Mom stood and interrupted with her usual confidence that she knew better than the rest of her family what they needed and when they needed it. It was characteristic of her and sometimes irritating. "It's getting late. I think we should table this conversation for tonight and talk more tomorrow."

Without waiting for a response, she gathered coffee cups and headed for the kitchen, calling over her shoulder that the dishes would wait till morning.

His father asked his opinion. "What do *you* say? Shall we head for bed?" *There* was the humor, Dad and he pretending they had the power to differ with Mom once she'd declared herself. Mom was already on the way upstairs. He wouldn't admit it, but she was right.

He watched her holding onto the railing to help her climb. He could see concern on her face. This was hard on her, too. He hugged his father. "Thank you, Dad," he said.

"Thank you, Son," his father replied.

Saturday they sat a long time over breakfast talking, recalling funny experiences from Richard's childhood and teenaged years. They called Richard's sister Sue to bring her into their conversation. Then they went for a drive to look up old haunts. At some point Mom told Richard that she had looked at the adoption records they had been given to see if there was any more information about his birth father. She found a note that the birth mother had never informed the birth father that she was pregnant, or when she gave birth. "He didn't know, honey. He didn't know about you. Forgive him."

Sunday Richard's plane left mid-afternoon, allowing time for them to attend the church Dad had served when Richard and Sue were children. Sitting in that familiar sanctuary, Richard tuned out the pastor's sermon and tuned in his memories. How proud he had been to be his father's son! To watch and listen each Sunday as Dad's words were received by the congregation and listened to with seriousness and respect. In that place he had been introduced to the music that inspired his creativity and directed his life. There he had been baptized, immersed, held in his father's arms and lowered into the baptismal pool behind the altar by his father, who wore hip-high rubber boots and waded into the water, immersing its youth one by one in the water, saying the ritual words, and safely lifting them upright. Summers at Kelley's Island Sue and he had practiced baptizing each other in Lake Erie. They were proud to be insiders who knew how it was done. "Keep your legs and back straight and just let my hand on your back hold you as I dip you back and down, and then raise you up," Dad had instructed. "I will never drop you. You are safe."

Remembering this, Richard thought that maybe that was what good parenting was all about— teaching your kids to relax and trust that they would not be dropped or abandoned, that you would hold them and not let them drown, would love them no matter what.

He looked to his right, to Mom, much recovered from her bypass surgery but looking older, and Dad, somewhat frail, his thinning skin speckled with brown spots and his eyes deeper set, eyelid folds leaning on them in a way Richard had not before noticed. He wondered how long they would be around to keep up their parenting performance. He heard their familiar voices raised in the hymn that was Dad's favorite, *Immortal, Invisible, God Only Wise.* Voices are like fingerprints, he thought, each unique and recognizable. Then he thought of Keisha's baby, *our* baby.

When he got off the plane at O'Hare, she was there to greet him holding a single daisy.

"It was an important weekend," he told her as he bent to kiss her. "I called Andrea Musleh from the airport. We're going to meet them at her house for lunch the day before Thanksgiving." As he held her, he could feel the baby gently kicking.

Keisha

Her last class over, Keisha walked home in the early November twilight. Chicago's big sky canopy gave space to dramatic contrasts—sweeps of sullen storm clouds vied with backlit sky-blue-pink fleece. The setting sun lit the horizon orange and red like a raging bonfire. She kicked the leaves puddled on the sidewalk and listened for the soft crunch they made. She loved this time of year, loved the smell of wood smoke perfuming the air as fireplaces returned to their work, loved the pungent, sweet scent of decaying leaves. She loved the nostalgia falling leaves evoked in her, their reminder of all that is lost. She loved autumn's juxtaposition of loss and hope, tangible decay and intangible new life, waiting beneath the blanket of dead leaves.

Words of an autumn song surfaced inside her, recalled from nowhere she recognized.

The bears are getting restless.
They are moving toward their dens.
The birds are on the fly to their winter homes again.

She had almost arrived at her apartment when she felt the baby moving inside her. Patting her tummy she said out loud, "Welcome, little one! May you love this world and delight in its beauty. May you know you are loved and wanted."

She rubbed her belly gently in a circular motion. No thoughts of fear or doubt now. Not tonight. If Richard didn't embrace being family with them, so be it. She could do this alone better than with him not wanting to be with them. Nothing worse than a person with one foot out the door.

She changed her mind and decided to keep walking. She was walking along the lake shore now, looking for a rock on which to sit for a while and savor the twilight. She climbed onto a large boulder and sat looking out at the quiet water. Ah, Richard! She acknowledged to herself that she loved this man more than anyone she had ever known and that she wished she could spend the rest of her life with him. She itemized what she loved about him.

His quirky and unpredictable nature.

The music he could bring forth so magically.

His intellect that made connections between music, history, literature, and art.

His respect and care for her.

His honesty and courage—that he says what he really means, even when it's difficult.

And his hands. Just thinking about his hands and how they moved across the keyboard—or across her body—made her shiver.

Even though I want him to want me—us—I know that whatever he decides, I'll be all right. She thought about the last words Gran Cora had said to her as they left for the airport.

"You have found your center, child, and this man you love will find his. No need to fret. Nothing you do can hurry the process. Do what you love, be who you are, and trust that God's universe will smile on you and your baby and on him."

On the plane flying home to Evanston, she'd decided on the name she wanted for their daughter. When she told Richard, he'd agreed. She would be Cora.

Edward, November

Edward answered the phone against his better judgment. He was enjoying being back in his apartment, alone, after the dramatic week in Nashville. He treasured being able to do whatever he pleased without intrusion, and the phone was definitely an intrusion. He reached into his memory to retrieve that voice. So much had transpired in the past eight months.

"Rev. Hardyway, this is Andrea Musleh, Connie's daughter. Did I catch you at a bad time?"

Edward mustered a timbre of reassurance, though he really would rather not be on the phone with *anyone* in his first week after nursing Arthur and helping Mama.

"Yes, Andrea, of course I remember you! How are you?"

"Actually, we're very good. We have located our brother and he's coming with his girlfriend to meet us the day before Thanksgiving. Of course, we're anxious that it go well, and Allison and I, in discussing this, decided it would be important to have you there to help with what'll probably be an awkward meeting, at least at first. You'd offered to come that day in Mom's apartment. Will you come? Please?"

"Well, my own family is gathering for Thanksgiving, a reunion that will make this Thanksgiving unlike any we have experienced before. I can't miss it, so I'm afraid I can't join you."

"But we're meeting him for lunch *Wednesday*, the day *before* Thanksgiving. That wouldn't interfere with your Thanksgiving reunion, would it? It'd mean so much to us if you'd come. We really need you, Reverend Hardyway. They're coming to my place for lunch, 12:00. We should be done by 2:00. Please, will you join us?"

Edward smiled at Andrea's clever use of all the right nuanced arguments. He thought over his family's Thanksgiving schedule. Arthur and Cora were arriving at 4:00 on Wednesday. He was to meet them at the airport and bring them to Ann and Don's home for dinner. He could make it.

"All right," he said. "I owe it to your mother to help you through this major moment in your lives." He wrote down directions for how to get to Andrea's and then entered the date on his wall calendar and cell phone. He was no longer confident he would remember everything he agreed to. They exchanged pleasantries and rang off. He wondered for a few minutes what this son of Connie would be like.

In his mind he lifted a congratulatory glass to Connie. This one's for you, old friend. The lost has been found. Then he turned on NPR to listen to the news, turning it off after a few minutes and settling into his leather chair with a glass of scotch, neat. He wanted no intrusions.

On November 23 he left his apartment, allowing plenty of time to reach Andrea's home on the west side. It was the busiest travel holiday of the year and the roads were congested with cars carrying family to each other. He was going to be late, something he detested. At least the airport was near Andrea's so he would definitely be able to get there to pick up the folks on time. He parked on the street, bundled up against the cold wind off Lake Erie, and strode to the front door of Andrea and Karim's frame bungalow, curious about what he would learn in the next hour.

Andrea ushered him into the living room and introduced him to her new-found brother, Richard Allen, and his girlfriend, Keisha, who was obviously pregnant. Keisha and Edward stared at each other, visibly shocked.

"Keisha?"

"Edward?"

"How do you know Andrea and Allison?" Keisha asked. Edward explained that his friendship with Andrea and Allison's mother,

Connie, connected them, and that they'd asked him to facilitate today's meeting. Keisha flashed one of her broad smiles to each of them and observed that this was going to be a good conversation with her Uncle Edward facilitating. Then Edward explained to Andrea and Allison his connection to Keisha and Richard, and someone said what a small world it is. The ice broken, Andrea called them into the dining room where a casserole, salad, and bread awaited them to ease The Conversation.

Edward worked hard at remaining focused on the task before them: Getting these young people acquainted with each other, giving them room to express their feelings about this poignant meeting, and helping them identify what they each wanted next, if they wanted anything next.

Andrea and Allison talked animatedly about Connie, wanting Richard to know his birth mother. They reiterated her love for him and her despair at not being able to provide for him. Richard spoke of his adoptive family, who he called his *real* parents, and of the good life he'd had because of their love and support for him. Edward reminded them all that both Connie and Richard's parents had been very courageous, caring people in the decisions they'd made, Connie to relinquish her toddler to people who could provide for him and Richard's parents to make him their son. "There are no bad people here," Edward stated, and they all nodded agreement.

"How are you feeling, Richard?" Edward asked.

"I feel that I love my parents and want them never to question that they are my parents. I am grateful to Connie for giving me life and loving me, which I'm sure made a difference in the person I've become. I'm grateful to her for providing a new and good life for me with Mom and Dad. And I'm grateful to you, Allison and Andrea, for caring so much about your Mom's wish to reunite us that you have spent time and money locating me. What you've done is impressive and I feel honored." Eight eyes focused intently on him.

"I like you both and I'm glad we're related. I imagine it'll be important to learn from you about the family health history, especially with Keisha's and my baby coming next month…"

He paused. He'd given a lot of thought to what he wanted to say, which was enabling him to be clear and articulate.

"I feel more like a distant cousin than your brother, and I think I'd like to have more of a cousin relationship to you in the future. At this point I can't see bringing you and my parents together or you and Keisha's parents, for that matter. We each are launched on lives that are quite satisfactory. I'd like to stay in touch, email news of our lives to each other, and perhaps see you when we come to Cleveland, which we will do because both sets of our parents live here."

He looked directly at Andrea and then Allison. "Does this make any sense to you? I don't want to hurt you or push you away. I just view you as distant relatives I've just happened to meet."

Edward asked the "How do you feel?" question to each of the women. To his surprise each gave a response similar to Richard's. Keisha cautioned that this being their first meeting, it was natural that they'd all be wary of too many expectations of intimate connection, but that over the years ahead, they probably would come to know and appreciate each other more and more, maybe leading to increased contact, even though at the moment each was happy in their separate worlds.

Allison noted the uncanny resemblance to Mom in Richard's eyes and chin. Andrea commented that he bore less resemblance to Connie than she'd expected or maybe feared. Edward didn't say it, but he saw no resemblance whatsoever.

"What do you know of Richard's father?" Keisha asked.

"Nothing. The court records are closed, and all parties signed a legal document that they would remain so. If we had a lot of money to spend on lawyers, we might be able to get them opened, but neither of us has that kind of a reserve."

The conversation shifted and relaxed to talking about their lives, interests, and families. It was almost 2 p.m. when Edward asked if they felt they had accomplished what they needed to accomplish in this meeting.

"Are there any other questions or concerns you want to raise?"

All four of them expressed gratitude for their meeting and thanked Edward for his skillful facilitation. They agreed to get together again the next time Keisha and Richard were in Cleveland.

"By then we'll have another family member to introduce to you," Keisha said smiling.

Then Richard, Keisha, and Edward donned their coats and gloves and departed just as Karim and Tony with the two-year-olds arrived. Edward guessed the timing had been prearranged, so that the husbands could meet Richard without the children distracting them from The Conversation.

They introduced themselves and shook hands. Nawal and Antonia ran to the house, and Edward and Richard slid into their cars, Keisha riding with her man. It seemed surprisingly anticlimactic.

Richard and Keisha met up with Edward a few hours later at Ann and Don's home. The rest of the family—Arthur, Mama, Mi-Young, her daughters along with Li's partner—had already arrived. There was no opportunity to process the time at Andrea's, although Edward found himself thinking about it. Anyway, Richard and Keisha seemed to have already moved on.

THANKSGIVING

Early Thanksgiving morning Don, Edward and Mi-Young gathered in the kitchen to prepare the turkey, having informed the others that the siblings were taking responsibility for this job. Edward and Mi-Young worked on the two kinds of dressings that represented Cora and Arthur's southern and northern traditions. Edward made the cornbread dressing and Mi-Young, oyster and bread stuffing. Don washed the turkey and put the giblets on to cook. Their conversation roamed stream of consciousness as they shifted from one task to another. Now they were peeling sweet and white potatoes.

Ann and Cora had baked mince, apple, and sweet potato pies the evening before and made several cranberry dishes. The younger generation was preparing green veggies and dips to start the meal. Edward told them he was known worldwide for his yeast rolls, which he'd made the day before. He offered his siblings a taste as a prelude to the serious eating that would begin once the rest of the household awakened.

Mi-Young discovered that her brother Don, for all his serious, distinguished demeanor, was really quite funny and the three of them competed in a steady stream of puns that warmed the kitchen with laughter.

When they finished preparations for the evening feast, they turned to brunch, warming and setting out Ann's special spinach and mushroom casserole and Cora's cheese grits as well as a large bowl of mixed fruit with Keisha's homemade yogurt and Richard's to-die-for coffee.

As they gathered around the dining room table, Richard commented, "This is a family that knows how to cook and how to eat."

It was a Johnson tradition to take a long walk before the Thanksgiving meal, to work up an appetite, to discover what surprises the woods would reveal in the chilly November afternoon, to chat one on one as they walked in Metropolitan Park. Keisha, swelling with child, begged off, as did Arthur and Cora. Ann decided she needed to remain at the house to make gravy, mash potatoes and do the other last minute food prep. So it was the younger set, led by elders Edward and Don, who took off for the Park.

Richard welcomed the opportunity for more conversation with Don and Edward. Besides, being the only male among the younger generation was wearing him out. The three men walked together several yards behind Kim, Li and Li's partner Katherine. Richard had been processing yesterday's time with Andrea and Allison.

"I don't know if Keisha told you that I'm adopted," he told Don. "Yesterday, Edward, Keisha and I met with the daughters of my birth mother—my half-sisters—for the first time. I keep thinking about that meeting, about the whole idea of having two families, one that raised me and one I'm biologically related to but know not at all."

Don was listening closely. "How did you learn about your birth family?" he asked.

"They found me after a search that was apparently initiated by my birth mother. She died last spring, and her daughters promised her they would keep looking for me and they found me. I'm not sure how much contact I want to have with them. They're very nice young women and, from what Edward and they tell me, my birth mother was a wonderful person. But I'm quite happy with my Mom and Dad. They've been terrific parents, and I don't want anything to cause them anxiety now in their 'golden years.'"

Richard suddenly realized that his parents were not much older than the two men he was talking with and hoped they were not offended by his choice of words.

Edward jumped in to clear the awkwardness. "Don and I are happy about our 'golden years,' Richard. They have brought us back to each other and back to our family, of which you are now an integral part."

Edward saw a stricken look pass over Don's face and chose his words carefully, intuiting that what he said would be especially important for Don.

"Yes, your birth mother was a wonderful woman, Richard. Connie Riegler and I lived in the same apartment building for ten years and got to know each other very well during that time. Some time I'll show you both the last gift she gave me. It's a carving of two interconnected shapes made from one piece of wood. I like to see it as a metaphor for family—for you, Richard, and those who are responsible for your birth and upbringing—actually, for all of us here this Thanksgiving, made from one human family, separate and intertwined, moving freely but never escaping our common connection."

They were quiet for several minutes.

Richard spoke first. "I've never liked change. I'm a person who does things the same way over and over and takes satisfaction from the repetition. At least, that is how I was before Keisha. Through her I've discovered that new experiences can be exciting. My composing has changed, expanded. So has my understanding of family."

Don responded. "I think I know what you mean. Ann and Keisha did that for me, too. Ann told me at the start of our relationship that as an only child she believed in 'making family' out of people. I've appreciated that more and more as the years pass. Keisha, Ann, Edward, Cora—none of them are blood relations of mine, but they are *my family* and the people I love most in the world."

Edward was paying close attention to Don.

Richard breathed in the chilly autumn air that was flavored faintly with the smell of burning leaves and the promise of winter.

"We'd best head back." Don stepped up his pace, striding ahead. "Wait, Don, I have something else to tell you," Richard said. "Keisha's probably told you that I have been scared by how quickly things have moved in our relationship, scared of commitment, of becoming a father so soon. I've done a lot of thinking about this. I talked with my sister and my parents. And I've finally decided what I want. I wanted to talk with you before I tell Keisha."

Don and Edward slowed their pace and made room for Richard between them.

"I realize my cowardice hasn't made a good impression on you and I appreciate how warm and inclusive you all have been to me, even knowing that I've had one foot out the door. I realized during the last few weeks that I don't want to live without Keisha in my life. I want to ask her to be my wife. I figured Thanksgiving might be the right time to do it…. There, I said it! That wasn't so hard." Richard was speaking to himself, but they heard his words and smiled.

"I love her very much, and I want to build a life and a family with her. I guess I'm asking your blessing and support for this, Don."

Richard's words were not what Don had expected. He extended his hand to Richard and then surprised them all by pulling Richard close into a bear hug.

"This year has been a time of tremendous change for all of us," Don said. "As Ann would say, it's been a time of lots of Maybe Crossings. I'm very happy that you've reached this decision, Richard. Welcome to our family."

Edward was grinning. "What a lucky man you are, Richard. You have three families—the family of blood and birth, the family of love and upbringing, and this family that Keisha connects you to. And all of them will love you forever."

Don called to his nieces, "We'd best head back. We don't want to keep the rest of the family waiting."

"When are you going to tell her, if I may ask?" Edward was thinking of the logistics. But Richard had taken off running before Edward finished the question. "Right now," he called over his shoulder.

Richard wiped his feet and entered the kitchen looking for Keisha.

She wasn't there. He greeted the family and when someone said she was upstairs resting, he bounded the stairs two at a time and entered her room. He sat on the bed beside her watching her sleep. Feeling his presence, she stirred, and stretched, knocking a box he had placed on her pillow onto the wood floor where it landed noisily.

"Everything OK?" Arthur came out of the bathroom across the hall to check on Keisha, who by now was awake and awkwardly pulling herself to a right-angle sitting position, her baby bump at the vortex where everything came together.

"What was that?" She looked somewhat disoriented.

Richard was on the floor reassembling the contents of the box and retying its bow.

"This is for you."

He handed her a medium sized box tied with an orange silk bow.

Puzzled, she opened it. Inside were a series of boxes within boxes. She opened each in turn. The next to last box contained a legal document and a piece of fine quality embossed paper that she unfolded and read it.

Arthur stood in the doorway watching them. Curious he spoke up. "What is it?"

"It is a marriage license, Grandpa. And an invitation to a wedding here at the house this Sunday, *three days from today*. It has my name and

Richard's. It says Edward and Richard's father will be officiating....Only I haven't signed it," she said, grinning at Richard.

Richard stood by the bed, his head tucked to avoid colliding with the dormer ceiling that angled down and met the wall where the headboard began. Curled downward that way he vaguely resembled a long-legged sea bird, his black curls framing the bald path to the back of his head, and his arms folded like wings over his chest. He hovered over her as she opened the final, smallest box. Inside was a wide ring intertwined with tendrils of silver threads that crossed and parted and crossed again like a thicket of vines.

"That's our Family, all of us, lives separate, connected, and reconnected in mysterious and amazing ways," he explained. "I've written a song cycle about it so we can always remember this moment."

Keisha sought his arms so suddenly that he lost his balance and fell forward onto the bed, holding her to him protectively. In falling he grazed his head on the low ceiling, and drops of blood darkened the pillow. They both began laughing.

"This is how we started, Grandpa, me cleaning blood—and bird poop—off Richard's head."

"So, Keisha," Arthur asked, his eyes twinkling, "Is this how you want to spend the rest of your life?"

"Yes, Grandpa, *YES!*"

From the stairwell they heard Ann calling them. "Come for dinner. The feast is ready and waiting!"

That evening Edward drove Mi-Young and her girls back to his apartment on Lake Shore Drive and got them settled in, Mi-Young in his guest room, the other three sharing his pull-out sofa and the loveseat perpendicular to it. They were all a buzz about the day, especially about Richard and Keisha's announcement and the wedding that would take place on Sunday. It would be a happening, and the young women chatted about what flourishes they could supply to enhance the celebration.

It was ten o'clock, late for Edward, but he knew he had one more thing to do before he slept. Quietly he left the apartment carrying a large package and his car keys. He phoned Ann that he would be briefly stopping by if Don was still awake. He was.

Ann greeted him in her bathrobe whispering that everyone else was already in bed. She ushered him to the kitchen and down the steps to the door to the back yard. Don was out there with Sam the dog, who ambled around the yard aimlessly, suffering indigestion from too many table scraps. When Sam saw Edward, he ran to him, rubbing against Edward's legs and licking his bare hands. There are good reasons for not having a dog, Edward thought as he wiped his hands on his coat.

Don sat bundled in his down jacket on one of two wrought iron chairs at a round wrought iron table, a set that Ann had picked up at an end of summer sale. He was leaning back, gazing at the sky. Edward wasn't sure Don knew he was there. He cleared his throat as he pulled the other wrought iron chair next to Don and sat down.

"I've been trying to figure out what that moon means." Don spoke without looking at him.

Edward looked up at the sliver of a crescent moon sliding out from behind the dark clouds of the night sky.

"It could be a smile or it could be a closed eye. For some reason it seems important to decide what it is." Don was still looking at the moon. Then he spoke again. "You knew her." His words were in between a question and a statement.

Edward breathed the cold air deep into his lungs. Okay, he'd come back for this. His brother needed him tonight and this would be an important conversation.

"She was my neighbor and my friend," he replied. "She was also the cause of all of us being reunited."

Don turned to face him, looking confused, suddenly remembering Father Joe saying he could call on Connie to help him.

Edward continued. "I went to see Connie's daughters before they moved everything out of our building, and they told me of the trust accounts she set up for the granddaughters through a Dr. Don Johnson. It was a long shot, but it started me searching for you."

"So you know." Don sighed audibly. "I'm glad. I need to share this with someone, and I'm glad it's you." He pulled a woolen blanket off the table, unfolded it, and passed one end to Edward. "Here, we can drape this over our seats. That wrought iron is butt-chilling, as Keisha would say." They stood and arranged the blanket so that it covered both chairs. Then they sat down again.

Edward welcomed the layers of wool between him and the icy metal. "Did you know before this afternoon?" he asked. He was sorting which of his many questions to ask and which to leave alone.

"I didn't know. For years I grieved for my lost son, my only biological child. Finding him leaves me deeply happy." There was a long pause and Edward resisted the urge to say something.

"I think I've decided that I can't share our connection with anyone other than you, at least not now. It might throw him off, raise more questions about his decision to marry Keisha. It doesn't seem to be important to him who his biological parents are. It's only important to me. I can feel my own private joy in knowing him, and he can be part of our family as my son-in-law. Does that make sense to you?"

Edward turned back to look at the Cheshire cat smile shining in the sky. "It makes sense. Will you ever tell him?"

"Maybe. I've thought about writing him a letter and putting it with our wills, for him to open at my death. That way he would know, but after we have established a relationship with each other as family. Or I may tell him in person later, just not now. Am I being a coward?"

"I don't think so. I think you are protecting your daughter and your son from unintended disturbance at this important time in their relationship.

You are all right with your decision?" Don nodded, then realizing Edward might not be able to see him in the dark, said, "Yes."

Edward stood and walked back to the door to the house. Bending down he picked up the package he'd brought from his apartment and carried it back to Don.

"Connie got this for me, but I think she would want it to go to you now."

Don unwrapped the heavy package and lifted from the bubble wrap a large wood carving, two carvings really, one within the other.

"Read what she wrote," Edward urged.

"Carved from the same wood, polished and glowing with age, inseparably connected forever." Don's voice was husky.
Edward looked up. "Personally, I don't see any disapproval in that sky.
I think the moon is both winking and smiling at us."

He stood and moved toward the house. "It is freezing out here and long past this old man's bedtime." He looked back at Don as he pushed open the door and the light from the kitchen poured out and covered him. "I love you, my brother," he said. "Sleep well."

EPILOGUE

Ann, Spring 2004

Images scraped Ann's consciousness, nagging to be recognized and nudging her from sleep. She lay in bed savoring them, reluctant to leave that vibrant state of in between. She shifted position and enjoyed the cool touch of a section of sheet not yet warmed by her body. It was so pleasant here. All things were equal as images paraded across her mind, coming into focus and then receding.

She saw with delight the newest member of the family, Baby Cora, their Valentine's baby, her intent, quizzical face so like her mother's, always puzzling about her world.

One by one she brought the others to mind: Cora and Arthur, Edward, Richard and Keisha, Mi-Young and her daughters, Richard's parents, Connie and her two girls, and, of course, Don.

Her parents hovered like trees planted by rivers of water, shading and sheltering her even now, almost a decade after their deaths.

Don stirred in his sleep beside her, his snores lifting the edge of the top sheet then letting it drop. She could see him, younger, lean and hard-bodied, prematurely gray and handsome, watching her, folded arms betraying his wariness. That was then. Long before this year when they had learned to fully trust each other and the universe. Before they discovered the fortification of family.

Yesterday walking their dog Sam in the promising March morning, she had heard someone knocking and looked up as she was passing her neighbors' house to see the source of the knocking. There in the second-floor window, framed by the triangular dormer and the dark interior of early morning, stood a beautiful one-year-old. His father's arm supported him as both looked down, smiling. It was a moment shining with tenderness. She felt time stop. They might have been a seventeenth century father and son captured on canvas by a Dutch Master, the father protectively holding his child, aglow with love, showing him the world out there beyond his current reach, repeating a role as ancient as time.

Her mind, skimming, paused on Death, wondering how much time they each had left.

She thought that she would like to have them all come celebrate with her at her exit. Let Keisha and Richard's children play around her bed, boisterous and always in motion. Keisha had confided that they were already talking about a second child. Let Keisha and Mi-Young's daughters share recipes and life adventures, work stories and laughter. Let them all know how good it is, this Life. How much she loved her expanding family!

Sam's barking jarred her into full wakefulness. Time to get up and get to work. She said thank you to whomever might be listening and threw back the covers. She swung her legs vertical and pushed off into the day.

Acknowledgements:

Thank you to John Monroe-Cassel, Hildred Cassel, Dr. Crystal Coles, Avery Marshall, Kaydee Haug, and Donna Ziegenhorn for feedback on drafts and especially to poet Michael Poage and novelist Connie May Fowler for telling me I had the gift and teaching me how to write more effectively.

About the Author:

Gretchen Eick is a historian and a writer of contemporary fiction. Her other books are *Dissent in Wichita: The Civil Rights Movement in the Midwest, 1954-72* (University of Illinois Press, nonfiction), *Herstories: Woman to Woman* (short fiction), *Finding Duncan* (her second novel), *They Met at Wounded Knee: the Eastmans' Story* (University of Nevada, nonfiction), *The Hard Verge: Britain, 2025* (a novel), *The Set Up: Classified Until 2064* (a speculative historical novel), *The Death Project: An Anthology for These Times* (edited with Cora Poage), and *Dark Crossings* (the sequel to *Maybe Crossings* set in 2019 and 2020).

Discussion Guide

1. Which characters in the first 100 pages did you find most interesting and why? Which characters did you care about and why in Parts 2 & 3?

2. What did you learn about the Civil Rights Movement that was new to you? Freedom Summer 1964 brought a thousand college students to the deep South to register voters and teach literacy. What did Ann learn in Mississippi? What did Barbara learn there?

3. Which scenes in the book are most memorable for you?

4. In 2003, the children of the Civil Rights Movement lived in a different context. How were their lives were different from their parents in attitudes, social behavior, assumptions?

5. How are Richard and Keisha different in personality and background? Have you been in a relationship where you were the Richard or the Keisha? Talk about what that was like for you?

6. Parts 2 and 3 are set in 2003. Coincidences drive the plot. Edward locates Don, Don finds his father after decades of no contact, Don discovers he has a son, Ann experiences her daughter's anger over being kept from knowing her biological father, etc. Thinking about your life, what moments have you experienced surprising coincidences, what Cora would call grace-filled moments? Share what you are willing to with the group.

7. Pregnancies in the plot: What would you have done if you were Keisha? Or Connie, pregnant and single in the 1960s? What shaped each of their choices? Even today going through pregnancy and raising a child as a single woman is difficult. How? What choices do women have today if they find themselves pregnant and unable to cope financially or medically or emotionally with a/another child?

8. Why do you think Don struggles with depression? His father, Arthur, also struggled with depression. In Arthur's case, Cora, his dear friend, "saved" him. Discuss the different ways Cora helped Arthur. Discuss Ann's relationship with Don. What did you like about it? Dislike?

9. How does religion or lack of religion play out in the characters' lives? [Note: none of them push their views on others.]

10. There are no evil people among the characters. Did that bother you? Where did you see evil? What do you imagine will happen to these people in the next two decades? [*Dark Crossings* picks up their story in 2019.]